"IT'S TOO LATE. DON'T YOU U...

Danielle swiveled in mid-sentence, and Ryan was there, touching her cheek. Emotion, a half-forgotten passion, captivated her. Little by little she turned her head; his hand followed until her lips pressed into his warm, callused palm.

Too late, he thought ruefully. *Too late for me to walk away.* His mustache was brushing her skin, tracing salty tears. Delicately he pushed down her sweater to free her fragrant skin for his lips.

"Ryan, please . . ." she moaned, and now the sweater clung precariously to her breasts. "Listen." Cupping his head in her hands, she held herself away. "For us love can never be comfortable. It was a fantasy we had once—that night never really happened. I'm not the same person anymore."

"Come to Malaysia, Danielle," he urged softly. "Let's meet once more—man to woman. . . ."

TASTE OF A DREAM

Casey Douglas

A *SuperRomance from*
HARLEQUIN
London · Toronto · New York · Sydney

First published in Great Britain in 1985 by
Harlequin, 15–16 Brook's Mews, London W1A 1DR

© June Casey 1984

ISBN 0 373 70131 4

11–0385

Printed and bound in Great Britain by
Cox & Wyman Ltd, Reading

PROLOGUE

ABOVE THE TANGLED STREETS of Kuala Lumpur, the darkening tropical sky showed patches of lurid yellow where flames and smoke licked up from the burning rubble.

Her heart pounding with fear, Danielle crept past the abandoned shop fronts. In normal times the arcaded sidewalks would have been alive with people dodging trishaws and bicycles in the crowded lanes. Now an eerie silence prevailed, punctuated by brief bursts of gunfire in the distance.

Kuala Lumpur was the most cosmopolitan of all the Southeast Asian capitals. Its multiracial character lent excitement and color to the city's life, but the tension was there, too. Falling rubber prices on the world market and the resurgence of guerrilla groups in Malaysia's northern hills had contributed to the potentially explosive situation. Still, Danielle hadn't expected it to blow up with such violent suddenness. All warnings to the contrary, she had insisted on visiting friends who lived in the old Chinatown quarter that crowded the muddy banks of the Klang River. The Chus had long since fled, and now she herself was alone and trapped.

Frightened by the crowds of panicky citizens thronging the bridges, she had retreated. That had been a mistake, she knew now, a potentially fatal one. Safety lay on the far shore, but separating her from it was a no-man's-land of sniper fire and torched buildings.

In the melee at the bridge she had lost one black pump and her matching snakeskin bag. Her slim white linen suit was torn and dirty, and the once-elegant French twist of her black hair was an untidy skein at her nape. Gone was the impeccable professional appearance, the air of cool self-possession, her hallmarks. She was terrified and exhausted.

Drawing in a ragged breath, Danielle stopped and closed her eyes. She prayed the nightmare scene would vanish, that when she reopened them she would find once again the Malaysia she had so admired, a land of unhurried courtesy and gentle charm. But the nightmare was all too real.

Her attuned ears picked up the quick heavy tread of boots against pavement, and with the stealth born of the instinct to survive, she withdrew into the deeper shadows of an arcade and pressed herself flat against the wall. A half-dozen armed men raced by; even from her fleeting glimpse of them she sensed their mood of murderous desperation. Long after the echo of their boots had died away in the distance, she stood petrified. The madness was on all sides now. She couldn't remain out in the open any longer.

Still pressed close to the shop wall and the meager protection it offered, she inched forward until she came to a short narrow alley. Swiftly she ran through to where it ended at the riverbank. On the opposite shore rose the downtown silhouette, where white domes shimmered against sleek skyscrapers. It was another world, unreachable.

The sound of footsteps in the street spurred her to action once more, and without hesitating, she crossed the alley and slipped through the only door standing ajar, scrambling down a steep flight of stairs that opened into a dark basement warehouse. For the moment, at least, she had found respite among the neatly piled bags of rice and casks of palm oil. A murky half-light filtered into the basement through a narrow barred window at street level. Suddenly she felt as though she'd found not a refuge but a lonely prison.

Too nervous to rest, she paced with the delicate sinuousness of a cat, pausing from time to time to listen for sounds from the street. Again she heard footsteps, and realized with dread that they were approaching her end of the alley. Holding her breath, she drew back and willed the unseen feet to return the way they had come. Her fear turned to terror as the door at the head of the stairs swung open.

Someone was coming down.

Panic-stricken, she backed up amid the casks. But as she reached behind her for the security of the wall, her hand brushed a funnel that had been balanced on the lip of a reed-covered jar and sent it clattering to the ground. She turned to run—her pursuer was too quick. An instant later hard fingers were digging into her arms.

"No, please, let me go!" she cried over her shoulder to the unseen assailant at her back.

Her plea ignored, she felt herself being dragged farther into the shadows, and she struggled futilely against the hand clapped across her mouth.

"Be quiet!" the voice commanded urgently in English. "Do you want to bring the whole place down around us?"

She shut up at once, as much out of surprise as fear.

"Now if I promise not to hurt you, will you promise not to scream?" the man said a little more gently.

Her head jerked in a quick nod, and the hands whose strength she'd already been made aware of pulled her around to face him. "A woman alone. You must be mad!" The accent was Australian, tension making it harsh and clipped. But rippling beneath it was a faint current of amusement.

She could only stare up at him, trembling still.

"Listen, it's all right now," he murmured.

That low lazy baritone might have convinced her of anything, if a burst of machine-gun fire and the splintering crash of a Molotov cocktail hadn't contradicted his words. She flung herself against his chest and clung to him. The man brought his arms up to circle her shoulders protectively as she shuddered against him. Then there was silence.

Embarrassed, she drew away, feeling the slow reluctant yielding of his arms. She raised her eyes, and their gazes met. They studied each other bemusedly, as if trying to puzzle out what quirk of fate had thrown them together in the subterranean depths of a strife-torn city.

His features were blunt and square, softened only by the thick brush of a mustache that framed his upper lip. But it was his eyes that riveted her. They gleamed in the shadowy half-light, lazily watchful. Yet the ironic amusement was there, too. He was almost enjoying the situation.

"What the devil are you doing here?" he demanded as his gleaming eyes swept the disarray of her elegant clothing, the long lovely legs in torn hosiery.

"The same as you, I suppose. Just trying to stay alive," she responded with tart wit, though her voice was still shaky.

"How did you wind up here in Chinatown, anyway?"

"I could ask you the same thing," she parried.

His lips curved in a grin of tigerish charm. "Maybe I just feel at home."

She stared hard at him, trying to fathom what he was all about.

"Do you live—" she began, but he shushed her again by putting one hand lightly to her lips.

Then she, too, heard the clatter of boots. In their wake came another barrage of gunfire and a muffled explosion that shook the earth beneath them. Reflexively the man acted, pushing Danielle down amid the rice sacks and throwing his body over hers as bits of plaster from the ceiling rained around them.

After the last tremor had died away, he pulled himself up on one elbow and looked down at her. "Are you all right?'' He lifted his fingers to brush away the streak of white dust on her cheek.

She managed a quick nod. ''Just frightened,'' she admitted. ''Do you think we should try to make a run for it?'' His unruffled courage had spurred her own.

''We wouldn't last two minutes in the streets. I'm afraid there's no place to run, love,'' he whispered with cool finality. ''We'll just have to make the best of it.''

Her blue-green eyes, dark with fear, seemed to fill the pale oval of her face. ''Do you think we'll die here?''

''Not if I have anything to say about it.'' The words were barely out of his mouth when another explosion rent the air. Again he threw his body across hers.

In a curious way Danielle's fear was tempered by a far more subtle feeling creeping over her. For the first time she was overwhelmed by her own vulnerability. Until now she had raced through life with arrogant self-confidence, knowing her own intelligence, or her ''connections,'' would get her through anything. In a world turned upside down those things had been stripped away.

Lying here with this stranger in the heart of destruction—his hard body protecting hers—Danielle sensed a hidden part of herself stirring. Suddenly it seemed that she'd traveled back ten thousand years, that she was a primitive woman dependent on the strength of one man for her survival. Under ordinary circumstances she would have laughed aloud at the thought . . . but not now.

When he pulled himself up, she was oddly reluctant to let him go. "You're a lot braver than I am," she whispered gravely, already missing the security of his warmth.

"I'm just more accustomed to tight situations, that's all."

He felt the stiffening of her body that met each distant crackle of gunfire, and the subsequent trembling. And all he wanted was to ease her fear, to somehow buffer her from the madness raging around them. This protective tenderness caught him by surprise.

Gently he slipped one arm beneath her and drew her close so that her head rested on his shoulder. When she lifted one hand, he thought she meant to push him away. Instead she laid it against his chest, as if to take sustenance from the slow steady beat of his heart.

He spoke against her hair, and his low expressive voice had a teasing lilt. "My old granny used to say to me, 'My boy, you're too reckless by far. One day you'll take one chance too many.'"

"Was she right?" Danielle asked, slanting a look up at him.

"I'm here now, aren't I?" he replied with wicked mischief.

Danielle laughed, a healing sound that was choked off by the deadly chatter of machine-gun fire in a neighboring alley. Her fingers dug into his chest. "I'm so frightened," she whispered.

He held her close. "Fear's a funny thing," he said

after a while. "I remember the first time I felt it to the marrow. It was the last time, too. I was ten years old, a city kid. My parents had sent me up from Sydney to stay with my grandmother on her sheep ranch, hoping the experience would be good for me. She was a tough old bird. When my grandfather died and left her a young widow, she took over the ranch without a second thought and ran it almost single-handedly for thirty years."

"Sounds like the type of woman I admire," Danielle couldn't resist observing.

He cocked his head to glance down into her face. "Kindred spirits?"

She laughed softly. "Maybe."

"At any rate, I was used to my parents' coddling and was miserable and lonely. The only thing that kept me going was the thought that it was only for six weeks.

"Then, one morning when there were only a few more days to go, I was out on the front porch. Gran had driven into town to pick up the mail and groceries, and as I looked out into the distance I could see the great trail of dust kicked up behind the Land Rover as she returned. I was waiting for her at the top of the steps. I was going to run down to give her a hand with the boxes, when suddenly she climbed out and stared up at me." He paused, as if reliving the scene again in his mind.

"Something in that dusty lined face froze me. There was a vacant expression in her eyes that I'd never seen before. She looked gaunt and sad. She came and stood at the bottom of the steps, staring up at me. 'Your mum and pop are dead—killed in a traffic bang-up. You're mine now, boy.' The matter-of-fact way she said it chilled me to the bone. I'll never forget the desolation that swept over me. For a long time I wanted to die, too. I was a lot more afraid of the future than of dying.''

"But you survived.''

He chuckled. "By the skin of my teeth. I thought I hated my old gran, but before the year was out we were thick as thieves. When she accused me years later of being too reckless by far, she said it with pride and satisfaction. That year was the dividing line for me between boyhood and manhood.''

He continued to reminisce, the slow easy cadence of his voice like waves drumming on a shore. Danielle saw the arid stretches of outback under a merciless blue sky, heard the melancholy howls of the dingoes and saw the little boy on horseback, patrolling against poachers with a rifle as big as he—his only companion the bone-cutting wind at his back.

She listened in fascination, and she was grateful to him, as well, realizing that he was talking to keep her mind far away from the bloodied streets above. Suddenly she wished to do the same for him, to give something of herself.

"I've known my share of fear, too, but maybe that's because I was born a coward,'' she told him, her gentle laughter self-mocking. "We always had horses, but I never quite trusted them. There was one black gelding, a real devil. He was a Spanish

Thoroughbred called Indio Negro. I was terrified of him, but on my seventh birthday my father made me get up on Indio's back. Even before I could take a breath the damned horse was running away with me. He'd sensed my fear. I was in a screaming panic.'' She paused, remembering. "It was a morning in autumn. Even now when I smell burning leaves or look up at a gray November sky I get a twinge of that old fear.''

"Your father sounds like a proper bastard.''

She shook her head. "It was a lesson he felt I had to learn. He wasn't about to have me grow up a coward. He was determined that I be as tough as he.''

"But you're a woman,'' the Aussie teased.

She teased him back. "Don't you think a woman should be tough?''

"That all depends.''

"On what?''

"On whether she loses something of herself in the bargain.''

"What would she have to lose?''

"Tenderness, maybe.''

His answer surprised her. Not knowing how to reply, she only nestled closer, and he seemed content with that.

THROUGH THE LONG NIGHT, he and Danielle talked, comforting each other with sad-funny stories out of their childhoods. It was as if they'd made a silent pact to forget the immediate danger. They found each other in a remembered world of innocence that hour by hour brought them closer.

"Why aren't you still on that sheep ranch?" she asked at last, snuggling more comfortably against his shoulder.

"After gran died I sold it. My life moved to a different rhythm by that time," he said simply. "In the end the outback was too dry, too barren, too silent." A sharp explosion rattled the narrow window in the basement wall.

Danielle shivered anew, but she managed to cajole him, "You didn't know when you had it good. I'd give anything right now for those barren silences." She was reluctant to give up their pasts and return to the terrible present.

He brought his free hand up to cup her nape, his broad thumb caressing the line of her jaw. "Now isn't that just typical of people?" he replied ironically. "Always missing what isn't there. . . and wanting what they can't have."

Danielle looked up at him. His eyes still shone their challenge at life, but there was a subtle undercurrent of sadness rippling through them that pierced her to the core. She realized that he not only understood her terror of dying, he shared it. Tomorrow was frightfully far away.

Yet she began to relax, and as she did so, Danielle drank in the man's faint musk scent and became disturbingly aware of their intimate proximity. Her head was still cradled against that muscled breadth of chest, and she felt the tangent pressure of their thighs, warm and firm.

Glancing up at him, she smiled tremulously.

Seeing her smile, he felt a stirring deep in his belly. These cool elegant beauties usually weren't his type at all, but some whisper of fragility within her called to him. He was achingly aware of every nuance of her body. The thrust of her pert breasts and the soft swell of her hip against his thigh elicited a hot-blooded male response. But his sudden desire was still tangled up with the tenderness he'd felt earlier. He found his reaction confusing...exciting, as if he were once again that boy on the brink of manhood.

Danielle sensed the subtle change in him. She sensed that his embrace was no longer simply protective, but was demanding something more of her. Now he, too, was aware of the exquisite apposition of their bodies, warm and alive, of the natural way she fit against him. Two strangers bound by a common fate, they were no longer strangers. They belonged wholly to each other.

He lowered his head as she lifted hers, until their lips were poised and waiting—a timeless moment that banished the world with all its terrors. In the promise of that kiss a new world was created.

Their lips met, hesitant and inquisitive. Then, with the inevitability of summer lightning, passion arced between them, tempestuous and electric. The kiss deepened, their tongues probing with the hungering intensity of long-lost lovers reunited. The fury and madness of the world above were purged in the white-hot ecstasy of mutual surrender.

Words were no longer necessary; their bodies spoke a primitive language of their own. Danielle was rocked by a passion she had never suspected could exist. He had awakened a deep instinctual womanliness that had nothing to do with feminine trappings.

Now an exultant wildness took possession of her, its unleashing softened by tenderness and an odd sense of gratitude. They had this moment, at least. For them time had accelerated, so that one minute might have been a year, one hour a century.

He dropped kisses on her temple, across her closed eyelids and the once-pale cheeks now flooded with the color of desire. "My God," he whispered huskily against her throat. "I don't even know your name, and yet I feel I know you better than I've ever known anyone."

His tongue followed the curving ridge of her ear. His lips closed over the lobe, and his mustache moved over it in a slow sensual brushstroke.

With impatient fingers he undid the tie of her black-dotted silk blouse to free the lovely expanse of her throat and neck. In a fevered rush his fingertips explored the silken smoothness of her flesh, as if driven by the fear of losing something infinitely precious that he was on the brink of discovering.

His mouth followed the gentle mapping of his touch until his lips found the pulsepoint at the base of her throat, lingering, almost willing her blood to pound as one with his. "You're so lovely...a beloved-stranger," he whispered, breathing in the scent of her that was like a green wood in spring—cool, dark and mysterious.

Her head thrown back, Danielle reveled in the

pleasure of his sensuous invasion. Each fingertip caress, each murmured endearment held the life-giving promise of a stormy summer sky after a long drought. And she held his head against her, ruffling the smooth dark hair with caressing fingers.

As his hand dipped into the open vee of her blouse and his fingertips skimmed the lace edge of her bra, Danielle sighed, her breasts rising to meet his fingers. Never had she wanted anything as much as she wanted this.

Driven by her own need to touch and caress, she unbuttoned his shirt and slipped her hand inside the rough cotton, so different from the expensive fabrics she was accustomed to. Different, too, was the hair-roughened texture of his broad chest. She tangled her fingers in the matted tracery, feeling a little shock of pleasure as they found the hard nub of his nipple. She slipped her other hand inside his shirt, sliding her arms around to embrace his bare torso.

Clinging to him with reckless ardor, she turned her head, inviting the nuzzle of his mouth against her throat. And as he kissed her, leaving a moist tingling trail of pleasure, his roving fingers dispensed with her buttons and clasps. Propping himself up on one elbow, he brushed the garments aside until they fell away against her upper arms in a crush of filmy lace and soft silk. The fiery-red glow of the night sky filtered into their hiding place and bathed her flesh in a wash of rose.

With a sharp intake of breath he let his eyes slowly drink in the beauty of her, the flushed skin defined against the blue-black tumble of hair veiling her shoulders. Now he was driven by conflicting desires, the urgent sexual demand of his loins countered by the equally powerful need to savor every inch of her—to emblazon on his mind the memory of that curiously wanton innocence when all the artificial constraints of civilization had been erased. Such magic could not occur more than once in a lifetime.

Their individual identities, the past and future, were irrelevant. All were consumed in the fire of that moment.

The yearning in his eyes inflamed her. Never had she been so aware of her own sexuality, of her own womanliness in every sense of the word, her need to cherish and love, to share the most intimate secrets of her being.

"Love me," she begged. "Love me before it's too late and we're lost to each other."

Her nipples, dark as currant wine, drew his lips downward again. He drank in their sweetness, his tongue a gentle marauder that flicked and curled, eliciting a rush of heightened sensuality along every nerve in her body.

She felt his hands caressing the enticing curve of her hips, felt them reach beneath the hem of her skirt to slide it up along her thighs. They savored undressing each other, and she reached with trembling hands to stroke the banded muscles across his back, to cup the lean tautness of his haunches and pull him toward her.

He needed no coaxing, and with delight she felt his

slow penetration, the hidden folds of her womanliness burgeoning in soft capitulation.

He was at once lover and teacher, the catalyst of her own self-discovery. She knew now the deepest meaning of being a woman, that awareness of her yielding femininity rising in exquisite opposition to his raw male power. Their bodies moved together in swift undulations, a primeval rhythm uniting in a bond as old as time.

The fierce sweet compulsion that had spurred their lovemaking ebbed in a burning mist, and they lay wrapped in each other's arms, unmoving. The ecstasy of their union had given way to the equally delicious awareness of each other as two separate beings: her hair fanning over his chest like a black banner, her perspiration-slicked thighs hot and smooth against his sinewy length.

"You're beautiful," he murmured against her temple. "Let those crazies out there bomb each other into oblivion. I don't care anymore. I could stay here with you forever."

"Let's," she whispered back teasingly, half wishing it could be that way. It was as if the rational side of her lay dormant. She felt more intensely alive than she ever had.

He was a man she knew nothing about. Yet she felt she had known him forever. Then it hit her: she loved this intimate stranger lying beside her, loved him deeply and completely. Sheer madness it might be, but she couldn't deny it, couldn't deny that he had touched her in a way no one ever had.

They murmured endearments to each other, their mingling breath and voices a foil for the ugly crack of gunshots far away. She knew that if she lived through this night and looked back on it from some distant future, the violence and danger would be long forgotten. What she held inside was protected, inviolate.

His low questioning voice was calling her back to him. "Are you still afraid?"

"Yes," she admitted as a light shiver touched her spine. "But somehow the fear is a little easier to bear."

Sporadic gunfire tore into the gathering stillness of the waning night.

He pulled her to him and held her tightly to still her trembling. After a while he drew back and reached for his slacks, digging into the pocket. "Here, take this," he said, handing her a small object. "It's a talisman... against fear."

She held it in the palm of her hand. It was a large fire opal, finely polished from countless thumb strokes. As she twisted her hand, its iridescent flame-bright core gleamed in the dim light. She closed her fingers around it.

Secure and warm in each other's arms, they drifted off to sleep, while gunfire burst from time to time in the distance.

THE MURKY GRAY LIGHT OF DAWN crept into the warehouse, pushing back the shadows. As her eyelids lifted heavily, the first thing Danielle noticed was the tall Australian standing below the street-level window, craning his head to glimpse outside. The gun-fire had ceased.

He turned to her. "It's over, love."

There was something curious in his voice that made her look sharply at him. "What do you mean?" she asked as she pulled on her clothes and joined him.

"Government troops have taken control." He craned his neck farther, eyes narrowing. "And it looks like they've got a contingent of U.S. Embassy police with them. The American ambassador must have lost someone important," he observed wryly.

Danielle bit her lip to keep from smiling. The two of them had discovered so much about each other, none of it having to do with the day-to-day reality of their lives.

"I can't believe the madness is over!" she replied, exuberant. The future existed, after all. "Come on, let's go up and show ourselves to the world."

Without waiting for his reply, Danielle raced up the basement stairs in her bare feet and called to the uniformed troops at the end of the short alleyway.

A shout and cry went up from the men in American uniform, and a young private yelled excitedly, "There she is, sarge, Ambassador Davis's daughter."

Sergeant Peters elbowed his way through the men, rushing forward. "Thank God you're alive, Miss Davis! You look like you've had an ugly time of it. Your father will be relieved to see you."

She smiled at the man. "It wasn't as bad as it might have been."

"Let's get out of here, then." He took her arm, but she shook it off.

"Wait, there's someone else with me." Danielle raced back down the stairs, the sergeant following. The basement was empty.

"Looks like whoever it was is gone now."

"But, no, that's impossible!" She hurried to the place where she and her lover had lain through the night—to the window. There was no trace of him.

Sergeant Peters crossed to the far corner of the warehouse and peered up another set of stairs Danielle had never noticed until now. "Must have taken off this way," he told her.

Numbly she fixed her eyes on the mossy dark stairway that led directly to the river's edge.

"We'd better get out of here, Miss Davis," the sergeant said at last, uncomfortable.

She fought to pull herself together. "Yes...yes, I suppose you're right."

A Jeep was waiting for them in the alley, and like an automaton she climbed into the back seat. But as the vehicle roared away she twisted her head to stare back at the blank row of buildings, the numb confusion in her mind giving way to a painful sense of loss.

CHAPTER ONE

A SLIGHT FROWN furrowing her brow, Danielle flipped through the stack of correspondence on her desk. The office was on the tenth floor of a high rise overlooking the Potomac River and sprawling complex of government buildings beyond. Her desk was oriented not to the view, but to the room and the expanse of white wall that was a perfect foil for her collection of brilliantly colored Malay fabrics. Framed batik prints vied for attention with the ceremonial wall hangings called *pua*.

Washington, D.C. ended at the threshold of her office, and a whole new world, more vivid and exotic, began. That exotic quality was part of what Danielle loved about her work, what made her so eager to protect endangered cultures from a drab industrial invasion.

She had worked hard these past several years and had risen quickly to the top echelons of the International Commission for Cultural Integrity. Now she headed the Southeast Asian division, as an adviser to the international banks that loaned money to foreign governments and entrepreneurs in that part of the world. Her role was to see that imported technology didn't threaten the ways of life of isolated tribal groups. When necessary, the bank loans were used to put muscle behind her decisions.

Danielle had been a natural choice for the influential position. A specialist in international law, she had lived and worked in Malaysia with her diplomat father. Such a cosmopolitan life-style had groomed her for her return to the U.S. capital—a city that was host to embassies and banking representatives from around the world—and for moving easily in the hub of power.

She was very proud of her track record. If a developer's plans appeared questionable, he had to answer to Danielle's office before the banks would even talk to him. As a result, the businessmen she dealt with were often very receptive to her recommendations.

But today her manicured nail tapped with angry impatience on the sleek letterhead of Kilpatrick Forestry, Ltd., a glaring exception to her impressive record. The firm had signed a long-term agreement with the Malaysian government to establish a timber industry in several outlying regions, and Kilpatrick was seeking additional funds for high-tech logging equipment. His camp in the remote mountain vastness of Sarawak state had come under fire from a group of anthropologists, a Dr. Strathmore chief among them. They feared the operation would radically change the lives of the Iban people, and Danielle had been called in to arbitrate.

Angered that this loan hadn't been automatically

approved, Ryan Kilpatrick, the firm's president, had been uncooperative to the point of rudeness in his response to the letters of inquiry Danielle had sent out. In his last letter he was threatening to come to Washington to settle the matter.

"Just you come, Mr. Kilpatrick," she murmured to herself. "Then we'll see how long you keep that contract of yours."

Working long into the afternoon, Danielle barely took notice of the darkening sky at her back. An antique desk lamp augmented the fluorescence overhead. She jumped when the intercom buzzed and quickly reached up to depress the switch. As she did so, the diamond engagement ring on her finger flashed in the lamplight. But Danielle was no longer aware of its icy brilliance.

"Yes, Jen?"

The cheery voice of her assistant, Jennifer Bondi, chuckled over the line. "You did it again, Danni," she teased. "I bet you've forgotten you're having an early dinner with Hal before heading over to the cocktail party at the Malaysian Embassy."

"Oh, Lord, you're right as usual!" She looked at her watch. "Has he called yet?"

"From the lobby. He's on his way up."

"Thanks, Jen. You might as well take off."

"Bless you, boss," Jen replied, her voice still full of laughter. "For once I won't have to race to make it to dance class. I'll have time to warm up properly, so my students won't think their teacher is a creaky old fossil."

"Come on, you're in better shape than I am," Danielle murmured distractedly as she riffled through her maze of reports and files. "I'll have to join you sometime."

"Good idea! I think you work far too hard, Danni, dear," Jen observed, and Danielle could envision the woman's wry but engaging smile. Only five years older than her boss, Jen nevertheless got a kick out of playing mother hen. But then that was Jen, caring and thoughtful beneath those bubbling good spirits. The secretary's big brown eyes were a lively complement to her generous mouth, and her simple pageboy haircut suited her unpretentious easy manner.

After wishing Jen a nice evening, Danielle leaned back with a sigh and rubbed her tense neck muscles. Her tired eyes caught a jeweled gleam on the desk top, and momentarily she forgot her exhaustion. The gem lay half-hidden in a shallow bowl littered with paper clips. Very slowly she moved it slightly so that its fire shone up at her. She had kept it these past four years, the only reminder of one distant magical night. The gem and all it represented might be forgotten for weeks at a time, but each time she saw it again the same feelings invariably resurfaced.

She had known a man, loved him deeply and lost him—all within the span of one short night. Twice her work had taken her back to Kuala Lumpur, and she had gone eagerly. Every waking moment she hadn't been working had been spent in search of that elusive stranger. But how could she find someone whose name she'd never known? Looking for him had been futile. Yet she hadn't been able to stop herself from trying. That one night had held a world of meaning for her; it had touched her profoundly.

But life went on, and Danielle could almost convince herself the incident no longer mattered. Still, she kept the burning memory of it deep inside, kept the stone that had been his talisman...and was now hers. "Where are you?" she whispered.

She had believed Hal Adams, an ambitious young attorney her father heartily approved of, would exorcise that memory. And she was doing her best to be a dutiful fiancée.

Resolutely she replaced the opal in its bowl and stood up, moving quickly to arrange the folders into neat stacks ready to be tackled the next day. Just as she was finishing, the office door swung open.

Her lips curved in a brief smile of welcome as Hal stepped inside. His narrow features gave him a look of sharp intelligence, boldly emphasized by the tortoiseshell glasses framing his alert blue eyes.

"Hello, Danni. Ready to go?"

She stood up and came around the desk, giving him an affectionate peck on the cheek. "Just let me freshen my makeup, and we can be on our way."

When she emerged from the women's executive lounge several minutes later, it was apparent she'd done a little more than slick on a deeper shade of rose lipstick. Though she still wore the soft cream gabardine suit, a subtle change of accessories gave her a sexy if no less elegant look. The sophisticated geometric print blouse had given way to a bare black camisole and two slender silver chains at her throat. She had replaced her dark pumps with strappy sling-backs.

But her hair was still drawn up in a simple chignon, softened only by a delicately etched comb. Danielle rarely wore her hair any other way. She was a woman, the look implied, but the softness only went so far. Her style was a no-nonsense signal to her male colleagues that she was every bit as ambitious and career minded as they. They respected her; some even regarded her as a serious rival—which pleased her. Danielle's life was bound by the dictates of her career, and tonight she reminded herself, rather too sharply, that it was all she wanted.

When she rejoined Hal in her office reception area, his eyes assessed her in his phlegmatic way. He slipped the papers he'd been studying back into his briefcase and snapped it shut.

"You should make a good impression tonight," he said, opening the door for her. "But I didn't expect you to take so long, Danni. We'd better hurry if we want the maître d' to keep our table."

"Fine," she said softly over her shoulder as she preceded him to the elevator. He missed the almost imperceptible sigh that fluttered through her voice.

THEY DINED at a small downtown restaurant known for its excellent food and impeccable service. The decor was unexciting, but then patrons were too engrossed in high-level deals over lunch or recaps of the day's strategy over dinner to notice. It was no lovers' retreat.

Danielle tried to be attentive as Hal discussed the conference sessions he'd led that day. A fast-rising State Department lawyer, he was in line for a key administrative post if he could win out over the competition, an equally savvy and ambitious colleague.

His fiancée listened, gave advice, suggested strategies, and Hal in turn did the same for her. The same age and of similar backgrounds, they were a well-meshed team, and Danielle knew Hal had no doubts that their marriage would operate on the same efficient, organized level.

He glanced down at his watch. "We'd better forgo the coffee," he told her crisply. "That invitation said seven-thirty, right?"

Later as he drove his comfortable sedan down Massachusetts Avenue, Hal glanced across the passenger seat to her. "Who's going to be at this Malaysian Embassy affair, Danni? Anyone I know?"

"No one from the State Department, if that's what you mean," she teased him. "We're focusing on my career tonight, remember?"

Hal shrugged. "Still, it always pays to keep your eyes open. Opportunities don't happen. They're made."

"You sound just like my father." Although her tone was still teasing, her smile was faintly rueful.

"I take that as a compliment," Hal retorted mildly. "There's one man I truly admire."

"I think dad will be here tonight, too, by the way," she told him. Danielle's gaze shifted back to the wide boulevard. The lamplit porticoes of exclusive hotels and elegant museum galleries slid past them in the darkness, but her thoughts were on her father. He was one of those high-energy men who had his finger on every power pulse in the capital. Once an ambassador, he was now an informal adviser to the president and to congressional leaders of both parties. For all her thirty years John Davis had been his daughter's mentor and guide. In many ways she was the son he had never had.

Her thoughts returned to the present as the car swung into a long curving drive, already lined with dozens of limousines. The embassy, set well back from the avenue, was housed in a lovely old mansion overlooking the lush darkness of Rock Creek Park.

The wide, high-ceilinged foyer opened onto a reception hall tastefully decorated with Malaysian appointments. Selangor pewter in simple contemporary designs contrasted with the antique beauty of Johore black ceramics gracing a long sideboard. The Malay love of color revealed itself in the numerous wall hangings. They made Danielle feel right at home.

She chatted easily with the Malaysian ambassador and his staff; then, as more people crowded around, she slipped off in search of others she knew. True to his own advice, Hal was already busy developing a rapport with a visiting United Nations official from New York and hadn't even noticed that his fiancée was no longer beside him.

She spotted her father across the room, deep in conversation with her boss, and made her way toward them. Davis was a distinguished-looking man, the attractive iron gray at his temples giving way to a smooth salt-and-pepper thickness. His nose was narrow and straight above a sensuous full upper lip that had been compressed by years of discipline. In fact, the profiles of father and daughter were remarkably similar, except that Danielle's was softened by high delicate cheekbones, inherited from her mother, and a pert but stubborn chin.

Davis looked up from his conversation as she joined them. "Danni!" he greeted her with an affectionate clap on the shoulder. "Clay and I were just discussing you."

In response to her inquisitive glance, ICCI chief Clay Perrin winked. "It was all good, I assure you," he teased his youngest but most able administrator. At the same time his shrewd eyes swept the rapidly filling hall. "It looks like everyone who's important in Southeast Asian affairs is here tonight."

"That's why we're here, I suppose," she interposed lightly.

Clay laughed. "Now that's the kind of talk I like to hear from my protégés."

The two shared a good working relationship. Danielle admired Clay, but she worried about him a little. His rapidly thinning hair and indifferently slouched shoulders bespoke a man aging far too quickly. She had come to work for him shortly after his divorce, and the years since hadn't worn well on him. Danielle's gaze shifted to her father. Though more physically fit than Clay, John Davis had the same perpetually tense look around his eyes.

Danielle's mother had been dead twenty years; Clay's marriage had been over for five. Why had neither man remarried, she suddenly asked herself. Perhaps because life within the circles of power sucked a person dry and left no room for emotion, for oneself. She shrugged off the uncomfortable train of thought as Clay ambled to the bar and her father fixed her with a questioning look.

"I'm sorry, dad, were you saying something?"

"I just said that we haven't had a chance to talk in quite a while. You've been a stranger to Foxhall lately." His smile was patient, but there was faint reproach in his voice, an undercurrent of loneliness that took her aback. "Now tell me," he went on with his usual briskness, "do you have everything under control at the office?"

She sighed, relieved he hadn't asked something more personal. "Don't I always, dad?", she said with a spunky grin.

As they chatted, father and daughter drifted into the easy if superficial camaraderie that had always bound them. But tonight she kept remembering the hint of loneliness in his voice. Was her vigorous, handsome father losing his grip?

John Forbes Davis had taught his daughter much through his own example. There was an old unspoken rule between them that personal feelings were never discussed. To let people see how you really felt was somehow an unforgivable show of weakness. Because of that lesson, she had been backing away from emotions all her life.

She was chatting nonstop now, amusing him with anecdotes from the office. "But you know how it is, dad," she went on in a determinedly lighthearted tone. "There's always at least one thorny problem in the works." She described her bristly exchange of letters with the president of Kilpatrick Forestry, Ltd.

Davis stroked his chin. "Kilpatrick," he mused. "There was a Ryan Kilpatrick in Kuala Lumpur. I don't know if the two of you ever met, but I ran across him several times at various functions. A good-looking man though something of a rogue, a scoundrel if the gossip was true. He worked for one of those big logging operations that exploited its workers as if they were slave labor. Eventually there were indictments. . . . I wonder if it was the same man."

Danielle perked up. "I never thought to research Kilpatrick's past," she replied, excited. "If he is the same man, that information might be just the leverage I need to make him come around." She smiled, a gleam of triumph in her eyes. "Kilpatrick has been threatening to come to D.C. and thrash it out with me in person. But I promise you, I'll make mincemeat of him when he does," she went on, only half-teasingly.

Davis nodded. "That's the way to handle him, Danni."

They were still chuckling in that conspiratorial way, when Danielle glanced idly around toward the entrance. Her whole body went rigid as her eyes riveted on the ruggedly attractive man who stood there with a petite blonde on his arm.

In that instant of shocked recognition Danielle went white. The elusive lover who had haunted her dreams stood, in the flesh, across the room. She felt the blood pounding in her ears like a storm tide.

"My God, it can't be him," she said dazedly.

Davis's eyes followed hers. "That's Kilpatrick, all right," he said with a trace of distaste. "But Danni, I thought you said you had never met Ryan Kilpatrick."

The words filtered through her fog, and her eyes widened. " 'Kilpatrick'?" she repeated in a strained voice. "You mean, the man with the blonde is Ryan Kilpatrick?"

Davis's smile was cool and calculating, as if he were considering a chess move. "That's your man. Looks like he's decided to come in for the fight." His eyes narrowed. "He doesn't seem to have changed much in four years."

Her mouth was parched, so that when she spoke her voice was little more than a quavering whisper. "No...he hasn't."

Davis was studying Kilpatrick with detached interest. "He still looks as if he could swing an ax all day long and not feel it. Danni, I think you've got your work cut out for you."

But she no longer heard her father's voice. Ryan's eyes had found Danielle across the crowded room, and it was as though they had been hurtled back across the abyss of time. No one else existed in that charged moment of rediscovery.

Slowly he approached, and she waited, her heart

thrashing in her breast like an imprisoned bird. Her eyes swept down him, taking in the dark hair against his tanned skin, the slightly rumpled linen suit and batik-patterned tie knotted carelessly at his throat. In the middle of that Washington crowd, among conservative suits and foulard neckware, he stood out as a maverick, a man used to setting his own rules no matter what the game.

As he drew closer she took in the details of him. His mustache was thick and full, its lushness reminding her with unbidden clarity of how silkily sensual it had once felt against her flesh. Those greenish eyes hadn't changed, either, lazily aware of everything.

Her pale face flooded with color as he stopped before her and extended his hand. "Miss Davis?" He inclined his head, the formality of his greeting mocked by the faint curve of his lips.

"You already knew my name?" She fought to keep her voice light as their hands met.

"How could I forget the daughter of an ambassador?" he teased her, his callused palm moving with subtle pressure against her own. When she sought to withdraw her fingers he held them fast.

The shock of seeing him again gave way to confusion and a prickle of betrayal, but she steeled herself to reveal nothing more than polite inquisitiveness. On that distant dawn he must have heard the relieved shouts of the embassy police. Then he had vanished into thin air. A man on the run? She remembered her father's words: "rogue, scoundrel."

John Davis stepped smoothly into the breach of his

daughter's silence. "Danni was just saying how much she was looking forward to seeing you, Mr. Kilpatrick." The irony in the former diplomat's voice was veiled but unmistakable.

Ryan looked momentarily nonplussed. "I had no idea I was expected." Even as he said this the pieces of the puzzle fell into place, and he felt curiously desolate. The beautiful, softly compliant woman he had made love to in a distant past had metamorphosed into something far different from the dream he held inside. A clever joke fate had played on him, but he didn't feel like laughing.

To cover his dismay, Ryan smiled mockingly. "So you're the hard-nosed little bureaucrat who's been giving me hell."

Danielle shrugged, and the gesture masked the trembling of her fingers, which he still held imprisoned. All he read in her features was a stony coldness, and his own expression hardened. "My old granny warned me there'd be days like this," he murmured, the words an ironic echo of the poignant intimacies they had once shared.

Danielle's eyelashes dropped against her cheeks as she recalled the boldly scrawled signature she had come to know so well in the past several months. Ryan Kilpatrick. Fate had played a devilish trick. How often she had prayed that she would find him again, little dreaming it would be like this! They had collided by chance again, but she was no longer a frightened, starry-eyed innocent. And he...? She shut her mind to the ugly questions lurking there.

When Danielle looked up again, the blond woman with him was assessing her. "Well, I declare," she drawled in a soft voice. "You two hardly seem to be strangers. By the way, Miss Davis, you remember me too, I'm sure? Charlotte Jenkins. My daddy's a congressman from Atlanta. I worked in your office several summers ago while I was still in school." Charlotte coyly held out her hand, a none-too-subtle hint that Danielle should have long since freed herself from Kilpatrick's lingering clasp.

"No, I'm sorry, I don't remember," Danielle replied with an exaggerated sweetness that mimicked the younger woman's ultrafeminine manner.

Unfazed, Charlotte smiled sweetly up at her date. "Shall we move on to the bar, Ryan, darlin'? I'm parched."

Ryan released Danielle's fingers, but his eyes still held hers questioningly. "We'll chat later, I hope?" he murmured under his breath. Then Kilpatrick led his date away.

After they'd gone Davis demanded, "What was that all about?" When she didn't reply, his wry amusement gave way to concern. "Are you all right, honey?"

Her father rarely used such terms of endearment, so Danielle realized she must look as upset as she felt. Nevertheless she reassured him, with a bright, patently false smile, "Really, I'm fine. It's just that I wasn't expecting to meet Kilpatrick without advance warning." She forestalled any further questions with a hurried, "Excuse me, dad. I'm going to get some fresh air."

Beyond the French doors at the far end of the room, a flagstone terrace lay empty and silent beneath the cool night sky. Danielle leaned against the low wall, staring out into the clustered shadows of a dark wood. Faint voices from inside mingled with the distant roar of traffic on the parkway, a soothing counterpoint to her jangled nerves.

"Ryan." She whispered it angrily this time, giving free reign to the suspicions that had lurked in her mind from the moment he had murmured her name with such damning nonchalance. All through those months, stretching into years, that she had suffered the private agony of her loss, Ryan had known who her father was. All that time, while she was struggling to come to terms with the painful realization that they were destined to be forever strangers, he could have found her easily. If he had wanted to, he could have contacted her at the American Embassy in Kuala Lumpur. If he had wanted to.... Danielle felt a cold hard knot forming inside her.

"So we meet again, ambassador's daughter." She froze as the familiar intimacy of that low easy baritone washed over her. How long had he stood there, staring down at her head bent beneath the weight of painful reminiscence? Slowly she turned, willing herself to appear composed. Never, she vowed in that instant, never would she reveal her weakness to him. "Danni...Danielle," he went on bemusedly. "I don't know what to call you."

Her eyes blazed up at him in the darkness. "Try Miss Davis, Mr. Kilpatrick."

The tentative gleam of humor in his eyes vanished. "So that's how it's to be between us?"

Ignoring that thrust, she crossed her arms and eyed him angrily. "I see you've carried out the threat in your last letter, Mr. Kilpatrick. You've come to Washington."

"I had unfinished business." He spoke each word with a measured intensity that cut her to the marrow.

"As far as I'm concerned it will stay that way."

"I don't give up easily."

"Really? I would have thought the opposite. I would have thought you were the type to turn tail and run at the first sign of trouble."

"It depends on the circumstances," he replied, suddenly angry himself. "If I've a reason for staying, wild horses wouldn't drag me away."

A charged silence arced between them. They were wounding each other intentionally, using pain to fill the emptiness where trust had been.

Her brittle animosity stunned him. The woman of substance and beauty he had loved one poignant, well-remembered night was nothing to him now but an impersonal name at the bottom of a letter. Ryan was so caught up in his own defensive anger that he didn't notice the trembling of her lower lip. She turned back to the low wall and sanctuary of darkness beyond, hiding her reaction.

"Listen to me," he said. "I've come to Washington for one reason only. I intend to circumvent all this bureaucratic nonsense. You're narrow and blind, the whole lot of you, attempting to legislate lives from twelve thousand miles away. I despise that kind of cheap arrogance.''

Her head whipped around. ''The bureaucracy you're so intent on condemning has only one purpose—to protect innocent tribal peoples from the likes of you.''

He regarded her narrowly, his expression unreadable. ''The likes of me? What the devil is that supposed to mean?''

''You're obviously the type who thinks only of himself.''

''So you think you know all about me from a six-month correspondence? How very clever of you.''

''You're wrong.'' Her soft voice was undercut with steel. ''I know all about your past, Mr. Kilpatrick.'' She was bluffing now, another of the ploys her father had taught her. The more you bluff, the more the other person reveals about himself.

But Ryan was ready for her. His answering laughter was short, harsh. ''You know damned little.''

''That little is damning enough,'' she flung back, undaunted. ''You're selfish and cruel.''

His eyes bored into her hotly, the passion in his look threatening to rip away her carefully built defenses. ''After what we shared together,'' he demanded, the murmur of his voice catching her in its sensual web, ''how can you accuse me of that?''

Suddenly they were confronting each other not as business adversaries but as man and woman. Her sharp badinage could no longer protect her.

She blinked hard to keep back the sting of tears. "That woman is dead."

"I don't believe that."

Danielle could feel her self-control slipping. "You killed her yourself, Ryan," she whispered, anguished. All the hurt she had tried to deny glimmered in her eyes and trembled her lips. Before she could stop them the bitter words were out. "That night meant nothing to you."

His hand closed over her arm, the pressure fueling the smoldering fires that threatened to blaze between them. "How can you believe that?"

She brought her fist up and pushed against his chest. As she did so the large diamond on her hand flashed.

Ryan glanced down at it, then slowly lifted his gaze to hers. "It looks as though I'm too late."

"Far too late."

For all the sharpness of the exchange their eyes said differently, calling to memory a furtive and exquisitely tender, all-consuming desire. Then reality intruded like a snap of impatient fingers, and the moment was gone. Boisterous laughter and warm air rushed out through the flung-open terrace doors. Lovers were once again strangers. Danielle and Ryan drew apart as if they'd been stung.

"Danni?" Hal's familiar voice, hesitant and rather irritated, called out to her. "I've been looking all over for you."

She took a deep breath to calm herself before responding, "In a minute, Hal." Satisfied, he retreated into the warmth of the embassy hall.

Ryan cocked his head down at her inquisitively. "'Danni' again?" he taunted. "You know that sounds to me like a nickname for a little boy."

"How dare you mock something so personal!"

He ignored her outrage. "So that woman I once loved is dead," he observed at last, amusement rippling through his attractive baritone. "Fine. Then we'll just have to start all over again...with you."

His cool amusement infuriated her. "There's nothing to start. The past is done, and there's no future in your staying. Our business is through."

His eyes swept down her, their depths turbulent, reckless. "You're wrong, Danielle. We haven't even begun."

Her name on his lips was sensual poetry, a gentle blandishment that enticed her.

Suddenly frightened by the devastating effect he could still have on her, she turned and rushed away. The lighted hall with its ambience of power and diplomacy, wit and cunning was her setting. What had occurred one night long ago was a quirk of fate, an accident. It would not happen again. She would not let it happen.

DANIELLE SAT HUNCHED against the passenger door as Hal drove through the empty streets toward Georgetown.

"Is something bothering you?" he finally asked.

"No," she answered, not looking at him. "Why should there be?"

"I don't know, Danni. You just seem so distant all of a sudden."

"Why do you call me that?" she said with un-wonted sharpness.

"Call you what?"

She frowned at him. " 'Danni.' "

His look was bewildered, though he retorted with unerring logic, "Haven't you always been called that?"

Without bothering to reply, she turned away again to stare out at the rows of expensive shops that filled the picturesque quarter.

After pulling up into the short driveway of her town house, Hal slid across the seat and put his arm around her shoulders. The kiss he bestowed on her lips was pleasant, perfunctory.

Dear Hal, she thought with an air of detachment even as he kissed her. She could count on him never to push too far or demand too much. Gently disengaging herself, she got out of the car and slowly climbed the dark stairs.

CHAPTER TWO

OFFICIALLY IT WAS SPRING, but the gray skies hovering over the Potomac still had the look of winter. Danielle stared out at the cheerless expanse, her back to the desk. She'd been fidgety and unable to concentrate all morning. Now, for the umpteenth time, she glanced at her watch. She scowled. Nearly noon.

Danielle jumped when the intercom buzzed.

"Mr. Kilpatrick is here for his eleven-thirty appointment," Jen announced, no hint of censure in her voice. "I'll send him in."

A moment later Danielle heard the office door open. Without turning, she addressed her visitor. "You're late." The words fell into a stony silence. The hairs on the back of her neck prickling, Danielle waited.

He was more patient, and she was at last forced to swivel in her chair to face him. Ryan stood just inside the door, his hands behind him on the knob. His stance accentuated the breadth of his chest beneath the well-cut but rumpled linen suit. He wore another of his outrageous ties, this one a yellow-and-gold Chinese silk with its ends rakishly askew. Vitality boiled beneath this token compromise to sophisticated Washington, as if he meant to show he would only compromise so far.

"I'm late, and I apologize," he acknowledged. "But that's no excuse for you to play your power act on me. I don't have any respect for people who grovel, or for the ones who force them into a position so that they have to."

Danielle arrogantly overrode his complaint. "I'm a busy woman, Mr. Kilpatrick."

"And I'm not busy?" he demanded. "I had to come away during the height of the dry season, when my company should be gearing up for full production. I had to travel twelve thousand miles to get what should have been okayed months ago. And you have the bloody nerve to chastise me for mucking up your 'busy' schedule?"

"Then you may have doubly wasted your time, because there's no guarantee you're going to get anything at all. I suggest you go back to Australia and leave the Malaysians alone."

"You with your laws and paperwork, your rules and regulations," Ryan answered, his voice rasping with impatience. "What in hell do you really know or care about the Malaysians?"

Danielle sprang from her chair and came around the desk to confront him, her whole body taut with outrage. "I once nearly died for them, Mr. Kilpatrick," she whispered between her teeth. Silently they stared at each other, and the quick angry rhythm of her breathing was like a ticking bombshell. "What in God's name do you think I was doing that evening in

Kuala Lumpur? I had friends in Chinatown I was terribly concerned about, but ironically I found out afterward that they had survived the night far more comfortably than I. . . ."

Unbidden, the potent shared memory of that long-ago night sprang to life, and the atmosphere between them changed. It crackled with a heavy expectant tension that left them burningly aware of each other.

Danielle backed off at once, furious at having let down her guard. The past was a dangerous mirage. "Shall we get down to business, Mr. Kilpatrick?" she suggested calmly, picking up the folder on her desk as if the emotional exchange had never happened. With practiced ease she became professional, objective.

The sham irritated Ryan. "I think we should settle our personal business first, don't you?" he challenged softly.

"The matter up for discussion is your application for a loan—for another helicopter, isn't it?"

Ryan exhaled explosively. "All right," he conceded, frustration clipping his syllables. "But for God's sake, if we have to discuss this now at least let's do it over lunch."

"No, thank you. I lunch only with my associates."

Ignoring her put-down, he laid his palms flat on the desk and leaned toward her. "Make an exception, now."

"I'm not interested in—"

"Well, I am." He straightened and took her gray

gabardine suit jacket from the coat rack, holding it out. "Besides, I've made reservations."

Meeting his look, she saw the teasing smile, and his unexpected warmth unnerved her. Under ordinary circumstances she would have insisted on conducting business on her own turf. But the office's Asian decor resonated with the aura of that distant world, evoking memories that had no business being re-awakened. Ryan himself was the catalyst, but she would no more admit to that than she would to any of the other confused emotions that had swept over her since he'd arrived.

"I suppose we could just as easily discuss the application over lunch," she conceded coolly. Snapping up her black leather envelope bag from a drawer, Danielle strode gracefully out of the office ahead of him and stopped in front of her secretary's desk. "I'm going out to lunch," she announced, smoothing her hand over the already-neat coil of her chignon.

"Very good." Jen's poker face slipped a little when her eyes flickered curiously in Ryan's direction. "If Clay stops by, how long shall I tell him you'll be, Danni?"

"No more than an—"

Her confident prediction was drowned out by Ryan's cocky voice. "Miss Davis will check back if she gets tied up." With that he took Danielle's elbow and grinned breezily at Jen. The smile was so infectious she had to smile, too—until she caught her boss's angry eye.

"I'll see you in an hour, then," Jen called loyally after them, though her eyes sparkled with telltale amusement.

While they waited for the elevator Danielle ignored him, using the time to straighten the collar of her black-on-gray patterned silk blouse and smooth down her skirt, as if she'd been alone. She continued the cold-shoulder treatment inside the elevator, staring straight ahead at the lit board marking their descent. Still, she was quite aware of his eyes on her.

"You know you shouldn't wear gray," he remarked conversationally.

Caught off guard, Danielle shot him a swift inquisitive glance. "Why not?" she demanded, regretting her response even as it tumbled out.

Never taking his eyes off her, Ryan tilted his head as if he were a portrait artist studying his subject. "A woman with your depth, your intensity should celebrate it with color. You should be wearing those bright batiks you have in your office," he went on in his half thoughtful, half teasing way. "If you were mine I'd want you to bloom, not fade into the crowd like army camouflage."

Danielle stared up at him, openmouthed. The unexpected intimacy in his mischievous, backhanded compliment unnerved her completely. Her restless fingers flew up toward her hair as if to seek reassurance in the tight neat coil of her chignon. Ryan had anticipated that defensive gesture, and with a breath of laughter he caught her hand.

Deliberately he brushed his thumb across the brilliant marquis solitaire on her third finger. "Don't worry," he murmured. "I don't have any desire to come between you and your fiancé."

All the same, he was slow in releasing her hand. The warm pressure of his fingertips sent a faint tremor through her, like wind licking at a stray spark.

The elevator slid to a stop. Relieved, Danielle turned from Ryan, and before the door had opened all the way she had slipped past the milling crowd waiting to go up.

Ryan exited more leisurely, his eyes following her across the spacious lobby until she disappeared through the revolving glass doors. He had meant to cut her down to size with that remark about her fiancé, but his intended mockery had backfired when he touched her hand.

Fool, he berated himself. He hadn't counted on his own response to her. All he wanted was to bring her down a peg or two, to get what he'd come for and be off again. Danielle had the world she wanted. *Let her keep it. The lady's nothing to me.* Ryan followed her outside, trying hard as hell to forget the elusive image of that soft trembling woman he had briefly loved.

Danielle shivered a little in the freshening wind off the river, though its bite wasn't quite as sharp as she'd expected. Sunlight peeked fitfully through the brindled gray of the sky, offering an illusion of warmth from where it glistened off a car windshield. At the curb she paused and turned, glimpsing the tall Australian as he emerged from the building. Reflexively he bent his head against the knifelike spring wind and hurried to where she stood waiting.

"Your kind of weather, I take it," he remarked, noticing the high color in her cheeks and her elegantly erect back, while he was hunched self-protectively against the elements.

"I'm not afraid of the cold," she shot back disdainfully.

"Yes, I can see there's a natural affinity."

Fleetingly she searched his eyes, wondering if he was laughing at her again. But all she found was an answering coldness. He had deliberately closed himself to her.

Ryan took her arm, and led her around the corner to his rented convertible Triumph, wedged insolently between a pair of sedans. After installing her in the passenger seat, Ryan climbed behind the wheel. Then, provoked by some imp of devilry, he reached up to free the hooks holding the cloth roof in place. A minute later they could see the murky sky glowering above their heads.

"Are you crazy!" Danielle protested. "We can't drive around with the top down in this weather."

"Very character building," he said, all innocence as he nosed out into the heavy traffic.

"Very funny," she replied under her breath, clamping her hands against her head as the convertible gathered speed on Constitution Avenue—not to smooth her hair this time, but to protect her ears, which were freezing.

To their left, the winter-bare lawns of the Mall

stretched toward the distant Capitol rotunda. A few people braved the cold, eating their sack lunches on benches, throwing the crumbs to the pigeons. When the sports car braked for a light in front of the courthouse, two men in warm-up suits jogged across the intersection.

Ryan's eyes followed them with interest. "I never could understand that sport," he said with good-humored contempt.

"Not everyone has the luxury of getting into shape on a sheep ranch or in a logging camp," Danielle countered dryly.

Her irony went right past him. "More's the pity. I don't envy them their eight-to-five lives."

"What makes you think they don't pity you yours?" Danielle felt compelled to defend her fellow Washingtonians.

Ryan shrugged, and it was obvious from the gesture that he didn't care a tinker's damn what anyone thought of him or his life. It pleased him, and that was all that mattered. He looked up to find her beautiful sea-colored eyes raking him impatiently.

"Here you are driving down the stateliest boulevard in the country, and you don't have a single word to spare for it," she accused. "Don't you find it beautiful?"

"Very nice, indeed. That is, if you go in for all those symbols of power."

"Well, I happen to love this city and all it stands for," she replied, offended. "You could at least keep your thoughts to yourself. Didn't your old granny teach you anything about diplomacy?''

Ryan's lips curved subtly in appreciation of her sharply aimed dig. ''Upon my word she did,'' Ryan said, enjoying himself. ''She always warned me to watch out for that kind of flimflam double-talk.''

Before she could reply the light changed again, and the convertible roared to life. Hugging her arms for warmth, Danielle glanced at the dashboard. She was sorely tempted to flick the heater switch, but in the end forbore.

The Australian drove with the swift panache of a man accustomed to the chaos of Kuala Lumpur's back streets, and within a mercifully short time they were pulling into the underground garage of a Water Street restaurant.

Sometime during that bracing drive Danielle's arrogant self-possession had slipped a little. Ryan grinned as he helped her from the car, resisting the urge to tweak the bright red of her nose. ''Maybe by the time I leave Washington I'll have developed a hide as thick as yours,'' he needled her.

Danielle's only answer was an exasperated sniffle, to which Ryan gallantly responded by pulling a handkerchief from his pants pocket.

Delicately she blew her nose. ''If I get pneumonia I'll have you in court for negligence,'' she complained as they climbed the stairs to the restaurant.

''Too right. Just sic that priggish, sharp-eyed little fiancé of yours on me.''

''We can leave him out of this.'' For all her anger,

Danielle didn't leap to Hal's defense as she had the joggers'. Ryan's contempt disturbed her deeply, perhaps because more than once she'd had similar traitorous thoughts herself.

The interior of the Mexican restaurant was cozy and attractively appointed with native pottery, baskets and handwoven throw rugs. "Good afternoon," the hostess greeted them brightly. "Dining room or patio?"

"Patio," Ryan replied at once with a slow wink down at Danielle as they fell into step behind the hostess. But to her surprise she found the patio with its little space heaters and glass wind walls every bit as cozy as inside.

They opted for hot wine mulled with cloves and sliced oranges, and as Danielle sipped the sweet aperitif quiet contentment unexpectedly stole over her. Beyond the restaurant walls the river channel stretched placidly toward the tree-lined quay of East Potomac Park. The sails of a lone sloop fluttered while the helmsman sought to bring her directly into the wind. It was as if a tantalizing hint of the sea had washed up with the incoming tide. Breathing deeply, Danielle caught the faint sharp scent of sea grass and, closing her eyes, could imagine herself on a low hill above Chesapeake Bay.

When she opened them again she found Ryan staring at her. "You don't get away like this very often, do you?"

She gazed into the ruby liquid in her glass, idly swirling it round and round. She said nothing, afraid her reply might reveal far more than she intended. Ryan had glimpsed too much already. His sensitivity was a threat to the carefully insulated world she had created for herself; no way on earth would she let those barriers fall again.

Danielle looked up, her expression shuttered. "Shall we get down to business?" she began crisply, as if he'd never spoken. "I have one question about your logging operation in Sarawak. Why did you have to penetrate so deeply into the upriver forests? From what I understand, that back country is rugged and virtually inaccessible. Wouldn't it have been easier to set up business in the lowlands, closer to the sea?"

Ryan's eyes held hers for an instant before flickering away idly toward the somnolent channel. Silence stretched between them, seeming to drown out the chink of cutlery and the murmur of other diners.

Suspecting that he meant to turn her own tactics against her, Danielle pressed him for a response. "Well?"

"It would have been easier, yes," he said finally, his eyes brushing across the lovely lips that impatience had compressed into a tense inflexible line.

"Then why Akan?"

"The mountains have the prime hardwoods I want. But even if the wood was less valuable I'd still be there, because I thrive on challenge. Do you understand that, Danielle?" Provocation was implicit in the murmured breath of her name, a warning and a promise both that set her blood pounding against her temples.

She looked down at her hands, gripping the stem of her wineglass, and desperately wished she'd never left her desk. Gone were all her office props, the applications and file folders she could have riffled through as a defense against him.

Her confusion infuriated her, but she took strength from her anger. "There are challenges and challenges," she answered him, lifting serene eyes to his. "Personally I think you've been in the wilds too long. Your bluntness is going to get you into trouble. It's useless against finesse and sophistication. You're out of your element, Mr. Kilpatrick."

"Am I?" He laughed again, more softly. "We'll see."

With renewed determination she took charge of the conversation. "Tell me more about your business. I'm intrigued."

He acknowledged her sarcasm with one subtly cocked brow. "In the first place, I don't need another chopper so I can ferry myself from place to place 'like a modern-day Napoleon surveying his domain.'"

The flicker of an eyelid was the only hint of Danielle's embarrassment at hearing her own overstuffed phrase quoted. That particular letter, she recalled, had been written in the heat of anger after one from him describing her as a "know-it-all, do-nothing bureaucrat."

She exhaled impatiently, eager to let him know

she'd found out a little more about his operation since then. "You need the helicopter for aerial surveying."

"Not just for surveying. We do the actual logging with a chopper. There's no bigger thrill than swooping in across one of those dragontail ridges in the Santubongs. After the ground crew has made its cut, you can pluck a ten-ton hardwood log out of the forest as if you were taking a posy from a bouquet." His body tensed with remembered excitement. "Once you've got that payload attached, you think you've stumbled onto quicksand. Getting out of there in one piece depends totally on finding your balance and solid space again."

"You've actually flown the thing yourself?"

"I did a few times and once nearly set the chopper into a nose-dive spin." He grinned. "It scared the hell out of me."

"Like fun it did," she argued, feeling his excitement. "What scares the hell out of you is the threat of boredom and routine, not danger. Am I right?"

"Is this your woman's intuition talking?" he parried in that lazy way of his.

"I think you're a man who takes too many chances. A man who doesn't care enough to hold on to what he has. A poor risk all around."

The accusation cut into him. "All I need, Danielle, is the chance to prove myself." Pride warred with the hidden hunger in his voice, and she felt the heat of recognition flooding up her throat. The straightforward conversation had detoured them to a hidden path. They were talking about emotional risks and losses that had nothing to do with business.

"There are no second chances," she whispered, her voice husky with the effort to keep it steady. "I know your type now. You're the kind of man who'll come in and say anything to get what he wants. You hurt whatever you touch."

Ryan leaned across the table, his eyes as lifeless as if a light had been extinguished. "Including you?"

Danielle was saved from replying because the waiter arrived with their order, steaming plates of crab enchiladas. They ate in silence for several minutes, neither really tasting the delicately spiced entrée.

Finally Danielle gave up the pretense of eating and pushed her plate away. "I'm afraid this has been a waste of time. Neither of us has had our questions answered."

Ryan glanced down at his watch, then signaled the waiter to bring two cups of coffee along with the check. "We still have a couple of minutes. Fire away."

"I am curious about one thing," she said, striving to put them back on a strictly professional footing. "How do you plan to recoup the tremendous capital investment in a helicopter if you do get a loan? Four million dollars is an outrageous sum to ask for." Her tone implied his chances were nil.

"I take the pick of the forest. The Japanese and the Arabs are willing to pay well for the high-grade stuff I log and mill. It's a challenge, but it pays damn well, too. I'm not ashamed of that." He said this aggressively, anticipating her next barb.

She didn't disappoint him. "I suppose you tear out gaping holes in the jungle."

"I take only what I need. I don't put in any logging roads. I don't bring in any Caterpillar tractors to haul the payload all over hell and back and tear up the undergrowth. When I'm gone it's as if I've never been there."

"Except for the several hundred lives you've damaged irreparably with your hit-and-run style of economics."

Abruptly Ryan sat back and draped an elbow across his chair, doing his damndest to keep his anger in check. It was there all the same in his eyes. "For pity's sake, Danielle, you sound like one of those bleeding-heart liberals who's never left the safety of his own office. You lived and worked in Malaysia. Haven't you ever been upriver in Borneo? Or did you never bother to get past the cricket clubs and diplomatic parties in Kuala Lumpur?"

Another flicker of her eyelid gave the truth to his accusation, but she covered herself smoothly. "I have my experts in the field."

"'Experts.'" He smiled grimly. "Sometimes I think the only thing they're interested in is keeping the Iban like specimens in a curiosity shop. Sure, their life-style is primitive by our standards, but they're no childlike innocents. They want the same things we all do—a better life for their kids, a chance to know what the rest of the world is like."

"And so you very nobly offered to bring it to their doorstep."

He muttered an oath beneath his breath. "You tell me the alternative, lady."

"To let them find the world on their own terms. If you were honest, you'd admit you need the Iban much more than they need the likes of you."

"Oh, too right," he mocked, his jaw tightening. "Their lives look so idyllic from your vantage point. But I've seen the reality—mothers losing two out of three babies, men who can't expect to live beyond forty-five. All you know are the sterile area studies from your so-called experts."

"And just what does Kilpatrick Forestry deal in—human feeling?"

"No less than you do."

"I can't afford the luxury of considering the individual, Kilpatrick. My responsibility ends with the group. If I can protect the whole tribe, the little guy will take care of himself. Maybe that seems cold and unfeeling to you, but it's the political reality."

"I've got just one question," he shot back insolently. "How long has it been since you've felt anything at all?"

Danielle pushed her chair back, her instincts urging flight, but Ryan's hand shot out to imprison hers on the table. She felt the strength flowing beneath that lazy grace of his, strength and a slow hot sensuality that unnerved her.

"Let go of me."

"Not yet. The other night I couldn't help watching

you and Hal Adams at the embassy, a programmed couple going through the perfect routine—smiling, shaking hands, conferring with all the right people.'' He paused, and when he went on his voice had dropped to a dangerously soft pitch. ''Tell me, Danielle, does he make love to you the same way? When he touches you is it ever a hot explosion?''

Even before he saw the answering pallor in her cheeks, Ryan knew he'd stepped far beyond the bounds of common decency. Yet he couldn't stop himself. He was caught up in his own punishment. ''Has he even once made you forget the world outside until nothing exists but his arms and his lips?''

''Stop it.'' She whispered the command between clenched teeth, so afraid he might sense her weakness. His words were a relentlessly intimate invasion. ''You have no right, no right at all to—''

He felt a stab of remorse and abruptly released her hand. ''Let's get out of here,'' he said tautly, standing up and dropping a twenty-dollar bill on the table. ''Your secretary will think you've been kidnapped.''

''Haven't I?'' She flinched when he went to take her arm. ''As a matter of fact, I think I'll find my own way back to the office. I don't trust you in the least, Kilpatrick.''

Outside the restaurant she marched toward a waiting cab, but Ryan deftly stepped in front of her, blocking the way each time she tried to go around him.

''I can't say I entirely blame you. Nevertheless, I

brought you here, and I'll see that you get back." A thread of steel ran through his teasing insistence.

"Your gallantry's a little late," she answered, still hoping to get even with him after the way he'd so deliberately set her world on end.

During their silent drive back across town Danielle searched for a way to return the favor. It wasn't until Ryan had pulled up beneath the portico of her office complex that she finally spoke. "I've been reading about the Tasaday tribe in the Philippines," she began with elaborate casualness. "The government's still trying to prosecute the unscrupulous loggers who came in and nearly wiped out a Stone Age culture. Just what makes you any different from them?"

She had flung the last bit over her shoulder as she snapped open the passenger door, intending the remark as a quick parting salvo. But Ryan reached across her lap and slammed the door shut again. "There's one hell of a lot of difference. I'm not destroying anything. Unlike those other loggers—unlike you—I really care about these people." He bit off each word, his face only inches from hers. "So I'll be damned if I'm going to let you get away with passing judgment on me."

Taken aback by his fierce explosion of anger, Danielle could only stare at him. Flecks of gray and brown stood out against the changeable green of his eyes, like sharp stones in a meadow.

Gone was the lazy sensuality that had so disturbed her. Yet she found this unrelenting toughness no less disturbing. Something volatile simmered below the surface. His reaction was a far cry from the smooth point, counterpoint of his correspondence. He was far removed from the type of men she was used to confronting. But bravado drove her on.

"Don't write me off so easily," she said into the tense silence. "My voice carries weight with the people who *can* shut you down. You may have come a long way for nothing, after all."

"Not for nothing." He smiled, goading her. "I found you again, didn't I?" He flung her door open then with vicious strength, a dismissive gesture that cut Danielle's pride to the quick.

"Unlucky me." With that she climbed out of the car and marched determinedly across the pavement toward her office building.

Ryan stared after her, his fingers clenched around the steering wheel. Somehow she always had to have the last word, using it like a dagger. He was accustomed to women going out of their way to please him, but this hard-talking woman took delight in doing just the opposite.

Sardonic amusement lightened his grim mood when he thought back over the afternoon. That tough facade of hers had cracked once, just once, and she'd admitted the bald truth: "I don't trust you, Kilpatrick." The words were every bit as tough as she was; still, he'd glimpsed the haze of pain behind them and been touched by it. He wanted to dismiss her from his mind; instead that traitorous urge to discover and possess her rose inside, an instinct more powerful than logic. With an effort he snuffed out the feeling. If he was going to win, he'd need all his wits about him.

You don't trust me, Danielle? He laughed harshly as he slammed into first gear and sped away from the imposing high-rise tower. *Believe me, the feeling is mutual.*

DANIELLE'S MIND WHIRRED as swiftly and smoothly as the elevator she rode in. The remark she'd made in the car about unscrupulous loggers had been a shot in the dark, but she had struck a nerve.

What was it her father had mentioned offhandedly—something about Kilpatrick once being named in an indictment? She would have to dig; she had to find out what this man was all about. Her job was here and now. Her loyalties lay with the ICCI, not with a memory that could never be entirely erased. Dear God, why had he resurfaced like this, a chimera to taunt her?

The elevator slid open at her floor, and she strode into the office, her brisk air blotting out all suggestion of doubt.

"Get the Malaysian Embassy on the phone for me, will you, Jen?" she said by way of greeting. "I want to talk to Marda."

While she waited for the call to be put through, Danielle leafed through her telephone messages.

"I've got your call," the secretary said. "Want to take it in your office?"

Danielle nodded and closed the door behind her.

A few minutes later Jen trailed in with her steno

pad. "It was nice to see you take a break for lunch today instead of working straight through. You know that old saying about all work and no play...."

Danielle sat back in her chair, distractedly rubbing her temple. "I should have stayed and worked, Jen. I have a feeling it's going to be a long fruitless battle. Kilpatrick's going to fight me all the way."

"Maybe it'll be an interesting fight," Jen replied with a twinkle, her eyes registering approval of the color in her boss's usually pale cheeks. "Ryan Kilpatrick is quite a hunk."

Danielle shrugged dismissingly. "If you like that type."

"Not me, Danni! Personally I have a thing for older men. I've always figured that by the time a man's hit fifty he's sown all his wild oats and knows exactly what he wants out of life."

"Freud would have loved you," Danielle teased her.

"Boy, would he ever!" Jen agreed, perching on the straight-backed chair before the desk. "Guess it goes back to hero worship of my dad when I was a kid. He's a real power figure in the union. People were always coming by to ask favors."

Danielle smiled. "Did you ever consider becoming a union organizer like him? You could have been a one-woman show."

If Jen found this rare indulgence in small talk curious, she didn't show it. She went gamely along. "Oh, I suppose I'm one of those people who's always admired power more than wanted it for myself. My dad and I weren't two peas in a pod, like you and that handsome father of yours,'' Jen replied, a quick little smile animating her features.

Danielle looked up with a distracted air. ''Why haven't you married, then, if you don't mind my asking?''

Jen burst out laughing. ''Danni, what's gotten into you this afternoon? Even when you and I have gone the typical female route of shopping and dinner after work, we've never talked this personally before.''

''Lord, we haven't, have we?'' Danielle replied, looking sheepish. ''I suppose I just felt like spinning my wheels a bit while this Kilpatrick business percolates through my brain.''

''Go right ahead,'' Jen teased good-naturedly. ''And while it does, what can I gossip to you about...um, how about the latest office item?''

''What have I let myself in for?'' Danielle was laughing, too, but underneath she was a little dismayed with herself.

It hit her that though Jen was the closest thing to a friend she had, Danielle knew little about her beyond their mutual passion for Indonesian food, French films and horseback riding. Even with Hal, her relationship wasn't all that different. She knew what his ten-year career goals were because she'd helped him formulate them. But what were his dreams and fears, the private thoughts that made a man unique? Danielle had never bothered to find out.

A mischievous half smile tugged at the corners of

her lips as she imagined telling Hal what had happened the night she'd been trapped in the Kuala Lumpur riots; he'd be horrified to learn about that side of his future wife.

"Care to share the joke, Danni?" Jen broke into her thoughts.

The smile faded, and Danielle reminded herself there was no other side to her nature, so there could be nothing for Hal to disapprove of. "I was just thinking about something that happened a long time ago."

Jen couldn't quite mask the concern in her voice. "I do think you've been working too hard lately. Why don't you take the rest of the afternoon off for a change?"

"And do what?"

"Oh, just relax. Or better yet, do something sinfully decadent like putting on your bathrobe in the middle of the day and watching a soap. You know, just take the weight of the big bad world off those shoulders for a while. We could survive a few hours without you," Jen went on, blithely deflating her boss's ego.

"Hmm," Danielle shot back in the same vein. "With that attitude I can see why you didn't go for the union presidency."

"Yes," Jen agreed, standing up. "But I'm happy."

Danielle relaxed a little in Jen's reflected warmth and on impulse said, "My father's having a party this weekend out at Foxhall. Would you like to come? If you're worried about the crowd being a little too stuffy, dad's arranged an amateur steeplechase before supper to liven things up. We've got several horses you could choose from.''

"It sounds marvelous! And don't you worry about me getting bored." Her nose wrinkled playfully. "I'll just pretend I'm Scarlett O'Hara floating through those antebellum drawing rooms.''

They laughed together. "Good. It's settled, then.''

Someone rapped on the office door, and they both looked up expectantly as a clean-cut boy in a courier's uniform came inside. "Your packet from the Malaysian Embassy.''

After he'd left, Danielle used her ivory-handled letter opener to slit the thick manila envelope, then swiftly withdrew the contents.

Jen looked on in amusement. "So much for our small talk, I take it?" Her boss's only response was to wave her out with a distracted air. Danielle had forgotten all else with the courier's arrival.

Switching on the desk lamp, she began to leaf through the transcripts of four-year-old Malaysian federal court proceedings, searching for some link to the Australian. Her father's vague reference to indictments and Ryan's reaction to her offhand remarks had spurred this avenue of research.

Two-thirds of the way through the stack, she hit pay dirt. But it was with curious reluctance that she began to read the transcript.

A logging firm Danielle had never heard of had been brought to trial by the government on behalf of an Iban tribe. The company had promised a permanent industry and profit sharing for its native workers. Instead, what it returned to the people was a systematically raped landscape and tribal fishery grounds nearly destroyed by the silt and debris that poured into the mountain river during logging operations.

Named as one of the principal defendants in the suit was Ryan Kilpatrick.

Jen poked her head around the door. "It's five-thirty, Danni. Do you want me to wait for you so I can lock up?"

Danielle pushed up her reading glasses and rubbed the bridge of her nose. "You go ahead. I have to finish this."

"Is everything all right?"

"Why shouldn't it be?" Danielle replied brightly, her smile forced. Shrugging, Jen left her alone again, and a minute later Danielle heard the outer office door closing.

Her tired eyes skimmed page after page anxiously until at last she came to Ryan's testimony—what little there was of it. The rugged Australian, whom she had found to be candid and outspoken to a fault, had had curiously little to say at his own trial, either in defense or as apologia. The court must have found the evidence and testimony inconclusive, because the case had ended in a hung jury.

She closed the file and swiveled in her chair. Lights sprinkled the sophisticated cityscape below. After a long day Danielle loved to gaze down on the Washington night, her mind still busily planning long after everyone had left. But for the first time her devotion to work had left a curiously bitter aftertaste.

Delving into Ryan's past had put her more in the dark than ever. She told herself she had to find out the truth because her official position demanded it. Deep down, though, she knew that wasn't the real reason. Danielle had to know for herself what kind of man Ryan Kilpatrick was.

CHAPTER THREE

DANIELLE BREATHED IN DEEPLY, savoring the cold country air. The ground was spongy beneath her feet, but with each step the sweet fragrance of spring wafted up to her.

Towering English oaks, their buds unfurling in a soft mist of green, grew along the curving drive that buffered Foxhall not only from the state highway but from the twentieth century. Though Thoroughbreds grazed where her ancestors had grown cotton and tobacco, the mood remained: pastoral, remote.

When she was a little girl Danielle used to daydream about raising her own children at Foxhall. Her life had turned out rather differently. She had inherited her father's life-style along with his ambitions, so that visits to Foxhall had never been more than brief interludes in a hectic, work-filled existence.

As she ducked under a weathered split-rail fence, Danielle came nearly nose to toe with the gray leather of her boots, and she remembered Ryan Kilpatrick's impertinent observation about her clothing. Damn, she hadn't meant to think of him at all this weekend! Now even the shade of her boots was sufficient reminder of how he had gotten under her skin.

For an instant she imagined the big Aussie against the rolling Virginia hills and realized this country would be too tame, too constricting for him. He was the type who had to carve out his own niche, not have anything handed to him on a silver platter. Danielle thought of her fiancé then. Once their marriage vows were recited, Hal would be wedded to Foxhall and the famous Davis connections as surely as he would be tied to her.

Shaking off the disturbing undercurrent to her thoughts, she hurried down the sloping meadow to the barn. A lanky man came out of the stableyard, and she called to him.

"Sam, has Lady foaled yet?"

Sam Larkin, the feisty trainer and farmer who lived with his family on neighboring acreage, ran Foxhall as if it were an extension of his own property. He waited with obvious impatience for John Davis's daughter to reach him.

"Not yet, Danni. She's having a hell of a time of it. I left Doc Martin with her. Cora just called down to the barn to tell me that damn-fool kid of ours ran the tractor into a ditch. I gotta go bail him out."

"Still trying to make a farmer out of Tim?"

"Tryin' to."

"From the sound of things maybe he should stick to football."

Larkin's ruddy face split into a reluctant grin. "Yeah, you have a point. If he makes the pros I won't complain. Well, I gotta run." And he did, his long loping strides over the grassy fields belying his years.

Danielle went straight to the barn, eager to look in on the mare. Once inside, she heard Lady's high whinny and the nervous rustle of straw.

"Sam, is that you?" old Dr. Martin called out.

Impelled by the urgency in his tone, Danielle hurried forward past the dim stalls. Pungent horse smells gave way to the hospitallike astringency of lime and disinfectant as she approached the big, well-lit foaling stall.

"Dr. Martin, how is she?"

"Oh, Danni, it's you." He looked up from the thin surgical gloves he was pulling on. A stethoscope dangled from his neck. "Would you believe I just heard two heartbeats?"

"Twins? How marvelous! Can I do anything to help?"

"Now don't go getting too excited," the vet cautioned. "I'm afraid they're coming a little prematurely."

She watched in fascination as he inserted a gloved arm into the birth canal. "Don't push yet, my girl, not quite yet," the vet crooned to the mare.

Gone was Lady of the Manor's delicate composure, the fastidious aloofness that matched her elegant name. Sweat streamed down her flanks, staining her glossy chestnut coat a dull brown. Her breathing was deep and quick between the agonized contractions of birth.

"Boy, there's a tangle of legs and hooves in there," Dr. Martin said finally, his words trailing off in a grunt of pain.

Danielle's eyes widened. "Are you all right?"

"Lady's just doing what she's supposed to, bearing down. When she does, it feels like my arm's caught in a washing-machine wringer."

"Good Lord. I thought horses could do this on their own."

"Well, Lady's a little narrow through the hips."

Danielle leaned down to touch the mare's wet straining flanks, admiration and encouragement in each gentle stroke.

"Still want to help?" the vet asked a trifle impatiently, taking in at a glance her cashmere sweater and the tailored corduroy pants shoved into the tops of her handmade boots. "It's a messy business."

"I don't think there's much choice now."

He laughed, then groaned. When the pain in his arm let up he sprang into action. "I finally got these legs disentangled. Here comes number one," he said softly. "Now pay attention, Danni."

As he withdrew his arm a clear membranous sac appeared. With a sense of wonder Danielle could see within it the front feet and tiny nose of the foal. The membrane ruptured spontaneously, freeing the foal from its protective sheath.

"Now what? Do we have to do anything?" she asked.

"Not just yet." Together they watched as the minute withers and elbow appeared. "Sometimes the little thing will get caught in its mother's hips, and then you give a tug downward on the legs—not out," he cautioned, demonstrating.

Seconds later the premature foal lay on the straw, and Lady spared a quick glance around with confused dilated eyes to see what all her pain and trouble had netted. The newborn creature lay unmoving, lifeless.

Danielle looked on helplessly as Dr. Martin knelt over the foal and massaged its sides, trying to force breath and life into the feeble chest.

He shook his head even as his patient hands worked on. "It seems hopeless, but I'm going to try to save it, Danni."

She nodded, feeling a curious ache inside. "What about the one that's left—will it be stillborn, too?"

They glanced up as the second membrane ruptured and another dark wet nose pushed through the pelvic opening. "We can only wait and see. Help Lady with the next one if she needs it."

Dr. Martin turned back to the first foal, and suddenly Danielle had never felt more alone in her entire life. Trembling with nervous excitement, she watched the head and chin emerge. With miraculous speed more and more of the beautiful foal appeared, until a pair of tiny gangly legs hung in midair. Danielle gave a gentle tug downward as the vet had shown her.

The last powerful rhythmic contraction propelled the foal outward, and reflexively Danielle cradled it in her arms when it landed in the fragrant straw bedding, saturating it with blood. She stared down at the fragile newborn, so afraid his fate might be the same as his twin's. Yet even as she watched, Danielle could have sworn his nostrils twitched.

Gingerly she poked at the thin little chest. With a convulsive shudder the foal took its first breath, and unconsciously Danielle did the same, fighting with him for life. "Doc, this one's alive!" she called, joyous warmth surging through her.

The old vet knelt to examine the foal, his tired smile mirroring Danielle's delight. "Your he's a she, by the way, and I'd guess she barely tips the scales at ninety."

Even for a slender-boned Thoroughbred, the birth weight was dangerously low. "Do you think she'll make it?"

"It's just like in humans, Danni. Little preemies like her are at a high risk. We'll just have to wait and see."

Eventually their patience was rewarded. The foal fought to rise, stood shakily for a second and then collapsed. Danielle shot the vet a look of alarm, but his answering look counseled patience. Holding her breath, she watched the foal pull itself up again with a mighty effort. It tottered drunkenly, half falling against Lady's rear leg. The mare's drooping head lifted, and she turned to study the newcomer. She must have decided the baby was indeed hers, because she gave it a thorough and unmistakably proprietary lick. Buoyed by this welcome, the foal staggered over to Lady's swollen udder and began to nurse.

"That little one's a fighter, Danni. I'd say she's got a fair chance." They watched the pair in pleased silence until Dr. Martin rose creakily to his feet.

Danielle's eyes followed his to the stillborn foal

that had had no chance at all. "Are you certain there was nothing more you could have done?" she asked in frustration. "Adrenaline to the heart—something?"

He shook his head and didn't speak again until they were out in the stableyard beside his truck. "Danni, I'll tell you. Part of the art of living is knowing when to accept the inevitable. And this was one of those cases."

Her eyes strayed to the gray blanket on the truck bed that covered the dead foal. "I rarely give in, doc."

"A Davis trait if I ever saw one." His eyes were twinkling now as, oblivious to the cold air, he toweled off the muck and rolled down his shirt sleeves. "By the way, thanks for the hand in there. I have to say you're the most elegant assistant I've ever had."

She looked down at her stained clothes and smiled back at him. "If I'm going to play the mistress of Foxhall, I have to dress the part. Are you sure you can't run up to the house for breakfast?"

"Thanks for the invitation, but I've got a half-dozen calls to make. I'll be back here in a few hours to check up on my patients. In the meantime, Sam'll know what to do in there." He gestured back to the foaling stall.

After a quick final peek to make certain mother and daughter were fine, Danielle crossed the fields back to the house in a buoyant mood. Passing the dining room, she called out a brisk good morning to her father, who was bent over his coffee cup and the editorial page of the *Post*.

His exclamation stopped her in her tracks. "Good God, Danni! What happened to you?"

"A bit of midwifery."

His eyebrows rose. "Lady?"

"Let me shower and change first, then I'll tell you all about it."

Over breakfast Danielle described the foaling in crisp, matter-of-fact terms. "If that little preemie makes it, she'll be a beauty, a rich deep chestnut."

"'If,'" Davis repeated, echoing his daughter's earlier frustration. "I was hoping for a good future contender in the Hillsborough Hunter Chase. What I might do is offer that foal in exchange for the stud fee I paid. Then I can breed Lady again next year and try for something stronger."

"Don't do that," Danielle put in quickly. "I'd...I think I'd like to buy that foal from you, rather than see it go to another farm."

Davis studied his daughter, amusement vying with a fleeting tenderness in his expression. "I've never seen this maternal side in you before."

"Don't be absurd, dad. It's not that at all. I'm simply gambling that the foal will eventually be worth a lot more than what I'll pay for her. It's a business investment, pure and straightforward."

"Hmm. I have a better idea," Davis suggested. "Let me give you Lady's offspring. In return you can buy me dinner at the Rive Gauche."

"Now who's going soft? You used to drive harder

bargains than that! But too late for you to back out,'' she hurried on, her turquoise eyes sparkling with triumph at a deal well concluded. ''This is definitely my kind of agreement—everything to gain and nothing to lose.''

''I've taught you well, haven't I, Danni?''

She relaxed and smiled. ''Of course you have.''

After a short silence her father surprised her by bringing up another matter entirely. ''Tell me, Danni, are you and Hal going to set a definite wedding date soon?''

She stirred her black coffee in a bid for time, realizing the subject hadn't really changed, after all. ''We haven't quite decided what month would be best.''

Vagueness was a useful tool at the bargaining table, Davis had told his daughter once; never show your cards until you're certain what everyone else is holding. When she looked up and caught his eye, Danielle knew he'd read her mind. Feeling oddly as if she'd betrayed him, she hurried on. ''We're going to wait until after the elections—see which way the political winds are blowing, what opportunities he'll have in the State Department.''

Davis ignored her rambling excuses. ''Hal will be good for you. You need a man like that.''

''Honestly, dad! These are the eighties,'' she teased him. ''You're sounding like an overprotective Victorian father now.''

But he was too shrewd to be manipulated into a more general argument. ''You've been putting Hal off for too long, Danni.''

"If you're worrying that he'll change his mind, I can set you at ease. He needs me as much as I need him. Isn't that what marriage is all about?" The words had a brittle snap to them.

Her father's mouth tightened. "Your mother and I built a highly successful relationship on that basis."

Yes, but did you love her? Danielle thought. She couldn't ask the question aloud, because it mirrored too closely the one she refused to answer for herself: did she love Hal? Damn, why was she questioning herself this way at all!

And then she realized her viewpoint had begun to change the moment the Australian walked back into her life. She had been infuriated by the taunting intimacy of his questions in the restaurant. Yet even now the memory of that intimate invasion, for all its mockery, had power over her. Desperately she had tried to deny the slow hot upswell of excitement, the rush of blood and memory his voice elicited. She didn't know how long her guise of disdainful anger could protect her from the infinitely more subtle weapons he brought into play.

"Danni." The slight query in her father's voice called her back. "Forgive me for pushing, but believe me, I know what's best for you."

"You couldn't possibly when I don't even know myself."

"This uncertainty isn't like you at all."

"How do you know what I'm really like?" The retort was softened by a rueful smile.

Clearly discomfitted, John Davis attempted to change the subject. "Have you settled that Kilpatrick business at the office?"

"Not quite."

"You've hit a snag?"

Her eyes glinted with subtle irony. "You might say that. I'm afraid he's one of those men who plays by his own rules."

"Smart men always do."

"So?"

"You simply have to be smarter."

Danielle relaxed a little. They were on familiar ground now. Together they would reduce Ryan Kilpatrick to a tactical problem that could be handled with a well-planned strategy. Logic and cunning were the only requirements. Emotion had no place.

"Any suggestions, dad?"

"Just one." He flashed the deceptively urbane smile that had lulled diplomatic adversaries for thirty years. "Deal with the man on your own ground, Danni, as if he were a bull that claims his territory in the ring. He's the most difficult one for the bull-fighter to kill. So you claim your territory, as well, my dear, and make Kilpatrick come to you."

"He's already come to Washington."

"Still not far enough. In fact. . . ." Davis stood up, clearly deep in thought. "What I think I'll do is give him a ring and invite him out for the steeplechase to-morrow."

Danielle looked up, startled. The idea of seeing Ryan at Foxhall unnerved her a little, but she hid her misgivings. "Why bother inviting him?" she replied casually. "I doubt he'd accept the invitation."

"Don't underestimate yourself, Danni," he told his daughter from the doorway. "You have something he wants. He's not going to give up easily."

"That's just what I'm afraid of," she murmured. But her father had already gone.

AT THE TOP of the curving stairway Danielle paused, flicking the cuffs of her white silk blouse beneath the black velvet riding jacket. She had exchanged her corduroy jeans for dove-gray riding breeches. The polished image was more armor against Kilpatrick. She was determined to pit her world against his, to remind him that he could never beat the circles of power she represented. And yet. . . .

Her fingers went up to the scarf she'd tied around her throat at the last minute. An intense royal blue, the color echoed the turbulence of her eyes beneath their surface serenity.

Despite all the roles she'd played—influential attorney, dutiful fiancée, the worthy successor to her father—no one had ever paid any attention to the woman inside. No one except Ryan. That was the potentially devastating hold he had over her, that simple awareness that forced her to respond in kind. Burying the disturbing thought, she moved with determination down the stairs.

Her father had invited most of his neighbors, so the crowd was a lively mix of foreign dignitaries, high-level politicians and old friends in comfortable hacking attire, eager to ride in the first race of the season.

Yet Danielle had the sensation of going through a time warp when Sam Larkin's wife, Cora, drifted through the foyer in a crinoline-lined taffeta gown she must have saved from an old Civil War pageant. With a theatrically bright smile in place, the woman offered cups of hot whiskey-spiked cider from a silver tray.

Danielle went down to join her. "What are you doing, Cora—a remake of *Gone with the Wind*?"

The woman laughed archly and reached up to pat her carefully coiffed blond hair. "I wore this when I played the lead in *Johnny Reb* last summer at our little theater. Adds a touch of class to your dad's party, don't you think?"

"Mmm," Danielle murmured noncommittally. "I feel as though I've walked into one of those English castles where his lord and ladyship are genteelly broke and have to open up the place to tourists."

"Well, you know I was supposed to be a guest today," Cora defended herself. "Two of the caterer's assistants didn't show up, so your dad corralled me into helping out."

"Has Sam seen you yet?"

Ignoring the question, Cora gave her neighbor a severe look. "This mansion was positively cryin' out for dramatic color, which I'm graciously supplyin'." Her soft drawl was growing more pronounced by the minute.

"If I see Sam I'll let him know where you are," Danielle replied with an innocent air.

"Danni Davis, don't you dare! You know how that man feels about my 'charades,' as he calls them."

Danielle laughed and drifted away toward the high-ceilinged drawing room, furnished with a pleasing mixture of Davis family heirlooms and comfortable chintz.

"Oh, by the way," Cora called after her, "that sweet secretary of yours offered to lend a hand, too."

Danielle spotted Jen at once, her dark hair falling forward over the neck of her red sweater as she bent to offer a guest something from the hors d'oeuvres tray in her hands.

Danielle pulled Jen aside, taking the tray. "I thought you wanted to play Scarlett O'Hara, not the butler, for heaven's sake," she whispered. "Come on and mingle."

"Snob! What do you think I've been doing?" Jen teased her back. "Offering people appetizers is a great icebreaker. I've already got a hot stock tip from one of the board of directors of Mid-Atlantic Railway, a terrific recipe for satay from an Indonesian businessman and—"

"You were born in the wrong century, Jen. You could have been a rival to Mata Hari. What do you do for an encore—charm the fur off a polar bear?"

"Charm's got nothing to do with it." Jen's warm grin was infectious. "I just listen and smile a lot."

"Maybe I should sic you on Kilpatrick."

"No way, boss. This is my day off. Remember?"

"Coward." They were both still laughing when Danielle's father joined them, looking fit and handsome in his tailored riding clothes. "Dad, you remember Jennifer Bondi, don't you?"

"Of course," he replied smoothly. "How are you, Jennifer?"

Jen extended her hand, a twinkle in her dark eyes. "I'd have recognized you anywhere, Mr. Davis. You're the spitting image of that Confederate general in the photograph on your mantel."

He looked momentarily taken aback by her irreverence. But he recovered at once and relaxed. "You think so?"

"Absolutely. I see that same feistiness and stubborn determination around the chin." She looked from Davis to his daughter, teasing them both now. "I think it runs in the family."

"We do run true to form," he agreed. "Have you seen the rest of the Davis family tree in the library?"

"No, I haven't." There was droll mischief in her tone. "And I have a feeling I'm about to."

Davis looked amused. "Most women would at least pretend to be impressed."

"Jen isn't 'most women,' dad," Danielle interposed. "She says just what she thinks and manages to keep my ego in line when it starts to swell."

"Another Davis fault, I'm afraid," he admitted to Jen with uncharacteristic candor, and the lines around his eyes deepened engagingly. "Now that you've been forewarned, would you still like to see our family tree?"

Jen smiled her assent, and the two moved off, leaving Danielle to stare after them in bemusement.

Hal found her a moment later. "Didn't your father hire caterers to take care of this?" he asked. "You really have more important things to do."

"What?" Her eyes followed his to the tray she'd taken from Jen, and she laughed. "Snob," she accused airily.

"Will you kindly cut out the games, Danni?" he replied, exasperated. "I have someone I want you to meet."

"Of course you do." She set the tray down hard on a table and linked her arm through his with an exaggerated show of propriety.

Something in her manner must have sliced through his usual haze of self-interest, because he gave her a long thoughtful look. "What's bothering you?"

"Nothing. Let's get on with it, shall we?"

Hal introduced her to Jacob Farrel, a member of the Senate Foreign Relations Committee. "So this is your fiancée, Adams." The silver-haired man nodded approval, his hawklike nose sniffing the political winds. "You know I'm a great admirer of your father, Miss Davis. His position on Southeast Asia is the most farseeing of any I've encountered. We should have more men like him in government. He has that rare gift of protecting American interests without antagonizing our allies." He addressed them as if he were being interviewed by the press. "Don't you think so?"

Danielle slipped effortlessly into the correct

groove, listening well and from time to time offering her own incisive comments. Yet she had the curious sensation of standing outside herself, watching her and Hal as they made all the right moves. They were performing an elaborately choreographed dance in which neither of them ever touched. Each step was flawless, but the movements held no passion.

Suddenly Danielle felt bloodless, cold. They had never quarreled; never once had they risked discovering what might lie beneath the surface. For the first time, when she envisioned the future it frightened her.

A bead of perspiration broke out on her forehead. "Will you two excuse me, please? I think I need a little fresh air." Without waiting for a reply, she turned and left.

Outside, the sun was shining. Long bars of shadow slanted across the terrace, as if the soaring columns of Foxhall's portico meant to enfold her. She resisted the impulse to leave, perching instead on the outermost corner of the white stone balustrade. Several foreign guests had found their way down to the elegant gardens, where English boxthorn hedges and flowering shrubs grew in stately patterns laid out two centuries before. But most of those outside were local horsepeople, eagerly discussing the upcoming steeple-chase.

The upper terrace overlooked the gentle sweep of meadow and field, site of the race. Pairs of bright-colored flags billowed and flapped at intervals along the challenging course, marking each post and rail. The race, at least, she was looking forward to.

Danielle turned at the sound of a car laboring up the long driveway. A Triumph, its top down, came over the rise.

She tensed. Then in spite of herself she laughed, watching as Ryan screeched to a halt before an impossibly small space between a horse trailer and a black limousine. Swiftly he backed into the opening, leaving barely an inch to spare on either side.

Unaware that he was being observed, Ryan unfolded himself from the driver's seat and lazily surveyed the countryside. Foxhall. The name itself whispered old money, tradition, a blue-blood lineage stretching back unbroken for generations. A far cry from anything he had ever known, much less wanted. Now here he was thrust in the middle of it all, forced to play their games so he could come away with the prize.

He crossed the driveway and put one booted foot on a paddock fence, extending his hand to the sleek pony that trotted up to greet him. These were the things he could trust—land, animals, the elements. Nature could be merciless and cruel, but at least you always knew where you stood with it.

Ryan debated whether to even bother going up to the house. His pride was worth a hell of a lot more to him than a loan. The ICCI could use someone else as its whipping boy.

And Danielle. . . . He shook his head. What was his pride worth there? Turning, he saw her perched on the terrace balustrade. He felt a tight ache inside, part regret and part hunger, that went beyond simple physical desire. He despised himself for wanting her so badly when he knew she wasn't to be trusted.

Slowly Ryan climbed the terrace stairs toward her. He noticed the cool splash of color at her throat and wondered if she had worn the scarf to please or mock him. *Never mind,* he told himself, his soft laugh lightening his brooding expression. Some connection, however faint and perverse, still linked them. All of a sudden he was looking forward to the game again.

She didn't disappoint him. "How good of you to come, Kilpatrick," she murmured, her tone making a mockery of the stock phrase.

"Your old man made it sound like I'd better be here if I knew what was good for me," he retaliated quietly.

"You read too much into his tone. He's not intimidating at all."

"Neither are sharks, if I don't dive in their territory."

"You mean they don't recognize a fellow predator when they see one?"

Just then Cora Larkin sailed out, her welcome-wagon smile zeroing in on the big handsome man at Danielle's side. "Welcome to Foxhall and Virginia hospitality, Davis style. Looks like I'm just in time with the hot spiked cider. Believe me," she cooed with a flutter of her false eyelashes, "it's one hundred percent guaranteed to take the chill off."

"Amen to that," Ryan murmured as he tossed back the cider.

Feeling like a fool, Danielle stared out over the fields. She wanted to strangle them both. Why didn't someone sound the horn to get the race underway?

"Cat got your tongue?" he needled her after Cora had drifted away in search of a fresh audience. "Aren't you going to resume the attack? That's why I was invited out here, wasn't it—to get the full brunt of 'Davis hospitality'?"

"If you're so certain of that you shouldn't have bothered to come."

"I wanted to see you again."

Though his directness unnerved her, she couldn't help being equally direct. "Why?"

He shrugged. "I suppose I'm more stubborn than wise."

"That's no answer at all."

"No."

Their eyes met, his bemused, hers wary.

Again that curiously potent alchemy between them was at work, bewitching away the rest of the world.

He reached up to finger the silk at her throat just for an instant, but it was long enough for her to catch the scent of his skin, undiluted by colognes or aftershave. "Is this standard racing attire?"

"Only for professional riders," she answered, her eyes involuntarily following his hand as he withdrew it.

"And you're a professional?"

"Only at my work."

His eyes glinted teasingly. "I'm surprised you take the time to play at all. But then again... you do seem like the scrummaging type."

" 'Scrummaging'?" she repeated, a reluctant smile curving her lips. "Is that some of your Aussie slang?"

"No, it's a rugby term. I'm a body-contact player from way back."

"I'm not surprised," she put in dryly, her eyes measuring the breadth of his shoulders and the size of his hands compared to her own. "The rougher the body contact, the better. Is that your motto?"

He shook his head, his eyes full of mischief. "It depends. I can think of games where you don't have to play rough to win."

"How often *do* you win, Kilpatrick?"

"Invariably."

His brashness nettled her, and before she knew it the challenge was tumbling from her lips. "You only ride range ponies, don't you? I'm sure you wouldn't be interested in sitting astride a Thoroughbred."

He leaned his elbows on the balustrade beside her and laughed into her eyes. "I might be interested. It depends on what the stakes are."

He was too close now, and she realized it wasn't so much his physical size but her own keen awareness of him that threatened to overpower her. But she resisted the impulse to draw back.

"Ah, Danni!" She turned in relief at the sound of her father's voice, and was surprised to see Jen still with him. "So our last guest has finally arrived." Davis's exaggerated conviviality held more irony than warmth. "What do you think of Foxhall, Kilpatrick?"

"About what I expected," Ryan replied, his words double-edged. "Money translates roughly the same no matter where you go."

Surprisingly, it was Jen who piped up in defense, "The big difference is that most people would be fighting like mad to hold on to what they have—but the Davises are donating theirs to the National Trust."

Danielle winced at having this very private family matter between her father and her aired before strangers. What could he have been thinking of to have confided something so personal, especially to Jen, whom he barely knew. She felt almost betrayed by the both of them.

"I see," Ryan was saying. "Now we're paying homage to a family with a real social conscience."

Davis, a master of the ironic dig himself, wasn't about to let his Aussie guest have the last word. "I'm sure you're familiar with philanthropy, Mr. Kilpatrick. But in case you're not, I'll clarify the meaning—we prefer to give, rather than take."

"I've given my share."

"Is that what you told the court when you were indicted with your cronies?"

Ryan's color deepened. "You're determined to have my ass, aren't you, Davis?"

Danielle had the grace to blush as Jen's eyes darted questioningly from father to daughter, but Davis seemed unfazed. "A man is known by the company he keeps, Kilpatrick."

"Too right." Ryan laughed shortly, glancing around the small group.

Clearly irritated at having his pithy criticism turned back on him, Davis was about to reply, when the hunting horn sounded. The two men continued to glare at each other until Jen diffused the tension by touching her companion's arm. "Loser buys the drinks at the Jockey Club. Remember our bet, John?"

All the tension went out of him. "Of course, Jennifer. Let's go."

Watching them leave together, Danielle felt an irrational surge of jealousy. She still couldn't believe how her father's expression had softened as his eyes met Jen's. *I'm imagining things,* Danielle tried to convince herself. She looked up to find Ryan watching her, and wondered how much he'd guessed of her feelings.

"You and your father are too much alike, Danielle."

Her eyes flashed. "I'm proud of that."

Ryan was about to turn away when Hal Adams hurried over, still wearing his dark-blue business suit. "Danni, honey, listen. I know I promised I'd ride in this race, but Senator Farrel isn't interested in horses. I feel obligated to stay with him up at the house. You understand that, don't you?"

"No. I'd think the senator would be very interested to see you test your mettle."

"You've become a real comedienne," he said coldly, his eyes sliding away to challenge Ryan where he stood unabashedly taking in the lovers' tiff. "You know I'm not comfortable on horseback."

"You're a competent rider," she persisted, mortified that Ryan had to hear this. "And you promised me."

"Now look, Danni—"

"Adams," Ryan broke in, "I'd be more than happy to take your place."

Danielle felt the hot flood of embarrassment rushing up her neck, wondering if Hal had caught the subtle mockery in Ryan's tone. If he'd noticed, he didn't show it. "Be my guest," Hal said shortly.

"Did you two happen to have a wager going?" Ryan asked.

"We have a standing bet—breakfast in bed for the win—"

"Hal!" Danielle broke in, chagrined.

Ryan was grinning openly now. "Sounds fair enough."

For a second Danielle thought Hal would come through after all, landing a solid punch on Kilpatrick's jaw. But it was a fleeting hope. If discretion was the better part of valor, then Hal possessed it in abundance. Ignoring Ryan as if he'd never spoken, Hal kissed his fiancée's unresponsive lips proprietorially. "Be careful, darling. You know how much you mean to me."

She jerked away. "Give the senator my regards."

With that she hurried down the stairs toward the waiting horses, her cheeks flushed with annoyance.

CHAPTER FOUR

THE TUMULT of two-dozen mounted equestrians vying for position shattered Foxhall's sleepy pastoral beauty. Excitement spread like wildfire, until the starting post fairly danced with curvetting Thoroughbreds, eager for the race to begin. Away down the hill, the flags billowed to life with a snap in the freshening wind, their streaming colors like medieval standards marking lines of battle against the bare landscape.

Danielle hurried over to the gray mare Sam Larkin struggled to hold in check well apart from the other competitors. One hand still tight on the reins, he gave her a foot up into the saddle. "Good luck, Danni. You're going to need it with this one. She's no Lady."

"I know that, Sam." She smiled fleetingly in acknowledgment of his pun.

Lizzie B, a high-strung mare with the reckless habit of rushing her fences, would suit Danielle just fine; she was in a pretty reckless mood herself. Nudging the mare's flanks, Danielle fought to take command as they wheeled toward the far edge of the field. Lizzie strained forward, every quivering muscle on edge. In response Danielle shortened the reins, well aware that this ride was akin to a tightrope act. How much did she dare to give the mare her head without risking pushing her over the edge?

Unconsciously her hands tightened on the reins, as if by mastering Lizzie's wildness she could master the same emotions lurking inside her. Danielle reached up to adjust the strap of her velvet-covered hard hat, pulling it tight beneath her chin.

Standing up in the stirrups, she could just see over the bobbing heads of the other riders. Unexpectedly, her spirits lifted as she watched Ryan swing up onto White Lightning—an absurd misnomer for the horse, given his placid, one-pace temperament. The gelding had suited Hal's personality and riding abilities perfectly, so it was going to be interesting to see how the confident Australian handled the mount. Where Hal ran cold, she sensed Ryan ran hot. Where one spelled predictability and comfortable security, the other spelled what—danger, excitement?

Danielle's competitiveness was honed to a fine edge now, and she even allowed herself a spunky grin, almost glad Hal had backed out. He was too easy to beat. Ryan, even on White Lightning, might be another matter entirely.

Her thoughts were interrupted when another horse and rider nudged in beside her at the far edge of the starting line. Kay Witherspoon, one of Fairfax County's more outspoken residents, nodded to her young neighbor.

"Danni, don't you think you've taken on a little more than you can handle? I've never seen you on anything but Lady."

"She—"

"Oh, yes, I know," the older woman interrupted with authority. "Dr. Martin was by my place and mentioned she'd had a difficult delivery. Pity all John's left with is one second-rate foal. If I were your father—"

"Thanks for the advice," Danielle shot back, nettled. "Actually dad's already gotten a very nice offer for the new foal."

"Who on earth would be foolish enough to buy it?" Mrs. Witherspoon demanded, her manner disdainful.

"I would."

The woman's discomfitted "oh" was swallowed up in the sharp report of a pistol.

The horses plunged forward, all except Lizzie, who shied and jerked sideways. Danielle lost precious seconds getting the skittish mare under control. Lizzie was still so rattled by the noise and bustle that she took refuge in her mistress's firm hand, jumping the first fence almost sedately.

Just as Danielle decided the race might be a piece of cake, after all, the headstrong mare spotted an open pasture gate across the field and veered in its direction, evidently deciding a shortcut back to the barn was more her speed.

"You lazy little hellion," Danielle swore, retaliating with a quick spurred jab to Lizzie's flank and a light thwack across the rump with her riding crop. Smarting under the reprimand, the mare laid her ears back flat against her head and dashed pell-mell for the next fence, choosing her own precarious

takeoff point over the brush barrier, completely dis-
regarding Danielle's frantic signals.

At this point all the rider could do was hang on
tightly and hope for the best. Risking a glance up, she
was delighted to see White Lightning's pale rump just
ahead. At least there was a chance she could dash
past Ryan to put him in last place.

Lizzie, in a frenzy of delight at having her controls
relaxed, plunged ahead. Thoroughly unladylike, she
charged each fence helter-skelter and bounded over
with hooves flying. Exasperated and a little unnerved, Danielle still had guts enough to urge the
mare on, until their mad scramble over fences bore
little resemblance to the elegant rich-man's sport
steeplechasing was supposed to be.

Ryan heard the undisciplined thundering of hooves
coming up on his left and risked a glance over his
shoulder. He laughed to himself. Danielle's hard hat
had tipped forward crookedly on her brow, and a
long strand of her dark hair had worked free of the
chignon to whip across her face. He stopped laughing
when she raced past, not even deigning to give him a
glance.

Until now the steeplechase had been fun, a reminder of the range fences and fallen gum trees he'd
jumped as a boy, with his grandmother's horses. But
Danielle awakened his fighting instincts.

Ryan had seen the contempt blazing out of her eyes
when Adams had backed out of the race. He got the
feeling she had little respect for the man she was going to marry. Yet somehow her contempt made her

feel safe with Adams: a weak man would never get the better of her.

Ryan grinned slyly, deciding then and there he wasn't about to let her get away with winning. He brought his riding crop up and rapped it sharply on the gelding's flanks, a polite wake-up call. Twice more he snapped the crop down.

"You're a dignified old man, White Lightning," he murmured to the startled horse. "But I've got a feeling there's still some fire left in you."

The once-placid gelding tensed, his ears quivering with anticipation. Ryan's thighs—taut, hard muscled, commanding against him—were the only spur needed. White Lightning drank in some of that raw driving energy.

They galloped in pursuit, nipping threateningly at Lizzie's tail. Shocked, Danielle heard the gelding's thundering approach and leaned forward in the saddle. That was enough hint for the supersensitive Lizzie, who sprinted ahead and leaped the next fence wildly. Their sloppy landing lost them precious momentum, giving the lead to their competitors.

Danielle spared a quick glance at Ryan's profile in passing. In those two seconds she sensed the advantage he'd gained over her—he'd won his horse's confidence. White Lightning was running now because he loved it, because the rider had communicated his daredevil love of life to him.

Danielle was so caught up in this unexpected turn of events that she didn't notice another opening in the pasture fence until Lizzie broke stride and started to make a run for it, her neck stretched as she strained at the bit.

"Damn your sneaky soul!" Infuriated by the mare's headstrong ways, she snapped her wrists as sharply as she could to bring Lizzie's head up and regain some semblance of control. Danielle pushed her toward the next fence with little warning spurs against her ribs as a constant reminder that the games were over and she was boss now.

Lizzie breathed one snort of protest, then settled down enough to give her mistress a mad roller-coaster ride in pursuit of the gelding. The chastisement paid off. Flawlessly they took the three subsequent fences, until they were nearly neck and neck with Ryan. Other riders had begun to tire and fall back, so the field was more crowded now, but neither Ryan nor Danielle noticed. For them it was strictly a one-on-one competition; no one else mattered.

Lizzie, in fine fettle and full of herself, nosed up close behind the hard-breathing gelding, and Danielle smiled to herself, listening to Ryan's muttered string of imprecations. With his large body straddling the horse, he seemed to her a Viking on horseback. He needed a big Morgan horse or a Clydesdale, a breed to match his stature. Yet he didn't look absurd on the fine-boned gelding because they moved so handsomely together.

Refusing to be impressed, Danielle drove Lizzie on, both of them reckless now. Four riders were bearing down on the tenth fence, with Ryan right behind them. White Lightning took the post-and-rails cleanly and Lizzie made a game attempt to follow.

The flick of a tail close to her face flustered the mare. Half closing her eyes, Lizzie leaped too soon and came crashing down square in the center of the thick sapling posts. Danielle, who had been leaning into the jump as style required, kept on going after Lizzie had stopped. She flew over the mare's head to the other side of the fence, landing on her backside in the churned-up field.

Hooves thundered past her head as the mare broke free of the barrier, and then there was silence. Danielle stared up at the cloud-filled sky, less hurt by the force of her landing than by the idea of losing.

Fighting back tears, she pulled herself up to a sitting position and gingerly felt her bones. She had just decided none were broken when she heard hooves pounding in her direction. She attempted to scoot backward, thinking it was Lizzie run amok now that she was riderless.

But it wasn't the troublesome mare who came at a gallop around the far fence. Ryan had doubled back, spurring his mount when he caught sight of Danielle sprawled in the dirt. He was beside her in a flash.

"Are you okay?"

The concern in his voice brought the tears even closer to flowing, but she fought them back. "Of course I am." Her sternness fooled neither of them, and she didn't refuse the hand he offered to help her up.

Twisting her head, she stared down at her mud-splattered behind. "Luckily it's nicely cushioned,"

Ryan consoled her. She glared at him, but the quelling look did nothing to diminish the teasing light in his eyes. "I was looking forward to being served breakfast in bed. Given the circumstances...." He stopped and grinned. "Maybe I should be bringing you a tray, instead."

"Look, you've won. Now let's drop it, shall we?" Realizing how churlish she must have sounded, Danielle added stiffly, "Thank you for coming back to see how I am."

"But I know you'd have done the same for me."

"Yes, to administer the coup de grace."

"That's what I love about you, Danielle—you're such a graceful loser."

"I like to win, Kilpatrick."

"I told you before, so do I. Why fight it?" With a grin he got back up on the gelding and wheeled away.

Danielle stomped up the hill, forgetting her sore back. Damn him! He always managed to get the last word.

THE BUFFET SUPPER was in full swing by the time Danielle returned downstairs. A long hot shower had eased her aches, and she had exchanged her muddy riding clothes for a cream-colored skirt and wraparound angora sweater anchored by a soft leather belt.

Picking up a plate from the end of the dining-room table, she filled it sparingly with fresh fruit, salad and a warm croissant.

"Is that all you're eating, Danni-girl?"

She smiled in response to the jovial voice, knowing

even before she looked up that her accuser's pudgy hands would be balancing a gargantuan plateful of food. A man of ample girth and genial wit, Callum Harding adored food, whiskey and a spot of gambling, in that order.

"Hello, Callum. I see you're making up for my picky appetite."

"What's the matter—still smarting from that fall you took?"

"Do I look it?"

Callum shook his head admiringly. "I can't figure it out. You Davises always have had that feline knack of landing on your feet. . . er, so to speak."

"Naturally." As she answered Callum imperturbably, Danielle was aware of Ryan sauntering into the dining room from the hall.

Oblivious to the newcomer, Callum chatted on in high humor. "How long do you think your luck's going to hold out, girl? I heard your daddy suckered you into taking a skinny little foal off his hands."

"You remember the old comic-book ads, don't you, Callum? Ninety-pound weaklings can turn out to be the muscled hotshots who take all the prizes."

"I never went in for that hogwash myself." Callum patted his belly in amusement. "And I do think you're talking rashly now."

She gave her old friend a level look. "You know me, Callum. I don't make idle boasts. . .or threats."

"Lordie, do I know you! Stubborn as the day is long. You won't let that poor little critter give up the ghost even if he wants to."

"I watched that foal being born. I'll watch her take first in the Hillsborough Hunter Chase two years from now."

"Whoo-ee, would you care to put your money where your mouth is, girl?" Callum's eyes sparkled in anticipation of a friendly little wager.

"Sorry," she teased him back serenely, "but I'd hate to see a grown man cry."

"Would you?" countered a husky voice from the other end of the table. Danielle's and Callum's heads jerked up at this unexpected interruption. "Any man would be a fool if he believed you meant that." Ryan's eyes were fixed on her, amused and subtly accusing at the same time.

Callum snorted. "Who are you, sir? By your accent I'd say you're an Englishman, but your manners say otherwise."

Ryan inclined his head at Danielle's gallant defender. "Too right, mate," he replied, accentuating his drawl. "I'm Australian. Kilpatrick's the name. Family tradition has it that one of my way-back ancestors was an Irish rebel who irritated King George so much that gentleman shipped him out to Australia with a bunch of other ne'er-do-wells."

"They say bloodlines run true," Danielle cut in.

"If you happen to be a horse."

She shrugged. "You mean there's nothing left of that old Irish rebel who lived by his own rules, and society be damned?"

He shrugged.

Meanwhile, Callum had been following their exchange with interest. "Just what do you do, Kilpatrick?" he inquired.

"I log hardwoods in Malaysia."

"Malaysia! I'll be danged."

Danielle couldn't resist getting another dig in. "Actually, he's being modest, Callum. What he is is an adventurer."

Ryan's eyes narrowed. "I suppose it depends on what you mean by the word." Tension crept into the air, fed by the sparks of mutual accusation that made a mockery of their surface politeness.

Callum broke the standoff with a hearty laugh. "Whoo-ee, now if it's adventure you want to talk about, I can tell you folks a few things about my time in North Africa after the war." He shot Ryan a look of mischief. "Never mind, young man. When you're my age you'll be regaling anyone who'll listen to your tales."

With a grin Ryan sauntered away, leaving them alone once more in the dining room. "I wouldn't mind hearing those stories again." Danielle smiled up at Callum, and he began to reminisce, absentmindedly adding goodies to her plate as they went past the table, since his own was already overflowing.

She stayed by his side most of the evening, grateful for the buffer of his genial expansiveness, which required only an occasional answering word from her. Danielle was more exhausted than she cared to admit, unconsciously aware that her fatigue stemmed from more than just the party and the hard spill she'd taken.

Jen and her father drifted through the living room at one point, deep in lively conversation of their own between interruptions from the other guests. Danielle's eyes followed her dark-haired secretary. This was a new side to Jen.

Danielle was familiar with her friend's intelligence, her unflustered capability in any office crisis, her unfailing good humor. As Jen moved easily from group to group at John Davis's side, Danielle realized she also possessed a lively sophistication that had nothing to do with snobbery or pretenses.

Danielle recalled the self-assured way Jen had replied when she had teased her secretary about not wanting to shoot for the big-time professional goals. The woman was happy in and of herself; there was no need to push herself relentlessly. Danielle felt a twinge of envy, getting a clearer idea of what might be drawing her father to Jen.

She was so caught up in her thoughts that she didn't notice Hal approaching until he perched on the leather ottoman in front of the wing chair where she sat curled up. "Are you sure you're okay, Danni, darling?" he inquired, placing a solicitous hand on her knee.

"Of course I am. You know, you missed one exciting race, Hal," she reproved him, sensing his concern was covering his relief that he hadn't been the one thrown.

"Yes, I heard White Lightning nearly stole the show with Kilpatrick. I thought you said that old Arabian was safe enough for a child to ride."

"I suppose there's some life left in the old man. You'll have to give him a go next weekend." Danielle tried hard not to smile.

Hal touched the knot of his tie with nervous fingers and deftly changed the subject. "While the rest of you were playing, Senator Farrel and I had a long chat," he confided, lowering his voice to a whisper. "There's a chance he's going to be nominated for secretary of state, and he's going to need a top-level assistant."

"Go for it, then. You've got the qualifications," she said. Unhesitatingly she slipped into her usual role of nurturing her fiancé, of smoothing down the insecurities that lay beneath his sharp competitive mask. Her position of relative power, knowing deep down she was stronger than Hal, had once been a source of satisfaction. Now his weakness only dismayed her.

"Danni, are you listening to me?" His words prodded her.

For once she rebelled. "I'm sorry, Hal," she apologized distantly, pulling herself up out of the comfortable chair. "But my back is bothering me more than I realized. I think I'll take a walk to try to unkink it."

Without looking back, she went out into the hall, taking a warm black shawl from the closet. Wrapping it around her, she stepped out into the night.

For all the chill of the air, Danielle felt a tantalizing undercurrent of warmth. The fragrant scent of herbs wafting up from the kitchen garden presaged summer. As she walked alongside the balustrade, her eyes adjusting to the crisp moonlit darkness of the country night, it struck her that her appreciation for the changing seasons and the wax and wane of the moon were tied to Foxhall. In the city she was always too distracted to notice; even a full moon paled against the harsh glare of city streetlights.

She wished her father would reconsider his National Trust pledge. She had gone along with his plan, understanding the tax advantages of such a move. Still, Foxhall had a special place in her heart.

Danielle had meant to walk only to the end of the terrace, but on impulse she continued down the stairs and struck out across the field, heedless of the dew that would probably ruin her kidskin pumps. The house with its blaze of lights was no longer visible. The pitched-slate roof of the old anvil workshop, adjacent to the barn, shone like tarnished silver in the moonlight.

No one was around. Danielle slipped inside the barn, pausing to take several lumps of sugar from a box on the supply shelf. At White Lightning's stall she stopped to rub his nose distractedly, thinking she would have to find another horse for her fiancé. After today's performance she knew Hal wouldn't ride him again. The gelding had proved too full of surprises, and what Hal wanted out of life more than anything else was guarantees. He wanted all the risks minimized. He wanted his life to run in a smooth grooved track.

Restless, Danielle moved on until she came to Lizzie's stall. Sniffing the sugar, the mare tossed her head in anticipation. "Why should I reward you, Lizzie? You and your wild headstrong ways." One of the high-school kids who worked part-time as a stablehand for Sam had found Lizzie after the race, placidly grazing down by the highway. Impatient now for the treat, Lizzie nudged Danielle's closed hand. "And you're bad mannered to boot," the woman scolded, but she was laughing softly as she offered the white cube.

Danielle went on down the long row of stalls, quickening her step. Lady had been transferred to a roomy end stall on the south side of the barn, much warmer and light filled in the afternoon when the westering sun poured through the low window in the wall.

Recognizing her visitor, Lady trod daintily to the fence and accepted the tidbit from Danielle's hand. A scrabbling came from the nest of straw behind her, and Lady whickered in response. The tiny foal staggered over, sleepy eyed, hungry for her mother's warmth.

Something leaped in Danielle at the sight of her. Quickly she opened the stall door and knelt beside the foal in the straw, stroking her gently. "You are a little beauty," she breathed. A stray moonbeam caught the dark ruby gleam of her coat, shining like fire against the surrounding darkness. "Foxfire," Danielle whispered, testing the feel of the name on her tongue.

She would name the foal after the farm where

she'd been born and the fiery gleam of her coat. Danielle knew it was foolish to give her a name, to become so attached to a creature that might never survive the week. But it was too late. The attachment had begun the moment Danielle had caught the foal in her arms. What she had found in that moment was an affirmation of the deepest emotions that lay buried inside, a part of her that only rarely broke through the surface.

Danielle reached into her skirt pocket for the last sugar cube, scraping a few grains into the edge of her nail. She held up her finger to the soft wet nose. Seconds later Foxfire was licking off the grains, her tongue warm and eager and hungry for life.

Danielle had no doubts then. The fragile newcomer would survive. With a little thrill of pleasure she leaned forward and touched her lips to the foal's muzzle, delicate and smooth as a baby's head.

The moment was shattered by an intrusion. "That's the first bit of tenderness I've seen in you, Danielle."

She whirled in surprise, like a thief caught out. "What are you doing here, Kilpatrick? Why did you follow me?"

He leaned against the open stall door, hands thrust into his pockets, and stared down at her. "Maybe I was looking for a little tenderness, too," he teased her.

She turned back to the foal, moving her palm down its sides in long gentling strokes. "You don't strike me as a man who needs tenderness," she said finally, not looking at him.

"Then you don't know much about a man's needs."

Ryan watched her hand go still. Her head was bent now, the tight chignon gleaming black in the moonlight. And he wanted to free her hair from its confining pins, to caress the long fragrant strands as they fanned across her shoulders—naked and soft. Once upon a time they had shared this and more.

The trick of the light streaming in through the window and the secluded shelter of the stall echoed that long-ago atmosphere. Because of that curious chemistry between them, Danielle felt the same dream resurfacing, but she beat it down. With gentle firmness she pushed the foal toward Lady and stood up. "I've got to get back to the house. They'll be wondering where I am."

"Let them wonder."

She stared at his mouth, remembering the feel of it against her own. She remembered the sweet solace of his fingertips against her bare skin and wanted to run from the memories, the heartache, the tiny nagging void that had grown inside since the morning she'd lost him.

"You should never have come here," she whispered.

"No. I should have been back in Malaysia days ago, and you should be up at the house with Adams. We're both here now, though. Why?"

His implication that a tenuous bond still existed between them rocked her. "I don't know." She clasped her hands together beneath the shawl to keep them from trembling. "Maybe it's because at heart we're two of a kind. Neither one of us can relax until we get what we want."

"What do we want?"

"To be left alone."

"Do you always lie to yourself that way?"

"I'm not lying. It's reality."

"Like hell it is. What we both want is to finish what we started a long time ago."

"That night was just an illusion." As she spoke she felt the gathering tension between them. Aware that she was perilously close to admitting her own hurt, she attacked, rebuilding the wall between them. "You were a wanted man. You were the foreman of that Kwan Hi company the government intended to prosecute. You were a fugitive from justice. That's why you disappeared that night."

"I've paid my debt," he grated.

"How could you have? You were never convicted of anything."

"I've had to live with my own conscience for four hellish years."

"If you're innocent, why are you so afraid to tell me what it was all about?"

"Why? Because your ambition and your ego scare the hell out of me. You seem to have this obsession with walking all over people."

She blanched. "If I do it's for self-protection. You of all men should appreciate that, Ryan Kilpatrick. Life's a game to you, isn't it?" The accusations poured out, and she was powerless to stop them.

"When the poker hand's over you can put down your cards and walk away without looking back. I can't."

"What the devil are you driving at?"

"I've only known your name one week." She drew a deep breath to still the unsteadiness of her voice. "You've known mine for four years. From the minute I walked out of that basement you knew who I was, but you didn't come after me. That night meant nothing to you, nothing."

The bruised look in her eyes exposed the pain of betrayal, but he refused to see it. Women used vulnerability as a weapon, too.

He said more roughly than he intended, "The night we shared was a beautiful moment, but that was as good as things could ever be for us, Danielle. Here we are fighting. This is the reality. This is what it's all about, isn't it?" He let out his breath sharply. "No, I didn't look very hard. You said it yourself a minute ago. We weren't part of the same world then."

"How much less so now," she replied bleakly, brushing past him to go out into the dark corridor, with each step widening the chasm between them.

"Danielle, don't go." The words were a command, a plea that called to her senses, compelling them to disobey the cold logic of her mind.

She stopped but didn't turn around. "It's too late," she whispered to the night. "Don't you understand?"

Yet even as she tried to deny the connection between them Danielle turned, and he was there. Slowly, tentatively, he reached up to touch her face. His hand was strong and warm, his splayed fingers gentle and sensitive as they traced the line of her cheekbone and furrowed brow.

Still unable to look at him, she gave herself up to the pleasure of his touch. Danielle sensed that through each fingertip he was remembering. Each point of contact evoked another memory, until both were caught up in the sensual tracery. Emotion and the half-forgotten flames of passion held her captive now, and she longed for the sweet sanctuary of his arms. Little by little she turned her head; his hand followed the movement until her lips were pressed to his warm callused palm.

With her last vestige of willpower she lifted a hand to push his away. But her own fingers betrayed her, clasping his more tightly against her fevered cheek. All the tenderness he'd asked for so teasingly flowed into her, an unexpected gift. . . a promise.

Dear God, how could it be a lie? Her uncertainty, conflicting feelings tormented her, until the tears squeezed through her downcast lashes, spilling over her cheek and their joined hands.

Ryan brushed the drops away with the broad pad of his thumb, but still more fell, like the slow steady rain that drums the frozen earth on a wintry day. He bent his head closer as she whispered something below her breath. He caught the words.

"Too late," she'd said.

His answering look was rueful, faintly self-mocking. *Too late, indeed,* he agreed silently. *Too late for me to walk away.* Though their worlds were in opposition, this raw physical need drew them to each other.

The same magic, the same reckless passion two strangers had shared had begun to work again. The world might pull them apart later, but neither cared about anything beyond this one exquisite moment.

Ryan bent his head even closer, until the dark fur of his mustache brushed against her skin and his lips found the wetness at the corners of her mouth to kiss away the salty tears.

Danielle felt weak, powerless. She swayed against him, then steadied herself, the tight balls of her fists unfolding to rest against his broad chest. Through skin and marrow she felt the low steady rhythm of his heart, a drumbeat beckoning to her most primitive instincts.

She let her head fall back; she was hungry for the dropped kisses that eased away the sting of her tears. There was nothing for her now but this pure reveling in a man's arms around her, the dark magic of his touch.

His caresses weren't hurried or demanding, but a gentle exploration—as if the shape of her jaw and the pale satin fineness of her skin were the most important things in the world to him. He wanted only to free the emotions locked in her heart, to communicate his desire through the hungry pressure of his lips against her throat, the sensual rasp of his tongue along the shelled indentation of her ear.

She felt sexually alive in the deepest sense of the

word—all female to his male. "Ryan." She whispered his given name for the first time, and the taste of it on her lips was like wine.

His hands moved to her shoulders, kneading, caressing. With an artist's delicacy Ryan pushed down her sweater to free her pale fragrant skin for the imprint of his lips. He kissed the hollow of her shoulder and the pulsepoint at the base of her throat, thrilling to her husky moan of delight.

"Oh, please...." Now the angora sweater clung precariously to the swell of her breasts, just covering them, and for all the coolness of the night air against her skin, they felt aflame. How eager she was for the completion of his lips, the savoring stroke of his tongue and the grazing of his teeth along the intimate curves he'd mapped long ago.

"Say my name again," he commanded, the words a fluid murmur washing over her.

"Ryan...." It came out in a soft strangled sigh. "No," she protested in vain, afraid of the overwhelming intensity of their forbidden encounter and the delicious pleasure she had no right to feel.

"And again."

"Oh, Ryan...stop." Shivering, she felt his hair, thick and smooth as an animal's pelt, teasing her sensitive skin. She cupped her hands around his head, driven by the conflicting urges to push him from her and hold him even more tightly to her breast.

He ignored her plea, hearing only the warm yearning language of her body that made him even more reckless and hungry for her. Her stockinged leg chafed his through the corduroy nap of his trousers, and he began to ease her down onto a soft bed of straw, eager to undress her so that no barriers remained.

She felt the exquisite sensual restraint of his touch giving way. Frightened, she tore herself from him. Ryan was neither lover nor friend; she couldn't find sustenance in his arms. She was betraying Hal; she was betraying herself.

And yet. . . dear God, how she wanted more! If he should touch her again she would be lost. She backed away, trembling, realizing how dangerous and foolish her behavior had been. Once Ryan appreciated the power he had over her, he would try to use it again and again.

"I have to go back, Ryan. This was a terrible mistake." She stood protected in the shadows while the moonlight limned his upper body in a cool silvery light: the gleam of his close-cropped hair, the curve of his passionate sensitive mouth, the rise and fall of his chest beneath his jacket.

Though he didn't move, his eyes caressed her, and when he held out his hands it was as if no other man had ever reached her. "Danielle," he said quietly into the darkness, "did you ever tell Adams about us. . . about what happened?"

"There was nothing to tell him. As far as I'm concerned it never happened." Her expression was distant, her gaze fixed not on him but the low window beyond.

"After this, can you still believe that?"

"Don't you understand!" The words came out in a

taut whisper, suppressing everything she had felt and desired. "I have to believe that night never happened. I have to believe it if I'm to go on with my life as it is."

"Danielle, don't you see you're cheating yourself, cheating us both?"

"No, you've got it wrong. It's Hal I'm cheating. I'm engaged to him. I've made my commitment."

"If your commitment were so strong you'd be beside him now, instead of here with me. If it were so bloody strong you'd hide your contempt of him a little better," he said with unflinching honesty. "Can't you see yourself, Danielle? You're running scared from a life that means bloody nothing to you."

"How in hell do you presume to know what I want or what I feel, what is or isn't important to me?"

"Then give me the chance to find out what you are, what you want. Let's meet on our own ground, Danielle," he urged softly. "Man to woman."

A frisson of warning raced up her spine. "I tried that once before. I won't be foolish enough to do it again."

"What's left, then?"

"All I want is to see you packing—to have my life return to normal."

"You're still lying to yourself."

"Don't push me, Ryan. Don't make me despise you."

"It's not me you despise. You despise what Hal Adams stands for. You despise your own cowardice." He stalked past her.

She wanted to crumple from exhaustion, but her stiff-backed pride forbade such weakness. "You can't talk to me that way," she called after him. "You're a stranger to me!"

Ryan heard her parting words echoing inside his head. *You bloody bastard,* he silently swore. *You had no right to attack her like that.*

As his anger with himself ebbed away, he tried to think more clearly. He had been sure their desire would be enough to link them. He hadn't counted on her pride, on a strength of will he had rarely seen before.

Her unexpected fierceness intrigued him as much as her soft yielding body had excited his senses. He saw in her an adversary and a lover, devil and angel, a beautiful chameleon who kept him off-balance with her coolness and her passion, with her quicksilver intelligence ready to battle his.

Reluctantly he admitted the truth: she reminded him of all that he'd been missing. She reminded him of all a woman could be.

CHAPTER FIVE

"THIS REPORT isn't up to your usual standards, Danni." Clay Perrin tapped his pipe bowl into the ashtray without looking at her. "It sounds too much like the backbiting stuff I get from rival department heads when they're out for revenge." Clay's eyes came up then, full of impatient questions. "What's going on?"

"I was writing from gut instinct."

"I got that impression," Clay observed dryly. "What you've given me is hasty, emotional and poorly documented."

She replied in a strained voice. "I made a recommendation based on the information at hand."

"Yes, and the loan committee's going to make a decision based on that recommendation. They'll have assumed we did a thorough professional investigation."

Danielle's eyes flickered downward, not missing his subtle emphasis on the word *professional*. "I'm not a magician, Clay. I can't pull evidence out of a hat."

"But isn't that just what you did?" Using his pipe stem as a guide, he ran his eyes down the typed page.

"For example, what the hell is this—'Kilpatrick once worked for a logging outfit that was shut down for illegal activities. Although he himself was never convicted....'" Clay looked up again. "Did you even bother to ask Kilpatrick what this was all about?"

She flushed at his sarcasm. "I asked. He was evasive."

Clay pushed the report across the desk toward her. "You're an attorney, damn it! You know innuendo and circumstantial evidence when you see it. The fact is, no matter what happened four years ago, in the eyes of the law Kilpatrick is an innocent man. What gives you the right to presume his guilt now?"

Because I had the childish urge to hurt him, she wanted to shout.

Usually Danielle relished these sessions with her boss. By playing devil's advocate over the years, Clay had sharpened her ability to distinguish between carefully reasoned arguments and fluff. But today she couldn't wait for the grilling to be over. She had committed the cardinal sin: she had let emotion come before professional judgment.

"Don't you have anything to say in your defense, Danni?"

"Clay, you know I've worked on this case for months. Kilpatrick hasn't given us one shred of proof that the Ibans aren't going to be hurt irreparably by his logging interests."

"And you haven't given one shred of proof that they will be hurt."

Danielle shifted uncomfortably. "Clay, it's no

use," she said finally. "I'd like to be taken off this project."

"Out of the question. It's been dragging on far too long as it is."

With a sigh Danielle got up and went to stand at the window behind Clay's desk. Far below a young couple stood arm in arm on the riverbank.

"I know the case has been dragging on," Danielle said at last, her gaze still fixed on the scene below. "Maybe that's the problem. Somewhere along the way I've lost my objectivity."

Clay swiveled to look at her. The bright afternoon light revealed all the tenseness of her expression, the faint shadows beneath her eyes. He addressed her more gently. "What is it, Danni—some personal problem? Did you have a tiff with Hal?"

Her eyes snapped up. "What does Hal have to do with it?"

"I was just fishing, Danni. I'm just trying to figure out what's going on." He leaned back in the chair, a smile hovering. "You're such a fine administrator that sometimes I almost forget you're a human being. I act like you don't have a right to your emotions."

"Careful, now. With talk like that you're dating yourself, old man," she teased him affectionately. "Nowadays it's the men who are supposed to be sensitive and caring while we women are tough as nails. It's the role reversal of the eighties, don't you know?"

"Just don't carry it too far."

Danielle stiffened as that little warning struck home. "I am what I am, Clay. I can't change that."

"You mean you don't want to change," he corrected.

She noticed that his gaze had strayed to the silver-framed photograph of his family, taken years before, and eager to change the subject she asked, "Do you still keep in touch with Patty, Clay?"

"Oh, sure. We had an amicable parting of the ways. She still writes from time to time. She's in Arizona now, involved with some guy who runs a rafting business down the Colorado River."

"You sound surprised."

"Not really," he answered, his expression far away. "You know what she used to call me, Danni? A knee-jerk bureaucrat."

She laughed. "And you said it was an amicable divorce?"

But he was off on his own train of thought. "I understand what she meant now. We're like paper watchdogs, you and I and the rest of us here. Our job is to make sure everyone else follows some pretty tough rules, so most of the time we wind up saying 'no,' and that attitude spills over into our personal lives, or at least it did into mine. All that rigid playing by the rules began to make me say 'no,' out of habit, to everything. I was afraid of my own impulses, until there was no excitement—no surprises—left. Patty got tired of that, I guess." He looked squarely at his young administrator. "I guess what I'm saying is, don't get trapped the same way."

"Why are you telling me all this?"

"Because you looked like you needed a lecture."
He was teasing again.

"You're crazy, Clay."

"I'm just trying to keep up with the latest trends."
His eyes twinkled faintly. "I'm being sensitive and
what was that other thing you mentioned? Oh, yes.
And I'm being caring."

"Keep it a secret, then," she said impishly. "All
your department heads will try to get away with
murder if they get the idea you've gone soft."

"You think so?" As he spoke Clay picked up her
case report and tore it slowly in half. "I want you to
do this over again, Danni. And this time do it right."

"I've exhausted all the files. How on earth do you
expect me to dredge up anything new?"

"I have every confidence in you."

"Brute."

His dry laughter followed her out into the hall.

Slowly Danielle walked back to her own office,
wondering what to do next. She longed to mark the
case closed and file it away, to forget that she'd ever
heard of Ryan Kilpatrick. But Clay was more right
than he knew. She was already too deeply involved.

Jen had her coat half on, ready to head out the
door, when her boss walked in. "How did the meeting go?"

In answer Danielle held up the two ripped halves of
her report.

"Oh-oh. That bad, huh?" Jen shook her head in
commiseration. "Now I suppose you're going to

work all night to have a new version for him in the morning.''

Danielle sighed. "I don't think so, Jen. To be perfectly honest, I'm tired of the whole damn business.''

Her secretary's eyebrows shot up in surprise, though her only response was a simple quiet, "I don't blame you."

"Well?"

"Well, what?"

"You mean you're not going to give me your standard line about how I've been working too hard?" Danielle couldn't resist teasing her.

Jen laughed softly. "Well, it's true, you know. Danielle, you are looking a little beat. I've never seen you so tense.''

"I'll get over it."

"You need to unwind."

"Will you stop your fussing if I promise I'll drink some hot cocoa and go straight to bed when I get home?"

Jen shook her head. "I've got a better idea. Come to jazz class with me. I'm not too bad a teacher."

"Jen, I don't know anything about dance!"

"So what. It's easy. And as the kids say, 'it feels good.' "

"And if it feels good, do it?"

"You got it."

They laughed together now. Yet Danielle still hedged. "Well, I don't know...."

"Come on, Danni. You can jump and kick and twirl all your frustrations away. I guarantee it."

"Well, maybe just to watch. My back's still a little sore."

"Forget it! I'm not going to let you weasel out that easily. I've got an extra leotard in my car."

The two women drove uptown. Beyond the glittering elegance of official Washington, the boulevard unraveled like a frayed collar. Block after block, there was nothing now but dingy rowhouses and mom-and-pop storefronts barred against the night.

Danielle stared out the car window, discomfitted by what she was seeing. "Why do you come down here?" she asked finally.

Jen grinned breezily. "The Davises aren't the only ones with a social conscience. Besides, I just plain enjoy working with these kids. If they can develop enough self-confidence and discipline to make it through my class, they'll be a lot more willing to try other things in the future."

"Well, I'm afraid even to drive through this part of town. It really isn't safe, Jen."

"Like father, like daughter. Your dad tried to lecture me, too."

"Oh?" Danielle replied with feigned casualness. "When was that?"

"We met for a drink after work on Tuesday."

"And then I suppose he took you out to dinner."

Jen's eyes slid over to her companion. "Yes, as a matter of fact, he did," she said coolly.

They drove on in silence until Jen pulled into the high-school parking lot, which was deserted and poorly lit. Danielle glimpsed two shadowy figures lurking near the gymnasium entrance. "Quick, lock the doors," she ordered nervously.

But Jen's only response was a silvery peal of laughter as she climbed out of the car. "Carlotta, Tami, hi. I hope you people practiced that routine we went over last week."

"Hi, teach," the teenagers greeted Jen. "Who's your frien'?" they demanded, checking Danielle out curiously. Feeling rather sheepish, Danielle got out and slowly came around to join them. She smiled in return when the introductions were made.

Inside the gym they were met by several more young people, mostly blacks and Latinos, who swarmed around Jen. "Okay, now, places everyone," she commanded in her best no-nonsense voice, which couldn't quite mask the sweetness beneath. "Where's Leetha—home sick again? We're going to have to lean on that girl. She's getting lazy."

Jen strolled over to retrieve a cassette tape from her tote bag, pausing just long enough before a young girl smoking in the corner to gently pluck the cigarette from her lips. "You're going to need every ounce of lung power you've got, Akanda," Jen admonished her with a smile. "You won't get even one toe in the door of a tryout if you keep it up. They want disciplined dancers, not a bunch of flakes. They want people with goals who are willing to work to get there. Do you all read me?" She paused. "Okay. Carlotta, put on this Shalimar tape and we'll get down to business."

Danielle thought horseback riding kept her in pretty decent shape, but ten minutes into Jen's pulsating jazz routine and the sweat was pouring down the back of her leotard and her face was beet red. Still she gamely kept up with them until the end, when everyone slid down effortlessly into a wide split.

Her tendons creaking, Danielle made it halfway. A dozen pairs of eyes were turned expectantly in her direction until the impish Akanda broke the silence with a tart, "Come on, lady! You gotta work to get there."

"Careful, though, Danielle," Jen added. "Don't push yourself too far."

Encouraged, Danielle lowered herself gingerly bit by bit, getting down as far as she could, grinning when the students cheered her attempt.

Danielle decided to sit the next routine out, even though the girls insisted she continue.

"Thanks," she demurred. "But, you see, I've always had this burning ambition to be a wallflower."

Jen whipped by, her eyes laughing, and called out, "Coward!"

Hobbling over to the bleachers, Danielle sank gratefully onto a bench and settled back to watch Jen in action.

"Once you've got the steps down pat here," Jen was coaching them, pointing to her head, "then you have to let it flow from here." She touched her heart. "You've got to feel the music deep down inside." She moved among the lithe acrobatic dancers, her eagle eye seemingly everywhere at once. "Akanda, save those improvisations for later. Take it from me, lady, you'll get a lot farther by following a choreographer's steps instead of messing around with his ego by making up your own. Enough said?"

And so it went. Danielle marveled at the way Jen directed them, sneaking in savvy advice on how to get along in life between all the technical tips.

Jen's body was a beautiful limber machine. She looked far younger than her thirty-five years. Danielle tried to imagine Jen and her father together—it was just too ridiculous. Not only was he twenty-five years older than she was, but their life-styles were totally different.

After class the two women drove back downtown, and Jen casually offered to treat her boss to cappuccino at a coffee bar.

"I'm getting the royal treatment tonight. First, you stretch out every tendon in my body to breaking point. Now what are you going to do, slip megavitamins into my cup?" Danielle needled her after they were shown to a cozy table overlooking Georgetown University Commons.

"Just call me 'mother hen.' "

"You do get a charge out of clucking over those kids, don't you?"

"I'd love to see them get a fair shot at life. They deserve it." Jen's candid dark eyes met Danielle's over their cups. "And obviously you think I'm crazy for doing this kind of thing."

"No, I admire you. You've made a very rewarding life for yourself." There was an awkward pause, and then she plunged on. "Which. . . which brings me to something I wanted to ask you. Do you have plans to see my father again?"

Jen's eyes narrowed. "Oh-oh, here it comes."

"What do you mean?" Danielle demanded with an air of injured innocence.

"As the kids would say, don't jive me, lady. You're an expert at hiding what you're feeling, Danni, but I haven't worked for you this long without being able to read the signs. You're really upset that your father and I—" Jen stopped and corrected herself. "That John and I might be interested in each other."

"Yes, I am." Danielle looked defiant, waiting. "Well, aren't you going to say it, Jen—it's none of my business."

"You're right. It's not."

The two women stared at each other in prickly silence.

Danielle sighed. "For heaven's sake, I wish you'd stop to think for a minute. Then maybe you'd realize there's no chance of your friendship coming to anything."

"What you're trying to say is there's no reason a man in his position should be interested in a secretary like me," Jen shot back, clearly hurt.

"That's not what I meant. You're young enough to be his daughter."

"And besides, my New York accent isn't quite upper crust enough for Jacques's and the Jockey Club."

"You're talking nonsense."

"I know that. But I'm afraid you might believe it. You've got just a bit of snobbery in you."

Danielle refused to be baited. "Shall we drop it, Jen?"

"You're the one who brought it up."

"Look—"

"Never mind. This conversation is pointless."

Danielle reached for her leather bag. "By the way," she began casually as if they'd never quarreled. "Have I ever shown you my mother's photograph?" She handed the open wallet across the table and watched Jen's eyes sweep down the patrician features.

"She was lovely."

"She was far more than that. My mother was the consummate diplomat's wife."

"And no other woman could ever come close—except maybe you? Is that the subtle point you're trying to make?" Jen smiled ruefully. "You know, Danni, I think John's getting just a little bit tired of his push-push-push existence. When I see the two of you together it's like I'm watching a couple of swordsmen constantly honing their skills. I think your father's hungry just to be himself, to be able to let down his guard for a change. He knows I'm not impressed by his status, so he doesn't try to impress me. He knows I'm not interested in games, so he doesn't have to play them when we're together."

"How lucky for you." Even as the sarcastic words slipped out Danielle could have kicked herself.

"Don't patronize me, Danni," Jen said angrily. "You've got your perfect job, your perfect fiancé, your perfect life all around. Why do you have to begrudge me wanting the same?" She stood up. "It's late. I've got to run. Do you want me to drop you back at the office so you can get your car?"

Danielle shook her head. "I'll take the Metro in the morning."

"I can drop you at your apartment, then."

How typical of Jen to be considerate of Danielle's comfort even when she was boiling mad! That made her feel more guilty than ever, but she was too stubborn to apologize. "No, thanks, Jen," she said in a subdued voice. "I think I'll walk. I need to clear some of the cobwebs out of my head."

Murmuring a stiff, "Good night," Jen was gone, and Danielle left the café a few minutes later.

Georgetown still bustled after dark. Laughter and music drifted out from elegant bistros sandwiched between antique shops and trendy boutiques featuring bald mannequins.

Danielle smiled ruefully as she walked along, remembering Jen's remark about her "perfect life." *If my life's so perfect, then what's missing?*

Once again she had the vague feeling that her father was betraying her. John Davis had raised his daughter to set goals and single-mindedly go after them. She had achieved most of them—now what? She wondered if the pursuit had been worthwhile. Wondered, too, why he should change the rules for himself now.

Danielle quickened her step up the tree-lined street, where gracious mansions had been subdivided into small elegant town homes. Her own was at the top of the hill.

As she let herself in the front door it occurred to her how much alike Jen and Ryan were. Neither of them believed in games, but the game was the only thing Danielle knew. She was afraid to look beneath those artificial rules, because she knew without them she would be lost.

JEN WAS IN AND OUT of Danielle's office all the next morning, taking dictation and double-checking the wording on a final draft of another case report they'd just completed. Although they addressed each other stiffly, the new constraint between them didn't affect their teamwork in the office. Danielle was grateful for that. As long as she was buried up to her ears in work she couldn't think about anything else.

The intercom on her desk buzzed, and Jen announced that she was sending Hal in. Before Danielle could protest, the door opened; her fiancé stepped inside.

"Hello, Danni," he greeted her. "I tried to reach you every evening this week, with no luck. So I decided to drop by. Senator Farrel and I were over at the International Monetary Fund headquarters for a meeting."

"It sounds as though you haven't left his side since Sunday afternoon," she remarked offhandedly, half her mind on the work he interrupted. "In fact, I'm surprised you're not dragging him off to lunch right now."

"I would have," Hal agreed, "but he had an important meeting with a group of lobbyists. That's why I came over here—to take you out to lunch instead."

"How nice to know I'm second choice," Danielle answered dryly.

"What are you so touchy about?"

"Thanks for the invitation, Hal, but I really am busy."

"But not too busy for that Australian."

Danielle dropped her pencil on the yellow legal pad in front of her. "What's that supposed to mean?"

"You had a long, cozy lunch out with him last week."

"That was business."

Hal lounged on the corner of her desk, toying with the antique brass temple bell she used as a paperweight. "And was it business when you disappeared from your father's party Sunday night and he followed you out?"

"Somehow the jealous-lover role just doesn't fit you, Hal," she replied, as cool and composed as ever but for the little telltale lines of tension around her mouth.

"I wasn't jealous, Danni. You know I trust you. Neither one of us is the type to fall prey to infatuation and all that tripe. We're two of a kind."

"Are we?" Her expression was ironic. "I'm so glad."

He eyed her narrowly as if weighing her remark. "Danni, you have to snap out of this strange mood. You haven't been yourself for a week. You're so distracted and self-absorbed, all you can talk about is this Kilpatrick case. You act like you don't care about anything else."

"Then make me care, dammit!" she flared.

He went on as if she hadn't spoken. "Danni, that big State Department dinner is Friday night. All I can say is I hope you'll work out whatever's bothering you before then, because I won't have you pulling your disappearing act in front of my colleagues."

"Oh, I see. All of a sudden I've become a potential liability instead of an asset. But I have a suggestion, Hal. Maybe you should cut your losses right now."

"What are you talking about?"

"Maybe we should call off our engagement."

His face went white with shock. "You're not making any sense. We've spent two years together. You can't throw them down the drain just like that."

Danielle stared at him with hard dry eyes, aware that not once had he mentioned loving or sharing. "I'm sorry, Hal. I need some breathing space."

"And I need you beside me."

"Couldn't you have said you needed me, period, and massaged my ego just a little?" Beneath the feigned wistfulness, her mockery was biting.

"Oh, for God's sake, you know that's what I meant."

"No, you said exactly what you meant. I'm an adornment, Hal, your entrée to higher political circles. You don't need a lover or a friend. All you want is a mentor."

"I haven't changed, Danni," he said with a proud dignity she hadn't known he was capable of. "I'm what I've always been, and that was good enough for you—until now. What's happened to change that?"

She shook her head helplessly. "It just has."

With trembling fingers she pulled the diamond engagement ring from her hand, but he refused to take it. "No, hold on to it. Once you've come to your senses you'll be wearing it again. We mean too much to each other."

Too drained to argue further, she slipped the ring into a drawer of her desk, locking it away. She looked up, and their eyes met.

"I'd still like for you to come to that dinner with me," he said almost pleadingly. "Danni, you know I can't make it without you."

She looked away. "Hal, I can't promise anything. I'm going through a difficult time."

He must have realized he would have to be satisfied with that because he didn't argue further, and Danielle was relieved when he left. She stared down at the pale circle of flesh on her finger, thinking of all the time it represented, time past. Her hand began to tremble again, but she ignored it.

"Jen," she spoke curtly into the intercom. "No more interruptions this morning. Please."

A half-hour later the buzzer sounded again. "Danni—"

"Jen, I meant what I said. Now you can tell whoever's out there—"

Before she could complete the sentence, the door burst open and Ryan strode in, his face flushed with anger.

"I've just been to Clay Perrin's office, and I'd like to know what in hell is going on. When I asked him if the papers had been signed or not, he told me to talk to you." His eyes bored into her. "I'm getting tired of this cat-and-mouse game. Do I get the loan or don't I?"

"You know very well if it were up to me alone you'd have gone home empty-handed long ago."

"Is this how you get your kicks?" he asked between his teeth. "How much longer do you intend to keep me dangling?"

"Don't push me." The warning in her voice was unmistakable, vibrating like tensile metal.

"'Push'?" he mocked her. "Don't tempt me. I feel like tossing you out that window. Lady, you're disrupting my life."

"Violence, too? What a delightfully charming picture you present, Kilpatrick." She was straining to the utmost to maintain her facade of cool aplomb.

"I think I've figured you out, Danielle." He was leaning over her desk now, his outrageously striped tie dangling before her nose so that she had to quell the urge to take her scissors to it. "You're punishing me because I had the bad luck to show you another part of yourself that you refuse to admit exists. You'd rather be a heartless, smooth-functioning machine, because it's a hell of a lot easier and less painful than being a woman."

"I refuse to listen to any more of this."

"So we made love to each other." His voice had risen over her objections. "Why do you have to make an international incident out of it?"

Her eyes flew to the door. "Will you stop shouting! The whole building will be taking sides in a minute."

"Let's get out of here, then. We're going to have it out, and I promise you, Danielle, I'm going to shout."

"Why don't we just get out the dueling pistols and be done with it? You and I are never going to agree."

"I prefer hand-to-hand combat myself." His eyes glittered dangerously. "It's much more satisfying. Now come on, let's get out of here."

"I'm sorry but I—"

"I know. You never go out to lunch except on important business." He came around the desk toward her.

"But I suppose I can make an exception in your case," she said haughtily, moving around the desk on the other side to keep him at bay. Without another word she turned and marched through the connecting door past Jen, who stared after her in astonishment.

THE WEATHER, at least, was warmer than the last time he'd dragged her out in his convertible. He flew down the sunny street at his usual breakneck pace. When he turned into the south entrance of Rock Creek Park, Danielle threw him a questioning glance. She should have known by now to expect the unexpected where Ryan was concerned.

Ten minutes later they had called a temporary truce as they faced each other over soft drinks and napkin-wrapped hot dogs slathered with mustard. A robin swooped down nearby , preening in the warm square of sunlight, which made his red breast gleam like claret wine. Danielle threw him a crumb, and with a sharp twitter he was off again.

Above those homey sounds came the incongruous roar of lions and the bray of elephants.

"Why the zoo, Ryan?" she asked, amused despite herself. "Is there something symbolic in our coming here?"

His lips twitched. "I thought if we were going to have a go at each other, we might as well do it in appropriately savage surroundings."

"You know you bring out the worst in me, Kilpatrick."

His grin broke out full force. "Maybe you're just now realizing how obnoxious and overbearing you really are."

"On the other hand," she shot back, "maybe I'm acquiring a few of your bad habits."

"Such as?"

"Your disgusting honesty, for one thing. *You're* the one who's abrasive to the point of being obnoxious."

"You'll learn to love it," he said, his eyes aglint with mischief. "It's a good tonic after all the bull—"

"Never mind!" she interrupted, and turned her full attention to her hot dog.

After two bites Danielle decided she was ravenous. Looking up, she saw that he was ignoring his own hot dog, concentrating on her. Self-consciously she dabbed at the corners of her mouth with her napkin, from time to time sneaking glances at him.

She had never noticed the golden highlights in his thick brown hair, the attractive tawniness of blond edging to gray. Her gaze fell to his hands. They were darkly tanned and mapped with veins, the palms rough with calluses. With a shock Danielle realized it wasn't with her eyes that she was seeing these facets of him. The texture of his body was embedded in her memory, so that when her eyes rested on his upper lip, the tiny scar running into his mustache, she was remembering the rippled feel of it against her own lips. And she knew the palms of his hands not with the watchful detachment of a fortune teller reading lifelines, but with a woman's intimate recall of their roughness against the burgeoning softness of her breasts.

Danielle felt herself torn in two, the one side determined to remain unaffected by him, while the other surrendered in all-too-willing complicity.

Then her eyes met his, and she flushed slightly. "Why are you staring at me?" The curt inquiry masked her fear that he might be making the same intimate discoveries about her.

"I like looking at you, since I don't dare touch," he teased her softly. "You're like a rose in a thornbush."

"You'd better beware of the barbs, then."

"You're full of threats, Danielle."

"But they don't frighten you," she said slowly.

"No."

The look in his eyes unsettled her. "What are you thinking of?"

"I'm wondering how much longer you're going to keep me on a tightrope."

She ignored the sexual undercurrent, his implication that they were quivering on the edge of an emotional abyss. "Until I have all the answers," she said as if she were in a committee meeting.

He sprawled back on the grass, his breath hissing out in frustration. "From what your boss said this morning, it sounds like you're still determined to convict me on the basis of what happened a long time ago."

"I'm through punishing you, Ryan."

"Are you? I don't think so. You've got to prove to yourself you're tougher than I am."

Her gaze slid away down the hill. From where she sat she could just see a pair of giraffes, their heads atop those improbably long necks lifted as if to catch an elusive scent. The diesel fumes from downtown traffic would contrast cruelly with the hot dry sweetness of their native grasses, and she felt sorry for them suddenly.

With an effort Danielle brought her mind back to the matter at hand. "You know how I operate, Ryan. I don't quit until I exhaust all possibilities."

"I don't happen to care for your style of doing business."

She lifted one brow. "That's what I've been saying about you all along."

"Let's walk, shall we?" he said abruptly. "I get bored being in one place too long."

Wide pathways curved through the hilly park, natural valleys and coppices of newly greening trees separating the animals' artificial habitats. The giant pandas were curled up peacefully beneath a bamboo tree in their glass-walled home, replete after their feeding. Most of the zoo animals, in fact, seemed poised between dream and reality, only the flicker of a tail or the flutter of an eyelid giving away their presence to the outside world.

The ape cages were a different matter. They fairly vibrated with life as monkeys of every size and color flung themselves from branch to branch, scratching and tickling and teasing one another mercilessly.

Danielle paused in front of a Malaysian siamang family. "Are these friends of yours?" she asked.

He cocked his head toward the elder of the tribe, a gibbon with a reddish-brown face, who glared back at them suspiciously. "I've made their acquaintance a time or two up in the mountains," he conceded. "They're a screechy quarrelsome lot, very family oriented...more or less like your local breed of attorney."

Danielle dropped her hand from the popcorn box he held out to her. "I may be quarrelsome, but I haven't screeched yet."

Ryan grinned. "Maybe no one's squeezed you hard enough."

Turning her back on him, she led the way to the elephants' enclosure, a hard packed dirt field separated from the pathway by a narrow moat. With their inquisitive trunks and loose, mud-caked hides crinkled in voluminous folds, they had to get the prize for the most whimsical creatures.

Noticing Danielle's fascination, Ryan said casually, "We have a couple of elephants up at camp. Strong and clever beasts. And they do a lot less damage to the forest undergrowth than caterpillar tractors would."

She gave him a look of utter disbelief. "I may not be that well-acquainted with Borneo, as you once reminded me, but I'm no fool. The only elephants on the island are in Sabah."

"Until now, yes."

"Go on," she said with a wry laugh. "I have to confess you've got me interested."

"The Malaysian government has yearly hunts on the peninsula because the country's overrun with elephants. They're trampling the plantations, so they have to be herded and shot."

"Oh, how sad."

"I thought so, too. That's why I got a permit to export a couple of babies across the South China Sea."

A smile tugged at her lips. "So you more or less contracted for foreign labor."

He was laughing now, too, a warm easy sound. "You could call them that, yes."

"You're a funny man, Ryan. Here you are fighting like mad to get a helicopter so you can do your space-age logging, or whatever you call it. And yet you're using elephants, too, which is downright primitive. It doesn't make sense to me."

His eyes traveled down her slowly. "Don't you

know me well enough by now, Danielle, to realize that I thrive on the unexpected?"

"That can be a dangerous way to live."

"Maybe I thrive on danger, too."

"It's not fair to force that philosophy on the people who work with you."

"I've had no complaints."

"Maybe the Iban are too confused to complain. The way you talk so blithely about helicopters, elephants...it's absurd. Doesn't it ever occur to you that with each new thing you bring in, you're further disrupting the fragile rhythm of their lives?"

His mouth tightened. "You really are too much. How in hell can you use phrases like 'the fragile rhythm of their lives' when you're twelve thousand miles from the Iban?"

"I have all the information I need," she bluffed.

"Like hell you do. You're being blinded by your anger toward me."

"I'm not angry anymore."

"Good. Then maybe you'll listen to what I have to say. You know you have only one option left, Danielle."

"What's that?" she asked suspiciously.

"You have to find out firsthand." His eyes sought hers. "Come to Malaysia."

Those three simple words, half plea and half command, sent her pulse racing. She sensed the inevitability of this juncture, as if subconsciously she'd been waiting for it since Ryan had reappeared in her life.

In a twinkling the well-worn rhythm of her own

life had been broken. Everything she was most familiar with seemed less real, less vital than this man who stood before her. They were strangers, there was no trust between them and she knew it was sheer madness. Yet for all that, she sensed the irrevocable logic to his invitation. Danielle knew that, for better or worse, they had to come full circle.

What had begun long ago in Malaysia, she prayed would be finished there.

CHAPTER SIX

"You know where you belong. You know where you belong. . . ."

The phrase drummed over and over in Danielle's mind, a drone that left her restless and at odds with herself. Then her father's persuasive authoritarian voice receded, and she woke up with a start.

The flight attendant was gently shaking her arm. "Are you all right, miss? You were mumbling in your sleep. May I get you a blanket?"

Danielle nodded gratefully. The cold air of the pressurized cabin had penetrated her linen suit jacket, making her shiver, and she snuggled down comfortably beneath the lightweight blanket the woman gave her. Despite the cozy warmth, sleep eluded her, and she stared out into the blackness of the night as the jet winged eastward en route to Malaysia. Again she heard the phrase that had been nagging her in dreams.

John Davis didn't approve of her making this trip. Danielle had driven up to Foxhall Saturday morning to see her father, a bit bleary-eyed after the State Department dinner with Hal the previous evening.

John Davis and Sam Larkin were bent over Lady's front hock, examining it, when Danielle approached them in the upper pasture. Out of nowhere Foxfire came gamboling down the field, rushing madly to her mother's side. Danielle quickened her step. Just watching the little chestnut-colored foal gave her a deep sense of satisfaction and belonging. Reluctantly she focused her attention back on her father.

For the first time she attempted to look at him objectively, wanting to see him through Jen Bondi's eyes. At sixty he was as fit and trim as a man twenty years younger. Though his hair was peppered with gray, his blue eyes radiated an electric vitality when he raised them to her.

And she got an inkling of what Jen found so attractive in him. John Davis was a man at the zenith of his capabilities and powers—strong, self-assured, totally in command. There was clearly no question in his mind about who or what he was. Jen admired that. Yet at the same time she had sensed a touching vulnerability in him that Danielle had never cared or troubled herself enough to see.

He straightened up to greet his daughter, and she put on a bright determined smile. "Good morning, dad. Sam. I see Foxfire is growing like a weed," she said, glancing at the little filly beside them.

Sam turned and grinned up at her. "I think you got yourself a real winner in this one. She may be a bit raggedy, but it's nothing time and mother's milk won't cure."

She nodded. "I wish I were going to be around in the next few weeks to watch the transformation, but duty's calling me away."

John Davis's eyes narrowed. "Where are you off to, Danni?"

"Malaysia."

It was Sam who broke the silence in the wake of her terse announcement. "Well, now, what's Foxfire going to do without you? She'll forget who her mistress is."

"I know that, Sam, but this is business. And business comes first."

"You know that 'business' should have been concluded long ago," John Davis said. "Here in Washington."

Perhaps sensing the tension in the atmosphere, Sam drifted off toward the barn, leaving father and daughter alone.

"I hit a stone wall," she defended herself. "Clay wants more answers, and it's my job to supply them."

"How long do you intend to stay?"

"I hadn't thought about it."

Another silence fell between them, and they began to walk up the hill. On the summit a light but invigorating wind touched them, insinuating its way into their bones. The clean scent of new grasses surrounded them, sharp and pungent with life. They both inhaled deeply, savoring.

"You haven't been back to Southeast Asia in a long time," Davis said finally, his eyes not on her but on the big white house in the distance. "If you stay more than a week, there's always the danger you'll succumb to that tropical mood. It gets under your skin."

His warning rankled. "Dad, this is work, not pleasure."

"Mmm," he said assessingly. "You know, Danni, you could turn this trip to advantage, after all. Have you thought about wangling an official invitation for Hal? You two could work together on this."

Danielle ignored the knot of tension in her stomach. "Hal's an armchair negotiator. On-site analysis isn't his thing. And besides," she couldn't resist adding, "he's allergic to mosquitoes."

"You're aren't really going into the Borneo hinterlands, are you?"

"Of course I am."

"You're playing into Kilpatrick's hands."

"Dad, I have to handle this my own way."

He studied her for a long thoughtful moment. "You want to go," he observed at last.

"I have to go," she hedged. "There's a difference."

"Not according to what Hal told me. We lunched together yesterday." There was an infinitesimal pause. "Hal seems to think there might be some personal involvement."

"He had no right to discuss this with you!"

"Is it true?"

"Of course not."

"Hal told me you've returned his engagement ring."

Danielle stooped down and broke off a grass stem, peeling it into threadlike slivers. "I'm not wearing the ring," she corrected slowly. "But I still have it."

Out of the corner of her eye she saw her father nodding at the distinction. And she remembered one of the early lessons he had taught her: always keep your options open. Suddenly she felt cowardly. No matter how much she might despise the thought, Danielle knew she was leaving herself an opening to return to the status quo. What galled her even more was that Hal would be there, waiting patiently for her recapitulation.

Her father broke into her thoughts. "When are you coming back, Danni?"

"I don't know. Clay seems to think I need a vacation."

Some of the tension eased between them. "That's not a bad idea," he conceded. "Go up to Pinang and just lie on the beach for a while—recharge your batteries. You'll be your old self when you come home."

Danielle didn't bother to argue that point. She stood up beside him again, and by tacit agreement they headed back toward the big house. They were almost to the driveway when she said, out of the blue, "May I ask you something, dad—why didn't you ever remarry after mother died?"

John Davis's features tightened reflexively at this unexpected intrusion into his privacy, but his reply was easy, almost light. "There was a certain panache in being an eligible bachelor, I suppose. Besides, the freedom was as much an advantage as finding and grooming another woman to fill your mother's place would have been."

"You never got lonely?" Danielle persisted.

"Not initially, no."

His clipped syllables warned her the interrogation had better end, and she took the hint. Still, those three words had said enough. With her attuned sensitivity, Danielle saw him not as her father but as a man a woman might fall in love with. She marveled at how Jen had sensed all this so quickly, and again she was jealous of the connection the two of them had found.

Davis, unaware of his daughter's irritation, attempted to change the subject. "Will you leave me a copy of your itinerary?"

"Jen has it," she replied more sharply than she intended. "I'm sure she'll be sharing it with you."

Davis stopped dead. "All right, Danni, I think it's about time we had it out. Just what is the problem?"

Intense blue eyes, cool mirror images, met in confrontation. Anger was simmering beneath the surface on both sides.

"The problem is you're dating my secretary, a woman who's young enough to be your daughter. It's just too improbable. You know how they love to gossip in this town about May-December flings. You have your reputation to consider."

"I'm not a man who goes in for flings, Danni, you should know that. You're insulting both Jennifer and me." He hesitated, clearly uncomfortable but determined to finish what he'd started. "I've never met another woman quite like her before."

"Forgive me, but I can't help thinking the novelty will wear off."

"Perhaps it will for Jennifer," he acknowledged, the bright blue of his eyes dimming a little. "But for me it's no novelty. I've found something in her I've been looking for my whole life."

This confession from the heart left Danielle aghast. "I...I see. I take it that this...this whatever it is—" she stumbled over her words "—is something you never had with mother."

"No."

As their eyes met again, the pain his admission cost Danielle was eased by the realization that for the first time he was speaking openly about what he felt. The trouble was, it was nothing she cared to hear.

Struggling hard to hide her disapproval, she asked in a tense voice, "You're falling in love with Jen, aren't you?"

"Really, Danni, this cross-examination has gone far enough. I don't know how we got off on this discussion of my private life."

"Oh, I see," she shot back, stung by his withdrawal. "But it's perfectly appropriate for you to discuss mine—behind my back with Hal."

"That's not the same. You need my guidance. Danni, my dear," he went on, his stiffness giving way to persuasive charm, "you'll have the whole world at your feet—a career, beautiful children along down the line, a man who adores you. Why risk losing all that?"

"But what if I'm not in love with him, dad?"

He shook his head. "At your age romantic love is deceptive. It can be totally false. There was a lot to be said for arranged marriages. The married couple may not start out loving each other, but over the years they learn to. It's eminently sensible.''

"It may be sensible, but I prefer to have control over my own life.''

"And didn't you choose Hal?" he reminded her.

"As I recall, it was a joint effort—you and I chose him.''

"And we did well. Hal's ambitious, intelligent—''

"I know his strengths," she interrupted, frustrated. "It's his weaknesses that scare me. I just have the feeling he'll always be leaning on me, and I'll have no one to lean on when I need emotional support.''

"People can change.''

"Basic character doesn't change.''

"Then you can mold him," Davis argued quietly.

"The way you molded mother to be the perfect diplomat's wife?''

Her father must have sensed the irony in her words, because he answered sharply, "Your mother was as dedicated to my career as I was.''

"She must have had her private dreams, though.''

He looked away. "If she did she never confided them to me.''

"Whose fault was that—yours or hers?''

"That's the past," he insisted.

"But what about me? Dad, this is my life we're talking about!''

"Danni, I'm simply asking you not to do anything foolish. You've worked too hard for what you have. You have obligations.''

"I think I have an obligation to myself first."

He looked at her steadily. "Do what you want. You'll come to your senses in the end. You know where you belong."

HER FATHER'S WORDS still reverberated in her mind, a chilling counterpoint to the tropical air that greeted her as she stepped off the plane.

It disturbed Danielle to think he saw her life in terms of a game, a series of delicate maneuvers. He had always told her negotiations were a process of settling for less. That might be fine for diplomacy, but she couldn't live her life according to that credo. Underneath she knew his real objection: Ryan Kilpatrick was alien to everything she had lived and worked for. But she refused to think of that now.

The heat rose in blistering waves from the runway; the blouse beneath her linen jacket was sticking to her back. She hurried toward the terminal, her eyes eagerly seeking Ryan's features above the faceless press of the crowd at the gate.

He wasn't there. Swallowing her disappointment, she followed the rest of her fellow travelers toward the baggage-pickup area. She was just heaving her suitcase off the conveyor belt when a hand rather diffidently touched her shoulder, and she turned to face a thin balding man in khaki shorts and jacket. His waxed mustache and prominent nose leant him a distinguished Charles de Gaulle air.

"Miss Davis?" he inquired in a proper English accent, as if it didn't matter a jot whether she was or wasn't. "How'd you do. I'm Harry Diamond, Kilpatrick's general manager. He sent me to fetch you."

She stared curiously at the man while he picked up her bag and led the way toward the parking lot. "How did you recognize me, Mr. Diamond?"

"Ryan was quite precise in his description of you, actually." Harry glanced down at the top of her head; the inevitable smoothly coiled chignon shone like black silk in the fierce tropical sunlight. "Beautiful but arrogant."

"How flattering," Danielle said dryly. "What else did he say?"

"He mentioned something or other about your legs." He sneaked another vaguely disapproving glance downward toward the lithe curve of her calves.

"I wouldn't be surprised." Her tone was getting drier by the second. "I've tried to land a kick or two."

But her companion was no longer listening. He had retrieved a set of keys from his pocket and was stopping beside a beat-up Peugeot covered with dust.

Danielle ran her finger across the side window. "May I clean this for you? I have some tissues in my purse," she offered after he'd stowed her suitcase in the trunk and come around to unlock the passenger door.

"Oh, don't bother," he answered absently. "Rainy season will be along soon enough to do the job."

Once settled in, Danielle peered doubtfully

through the windshield. The man seemed as indifferent to the impaired visibility as he was to her. He picked up one of the two cassettes lying on the dashboard. "I had a frightful drive out here today," he complained. "It took me so damnably long I had to listen to the same tape twice through."

"Why didn't you just play the other one you have there?"

Harry looked at her as if she were mad. "That opera is for the drive back into town," he explained with irreducible logic. "Wagner on the drive in and Verdi on the drive back, of course."

"Of course." With a heavy sigh Danielle rolled down the side window.

The rickety little automobile lurched forward as though boosted by the grandiose strains of *La Traviata* pouring from the speaker. Reluctantly Danielle admitted that the rich drama of Italian opera somehow fit the panoply of human activity converging alongside them. Mopeds, trishaws, bicycles and smoke-belching trucks vied with the dirt-camouflaged Peugeot for the right of way.

In between operatic movements Danielle ventured a question. "Have you worked for Ryan long?"

"We've managed to keep each other out of trouble over the years."

"I suppose you were involved in that court case a few years back," she remarked, finding it difficult to sound casual when she had to shout over Pavarotti's roaring baritone. When they squealed to a stop for a flock of chickens straying onto the highway, Danielle took the opportunity to surreptitiously lower the volume.

After uttering a few choice curses in Malay to the chickens' owner, Harry surprised her by effortlessly picking up the thread of conversation. "That Kwan logging business, you mean? Sticky wicket that," he opined. "But Ryan wouldn't listen to me there. Sooner or later, women are always a man's downfall."

Danielle kept her astonishment to herself and asked simply, "In what way?"

"He's too fond of them by far." Harry shot her a darkling look so rife with meaning that she shifted uncomfortably.

"Don't worry, Mr. Diamond. I can assure you there's no danger in this case."

"I should bloody well think not." His voice quavered with indignation. "I doubt he'd trust his own sainted granny if she were to put in an appearance from the grave."

"But you were saying—about the women?" Danielle prompted.

"Oh, bloody hell!" he swore, his expression full of self-reproach.

"Ryan warned me you would try the cross-examining bit and that I wasn't to fall for it." Harry gave her another faintly condemnatory look. "I must say you do have that barrister's air about you."

She had to laugh at that. "Are they the same in England as we attorneys are in America—slick as eels and too clever for our own good?"

His lips twitched. "I must say, Miss Davis, you aren't nearly as awful as Ryan made you out to me."

"You're full of compliments, Mr. Diamond," she mocked him, but she was smiling, too.

Harry eyed her in a comical way. "I must say he was off about another thing, as well."

"What's that?"

"Ryan said you had eyes like a cobra, hypnotic and threatening. But I don't agree. More like a mongoose, I'd say," he decided judiciously. "Sharp and lively, but not terribly dangerous."

"Thanks," she answered coolly, "but I prefer the cobra."

"Indeed. Ryan rather thought you would."

Danielle's head snapped up. "What else did your observant boss have to say about me?"

"Oh, the rest was rather less polite, I assure you."

"Indeed."

Oblivious to her mockery, Harry tromped on the accelerator, and his disreputable vehicle rocketed onto a wide thoroughfare leading away from the urban sprawl of Kuala Lumpur. Danielle lightly tapped his arm. "Mr. Diamond, I really think I should check into the Sheraton first. They might not hold my room."

"Oh?" he replied vaguely. "But we had already made arrangements for you. Of course I'll do as you wish, but I would hate to see Racha disappointed. She is so looking forward to meeting you."

"Who is Racha?" she asked, her curiosity piqued.

"Let's drive on ahead to the house, shall we? You

can meet her, and we can avoid early-afternoon rush hour in the city, in any case.''

Gradually the ramshackle jumble of industrial warehouses and refineries gave way to dense thickets of greenery. The swampy jungle where tigers had prowled a hundred years earlier was now a lush suburban enclave with multiacred estates bordering the river.

"This isn't exactly how I envisioned Ryan's rough-and-tumble life as a logger,'' Danielle said after a while.

"He spends very little time here, actually, though the past week he has been flying back and forth between Kuala Lumpur and Borneo. I told him Racha and I would see to your arrival, but he's been as restless as a cat on hot pavement.''

"Good. He's worried.''

"Nonsense!'' Harry rounded on her. "The fool's been licking his chops. He's been anticipating this... this showdown. The women we're accustomed to in this part of the world are gentle, barely heard. They kowtow to a man and use all the soft wiles, as it's always been done. You're a shock to his system, Miss Davis. And I'm afraid you could become addictive.'' Harry shook his head in frustration. "He's mad about hot peppers, too, but it's a fatal attraction. He invariably gets heartburn.''

Danielle didn't know whether to be insulted or amused. "Thanks for the warning. I like to know a man's weaknesses.''

"I was afraid you would be this way,'' he tut-

tutted. "And all the man ever wanted was a life free of entanglements."

"That's what I'm trying to give him," she argued, her eyes full of devilry. "If I deny the loan, there's no point in his continuing in business. Then Ryan could just skip back to Australia and finish up as a playboy on a Tasmanian beach."

"What an appalling sense of humor you have. Ryan evidently forgot to mention that when he was cataloging your traits."

Abruptly he slowed down before a narrow gravel drive half-hidden by trees. Just as he was about to turn into the property, a gray Mercedes Benz that looked as if it had seen better days burst out onto the highway in front of them, forcing Harry to slam on the brakes.

Danielle just glimpsed the woman driver. Her delicate Oriental features were at odds with her wild ruthlessness behind the wheel. Harry was staring after her in the rearview mirror, a worried speculative look in his eyes.

"Damn all! When it rains it pours."

"It looks as though you're the one with heartburn," Danielle said sweetly. "Is she your friend or Ryan's?"

He refused to dignify that with a response.

The driveway curved in toward the river for a good quarter mile. Delicious fragrances wafted in through the open car windows, the sweetness of frangipani mingling with the heavy musk of laburnum blossoms, which had fallen from their branches to carpet the dank earth in molten gold.

Perhaps because she was expecting something on the order of Foxhall, with its soaring columns and imposing architectural statement, Danielle was surprised by the sprawling, ranch-style house at the end of the drive. It might have been a home in any Virginia suburb, but for its unusual wood siding and luxuriant tropical garden.

In a distracted mood, Harry parked and came around to open Danielle's door. Together they went in through the side door of the garage, which had been converted into an efficient office complete with a small computer, telex machine and several desks.

"I see Mei Kwan was here stirring up old dust," Harry addressed the young woman whose back was to them, her head buried in a file cabinet. "Did she bother you?"

As the woman turned to face them, Danielle was struck by the almost ethereal delicacy of her features. Her skin was a lovely pale bisque color, and her almond-shaped eyes were gentle.

She had a sweet smile that encompassed them both. "No, she did not bother me, Harry," the young woman said in liltingly accented English. "There is an old saying of the Malaysians—'the mouse deer should keep clear of the wrestling elephants lest it be crushed.' If she and our Ryan wish to lock tusks, it is no concern of mine."

"Quite so," Harry said, though it was obvious he shared no such gentle philosophy. "Racha, I have brought Miss Davis. Miss Davis, this is Racha Sabatin."

"Welcome to Malaysia," the woman greeted Danielle with a charming incline of her head. "Or should I say, welcome back? Our Ryan tells us you are no stranger to Southeast Asia. Please, sit down. I read a question in your eyes, Miss Davis," she prompted, still smiling.

"Call me 'Danielle,' please."

"I shall, then."

"You seem different from other Malays."

"My home is on Borneo in the state of Sarawak. My people are Iban."

Danielle's eyes took in the elegant pearls in her earlobes, the tasteful shirtwaist dress that might have been a twin of one of Jen's.

Seeing her surprise, Racha smiled more deeply. "I have one foot in the past and one in the future. How do your Western psychologists say—I am schizophrenic? When I go home, I take up my sarong again."

Harry, who had perched on the desk edge, nodded. "We have an old saying, Racha—when in Rome do as the Romans do."

She laughed. "Yes, that is my new philosophy." But when she looked back at Danielle her eyes were serious. "Our Ryan says you fear for the peoples in my state."

"Some of us in Washington are concerned that unique cultures like yours will disappear," Danielle explained earnestly. "My job is to keep that from happening."

"You can save endangered animals, like the white

tiger," Racha said with a shake of her head. "But as for me, I would not care to live in a zoo. We have a wonderful museum in Kuching preserving all the beautiful artifacts of my peoples. But as for me and my family and our kin, we cannot be kept as museum pieces. You understand, Danielle?"

"Of course. All I'm saying is my agency wants to ensure that you have the right to maintain your unique way of living without other people barging in to change things you don't want changed."

"Yes, there are bad peoples like that."

"Ryan?"

Racha frowned. "Our Ryan is bad and good. One must be weighed against the other."

Harry stood up. "While you two engage in this fascinating character dissection, I'm going to repair to the bar."

"No, Harry," Racha protested with surprising force. "Our Ryan say no beer, no gin before five o'clock."

"Oh, fuss and bother! I don't need a nursemaid." Nevertheless he sat down again and picked up a newspaper, rattling the pages in irritation.

"Come, Danielle." Racha stood up, ignoring the Englishman. "I will show you the grounds, if you like. The river is quite tame compared to the mountain streams above my native kampong, but it is still pretty here."

Outside, Racha led the way to a brightly painted golf cart.

"Wouldn't it be more interesting to walk?" Danielle suggested. "Besides, I've been sitting in a plane for hours. The exercise would be nice."

"I . . . I am afraid I cannot walk too far."

Seeing the young woman's distress, Danielle wished she hadn't said anything. "Oh, I'm sorry. Forget I asked. Really, the cart will be fine."

Once they were settled inside, Danielle glanced over at her companion, and without meaning to she rested her eyes on Racha's thin wrist where it was poised over the starter button.

The little motor hummed to life, and the two women were off. Racha cast a faintly envious glance at Danielle. "To think of your flying thousands of miles here! I have never been outside Malaysia. How exciting jet travel must be."

The American smiled a little ruefully. "To tell you the truth, I slept most of the way."

"No! I would have my face pressed to the window the entire time. You see, sometimes I feel my life will be short, so that I must experience all that I can quickly . . . and deeply." Danielle sensed Racha's wistfulness, but it was fleeting, and soon she was pointing out pretty shrubs along their path.

Closer to the river stood a bungalow on stilts, very much like a traditional Malaysian home but for the encircling wall of windows and a plastic-domed skylight protruding through the thatched roof.

"That will be your abode for tonight, if you wish."

"I don't know. . . ."

"Please stay," Racha asked simply. "I have met few Western women, and I am interested in you."

Danielle wondered if this was where Ryan had acquired his habit of speaking with such unsettling directness. Her gaze slid away toward the dark undergrowth of lianas and wild orchids that were kept at bay around the perimeter of closely cropped emerald lawn.

"Forgive me, I should have not dragged you out here after your long journey," Racha said at last, taking Danielle's reticence for tiredness. "Would you care for tea?"

"Yes, please."

But instead of returning to the house, Racha skirted the rock-lined swimming pool and doubled back to the tree house, as Danielle had already dubbed it in her mind.

The bungalow's air of rustic authenticity was heightened by a notched bamboo pole, sole means of access to the upper reaches. Slipping out of her heels, Danielle clambered up the primitive staircase. At the top she turned to wait for Racha. The slender young woman took each step slowly, and Danielle couldn't help noticing she was out of breath by the time she reached the top.

At last they stood together on the narrow veranda. Racha's smile banished the telltale lines of exhaustion around her lips. She led the way inside. The interior was cool and light, the screened walls allowing every stray breeze off the river to whisper through. Curved shelves crammed helter-skelter with books fit beneath the windows. The big room's only other furnishings were an enormous bed covered with a dark-green batik spread and a low table set with a kerosene lamp.

After rolling out two grass mats and laying them beside the table, Racha swiftly made their tea. "I am fond of this place," she told Danielle as she settled down cross-legged on the mat, "because it reminds me of my home. The peoples in America do not live this way, I understand."

"No, it's very different."

Racha set down her teacup, and the wistful look came over her face again. "Sometimes I feel I do not belong anywhere. When I am here keeping the books I am always hungry for home, and yet when I go there it is high up in the air, you understand, and so it is difficult to breathe."

Danielle shifted uncomfortably. She had begun to suspect the girl's frail beauty had more to do with a health problem rather than delicate bone structure.

Racha chatted on, oblivious to her companion's discomfort. "I am told Western women have much energy. I long to be like them. I want to work, and yet I would like a family, too. That is my falldown, my friends tell me. I wish to do too much."

"American women face the same dilemma," Danielle answered quickly, relieved to have the conversation return to generalities.

"Dilemma?" Racha asked. "What is this?"

"A problem you have to solve in your own mind— like whether to work or to have children." Danielle paused to sip the fragrant tea and glance around the room, trying to find some stamp of Ryan's personality. Perhaps the evidence was there in the casual scattering of books, the harmonious blending of the room with its surroundings, in that conscious act of stripping down to bare essentials that she found at once so frustrating and fascinating in the man.

She was called back, startled, to her companion's presence when Racha asked in her forthright way, "You are married?"

"No."

"Neither is Ryan."

"I got the impression he's not the marrying kind."

"He had a woman."

"Just one?" Danielle replied lightly.

"I think you are joking with those words." Racha frowned slightly. "I have heard how in the West people discard lovers as if they're old clothes. To the Ibans that is scandal. In our old times adultery was punished by death. No, I think Ryan is like my people's men—one woman is enough."

Danielle swirled the last of the tea in the cup bottom. "What happened to Ryan's woman?"

"You saw her."

Danielle's eyes shot up. "Who?"

"She was driving off as you and Harry arrived. Mei Kwan. She is not a nice person," Racha observed with surprising coldness.

Danielle was bursting with curiosity, but before she could phrase a question Racha had changed the subject again. "I hope you will come to visit our village."

"Thank you. I intend to."

"That is good. But...." Racha sighed. "I must warn you before you meet my younger sister, Marie. She is going through a difficult stage. You see, it is Iban custom now that the older child go out into the world to work and the younger daughter stay home to carry on tribal tradition. Marie is jealous that I have this life, while my father makes her stay in the longhouse and weave."

Danielle frowned slightly. With each ingenuous remark the younger woman made, she felt herself being drawn into a personal web that was beyond her experience. She deliberately tried to put things back on a strictly impersonal footing.

"I'll look forward to visiting an Iban longhouse. I've never been inside one before."

"You live alone?" Racha asked, innocently undermining Danielle's attempt.

"Yes."

"You have no brothers and sisters?"

"No."

Racha didn't seem put out by the almost rude abruptness of Danielle's responses. "And do you wish to have children of your own?"

"Most women do, don't they?" Danielle hedged. "Especially if their own family life was happy."

"I think we have children not to remember the past but because we hope better for the future. In my family I think we are not so lucky, though. I do not know if my brother Sing can ever marry. He is paralyzed in his legs and can no longer walk."

Danielle was drawn in despite herself. "What's wrong with him?"

"He was in a logging accident. They were working on a muddy slope when the tractor fell back on him."

"He was alone?"

"No...our Ryan was with him." Racha looked away evasively. "It was not Ryan's fault. It was not!" Her very insistence implied otherwise, as if she didn't want to believe he could have been responsible.

"When did this happen?"

Racha waved her arm dismissingly. "Many years ago—Danielle, again you must forgive me. Here I sit chatting when surely you must wish to rest after your travels."

"To tell you the truth, I'm wide-awake and a little restless."

"Perhaps you would like to drive into the city, then. Our Ryan said it was your home once."

Danielle smiled. "Only for a very brief time, but, yes, I think I would enjoy that."

"It is settled, then. We shall go fetch Harry."

"Won't you come, too?"

"Such big cities are frightening for me. I will stay and work. There is much to be done before Ryan returns this evening."

WAGNERIAN OPERA blasted out of the cassette player like a Nordic wind. Harry seemed lost in the music's harmonic complexities, and Danielle was just as glad he made no effort to pick up the prickly threads of conversation they had dropped earlier. She had enough on her mind.

Bits of another conversation teased her. What was it Ryan had said? "I've had to live with my own conscience for four hellish years." She wondered if the accident that had left Racha's brother paralyzed was somehow connected with those agonized words.

Danielle laid her head against the seat and tried to relax. Too much was happening too quickly. She realized her judgment of Ryan was already being affected in subtle ways, now that she had begun to see him through the eyes of his employees. Harry's chance remark about the hot peppers and heartburn made Ryan seem endearingly human. And there was Racha, who, though she seemed to adore her boss, appeared troubled by some darker side of him. What was Ryan really?

Danielle gave up the puzzle as the little Peugeot entered Kuala Lumpur proper. Harry hunched over the wheel grimly like a fighter pilot at his controls, determined not to be knocked out of the cutthroat battle driving in the city had become.

He dropped her off at the central marketplace with the promise to come back for her in two hours. Danielle stared around in amazement. From time to time the ground shook as work crews blew craters into a nearby construction site. Soaring office buildings and expensive condominiums were going up everywhere.

For an instant she shared Racha's instinctive avoidance of the big-city madness, and was glad to turn into the crowded colorful bazaar. She strolled along from stall to stall, avoiding the spray-painted parasols and gimcrack souvenirs. Yet there were still craftsmen at work, in abundance, hand-lettering delicately on silk banners, carving rosewood chests.

She stayed longest in the little open-air fabric workshops, watching the men apply swirling designs in hot wax to long bolts of fabric before steeping them in tubs of cool vegetable dyes. Unable to resist, she bought several lengths of the finished batiks in shades ranging from a muted turquoise to a rich jade green.

Harry was punctual in calling for her, but she noted with a tremor of misgiving the telltale ruddiness of his cheeks. Evidently Ryan's dictum of no liquor before the cocktail hour didn't apply as long as Harry was out of range of Racha's eagle eye.

"Ah, ha," the Englishman announced with a satisfied gleam when she'd settled into the passenger seat with her packages. "I've never met a woman yet who doesn't like to shop. You're running true to feminine form at last."

"How did you survive this far into the twentieth century with such fossilized opinions, Mr. Diamond?" she teased him.

His chin quivered. "I can assure you I am most liberal in my thinking."

"Except where women are concerned."

"Damnable impertinence," he muttered, his expansive mood dampened a little. "What Ryan finds so captivating is beyond me."

Danielle gave him a bright questioning look. "Is he captivated, Mr. Diamond?"

"Like a hare is captivated by a cobra."

"But you were comparing me to a mongoose earlier, don't you remember?"

"That *is* your style, Miss Davis," he retorted, aggrieved. "You provoke one relentlessly until one has no recourse but to strike back."

"You're just angry because you know the mongoose eventually wins."

"Rot!"

She was laughing. "Now that we've aired our differences, should we put Verdi on and ignore each other in a civilized way?"

Harry's lips curved in an unwilling smile. "It's early yet, I must say, and Ryan did give orders that you be taken wherever you want to go. I am at your reluctant service, Miss Davis."

They were inching along now in bumper-to-bumper traffic. Since there seemed to be no danger of Harry careering into a telephone pole, Danielle relaxed. "All right, then. If you really don't mind driving, I think I'd like to go across the river into the old part of the city." Her tone was distant. "But I'm afraid it'll be as changed as all this."

The narrow lanes of Chinatown pulsated with life. Yet Danielle saw the district as it had been four years earlier—a lonely dangerous outpost where the only reality was the acridness of gunpowder and fire. Now the air smelled enticingly of fresh fruit, spices and fishballs simmering on vendors' grills. Business was brisk in the traditional shop houses lining the sidewalks.

The terrain was becoming more familiar, and Danielle's heartbeat quickened at the patchwork of memories. She had hurried down this same arcade, running blindly from the madness, and at that corner just ahead she had veered into the alley in desperation. . . .

On impulse Danielle turned to Harry. "I'd like to stop here, please."

"Did you see something you fancied in a shop window?"

She climbed out of the car without replying. On the sidewalk shoppers in their colorful attire buffeted her, but she was unaware of them. Slowly she made her way to the remembered lane. The scent of palm oil wafted over her. It must have been a trick of her imagination. Because she saw with a shock that all the old rickety warehouses had been torn down.

In their place rose a modern office complex, the glass facade brilliant in the late-afternoon sun reflecting off the river. Where muddy slopes had led down to a rotting wharf there was now a shady lawn with benches for the office workers to relax while they took their lunch. This might have been a park at home.

Walled in by the impersonal block of new buildings, Danielle sat down on a bench. Bit by bit she got over the shock of seeing a familiar corner wiped out. She felt relieved, actually. The past had been eliminated as if it had never existed.

Even as Danielle told herself all this, the sun crept toward the horizon through the brownish haze blanketing the city. A murky yellow-red light suffused the

sky. She shivered. Fear and bittersweet memory
washed over her, mocking her detachment. Without
warning the past and the future grew hopelessly entwined.

Danielle took several steadying breaths, until
gradually she became aware of the clangor and
tumult of old Chinatown at her back. The moment of
weakness passed. She stood up and made her way to
the car, wondering what lay ahead.

She was wary of the coming meeting with Ryan.
He was the one on familiar terrain, while she would
have to watch every step. Had he engineered that tea-
time interlude with Racha? If he had, it was a clever
move, a move she herself might have made. When
they were still in the States, Ryan had seemed too
naively open. Belatedly Danielle realized that for all
his "openness," she knew next to nothing about him.
The idea was both disturbing and oddly exciting.

Quickening her pace, she slid in beside Harry, and
the dusty Peugeot obediently wheezed to life.

CHAPTER SEVEN

DANIELLE TURNED one shoulder and then the other, glancing critically down her figure in the lamplight reflected off the dark window. The "treehouse" had only one small mirror, over the bathroom sink. She smiled wryly as she braided one of her new scarves at the waist of her white silk trousers. She might have guessed Ryan wasn't the type to primp before mirrors. Still, the man had to have some weak point. Idly she wondered how long it would take to find the crack in his facade....

A soft knock at the door interrupted her thoughts, and she hurried to answer it. Ryan's petite houseman, shy and solemn faced, beckoned her to come to dinner.

They crossed the dewy lawn in silence. The main house was ablaze with lights, as if it had sprung to life in the relative cool of the tropical evening. But the garden lay in shadow, the rock-bordered pool now a dark and mysterious lagoon.

The houseman left her alone on the terrace, where a table had been set for two. Danielle wandered over and picked up one of the dishes; she lightly traced the blue willow pattern with a finger. The rounded edge was marred by a chip, and aging lines crisscrossed the underside. The plates, old-fashioned and homey, seemed out of place in such elegant surroundings. They belonged on a scrubbed pine table in a farmer's kitchen.

The whoosh of a sliding glass panel made her turn. Ryan lounged in the open doorway from the living room, his eyes moving slowly from her face to the plate she held, then back again. He wore pale slacks and a dress shirt, the sleeves rolled above his elbows. On his feet were simple leather thongs, and she noticed his hair was slightly tousled and still damp from the shower. Everything about him bespoke ease and lazy assurance.

Affected by that aura, she found her tenseness beginning to ebb a little. All day she had been half dreading this moment. Now that he was here, she faced him with a light and curious expectancy, an enigmatic half smile on her lips. Once again she felt disarmed by his surprises. Every encounter with him would probably be like this, leaving her unsettled and not quite the same person she had been.

He stirred finally and moved across the terrace toward her. "Do you approve of my taste in china?" he asked, his low voice mellow and faintly teasing.

"I'm sure your famous old granny would have approved."

He grinned. "How did you guess the dishes were hers?"

"Oh, everything about them. They seem so sturdy

and practical—enduring. They're just as I pictured her."

"Yeah, she was all those things. I still miss the old girl sometimes," he admitted, his eyes alight with humor. "Every time I sit down to a meal with that blue pattern staring me in the face, I can still hear her filling my head with hard-nosed advice about how she intended to make a real outback man out of a puny city kid."

"Did she succeed?"

He took the plate from her, and their fingers accidently touched, sending delicious tremors of awareness up her arms. "You tell me," he parried softly, no longer teasing.

Their gazes locked just for an instant, until her eyes skittered away to neutral ground, settling here and there on rich oil paintings and exquisite contemporary wood sculptures adorning his contemporary living room. "Would your old granny have approved of all this opulence?"

The subtle dig annoyed him. "You know bloody well she wouldn't have. This house has to be impressive because my clients expect it. Those ironwood tiles on the roof, the ebony cabinets in every room are proof that what I'm providing is out of the ordinary and worth every cent my milled lumber costs them. I use this place the way you and your father use Foxhall—to prove to the rest of the world that I can deliver."

Danielle eyed him sharply, reluctantly acknowledging a point taken. "I wouldn't put it quite so bluntly."

"No, you wouldn't." He was grinning again. "But, then, you're the diplomat."

"And you're the humble logger, eking out his rugged existence in the wilds."

"Usually, yes," he agreed amiably. "I've made an exception for you, knowing the life-style you're accustomed to."

"If I'm so addicted to luxury, then what am I doing in your rustic tree house?"

"I suppose I just liked the idea of having you in my bed."

"Oh, really? I'd hate to see you suffer from any false expectations. So maybe you should move back into the guesthouse, and I'll go to the Sheraton. I think we'd both be happier all around."

"Is the Sheraton your idea of experiencing Malaysia, Danielle—shopping in the hotel handicrafts boutique and pretending you've seen a native kampong?"

Their repartee had been mischievous and cutting, but the unfairness of this last dig hurt. "I'll sleep on a pandanus mat in the middle of a rain forest if I have to, Ryan Kilpatrick. I'll admit I'm not used to roughing it, but I will. I'm here to find the truth, and until I get it I'll put up with anything."

"I'll hold you to that, Danielle. Believe me, I will," Ryan parried with surprising intensity. He had perched on one of the tubular steel chair backs, his face only inches from hers. She met his look without flinching, captivated by the stony light in his eyes and the clamped-down stubbornness of his jaw. How she would enjoy this game.

"Good," she said softly, her gaze still lingering on his face. "But I'm wondering—are you going to begin by trying to starve me? I haven't eaten since breakfast on the plane."

"I see my bluntness might be contagious," he said, trying hard not to smile as he stood up and called Talib. An instant later the houseman materialized out of the darkness, nodding in response to Ryan's fluent instructions.

"You have well-trained staff," Danielle observed after Talib had returned in a twinkling, bearing drinks on a brass tray. "I envy you."

"I try to treat them right."

"You 'try'?"

He turned the irony back on her. "What did you think of Racha? Is she everything you imagined a primitive tribal woman to be?"

Danielle shrugged. "Women have a talent for getting straight to the heart of matters. Underneath we're all pretty much alike."

"Somehow I don't think Racha has quite so sophisticated a viewpoint." Ryan was needling her again, but gently, as he poured her a drink. "You're an exotic creature to her, Danielle. You're the first Western woman she's met face to face. She says your eyes have a faraway look in them, like an evening sky."

"I hope you set her straight," she replied with an air of innocence. "My eyes are more like a cobra's, wouldn't you say?"

"I can see it was a mistake to have sent Harry to fetch you," he said, laughing.

"No, you knew what you were doing, Ryan. You wanted me to find out what you really think of me." She barely moistened her lips with the bracing rum-and-lime-juice concoction. "The problem is I don't care what you think. I'm not the one on trial."

Ignoring that thrust, too, Ryan picked up the cocktail shaker and walked over to refill her glass, though he could see she had barely touched her drink. The gesture was an excuse to come closer, Danielle realized, and her pulse quickened. Steadying both hands around her glass, she lifted it to her lips.

Ryan's eyes never left her face. When he finally spoke his conversation had nothing to do with what had gone before. "Racha tells me you seem to want children but there's no husband in sight." Even as he teased her he lifted his hand and slowly brushed her bare ring finger with one knuckle, each deliberate downward stroke full of questions.

The hairs prickled deliciously along her bare arms. Her susceptibility to him was a sweet curse. Even that simple touch of his hand against hers was enough to throw her into confusion. She said nothing, afraid the revelation of her broken engagement would leave her too vulnerable.

Finally he released her hand, but the questions were still there in his eyes. "You know, Danielle, I half expected you to bring your fiancé along on this trip and let him run interference for you."

She found her tongue at that. "I fight my own battles, Ryan. You should know that much about me."

"But didn't Adams want to come?" he persisted

quietly. "If you were mine I wouldn't want you to be so far away."

If you were mine. Danielle closed her mind to the hypnotic thought. "I...didn't ask him to come. He's unhappy unless he knows what's going to happen next." She struggled to keep the conversation going. Her confusion and her tiredness from the long journey were beginning to take their toll. "Asia's too full of the mysterious and unexpected for his taste."

"You mean, Asia's too much like real life," Ryan countered softly, his eyes seeking hers in the darkness, though he made no move to touch her again. "There are no long-term engagements here, Danielle, no concrete-and-glass towers, no handbooks full of meaningless regulations to keep life at bay."

She bit her lip as their eyes met. They weren't talking about Hal; they never had been. "You don't play fair," she whispered almost angrily.

He watched her slip into one of the chairs, certain her aura of fragility was a mere trick of the moonlight. His eyes followed the vulnerable curve of her smooth nape as she turned away, and he knew it was no trick. She was exhausted; her defenses were down.

Some men liked winning no matter what the odds, but he'd feel like a bastard if he won this first skirmish through default.

He remembered something Mei had once told him about flowers: they had to be picked in the early morning, when the dew was on them. The ones you picked at midday never lasted. Staring down at

Danielle, he thought of that now. He had come on tough when she was at her lowest point, and without realizing it, she had given him a glimpse through her defenses. She was a woman on the run from herself. He had the crazy urge to pick up all the protective petals she had dropped and give them back to her intact.

Ryan might hunger for that sweet vulnerability she had once shown him, but he felt safer with her harsh side, because it was no threat. As long as she was tough he could deal with her on a businesslike basis. He could ignore the deeper feelings she aroused. Commitment was too risky. His last affair had proven that. Mei Kwan was one of those women who hid her rapacious instincts behind whispery girlish laughter and supposed ultrafeminine helplessness, lulling him into being her fall guy, more fool him. There had been no excuse for his own stupidity, either.

Now here was Danielle, confusing the hell out of him because she was tough on the outside and fragile within, and he had no idea which part of her he wanted.

Danielle stirred, shaking off her exhaustion. She glanced impatiently at Ryan over one shoulder. "I warn you," she said dryly. "When I'm hungry my blood sugar gets low, and I can be very mean."

Relaxing, Ryan slid into the chair opposite her. "Is that so?" he said wickedly. "It must happen a lot, then."

Danielle was about to phrase a suitably waspish retort, when the miraculously efficient Talib appeared with several steaming dishes. She helped herself to everything, from the sliced rambutan fruit that tasted like grapefruit-splashed cherries to the steamed vegetables and baked fish from the river. She didn't look up again until her plate was empty.

"A wonderful meal," she said simply after the last plates had been cleared away. "Thank you."

"It's a nice change," he agreed with a relaxed smile. "Up at the Iban camp it's wild boar three times a day with a handful of rice thrown in, if you're lucky."

"Thanks for the warning. I'll manage. Boar can't be any more exotic tasting than roast goat or stewed octopus."

"I had no idea you were a gourmet."

Her look was wry. "I'm a child of diplomacy, remember? If you're a guest, you eat whatever's served and compliment it lavishly, no matter what it tastes like."

"No wonder you're so expert at hiding your feelings. You've had years to practice."

The shuttered look came over her face, but not before he glimpsed the distress his remark had caused. He got up from the table and went to stand by the pool, staring down into it. Without turning he said, "Harry tells me you and he went into the city today." There was a slight pause, then, "Was it as you remembered?"

"All the bustle and vitality is the same. Kuala Lumpur wouldn't be itself without that," she said slowly, seeing his wide shoulders where the house lights touched them and wishing she could touch them, too; they looked so strong, so capable of bearing anything. "But I was stunned by all the new construction." Her sigh was barely perceptible. "The bazaar, at least, hasn't changed. I bought a lot of batiks."

"To wear, I hope," he said, turning to face her.

She smiled tiredly and shook her head. "No. They're to add to my office collection."

"Having the stuff framed is a poor second to the real thing. Those patterns are meant to complement the body. They take on the life of the wearer."

"I'm afraid it isn't the fabric of my daily life," she told him softly.

"It should be, then." He moved back toward her, his hands thrust into the pockets of his trousers and his head playfully to one side as he studied her—the long silk-clad legs thrust out casually in front of her, the rounded smoothness of her shoulders that the elegant white camisole left bare. "When you're relaxed you have a very sensual way about you, Danielle. I'd love to see you walk when you're not in a hurry, when you're not angry or pressured and ready to do battle. I'd love to see your hair down and you brushing it with long slow strokes."

Each huskily whispered word brought him a step closer, until she felt herself enveloped in his confided wishes. The words were like a warm caressing wind, and for all her tiredness she felt a flutter of excitement deep inside. She took refuge in conversation, still fighting him, however subtly.

"Ryan, did Harry tell you that I asked him to drive me through Chinatown, too?"

For a long time he stared down at her. "Did you go back to High Street?" he asked finally.

"Yes. It was a shock. Everything's changed. I...." She faltered a moment. Then, finding her strength, she lifted her head and met his look evenly. "I could find no connection. It was too long ago."

The implication was clear: they were not the same two people they had been.

"So what if four years have passed," he countered with his characteristic frankness. "Time has nothing to do with it. Losing the connection was a matter of choice. It was what we both wanted."

"What you wanted."

"Not now, Danielle. I don't want to lose you now."

The simple words were devastating. "But don't you see?" she said passionately. "Those threads between us were cut—irrevocably."

"There was nothing 'irrevocable' about it. If there were, you wouldn't be here now. Danielle, you came back because it was important to you. I don't know if it was me or the country that drew you. But whatever happened here, it has changed us both. We share that."

She stood up, unwilling to face that stark truth. "Walk me back to the bungalow, will you? I'm really too tired to talk anymore."

He nodded and took her arm, content to bide his time.

She had taken only a few steps when her legs grew wobbly, the inevitable effect of jet lag. Leaning against him as she slipped out of her high-heeled sandals, Danielle was aware once again of his easy strength. How tempting it would be to lose herself in his arms. Immediately she recoiled from the idea. She tried to draw away from that warm steady hand on her elbow, only to realize that he held her all the more firmly.

The dewy grass felt deliciously cool and soft against her bare feet, and gradually she succumbed to that small pleasure, at least. Ahead of them through the trees, the quiet, slow-moving river shimmered against the night. Ryan had created a delightful private world, like Foxhall in a way, a retreat and a haven where a person could be totally himself. Yet it seemed he spent so little time here.

Ryan must have sensed her appreciation. "I'm glad you've come, Danielle," he said, a hint of his usual teasing in that baritone drawl. "It's only a matter of time until we work out the terms."

Surprisingly feisty once more, she shot him a quick sideways glance. "I think it's only fair to warn you, Ryan. I'm one hell of a negotiator."

"I'm sure we'll come to some straightforward terms of agreement."

"Just so long as they aren't terms of surrender."

They had reached the tree-house bungalow and stood facing each other at the base of the bamboo stairway. He smiled down at her crookedly. "What's that Latin phrase you lawyers like to bandy about when you're negotiating?"

"Quid pro quo?"

"Ah, yes. One has to give something...isn't that how it goes?" He leaned down and ever so gently brushed his mouth against hers, the merest tantalizing taste of a kiss. "In order to get something in return."

Though he. released her, neither of them moved. Their eyes held each other, tentatively searching for answers to questions both were afraid to ask. Danielle turned away and began to climb the steep stairs, feeling his eyes on her back.

On impulse she turned and retraced her steps, pausing on the first rung. Without stopping to think what she was doing, Danielle caught his face between her hands and kissed him back. Her teeth nipped his lower lip gently, and a gurgle of laughter rose in her throat.

He reached for her, but she was too quick. This time she ran up the stairs to the top without pausing.

Ryan stared after her hungrily. Only once the door had shut and he'd heard the bolt being firmly slid into place did he move away. He sauntered down toward the river, feeling curiously light and boyish.

As usual he tried to remind himself that wanting something so badly was dangerous. It tended to blind you. Then he laughed. He was hardly blind to Danielle's faults; she was a high-handed, beautiful snob who let power go to her head. Yet he craved her the way he craved challenge. She was an equal, a woman who knew bloody well how to take care of herself. He tried to tell himself they could both finish what they'd started so long ago and walk away from the affair intact.

He turned back and stopped, only moving on after the dim light from the old kerosene lantern had been extinguished. Walking across the grass, he remembered the feel of her body as she'd leaned against him, and he knew he was lying to himself. Deep in his gut, he was afraid of what Danielle could come to mean to him. After all he'd been through, the last thing he needed was any form of commitment, lasting or otherwise.

DANIELLE UNDRESSED in the dark, pattering around with an edgy awareness. Everything in the room was a reminder of Ryan. Opening a closet, she found a short robe and slipped into it. His scent rose lightly from the folds. She buried her face in the collar and pulled the belt more tightly, savoring the feel of the cool cotton against her nakedness.

She lay down on the bed—his bed, as he had so wickedly reminded her—and stared up through the skylight dome. Though high clouds blurred the velvet night sky, a few stars were visible, their diamond brilliance pinpointing her fugitive desires. She found a pillow and hugged it to her tightly, giving herself up to the soft explosion of her senses and emotions.

For longer than she could remember she had managed to keep the world at bay. Even with the people she was closest to—her father, Hal, Jen—there was that inevitable sense of detachment. But not with Ryan. He was a transgressor. Somehow he had found his way into locked recesses and touched her where she was most vulnerable.

That carnal knowledge they had shared so long ago was a prelude, she knew now. What chance had begun, the two of them would finish. Her body had intuited that long ago, and only now was her mind reluctantly following.

Where was it all leading to?

CHAPTER EIGHT

THE SOUTH CHINA SEA stretched far below, an emerald-and-blue carpet separating the two halves of Malaysia. Sarawak state, where their little twin-engine commuter plane was bound, lay four hundred miles inland to the east. They would be touching down at Kuching in a couple of hours.

Danielle recrossed her legs and tapped impatiently on the notepad in her lap. After a good night's sleep she was her old self, crisp and businesslike and ready to tackle the world. Racha Sabatin sat in the window seat next to her, her face pressed eagerly to the small porthole.

Reluctantly Danielle looked up from her notes when Racha touched her arm.

"Every time I go home to Akan, I bring a few little gifts for Marie so she will not feel so left out," Racha confided, pausing for breath between words. "Today I have brought some pretty earrings and a bolt of lace fabric for her marriage chest. She is promised to a boy in the kampong. He is our cousin, and they will marry next year when she is sixteen, though she says she does not want to. My parents never arranged a husband for me when I was born because they thought I would not live." A dimple showed briefly in her cheek. "I surprised them. Now here I am twenty and still not married. By my people's custom, I am a spinster." Her eyes rested thoughtfully on her companion. "How old are you, Danielle?"

"I'm thirty."

"Ah, yes." Racha smiled, once again disarming the American by her directness. "And you don't mind not having a husband?"

Danielle's eyebrows lifted slightly, and she was aware of Ryan, eavesdropping from where he sat up front next to their pilot. "It has its advantages." Did she imagine his laugh, or was that the engines?

Quicksilver in her moods, Racha had turned back to the window already. She touched Danielle's arm excitedly. "There is an immense ship down there! How my father would be amazed to see it next to his fishing *perahu*."

Danielle leaned over to stare down into the blue expanse. "Looks like an oil tanker. Probably from the refinery at Miri," she replied with authority.

"How wonderful your knowledge of the world is. If I could have just a part of your experience I would be happy."

Embarrassed by Racha's uninhibited admiration, Danielle deliberately changed the focus of their conversation. "And I'm impressed by your command of English. Where did you learn to speak it so well?"

Racha glowed at the compliment. "We studied at the high school in Kuching. Also, Ryan and Harry and the pilots have coached me. I can speak Malay and some Tamil, as well. Ryan says I would make a good ambassador.'' The dimple appeared again.

An ambassador of goodwill, maybe, Danielle assessed. Racha was too open in her feelings, too naive to make it in the real diplomatic world. Another ten years wouldn't give her that calculated *savoir vivre* necessary for career survival; those kinds of lessons had to begin early. Fleetingly Danielle envied Racha's fresh innocence, just as the Iban girl had envied her her worldliness.

With a sigh Danielle leaned back against the seat and tried to concentrate on the fact-finding mission ahead. She remembered Clay Perrin's admonishment not to let her emotions get in the way of her critical judgment. *You have a job to do,* she reminded herself.

''Do you like books?'' Racha was asking now, clearly not about to let the conversation falter.

''I'm afraid most of my reading has to do with my work. There's not much time left for anything else.'' A private half smile hovered as she remembered the book she'd leisurely skimmed through last night when she'd woken up, restless, in the quiet predawn hours. Ryan had left a volume of Malaysian poetry and proverbs on the bedside table, another of those unexpected glimpses into his private self. The beauty and lyricism of the verses had gradually lulled her back to sleep.

Racha was chatting on, but there were definite pauses between words now. The plane had climbed a little to avoid the turbulence, and her lungs must be feeling the strain. "I...I am lucky that I love to read, since I cannot be very active. I even taught my brother, Sing to read English...." She lowered her already whispery voice. "After the accident."

"Will I meet Sing?" Danielle asked at once.

"No. Ryan has found him work in Pinang." She paused for another breath. "It is work that he can do with his hands. Electronic assembly, I think you call it."

Racha choked on the last word and began to cough and wheeze, unable to catch her breath. Alarmed, Danielle called, "Ryan! Do we have water or something for Racha?"

He was out of his seat in an instant, but the pilot grabbed his arm. "'Ere, mate. I've got a flask of brandy tucked away that'll do the trick better. Take the stick, and I'll get it."

Ryan slipped behind the controls as the grizzled pilot climbed back toward the two women. True to his word, he found the battered flask in seconds and, reaching across Danielle, held it to Racha's lips. She sipped and choked a little from the strong alcohol, but almost immediately her color returned and her breathing was easier.

"I knew you were a rough little bloke," the pilot teased her gruffly.

"It was just the excitement, Jim. Perhaps I should not have come. There was still filing to do, and someone should be there to look after our Harry."

"That one won't go to 'ell overnight, so don't you worry," the pilot pronounced with puckish irreverence. "'E's been pickled before and 'e'll get pickled again—nursemaid or no nursemaid."

Saying that, he shifted his attention to Danielle with a slow wink. The gruff fatherly air he apparently reserved for Racha was no longer in evidence, and the long glance he bestowed on the vee of Danielle's blouse was distinctly appreciative.

She shifted uncomfortably. Ryan, who must have eyes in the back of his head, intervened. His curt voice cut into the engines' dull roar. "I'm paying you to fly this crate, Black, not to play stewardess to the passengers."

"Right-o, mate," the pilot said cheerfully, not a bit abashed at having his fun curtailed.

After Ryan had slipped out of the pilot's seat and back into his own, Danielle gave him a quick wry glance that conveyed her thanks. He gave her a grin that made her want to laugh. Out of the corner of her eye Danielle was aware of Racha observing this silent little exchange, but when she turned to her the girl hastily looked out the window.

Minutes later Black announced, "Land dead ahead, mates. Be prepared to swim if I overshoot the runway." And Danielle had to laugh at that, too. His rough Aussie drawl was a far cry from the delivery of commercial airline pilots, whose easygoing professional voices wrapped the traveler in a little cocoon of safety.

She leaned over Racha's shoulder to get her first glimpse of the vast island's eastern shore. A flat coastal plain was rising up to meet them. Tangled mangroves bordered a great muddy river snaking its way torpidly through the swampy flatlands. Kuching rose on slightly higher ground, a rim of civilization between the ocean and the dark-green hills folding upward endlessly toward a mountainous, barely explored interior.

Protruding out of native ironwood shingles, the spires of two cathedrals pierced the tropic sky. Even from the air the river port had a charming quaint air. Danielle remembered reading that it had been spared the heavy bombing during World War II that had destroyed ports farther north.

After that first brief glimpse, the city dissolved into the background. The hot black tarmac of the air strip rushed up to enfold them, and for all Black's joking, the little plane touched down faultlessly. They taxied to a stop at the end of the field, where a big snub-nosed helicopter that looked like Korean War surplus waited to ferry them upriver.

As if on cue, the powerful propeller blades cranked to life. Ryan clambered out of the plane, reaching up a hand for Danielle and Racha. Motioning for them to crouch low because of the rotor-wash winds kicked up by the whirling blades, Ryan hustled them toward the waiting helicopter. Pilot Mike Swanson gave them a hand up. After checking to see that his passengers were belted in, Swanson lifted his craft off the ground, sparing a laconic salute for Black, who grew steadily smaller on the runway below.

Swanson was another Australian, Danielle decided. In fact, the tough-looking man might have been a

twin to Black. They were part of the network of
pilots Ryan called on to run his aerial logging business in the hinterlands. From what Danielle could
judge of them, they were a unique breed—cocky,
confident loners who depended solely on themselves,
men to whom women were either inconveniences or
playthings, depending on the mood. She wondered if
Ryan would be the same way in another ten or fifteen
years.

Danielle turned at the sound of Racha's labored
breathing. "Are you all right?" she asked, uncap-
ping the brandy flask Black had given them.

Racha took a dainty swallow, and most of the
blueness around her lips disappeared. "I should not
have run. But I...I will be fine now." She put on a
brave smile and gestured for Danielle to look out the
porthole. "You must see my home state."

The powerful helicopter had continued its vertical
ascent for a couple of hundred yards, until it was
whirling toward the northeast, climbing steadily.
Below them stretched a verdant patchwork of pepper
plantations interspersed with vast growths of bamboo and nipa palm. An occasional water buffalo, its
undulant bony hips reminding Danielle of a broken-
down rocking chair, grazed hock-deep in water. As
slow-moving as the river, the beasts seemed oblivious
to the mechanical roar overhead.

The helicopter's flight path roughly followed the
river basin far below, and with dramatic swiftness the
terrain was changing. The river lost its meandering
character as hills closed in on the banks from either

side, compressing the water into a sinuous ribbon, white flecked where it bounced over thunderous, boulder-studded rapids. Narrow gorges dissected the hills into unconnected ranges. And looming ever closer was the forbidding mountainous crest marking Sarawak's interior border. The green-black ridge knifed the horizon like a dragon's tail.

Danielle's eyes were riveted on the fierce scenery. The rushing, foam-splashed waterway below bore no relation to the coffee-colored rivers on the mainland, and she could understand a little better Racha's pride and her longing for her native upland country.

After skimming miles of such primeval splendor, Danielle's sharpened eyes were ready for the first faint proof of human habitation. There it was at last. A curl of woodsmoke rose up out of the rain forest.

Minutes later they were flying over a tiny village on stilts, half in shadow where the mountain loomed above it. Looking like dolls on a museum shelf, men and women in low-slung sarongs walked back from their fields. Some of the women carried babies on their backs, in knapsacks decorated with bits of colored cloth and shells that caught the late-afternoon light.

Ryan gave an order to the pilot, and instead of bringing the helicopter down in the small cleared field below, they flew on over higher ground.

Danielle craned her neck to take in the construction site straddling a stream. She was looking at the core of a modern logging operation, complete with sawmill and several dozen workers' barracks. Widegirthed logs, some of them more than two hundred feet long, lay bundled like kindling in a cleared yard. Reminding herself that she wasn't on a sight-seeing trip, Danielle reached for the camera in her handbag. She hoped her film was fast enough to capture what fading light remained. There might not be another chance to get pictures from this vantage point, and she had to have as much documentation as possible for her report.

Despite the beehive of activity in the logging yard, Danielle couldn't yet see any evidence of abuses. The rain forest surrounding the site was almost untouched but for a narrow trail and a clearing where a stand of trees had already been harvested. Still, her camera clicked away.

She was startled when someone touched her shoulder. She looked around to meet Ryan's eyes. "I've already done aerial mapping of the area," he told her dryly. "I can make copies for you if you're that interested."

"No, thanks. I prefer to collect my own evidence."

He shrugged, unconcerned.

They continued to fly up into the forest, using the clear, fast-moving mountain stream as a guide. Looking down, Danielle drew in her breath sharply. Here was the destruction she had suspected all along. Pockmarked and destroyed, the land looked like a gouged emerald. Long strips of forest had been clearcut in places and burned to stump in others. The waffled tread marks of Caterpillar tractors crisscrossed the area like gigantic teeth marks. What had once been rich loamy earth was nothing now but unstable punk, a useless scar that could support neither trees nor wildlife.

She stopped taking photos and just stared down at the wasteland.

"This was where the Kwan Company operated," Ryan told her in a taut voice.

Danielle turned swiftly, her glance accusing. "And you had the nerve to come back here?"

"It's hard sometimes, knowing I played a part in this."

The ambiguous words were almost swallowed up in the high-torque whine of the engine as Swanson maneuvered the rotor controls. The aerial tour was over. They were heading back in the gathering dusk to the village.

A welcoming committee of a half-dozen Iban men, their flat-bottomed fishing boats pulled up close to the river bank, waited to taxi the visitors from the primitive heliport. Bare-chested and wiry, yet powerful-looking, the men burst into voluble conversation as soon as they saw Racha. She greeted them happily.

Only Danielle, walking close beside her toward the boats, saw the physical strain she was under. Although the village stood at only thirty-five hundred feet, for Racha the thinner air was almost intolerable. With a pang Danielle asked herself how many more times the girl could make this trip, and intuitively she knew Racha must be wondering the same thing. Before long she would be a prisoner at sea level.

In a put-putting cacophony of outboard motors, they were ferried over to Akan, which consisted of one long communal dwelling and a cluster of smaller huts all elevated on stilts. The village was built on a rise a few hundred feet back from the river. A litchi tree grew close to the sloping muddy bank, its exposed roots conveniently serving as steps up to the village pathway.

Brushing past an indifferent honor guard of pigs, roosters and skinny little mongrel dogs, Racha led the way to the longhouse, which in essence was a Main Street of individual dwellings nestled under one ironwood-tile roof. Dim lamplight spilled out into the darkness from a seemingly endless line of open doorways perched ten feet off the ground.

Racha politely insisted that Danielle climb the notched bamboo pole to the community veranda. A group of children hung over the rails, eyes round with curiosity. There was a pretty stranger in their midst, and not a peep escaped their lips. At a gentle reprimand from Racha, they all dispersed in a twinkling.

The villagers, gathered in casual clusters outside their apartment doors, stopped their lively discussion of the day's events long enough to greet Racha and smile a shy welcome in Danielle's direction. While many of the younger Ibans wore simple Western attire, it was apparent their elders clung to more traditional ways. Above their brightly patterned sarongs the women's breasts were bare. One woman with a timid five-year-old boy peeking out from behind her skirts approached Racha, clearly worried. As they chatted, Danielle couldn't help noticing the sores on the child's mouth.

Racha nodded quickly to her kinswoman and, leading Danielle away, explained, "That is my cousin Landa. She wishes me to bring back medicine for her son the next time I return, and I told her I would try."

The Sabatin household was halfway down the long corridor, the ninth doorway in a row of eighteen. Outside, Racha's father sat smoking a cheroot while his wife started preparations for the evening meal, skinning a joint of boar and shoving the debris through openings between the bamboo flooring. The parents greeted Danielle courteously and urged her to rest inside.

She was debating what to do when Ryan, hurriedly threading his way through the little knot of villagers, came up to join her. "Good, you made it okay. Not too much cultural shock, I hope?"

"I'm fine."

"Right. Listen, I have to run up to the logging camp now."

"Can't I go with you?" The quick question, not quite a plea, revealed her nervousness at being left in a village of strangers.

"Swanson can't fly that chopper after dark, so it's going to be a half-hour trip by boat. I think you'll be better off here."

She had no choice but to nod in agreement.

He grinned. "See you later on tonight, then. Enjoy your dinner."

Racha gracefully ushered her inside the home after Ryan left. An elderly man sat dozing in a corner of the dim, high-ceilinged room, which was nearly empty but for the rows of rolled-up hammocks on the walls. The only other furniture was an open rattan cupboard standing in one corner. It held shotguns, fishing nets and a lantern, as well as precious family heirlooms—antique earthenware Chinese jars and sets of highly polished brass gongs passed down from one generation to the next. In years gone by, such pieces were the currency of bride price when marriage settlements were negotiated.

After whispering to Danielle that the man was her grandfather, Racha led the way up another ladder to the snug attic space where she and her sister slept. The loft, with its low balcony, overlooked the main living space.

"Would you like to rest for a while?"

Danielle nodded gratefully, sitting down cross-legged on one of the grass mats. While Racha busied herself unpacking the few things she'd brought home, Danielle took pen and notepad from her handbag. She began to jot down random observations and a list of questions she wanted to ask the men who worked for Ryan up at camp.

Momentarily closing her eyes, she saw again the little boy with his infected mouth and the worried look in his mother's eyes; she saw the women pushing kitchen refuse down to ground level, where the rooting animals served as efficient garbage disposals. And she wondered how Racha dealt with her schizophrenic existence. Her mind fomenting with plans, Danielle bent her head and began to write swiftly.

Some time later she looked up to find Racha studying her. "You are a busy woman," she teased the American.

Danielle nodded. "There's so much to do. Racha, have you ever considered starting a rural women's group here to teach the other women about health and nutrition matters? Eventually you could arrange for pediatric exams and even have a regular health clinic with visiting doctors."

Racha's eyes gleamed bright with hope. "Someday, perhaps. It is my wish that even specialists will come. I have mentioned this to the heart doctor I saw in the city, but he says there are too many remote villages to be reached regularly. . . but someday."

Danielle's eyes narrowed thoughtfully when Racha mentioned her visit to the cardiologist. All the pieces had begun to fall into place—Racha's fragility, the physical activity that put such a strain on her, the parents who thought she would die as an infant—all the result of a heart condition.

Racha went on. "Perhaps if the specialists had seen me as a baby I could have been helped."

"'Could have been'?" Though Danielle tried to tell herself Racha's problems had nothing to do with her, she couldn't help being drawn in.

"The doctor told me the surgery I needed could

not be done here. Only a few hospitals in the world have the facilities. And I could not burden my family with this."

"But surely Ryan knows all about it."

Racha touched a finger to her lips. "He knows only that my heart is a little weak. I have told no one that it grows worse, especially in this past year. I have no desire to trouble Ryan with the responsibility. It is my wish that he not—how do you say—coddle me."

"But if you need help—"

"It is my decision," Racha insisted stubbornly. "Still, I must admit I have a little hope."

With a secret smile she went over to a small rattan trunk and pulled out a magazine, which she handed to her companion. It was an issue of *Science*, the pages raggedy and limp and obviously well thumbed.

"I found this in Ryan's library some time ago, and ever since I have been trying to read and understand it," Racha said, her delicate fingers flipping the pages open in Danielle's lap to an article about the use of pig valves as a replacement for defective heart valves in people. Her luminous dark eyes sought Danielle's. "Will you explain it to me, please? You see, my problem is also with the valves."

Danielle swallowed hard. Well, dammit, she could do that much for Racha.

They unrolled one of the hammocks and strung it to the opposite wall. The two women sat side by side, and Danielle began to read and paraphrase aloud. Some of the technological jargon went right over Danielle's head, too, but luckily most of it was pretty straightforward. She did her best to explain the complicated bits, while Racha nodded solemnly from time to time, eyes fixed on the illustrated diagrams.

The women's heads were so close together now that Danielle caught the younger woman's every labored breath, and she sensed the distance she herself was so determined to maintain rapidly fading. Danielle didn't want to care about Racha's problems; her father had warned her that she didn't have the luxury of caring about the individual. That was one of John Davis's central maxims. "Concentrate on the big picture," he had said time and time again. "We diplomats operate on that scale always. You can't get bogged down with the little man's concerns when you have whole countries to deal with."

And yet, she had begun to care all the same.

Their quiet interlude of reading in the dim lantern light was shattered by the arrival of Racha's younger sister. Two women couldn't have been more different. Where Racha was slim and fragile, Marie had a sturdy, compact, quite athletic frame. Her mouth was sulky, set in rebellious lines. She had a wide-eyed baby slung on one hip, and judging by the din starting up below, it sounded as though the baby's mother wasn't a bit happy at having her offspring commandeered. The little girl, naked but for a beaded necklace and twin circlets of shells around her chubby ankles, at least seemed content enough. The mother stared up at them through the openings in the bamboo loft railing, and when Marie started to hand the child to Danielle the mother shrieked her objections.

A rapid-fire exchange ensued between Racha and her sister. Racha apparently won the skirmish, because with an exaggerated sigh Marie turned and climbed down the ladder. Peeping over the edge of the loft, Danielle watched her return the baby to its mother, who scurried back outside in obvious relief.

"What's going on?" Danielle asked.

Looking rather shamefaced, Racha explained, "I am afraid there is an old Iban belief that a baby should never be shown to a stranger because he is not yet strong enough to bear such a sight, and many women still believe it. I am sorry for the uproar. Sometimes Marie is very, very bad."

The teenager had come up to the loft again and now perched at her feet, jabbering animatedly.

"What's she saying?" Danielle asked.

"She is telling me all the gossip I have missed while I was away." Racha shook her head. "It is a silly story about one of our kin in another village who is jealous of my uncle and his wife. This woman made a divorce amulet out of entwined dog and cat hairs and hid it in a betel-gum mixture, which she gave to our uncle to chew. Because the dog and cat don't get along by nature, the amulet is supposed to have the same result on the married couple, you see?"

Danielle laughed. "Believe me, in my country there's no need for amulets. People do quite well getting divorced on their own."

Racha listened with interest, then translated Danielle's words to Marie, who at that point seemed far more interested in studying this stranger inch by inch.

Her eyes traveled up the tan espadrilles, over the expensive linen of her slacks and the woven rope belt at her waist to the long-sleeved plaid muslin shirt in smoky shades of lavender, blue and gray.

Racha evidently disapproved of her sister's behavior, because another sharp word sent Marie scuttling off downstairs. After she had gone Racha began to chuckle softly. "Is it difficult for you to believe that I miss all this when I am alone in the city house?"

"Not at all. This is your home and your family. They seem very proud of you. Even Marie," Danielle added, a smile hovering.

Racha nodded. "It is great prestige to have a job in the capital. All Akan is proud of that. I only hope I do not disappoint them."

"But how could you?"

"By dying."

"Don't be silly," Danielle quickly replied.

Racha looked at her again with intense curiosity. "I have heard this about Westerners, that you are afraid to talk of death. To no one else have I mentioned my deep concerns. Forgive me. I think now that I have placed a burden on you. Perhaps I opened myself to you because I know you will not be here long, and you will be free to forget me once you return to Washington."

The simplicity of Racha's confession made Danielle's own heart ache, and for once she was at a loss for words.

Racha took no notice. "Please come down now.

My mother will have dinner nearly ready, and we can lay the mats on the floor.''

The meal was a lovely affair. The family sat in a circle on the grass mats; everyone helped himself from the communal bowls in the center of the floor. The wild pig was a bit tough and gamy, but no less palatable than the venison steaks Sam Larkin would stew each winter after one of his hunting trips. And the rice, hill grown on the family acreage, had been steamed to tender perfection in a hollowed-out length of bamboo cane.

The conversation whirled around Danielle. She knew she was the chief topic of conversation by the frequent interested glances cast in her direction. But she didn't mind. Some of the strangeness of her surroundings had worn off, and she was beginning to relax.

Glancing around the high-ceilinged apartment, Danielle saw another heirloom of the past dangling from an obscure corner of the rafters, and she nearly jumped. In the earlier dimness it had escaped her notice. Now in the smoky yellow light of the kerosene lanterns burning fully, the thing seemed to leap out at her. Danielle did her damndest to hide her shock, but it wasn't every day she was confronted with a shrunken head.

The elderly grandfather picked up on her interest and smiled benignly. Danielle noticed the smattering of blue tattoo marks on his knuckles and remembered reading somewhere that Iban warriors had logged their successful head-hunting jaunts in just this shorthand way.

Racha smiled, too. "Taking such trophies was banned fifty years ago, but a few of our men continued to practice it through the war."

Danielle didn't have the nerve to ask if Racha's sweet-faced grandfather had counted himself among those determined warriors, so she murmured instead, "A fascinating custom."

"Yes, but the times change. We Iban must find other ways to appease our ancestors' spirits now that we can no longer live up to our reputation of being the 'wild men of Borneo.'"

Danielle, realizing she was being teased, joked back, "Don't be so smug. Every society has their share of wild men . . . and women."

"Even America?"

"Yes, of course."

Racha translated this interchange for the rest of the family, and now five pairs of eyes gleamed back at Danielle expectantly. She hadn't foreseen that her remark would be taken literally.

It was obvious they were expecting some sort of tale, and seeing no way out, she launched into a recital of the first one that came to mind: the grisly story of Lizzie Borden, the New England girl who was reputed to have chopped up her father and stepmother with an ax in a fit of pique back in 1892. The family listened raptly to her highly embellished version of the story.

She fell silent at last, and a swell of murmured admiration filled the room. Danielle brushed her forehead with the back of her hand, looking rather sheepish.

"I'm sorry, Racha," she apologized. "I don't know what got into me, but your family seemed to be expecting something of me."

"No. It was wonderful. We have strong storytelling traditions here. In the old days, before a new kampong could be built or a new field planted, the Iban priests' stories of the spirits and our ancestors would go on sometimes for five days and nights uninterrupted, to appease the gods. You would make a good Iban, Danielle," she added with a smile.

"Yes, bravo."

The deep Aussie drawl, so familiar to both women, brought their heads up in surprise. Danielle saw the adulation in Racha's eager, unguarded gaze. No matter what sins Ryan might have been guilty of in the past, the young Iban woman had clearly forgiven him.

Annoyed without knowing why, Danielle said sassily, "How long have you been eavesdropping, Kilpatrick? For someone who pretends to be so up front, you're a very accomplished sneak."

"Thanks. I knew you'd find something good to say about me eventually."

Before she could reply he turned to Racha, gently laying his hand on her head, and greeted the rest of the family with equal warmth. That done, he surprised Danielle by holding his hand down to her, and she let him pull her to her feet.

"Do you want to take a walk? Or don't you trust me in the dark?"

She gave him a long level look. "I'll take my chances."

As they left Danielle deliberately blanked out the awareness of Racha's disappointment. Ryan wouldn't have noticed a thing, she was certain. Men were attuned to action, not feelings. She had been that way herself once. She had begun to change a little since yesterday, becoming more aware of emotions and sympathies she had never bothered about before. She felt like a cobra shedding its skin. The only trouble was, the sloughing-off process left one terribly exposed.

"A penny for your thoughts," Ryan said, head turned and slightly bent as they walked along so that his eyes looked into hers.

"Nothing, really," she lied. "I was just wondering if we'd meet any snakes down there in the dark."

"Life's full of risks," he gibed softly, even as he nodded a pleasant good-night to the people along the bamboo boardwalk who sat mending fishing nets or having a last smoke of the evening.

When they descended the bamboo ladder they left behind the companionable bustle and activity of the kampong. Side by side they strolled back along the path to the river.

The night loomed silent and mysterious, fed by the murmur of the water and vague rustlings that made the encroaching forest come alive. Danielle breathed in deeply, aware of the mingled fragrances of wet leaves and rich earth. The vast canopy of stars shone brilliantly, but she was less aware of their light than of a curious phosphorescence flashing among the trees.

They moved closer to the woods' edge, the rampant lushness of ferns, vines and flowering bushes a soft blur against the surrounding night. Illuminating the darkness were enormous butterflies bearing green lanterns of light on their breasts. The random pattern of their flight was an aerial ballet, eerie yet beautiful.

"Lovely, isn't it?" Ryan murmured.

"Mmm. I had no idea such things existed. This place has an incredible aura of peace about it."

"It's not quite so peaceful by day. You can hear the saws and the mill, the chopper working. Our logging site's only a mile and a half upstream."

"Are you trying to prepare me?"

"I'm just telling it like it is. I've got nothing to hide."

Danielle's eyes snapped with their old fire. "You *can't* hide the desecration up at the older site." She paused, and the air between them was heavy with accusation. "You were Kwan's foreman then."

"You've really done your homework, haven't you?"

"That's my job."

"How much do you already know?"

"Only what I learned from the transcripts of the Kwan trial. There are a lot of gaps in the testimony...yours especially."

"I'd only done the initial survey for Kwan," he said curtly. "After that most of my time was spent in Kuching coordinating supply schedules. I had no idea of the systematic rape that was going on. The next time I came up it was too late to undo the damage.

All I wanted at that point was to get the job over with as quickly as possible.''

"So that was when you and the Sabatin boy teamed up?''

Ryan glanced at her sharply. "Yes. I was driving the cat. When I gave the order to set the winch line on the logs, Sing Sabatin jumped off. A lot of the time we were on very steep hillsides, so it was hard going. At one point we were fighting an uphill log, the toughest of all to bring down. After Sing hooked it up, I got the winch in gear. Then the damned cat started to slide backward. I jumped off, yelling for him to get out of the way. But he got tangled in the cable line, and that log came down on his back...."

Danielle felt the agony of his reminiscence, sensed the hidden anger there, too—anger at himself, anger at Kwan for his irresponsible greed.

"Why didn't you at least defend yourself at the trial when it came to the ecological issue? Didn't you see how damning your silence would be?''

"Of course I saw it," he snapped. "At the time I felt I had no choice. Talking couldn't have done anyone any good. It would only have done more harm.''

Danielle didn't ask the obvious question: whom had he been trying to protect? She recalled Harry Diamond's bitter remark about women being Ryan's downfall, and she remembered the beautiful specimen behind the wheel of the Mercedes. Even from that brief glimpse of her, Danielle had sensed she was the type who could convincingly act the gentle innocent, and Ryan's weakness was that strong protective instinct of his. Mei Kwan had come back into Ryan's life now, no doubt to play on his sympathy again after her father's last penny had been spent. And Ryan would probably arrange something for her out of pity.

The idea upset her, even though she knew his personal affairs were none of her business. Somehow the thought of his ever having been vulnerable to a woman made him too human, too reachable. Then Danielle thought of Racha's worshipping look, and realized she was jealous. Ryan couldn't remain oblivious for long to the girl's meek and loving devotion.

"So what's next, Ryan?" Danielle asked, forcing herself to concentrate on the issue at hand.

"Isn't that up to you?"

Danielle's breath caught in her throat. Only after a moment did she read the irony in his tone and realize he'd been referring to his business. "I was just wondering how long you intend to stay here."

"What the hell has that got to do with anything?"

She turned her back on him to stare out over the silvery black expanse of the river. After a long while she said, "I picked up that English translation of Malaysian proverbs from the bed stand last night when I couldn't sleep. One of them sticks in my mind." She quoted softly into the night, " 'One can pay back the loan of gold, but one dies forever in debt to those who are kind.' Isn't that how it goes, Ryan? You've been very kind to the Sabatin family—so kind that maybe they're beginning to believe you're going to stay around forever. That... that doesn't seem quite fair to them—or you."

"This is my life, Danielle. And how I live it is my own bloody business."

She felt as if he'd slapped her. She had been trying to reach out to him, but he had misread her intention. Small wonder, she berated herself. She had been so eager to attack him all along; why should he believe she might do anything else now?

"Will you be ready to go up to camp in the morning?" he asked roughly. "I'd like to get this medieval inquisition over with as soon as possible."

Stung, Danielle retreated further into herself. "I'll arrange my own schedule, if you don't mind. I want to interview some of the men first."

"Be my guest."

"Ryan, there's another thing I want to discuss with you."

He eyed her warily. "What?"

"I've been doing a lot of thinking, and I'd like to look into arranging some social-service programs for the village. From what I've seen so far, it could use a health clinic, a school, some sort of preventive-medicine program—"

Ryan had been listening to this recital in growing disbelief. "Now wait just one minute. Aren't you forgetting why you came here? You were so quick to criticize the effect of my operation on this culture. Now what the hell are you trying to do but put your stamp on it? You don't give a damn about how much change this community suffers through, as long as you're the one leading the way."

"My changes would be for their own good," she said, stunned by his reaction.

Ryan's voice dropped menacingly. "You self-righteous Pollyanna. What makes you think they want what you have to offer? These people aren't fools. Most of them have been down to Kuching. They've had a taste of the modern world. Sure, they like the outboard motors and butane stoves and the other things that make their life easier. But maybe they don't want the rest of the claptrap of civilization. Maybe they don't want the government breathing down their necks, which is what they'd get once you brought in a clinic and a school and God knows what else." Angrily he kicked at a tree root.

"So you think it's right to deprive girls like Marie of an education? She's so bored she has to create mischief."

"Why do you think she'd be any different in school? Her dad's no fool. Here he can keep his eye on her, and at the same time see that she passes on the family's cultural inheritance. Has she shown you any of her *pua* weavings? She's damn talented when she puts her mind to it."

"But maybe that's not what she wants to do," Danielle argued.

"Come on! Everyone has his responsibilities, no matter what the society. Marie will inherit the house and land when her parents die. She'll marry her cousin, and they'll have a bunch of kids. Some of them will go to school in Kuching, while the rest carry on the old ways. That's how it's done here, and you have no bloody right to interfere.''

''You were the one who brought me up here. I've seen what's needed, and I can get it done. I have plenty of contacts in Kuala Lumpur. My father has a friend in the Ministry of Health who owes him a favor, and my office has close ties to the housing ministry. I can cut through the bureaucracy in a matter of—''

''Will you stop and listen to yourself?'' Ryan broke in. ''You don't give a damn about these people. You can't know what they want or need when you only met them a couple of hours ago. This is just another exercise in power for you, a chance to flex your political muscle. You're a real chip off the old block, aren't you?''

''I can't help what I am,'' she said coolly. She saw little point in trying to defend herself.

''Yes, I can see that now,'' he whispered between his teeth. They stared at each other. When he spoke again each word was slow and deliberate. ''I don't happen to like the way you and your old man operate. In this life I've always paid in a personal way. When I love, I love. And when I hate, I hate. I don't hide behind any facades. My life is ruled by my passions. What rules yours, Danielle—chicanery and deals?''

She felt herself crumbling; still, she had to fight back, to regain some vestige of self-respect. ''I have certain ideals, Ryan, whether you choose to believe it or not. I happen to have faith that I can change things I don't think are right. I wouldn't call that chicanery," she said stiffly, her bearing radiating pride.

And as she defended herself Ryan's eyes slowly drank in the details of her—her eyes luminous in the darkness, the angry pulse in her temple, her long expressive fingers pressed to her thighs. In that instant he found her heartbreakingly beautiful and desirable. Despite their irreconcilable differences, all he wanted was to fold her into his arms.

He moved toward her. "Danielle...."

Fiercely she shook her head. "No! Leave me alone!"

Turning, she stumbled back up the path toward the silent longhouse. Ryan's words had devastated her; her first instinct was to run, to conceal the knifelike hurt he'd inflicted.

She climbed the ladder and crept on tiptoe down the long deserted veranda, the only sounds an occasional whisper or snore, the distant barking of a dog. The village was wrapped in a cocoon of peace that excluded her.

Outside the Sabatins' doorway, she slipped off her shoes and threaded her way around the recumbent forms of mother, father and grandfather. But upstairs in the loft, Racha lay awake waiting for her.

"You are all right, Danielle?" she asked, concerned.

"Yes, I'm fine." Danielle stared up at the thatched roof where wisps of smoke lingered from the evening fire. For the first time in her life she was consumed by self-doubt.

She remembered Ryan's angry declaration: "My life is ruled by my passions." How she had felt that whenever she was near him! Passion radiated from him like a life-force, seductive and vital. And what was her own life in comparison?

CHAPTER NINE

"MY KINSPEOPLE work very hard, as you see," Racha was saying.

Turning back from the riverbank, Danielle was moved by the rustic beauty of the setting. Though the village still lay in shadow, the sky beyond the mountain had already brightened into a rosy golden dome. Dozens of people walked up and down the longhouse ladders, the men hauling fishing nets and hoes to weed their fields, while the women lugged buckets of water from the river.

"They do, Racha. I don't know if I could keep up with them."

"Now perhaps you can see why I live in the city."

Danielle turned to her. "Will you be coming up to the logging camp?"

"The boat trip is too strenuous for me," the young Iban said, shaking her head regretfully. "Akan is my limit, I'm afraid." She hesitated. "Tell me, Danielle, will you give Ryan the loan he asks for?"

"I can't answer that yet."

"He is in need of it."

"And your people?"

"They need the camp and the work it provides. Without it they would be much poorer."

"And when they have enough outboard motors and lanterns and the other things money can buy, will they build a school? Ryan doesn't seem to think the village wants one. I disagree with him."

Racha smiled a little. "You are thinking of Marie. But I know my sister. She would get bored behind a desk. Come, I would like to show you something."

Together they walked to one of the outlying thatched-roof huts and climbed the ladder. Inside there was nothing but a weaving loom strung with a work in progress. A rich spectrum of green threads climbed and interlaced along the natural-colored warp, creating a subtly textured tapestry of unusual beauty.

"This is Marie's work," Racha said.

"And she's had no training?"

"She has, yes. The elder women always teach the younger the techniques of *pua*."

"I meant that she's had no professional art classes?"

"Here in Akan?" Racha's tone was disbelieving. "No."

As they left the hut a glimmer of an idea took shape in Danielle's mind. What Marie might really benefit from was a scholarship to a design center. Then she could share what she learned with the other village girls and widen their artistic horizons even if they had to remain within the bounds of the village. Danielle made a mental note to look into the idea as soon as she got back to Kuala Lumpur. She knew of several agencies involved in funding the arts.

She was prodded back to the present by an incredible din overhead, fracturing the mountain silence. The big helicopter that had ferried them upstream from Kuching was carrying a different payload today. A fifty-foot log dangled like a matchstick from the end of a cable line.

"Where's he taking it to?" Danielle asked Racha as their eyes followed Swanson's downstream flight.

"A crew is waiting to release the log at the shallows. When they have accumulated many they will be transported downriver to the sea. Some of the lumber will be milled at Ryan's factory on the coast, and some will stay raw timber. From there ships take it to Japan and the Mideast, wherever our buyers are."

Danielle caught the note of pride in Racha's voice, and fleetingly she envied this girl who was a part of Ryan's life and his work, while she herself was an outsider.

"Look, Danielle—my father comes. We should get your things from the longhouse."

Ten minutes later Danielle was settled in the prow of the shallow-bottomed *perahu* facing Mr. Sabatin, her overnight bag wedged safely between her legs. The small outboard motor chugged to life, and the boat headed slowly upriver against the current, past a group of gleeful naked boys taking turns swinging off a vine into the river. Beyond them rose a neat checkerboard of fields, where the villagers grew maize, cassava and rice. Men and women worked side by side, their strong backs bent beneath the morning sun as they moved between the verdant rows.

The boat rounded a bend in the swift river, and Akan disappeared from sight, as if it had never existed. Now the world was bound by two impenetrable walls of jungle forest so dense it had the black-green richness of jade. As the channel narrowed the boat began to tip and sway wildly over the white-flecked water. The forest encroached overhead. At one point a feathery mengaris tree spread its canopy from bank to bank, sheltering them in dappled sunlight.

Speaking in surprisingly good English, Mr. Sabatin pointed out things along the way that Danielle's unschooled eyes would probably have missed. There were birds in profusion, hornbills and sweet-voiced bulbuls, parrots and an exquisitely feathered pheasant with long brilliant blue wattles and a pure white tail. They spotted an elusive gibbon. His black, heart-shaped face appeared for just an instant in the treetops and vanished again, but not before his gibberings set off a wild orchestra of other cries.

"The rain forest is beautiful, Mr. Sabatin. The colors remind me of the colors in Marie's weaving."

He acknowledged this bit of praise. "When she works hard, she is a good daughter. But she is lazy."

"Perhaps she needs more challenge," Danielle suggested. "She might enjoy art school. There are many scholarships for girls like her."

The man regarded his guest somewhat suspiciously. "Has Marie asked this of you?"

"Oh, no." Danielle brightened. "It is my idea."

At that Mr. Sabatin hunkered impassively over the tiller and gave his full attention to maneuvering the bucking canoe through a series of rapids. There was no other chance to press her point.

With scant inches to spare they threaded between half-submerged rocks, and once he and his passenger had to disembark to carry the lightweight canoe several feet across bouldery shallows.

Danielle's tennis shoes squished by the time they reboarded. She was glad she'd worn khaki walking shorts, though even in such surroundings she managed to maintain a vestige of her usual cool elegance. The white silk camp shirt was water-splashed, but at least her pearl earrings were still in place. With any luck at all the ICCI would appear intact at Ryan's jungle door.

As the little boat fought its way steadily up the twisting river channel, the screech of jungle birds and the thrum of the outboard motor were swallowed up in the whine of power-driven saws. The helicopter was returning. Danielle felt its distant whirring as a vibration in her chest before she actually heard it overhead.

Now that she was almost at camp, the self-confidence that had buoyed her all morning began to waver. She had told herself she wouldn't let Ryan's blistering personal attack of the night before affect the job she'd come to do. But that was a lie. Her usual cold-bloodedness, that armor she had always depended on, had begun to fail her. She cared far too much what Ryan thought of her. That was her weak point; she knew it, and she would have to hide it.

Ahead of them a curving finger of jungle jutted

into the river, creating a tiny, still-water bay. Their *perahu* shuddered sideways for an instant. Then Mr. Sabatin opened the throttle all the way, and the boat leaped out of the fast-moving current toward the shore. Together they pulled the vessel up onto the muddy bank, leaving Danielle's overnight bag tucked beneath the plank seat.

Ryan's camp was a compact, well-organized logging center hacked out of the surrounding rain forest, a backdrop of towering hardwoods. Mr. Sabatin had already lost himself among the workers scurrying between storage sheds and the mill, so Danielle was left to find her own way. Ryan was nowhere in sight. She poked her head in doorways here and there, covering her ears against the whining band saw.

A ruckus in a bush-enclosed yard caught her attention. She went behind one of the big sheds to investigate. Rounding the corner, she came face to face with an elephant noisily shoveling in breakfast. The enormous beast curved his trunk up to his mouth and deposited a sheaf of palm leaves inside. That done, he extended his trunk curiously toward the woman who stood stock-still before him. The fleshy, hairy lobe at the tip of his trunk examined Danielle's hair and arms before swaying down to nudge her hand.

Petrified, she dropped the small string bag she carried. Before she could stoop to retrieve it, the elephant lowered his head, scooped up the bag and, after a brief sniff of inspection, dropped it again. Danielle hurriedly snatched it up and backed away from the animal.

Outside in the clearing she recovered her dignity as best she could and headed along a heavily traveled path, following the throb of the helicopter engine. The shadowed forest opened eventually into a small clearing. Squinting up into the brilliant sunshine, she saw the big green chopper hovering, its swaying cable a whiplash that the men on the ground leaped nimbly to avoid. Sawdust, dirt and leaves whirled into dust devils beneath the craft's strong, rotor-wash winds. Through the haze of debris Danielle recognized Ryan's tall muscled body. He wore khaki shorts, his tanned shoulders and blond-streaked hair glinting in the sun.

The conditions he worked under shocked her. Rotted limbs on neighboring trees, knocked loose by the intense artificial winds, crashed down around him. He seemed oblivious to that particular danger; he was too busy dodging the bouncing cable. In one quick, deft maneuver, he latched on to the dangling tag lines and hooked them to the choker collar around the felled tree. The attached log snapped to life, and Ryan had to duck and jump back in one movement to escape its furious prancing. With a quick wave up at the pilot he signaled the all clear, and the awkward payload lifted clear of the ground, swinging like a great pendulum above the jungle.

Danielle let out her breath in a long sigh. As he stripped off his heavy work gloves and made some bantering remark to the men, making them grin, Danielle sensed he relished all the risks and danger inherent in the job. But more than that, she understood he meant to show his employees he was willing to share the risks along with the rewards.

Ryan spotted her then and strode over, still smiling at the joke he'd shared with his men. Sweat glistened across his chest and down his long bare legs. Dust caked in the laugh lines around his eyes and feathered his lashes, making her want to brush it lightly away with a fingertip.

"Morning, Danielle," he greeted her, as if last night's argument had never occurred. "Are you taking lots of notes?"

"Mental notes. For a man who uses himself as collateral, you seem to take a lot of chances."

The laugh lines deepened. "That's not your problem, lady. If I die and default on the loan, the manufacturer will get his chopper back. Besides, I think I'm a hell of a lot better risk than some joker who counts his worth on paper."

"You're one of a kind, aren't you, Kilpatrick? One of those old-fashioned tycoons who's determined to carve out an empire single-handedly." Her light needling veiled what she was really thinking—that he needed no one, least of all a strong woman. All he wanted from Danielle was a signature on a piece of paper. If he had use for a woman at all it would be for the subservient type, someone to provide his evening comfort and a pleasant diversion from the real business of living.

How ridiculously ironic, to be mourning in Ryan what she had secretly despised the lack of in Hal. Her ex-fiancé's stifling dependence had given Danielle power, but it had also made her lonely. Either way, she couldn't win.

"Come on," Ryan was teasing her back. "This tycoon wants to shower. I'll show you around afterward." He picked up his T-shirt and a rifle leaning against a tree stump. Then to her surprise they moved down the path, deeper into the surrounding forest. The only sound as they walked was the brush of their feet against the soft earth underfoot. Here the silent green forest had an unexpected cathedrallike quality. The towering trees, their trunks bare, rose straight up to distant leafy canopies.

Gradually, rushing water in the distance intruded on the silence, growing louder as they drew closer to the source. A cliff loomed ahead of them. Water bounced down the craggy face, foaming into a bouldery, fern-bordered stream that meandered deeper into the ancient forest.

While Ryan unlaced his work boots and pulled them off, Danielle perched on a flat-topped rock that caught a stray beam of sunlight. Still wearing his khaki shorts, Ryan waded into the calf-deep water and stood beneath the falls. He turned from side to side, running his fingers through his short-cropped hair until all the dust and sweat of the morning were sluiced away into the clear cold stream.

Danielle tried not to stare, but it was difficult. Her eyes drew appreciatively, again and again, to that strong male body. Yes, Ryan was a man of action, and his fine physique was proof of that.

There was something so irresistibly attractive

about this headstrong loner. Danielle knew she might belong with the sophisticated cerebral types back in Washington, but it was Ryan she wanted.

With reluctance she shifted her attention away from him. Beyond the foaming splash of the waterfall the silence stretched, unbroken. Her eyes swept the vast leafy canopy above her, but the colorful birds and chattering monkeys she'd seen in abundance downstream were nowhere to be found.

A shadowy movement across the stream caught her eye. She stared in fascination, certain she'd glimpsed a furry profile. But the animal seemed much too big and bulky to be an ape. "Ryan!" she called. "I think we've got company."

He stepped out of the falls and followed the direction of her gaze. Seconds later a deep growl tore through the air; a bear lumbered out from behind a tree only a couple of hundred feet from them. He sniffed around him and glowered at the humans, cuffing at the air with one long-clawed paw.

"Don't move fast, Danielle," Ryan said in a low calm voice. "Just pick up that rifle and toss it to me."

With shaking hands she did as she was told, and watched him raise it to his shoulder, aiming the barrel between the animal's eyes. "Now pick up my things and come slowly up behind me on the bank. Bears don't usually come down this far out of the mountains. This guy's obviously lost."

"Oh, terrific," she mumbled, willing herself not to run. "Aren't you going to shoot?" she whispered from the safety of the bank.

"Not unless I have to." Together they inched back up the bank while the animal watched their retreat. Ryan touched her arm, and they began to climb the hill behind the falls, swiftly putting as much distance between them and him as they could.

"Are you always so reluctant to shoot?" Danielle asked, full of curiosity once the danger had passed.

"I guess I am. As long as I'm not directly threatened, why should I kill an animal? I respect their territory if they respect mine."

Danielle shivered a little. "Respect just goes so far, Ryan."

"Too right. All that talk about preserving Iban jungle life gets conveniently forgotten when your own beautiful neck is at stake," Ryan mocked her, and she blushed. "Besides, I think of myself as being here on sufferance—because these people want me to be here."

They tramped uphill in silence for a while. Her embarrassment forgotten, Danielle asked quietly, "Do you think the Ibans will want you to stay here forever?"

Ryan shrugged. "I haven't asked them."

"You must have done some thinking about the future."

He gave her a bemused look. "Why should that concern you?"

"Just idle curiosity, I suppose," she said with a shrug of her own. "If you get your own helicopter and the gamble pays off, you'll be a wealthy man. I'll always wonder if your riches corrupted you."

"No chance of that," was his quick reply. "I've been taking lessons from those rich eccentric Yanks I read about in the papers—you know, the ones who leave their millon-dollar estates to seventeen homeless kittens." Danielle smiled at that, but he wasn't done. "What I think I'll do is set up a trust to finance the stamping out of bureaucrats."

The mischievous jab had struck home, and Danielle's smile faded. "You wouldn't get to first base without us bureaucrats," she said coolly. "If you didn't have international agencies it would take years to get projects approved. Admit it, Ryan. You need me."

His laugh was derisive. "God help me, then." Before she could say anything more he gave her a gentle little push toward the crest of the hill. "I thought you'd enjoy the view," he explained, taking pleasure in her astonishment.

"Orchids everywhere. It's incredible!" She laughed her delight, their argument forgotten.

That morning when she'd looked up into the jungle from the middle of the river, all she had been able to see was an unrelieved mosaic of greens, the pale soft apple hues on the bank shading almost to black farther inland. But from a height the rain forest presented an exotically painted face to the sky.

Orchids seemed to explode out of the treetops, their colors an extravaganza of speckled yellows, pinks, mauves and creamy white. Some of the blossoms looked as small as pinheads, while others clustered showily along the tips of three-foot spikes.

The pendulous roots clung to the host trees like giant spider webs.

Danielle's eyes sparkled up at Ryan. "How can you bear to cut all this richness down?"

"I don't work that way—" he shook his head "—I've told you. That's what selective harvesting is all about. With the helicopter we can literally pick and choose the trees we want, leaving the rest intact."

"It sounds impressive," she said after a moment, her expression thoughtful. "But don't you feel guilty sometimes about taking the very best?"

He ran his fingers impatiently through his damp hair. "Yeah, I know. It bothers me when I think of cutting down a specimen that's centuries old, and I don't know if it will ever be replaced. On the other hand, I sure as hell prefer my way to what Kwan and his company did to the land farther upstream. Yet who's to say if I'm any better."

"I can't answer that."

"That's why you're here, isn't it, Danielle, to find out what kind of man I really am?"

In her mind's eye she saw him side by side with his men, dodging the big logs; she saw him taking deadly aim at that menacing bear without shooting it. "You're a man who's full of surprises," she said slowly.

"Don't you like surprises?"

"Only pleasant ones."

His eyes narrowed. "Have I given you any unpleasant ones?"

"Your impatience, for one. Your quick temper, for another."

"My Irish blood." He grinned. "It can't be helped."

"You'd be a dangerous man if you held grudges."

"Do I frighten you?"

"No."

"Pity. I was hoping I could intimidate you a little."

"I'm not easily intimidated."

"So I'm finding out. I suppose I'll just have to find other ways. . . ."

She pretended to be unmoved by his teasing. "I'm immune to charm, Ryan."

"Oh? You think I have some?"

"Stop playing innocent. You know damn well the effect you have on women."

"No, I don't. Tell me."

Afraid he might read the truth in her eyes, Danielle turned away and hurried ahead.

Ryan followed, a rueful smile twisting his attractive mouth. *What about the effect you have on me,* he asked himself. How would Danielle react if she knew he dreamed about her at night, remembering the taste and texture of her skin, the extraordinarily soft promise of her breasts when he'd cupped them in his hands. More than anything, he wanted her in his bed, beside him, to have her fall asleep in his arms and wake up beside him. At the same time, he wouldn't feel safe until she was out of his life and jetting back to the opposite end of the world, where she belonged. This confusion was maddening. It made him meaner to her than he meant to be. Without intending to, he had learned her tricks, using them to protect himself.

A sharp wind sprang up, carrying with it the damp breath of the trees. Ryan's eyes swept the massing clouds.

He lengthened his stride so he could catch up with her. A tree had fallen across the path, blocking it. Lithely Danielle climbed up and balanced for an instant on the rough curved surface. Before she could leap down to the far side, Ryan's hands circled her waist and he gently lowered her to the path.

The gallant, impulsive gesture was done in a twinkling. Yet something of his touch lingered. She sensed the hot tension dammed up inside him. It excited her. It deepened her awareness of him. His whole body exuded taut power, a barely leashed sexual energy. She sensed it in the hard thigh brushing hers as they walked side by side down the narrow path. And when she felt his eyes flickering down her bare legs she grew aware. He wanted her.

Desire feathered over her breasts and down her stomach like a warm prickling wind. Never had she felt so strongly the simple power of her womanliness, the communion of her body with his. This unspoken knowledge put them both on edge.

A stray droplet of rain touched her cheek, and she looked up through the trees. A great black cloud had blotted out the sun. Rain was imminent; any second they would be caught in a downpour. Maybe it would wash some of the tension out of the air, she thought as Ryan caught her hand.

They began to run, and it struck her that she didn't know where they were running to. She would have to trust him. Oddly, she took comfort in letting him take over. Deep down she knew what she trusted about this man were his protective instincts. Once long ago he had sheltered her in his arms. Perhaps the same magic would happen again. . . .

Then the storm began, pelting them with raindrops that wet them through to the skin. Damp sticky vines whipped against her ankles, causing her to stumble.

"How much farther?" she gasped.

"Too far in this storm," he shouted down at her over the din of the storm. "We'd better sit it out somewhere."

They cut sharply right off the path and very soon were climbing up a mossy embankment. Ryan pushed her on ahead, ready to give another boost each time her rubber-soled shoes began to slide backward. She dug her fingers into the moss and felt hard rock beneath. At the top of the embankment the ground leveled off, miraculously dry beneath an outcrop of limestone cliff that formed a shallow cave against the hill. As Danielle tumbled inside, a flock of swifts rose up in shrill protest, winging out into the rain to find other shelter. The floor was overgrown with moss.

She sighed with relief, slicking back her wet hair, still smooth and flat against her scalp, to where it joined the tight coil of her chignon. Ryan grinned down at her as he dug deep into the pocket of his shorts.

"Quite impressive," he teased her. "Not even an earring out of place. Emily Post would give you full marks for ladylike comportment in a storm."

She licked the raindrops from her lips and laughed, watching him scoop a big pile of twigs against the back wall and light it with waterproof matches. "They didn't quite prepare me for this when I was a twelve-year-old in charm school. How did you ever find this place?"

"The area's littered with caves. Here, give me your shoes. Maybe we can dry them out."

"Fat chance of that. They're soaked." But she took them off, anyway, and handed them across.

"Want to give me your blouse, too?" he asked innocently.

"Thanks, but I don't think Emily Post would approve."

Ryan took off his shirt, wrung it out, then used it to towel off his face and head. As he raised his arms, the firelight illuminated the damp soft matting of hair beneath his underarms. When he caught her eye she looked away hastily.

Danielle moved near the ledge and stared out into the storm. The slanting wetness was a sheer silvery veil protecting the forest from intrusion. Where the rain pounded the earth, Danielle was reminded of the primitive rhythm of beating drums.

"Are you cold?" Ryan asked, sitting down and leaning against the cave wall.

Aware of the warmth and brightness of the fire at her back she shook her head. "Not at all. I feel as though I'm lost in a fairy tale."

"Which one—Hansel and Gretel?"

"Actually, I was thinking more along the lines of Billy Goat Gruff."

He chuckled richly. "And I'm the troll under the bridge?"

"You said it, not me."

She smiled to herself when she looked over at him. Nothing could have been less trolllike than him, lounging against the cave wall, one leg casually outstretched, the other knee bent to support his arm.

Their raillery was erasing the tension lingering from their quarrel of the night before. Outside the shelter the elements still raged. A new feeling crept over her; she felt uncertain and yet secure, protected by a curious magic.

Drawn by her stillness, Ryan leaned forward and touched her back through the damp silk of her blouse. His fingers moved lightly and gently, causing her to tremble with awareness.

"I thought you said you weren't cold."

"I'm not," she answered, afraid to look at him. "How long do you think the storm will last?"

He withdrew his hand and followed her gaze out over the forest. "It's hard to say—could be minutes or hours. The storms this time of year are unpredictable and violent."

Danielle shivered again but said nothing.

Slowly the minutes ticked away, marked by the

plop of raindrops on the narrow ledge outside the cave. She heard the deep regular rhythm of his breathing and imagined laying her head against his chest, succumbing to the delightful strength of his arms, however brief the sweet solace he had to offer. Fear and pride held her back.

Finally Ryan spoke into the silence, his lazy voice seemingly far away. "I was caught in a storm like this one winter. I was sixteen, and I was in charge of the ranch when my old gran went into the city. You always lose a percentage of your lambs to dingoes or disease under such conditions. But it got to a point of pride with me—I wouldn't lose any while she was away.

"Then, of course, it happened. One little guy I especially liked didn't come back down from grazing with his mother. So I went after him. I knew a storm was coming, but I was willing to chance it. I found him. He'd fallen into a gully. I got him up just as the storm broke. Luckily I remembered there was an old shed nearby, so we huddled inside. I sat there just as I am now, watching the water rise in those rain-washed gullies and knowing no one would come to look for me."

Danielle glanced up at him. As he had once long ago, Ryan had confided another of his rites of passage into manhood. There must have been many, each making him a little tougher, more used to being alone in that remote vastness, until he was utterly self-reliant.

While Ryan's trials had been physical, Danielle's

had been emotional and intellectual. She had kept her own counsel, schooled herself to distrust her own feelings, until she had developed a steely core, immune to all those little vulnerabilities, to loving and caring. She wondered how much alike she and Ryan were inside.

He met her gaze straight on then. Those blue eyes of hers were deep and cool, unreadable. "As I said, we might be here awhile, Danielle. But I can offer you a shoulder to lean on."

"That's a kind offer to a woman you said last night you couldn't stand."

"I was angry. Maybe I got a little carried away."

" 'A little'?"

"Do you want me to apologize for what I said?"

"It wouldn't help, because I'd know you weren't sincere—" her words were wiped out by a distant roll of thunder off the mountains. It awakened all her harrowing memories of the riots in Kuala Lumpur, when she and Ryan had believed they would die in each other's arms. Fear washed over her, but with her usual bravado she tried to ignore it.

Through that curious chemistry of awareness between them, Ryan sensed her fears. She was vulnerable now; she needed him. But that knowledge didn't give him power. It made him more vulnerable, too. He couldn't help but respond to fulfill her needs; he couldn't help but be drawn into her feelings.

Not wanting to think, he opened his arms. "Come here, Danielle."

Her pulse quickened until her own heartbeat thun-

dered in her ears like the rain hammering against the
palms. And wordlessly she went. He enfolded her,
one hand coming up to press her head close to his
shoulder, to blot out the storm. She was a trembling
reed, slight and fragile, yet resilient. His thumb gently caressed the velvet smoothness of her cheek, and
he bent his head over hers. The scent of her, fresh
and alive with a hint of wild roses, excited him. The
hot coil of desire snaked along his belly.

"Danielle," he whispered, his breath fanning the
half circles of her drooped eyelashes.

He pressed his lips to her temple and felt the strong
surge of her pulse through the cool skin. He was
aware of the curve of her hip against his groin, of the
tight ache of wanting, deep inside him. *Here is woman,* his senses clamored. *Make her yours.*

"Oh, Danielle...." She heard her name as a rum-
ble in his chest, and drawn by his desire, she lifted her
mouth to his. Their breath mingled deliciously.
Through half-closed eyes she saw his lips part, ready
to take hers.

Ryan's kiss was probing and intimate, a provocatively deliberate exploration. Each point of contact,
tongue and teeth and flesh, was a new boundary he
meant to transgress, like a climber leaving his mark
on a virgin peak.

A more passive woman might have stood for that,
but Danielle wasn't one of them. Laughing softly
against his mouth, she took control of their languorous game. Her usual reluctance gave way to a
contained explosion of passion.

The sensual battle raged in exquisite, charged silence. With the tip of her tongue she teased the corners of his lips and the warm spiral of his ear, and was rewarded by his muffled groan against her throat. Sliding down a little, she used her slightly parted lips as a brush to stroke the dusting of hair on his chest, to tease the flat nub of nipple. Another despairing groan of delight escaped his lips; she thought he was captive—until he surprised her with a quick twist of his torso, putting him above her. Now she lay supine as the crackling fire warmed them both. His laughing eyes glinted down at her.

But she refused to bow to the inevitable. Tantalizing, she brought her hands up to his chest again and let them glide in a slow sensuous serpentine down his bare abdomen to the waistline of his shorts.

Ryan's breathing quickened, and she must have felt his belly muscles tighten at the pleasure her wantonly roving fingers evoked. He sensed the battlelines drawn behind her provocation. She still wanted to be the one to call all the shots, to draw back at the last minute, to prove her control was greater. But he had also sensed her passion and knew what a deliciously taut line she was walking. Two could play at this game. . . with pleasure.

Thoroughly aroused, Ryan let her tease him an instant longer. Then his hands swept down to catch her wrists. With playful roughness he pulled them above her head and held them there with his right hand, while the left was free to explore at his leisure.

His fingers marked a glissando down the row of

buttons and up again, dipping teasingly inside the vee of her blouse. She brought her knee up, but he had anticipated that move and flung his own leg across to imprison hers.

Far from feeling trapped by his weight, she felt enveloped in a circle of warmth by the intimate pressure of thigh against thigh. Her hips yearned against his, as her mouth had yearned for the pressure of those mobile lips.

The game of conquest and surrender became a breathless duet of give and take. His hands relaxed on her wrists, and she slipped her fingers through his grasp, trailing them across his palms, down the sensitive inner surface of his forearm, then up. She kissed the crook of his elbow and, catching one of his hands, pressed her lips to his inner wrist, teasing it with the tip of her tongue.

With a secret smile Ryan bent his head to her throat, burying his lips against the pulsepoint. "I love the scent of you, Danielle—just you with no perfume to mask it."

The words touched and excited her. "Oh, Ryan, you have the gift of making me feel special, as if no other woman had ever existed until now," she whispered.

"None has."

She found his hand once more and brought it up to the buttons on her blouse. Together they unfastened them one by one, until her breasts and shoulders were free of the white crushed silk. Lightly he grazed the ridge of her collarbone with his teeth. From that gentle height dropped a fragrant valley that lips and tongue took their own sweet time to enjoy.

Her breasts strained against the flimsy bonds of lace, eager to feel his lips closing gently around each nipple. Danielle felt a great wild river of sensuality unleashed inside her, and suddenly she was powerless to control the flow. The drugging heated magic of his kisses blotted out the crackling warmth beside her, the gray daylight beyond their shelter. She knew only the reality of his lips, each hot whispered pressure from them pulsing through her like the drumming of the rain against the fertile earth.

Ryan began to chafe his leg against hers, and she moved beneath him, opening a passage for his knee. Slowly he slid it between her thighs until it came to rest against cushioned softness. A low soft moan spilled from her lips. Dear God, how she wanted him inside of her, and yet she was afraid.

"Tell me what you want, Danielle," he demanded huskily, his eyes flashing the burning question deep into hers.

Ryan pressed his face into the shadowed cleft between her breasts, driven half-crazy by the storm of passion he had aroused in them both. They lay locked together, poised on the brink.

From a distance they heard voices calling Ryan's name. Time resumed with the slow monotonous plop of raindrops from the cliff overhang to the ledge below, measuring the seconds. Reality had intruded with its own demands. They drew apart.

With her back to him, Danielle buttoned up, slipped

into her shoes and climbed out onto the ledge. The rain had stopped; watery sunshine filtered through the dripping trees. She stood there, wondering if Ryan was as grateful for this reprieve as she was. Surely he understood—as she did—that the simple act of giving could only mean surrender on both sides. Loving was a kind of war. On such an intimate battlefield there were no victors—a chancy maneuver for two people who were too accustomed to winning.

CHAPTER TEN

RYAN CLIMBED DOWN the mossy embankment ahead of her, calling out to his men. At the bottom of the hill the runner met them and broke into urgent, rapid-fire speech. After listening impassively, Ryan said a few words. Satisfied, the workers turned and hurried back toward camp.

"Problems?" Danielle asked after they'd gone, relieved to have something to talk about other than themselves.

Ryan nodded distractedly. "Yeah. The usual things after an unexpected storm—a log broken free downstream, some flooding in the mill. They'd take care of it without question if I weren't here. But when I'm around they defer to me more or less out of courtesy. On the day-to-day stuff I really don't have much to do."

"If you're so expendable why do you stay?"

"Because I think I owe these people something."

"You're taking on Kwan's guilt?"

"Believe me, Danielle, I can do without the psychoanalysis." For all the dryness of his retort, she sensed she had struck a nerve.

"This wild greenery is beautiful, but it must make

your job twice as hard,'' she ventured, reaching out to run her hand down the wet face of an elephant-palm leaf. ''I can see why Kwan didn't do any cutting here.''

''You got it. Time was money on that operation. He got in and got what he wanted in less than a year. He made his fortune fast.''

''And spent it just as fast?''

''How in hell did you know that?''

She didn't answer directly. ''That day I arrived in Kuala Lumpur, Mei Kwan was just tearing out of your driveway, looking peeved at the world.''

''And Harry opened his big mouth?''

''No. I'm a lawyer, remember? I'm adept at putting two and two together.'' Danielle smiled, but the teasing upcurve of her lips was fleeting. On the surface she might be clever at drawing conclusions, but the emotional undercurrents eluded her, because she had no experience in dealing with them. Had he been in love with Mei? He must have been to have done what he did for her—to sacrifice his own integrity.

''Just what else has that clever little mind of yours put together?''

''Nothing. Shouldn't you be getting back?''

''No. For once I'd like to know what you're really thinking.''

She gave him a long level look before replying. ''All right. I was just wondering why a man who so prides himself on his honesty would deliberately sacrifice his reputation for someone else.'' At this point she was still guessing, really, but his reaction confirmed her assumption.

"Because I was a fool," he said shortly. "I've grown up since then. I'm not about to let my passion for a woman override the rest of my life again."

"Very wise."

The indifference in her tone annoyed him. She was implying that she herself was immune to passion. "Aren't you going to try to convince me otherwise?" he prodded, determined to put this exchange on an intensely personal level. He was tired of her backing away.

"Why should I?"

He glanced down at her left hand, where her fiancé's ring should have been. "Because we're both free now. We're both adults. I was hoping we might open up a little. I'm tired of fencing with you, Danielle. We know what we want."

But the depth of such a plunge terrified her, and she retreated. Though this man might be capable of transporting her to great heights of joy, she was sensitive to the fact that he was also capable of hurting. Danielle's tough shell had easily deflected all the scratches life threw at her—she wasn't certain she could survive an all-out emotional battle with Ryan. He was the reckless type, going straight for the jugular—no quarter asked, none given.

No, her father had been right as usual; coming to Malaysia had been a big tactical error. The stakes were far too high. Never before had she risked everything for a man's love. She couldn't be tempted to now.

"We'd better get back," she said with determined briskness. "The morning's almost gone."

"Do you expect an apology for that, too?"

"I don't expect anything from you, Ryan."

"How about if I make it up to you with lunch?" he said as they came out into the clearing where she'd first seen him at work. "Come up to the bungalow at noon."

"You're too kind," she said, her tone implying he was anything but.

He laughed and turned away.

Danielle spent the next hour poking around camp, taking a few photographs to attach to her report and, when she found anyone who could speak English, asking questions about the job underway and the workers' feelings about the logging operation. Though the outcome was far from settled in her own mind, it was obvious the Iban were staunch supporters of Kilpatrick Forestry, Ltd.

Grudgingly she had to admit the twentieth century would encroach on this culture no matter what, and Ryan's logging venture was probably no more damaging than any other modern "invasion" would be. The situation might be different for the Penang and other more primitive, isolated tribes farther up in the mountains. Those could be causes for her to champion a few years down the line.

At noon she climbed the cliff path above the river that led to Ryan's bungalow, feeling oddly let down. She had followed Clay Perrin's orders: she was getting the facts and would set them down impartially in her report. But once the bank committee made its decision and her job was done, what more reason would there be to stay?

Open to the sky and the cascading rapids, Ryan's bungalow perched on a narrow promontory above the river. Unconsciously Danielle quickened her step, eager to know more of the man. The last hundred yards of the path climbed steeply, ending in a narrow garden below the veranda. She walked up the steps and knocked on the screen door.

A barefoot elderly woman drifted out of the shadows from the back of the house and, in graceful pantomime, gestured for Danielle to come inside and make herself at home. The bungalow consisted of one airy, high-ceilinged room with a tiny kitchen off the back and a loft reached by rustic spiral stairs.

In one corner of the main room stood a desk and bookshelves. The "dining room" in the opposite corner was furnished with a low table ringed by batik pillows and a cotton lacework tablecloth, incongruous-looking until Danielle realized the cloth must be another family heirloom, at once treasured and well used. The only wall adornment was an attractive oil painting of a vast prairie. She realized the setting must be the Australian "west," the outback where Ryan had spent his boyhood.

Danielle was still studying the painting when the woman came out once more through the kitchen door. She handed the American guest a cup of cool water and gestured for Danielle to sit on a low, pillow-backed divan on the veranda, overlooking the logging village at the bottom of the hill.

"*Terimakasi.*" Danielle murmured her thanks in Iban, glad she had troubled to learn that one phrase, at least, when the woman's face lit up with pleasure.

"You are welcome," came the answer in English.

The ice broken, they began to talk. Danielle learned that Tida had four grown sons, working down in the camp, as well as thirteen grandchildren. She had traveled once long ago to Kuching as a young bride, and Danielle gathered that that one taste of civilization had been enough for the perky widow, who cooked Ryan's meals, washed his clothes and tended the small garden she'd planted.

Tida admitted to being sixty. For all her wrinkles and the odd missing tooth, her spry sturdiness belied her years. Danielle thought of Racha Sabatin, wondering if the gentle outspoken Racha would ever be a mother, much less a vigorous matriarch like Tida, who had outlived two husbands.

As they chatted Danielle found herself being enveloped in the harmonious texture of these women's lives. There was something enviable in the way Tida glowed with quiet satisfaction after Danielle complimented her on the lovely colors in her sarong. It had been a long time since her own life had been that touchingly straightforward, if it had ever been.

Danielle couldn't think of anything that gave her such pleasure, except perhaps for the little foal fate had dumped, literally, into her lap. And even Foxfire couldn't compete with career preoccupations. Her being in Malaysia was proof of that.

Tida, delighted by Danielle's attentiveness, gestured to the American's walking shorts, and with a mischievous expression suggested that they should exchange costumes sometime. Danielle smiled appreciatively at this joke, which delighted the house-keeper all the more.

They were still laughing conspiratorially when Ryan walked in, rather less amused himself.

"What are you up to now, Danielle—trying to convince Tida she ought to study at the Cordon Bleu in Paris?"

Tida, sensing the mood he was in, tactfully with-drew, while Danielle stared up at him, thunderstruck by his sarcastic attack. "I wasn't trying to convince her of anything. We were simply having a pleasant conversation, until you walked in."

"Come on," he drawled. "I've left you alone for an hour. Surely there's someone around camp you've managed to convince that their life is deprived in some way, and you can quick-fix it for them with your connections."

Angrily she stood up, shoulders lifted, chin tilted, ready for battle. "What the hell are you raving on about?"

"I was just talking to Ben Sabatin. He says you've concocted some harebrained scheme to have Marie sent off to art school."

She blinked, hoping her surprise wasn't showing. She had forgotten all about the sales pitch she'd given Mr. Sabatin. "I don't think it warrants all this melodramatic outrage," she replied icily. "It was just a suggestion."

She watched his jaw tense, and wondered uneasily if she'd gone too far.

"'Just a suggestion,'" he repeated slowly, his

voice pitched dangerously low. Each word brought him a step closer, until his face was inches from hers and she had to quell the urge to take a step back. "Don't you see, dammit? It's been nothing but one suggestion after another since you got here—clinics, scholarships, women's groups—"

"I stand by every one of my suggestions."

"I'm surprised you haven't tried to sell my own house out from under me and make it into a bloody Montessori School, or something."

"That's not a bad idea, Ryan. You could use a few basic lessons in common civility."

He glowered at her, but whatever rude retort he might have made was stifled when Tida reemerged from the kitchen to set a steaming bowl on the low table. The rich pungent scent of curry and other more exotic spices filled the air, reminding them both how hungry they were.

"Would you care to dine, Miss Davis?" he asked between his teeth. "The chef's prepared one of my favorites."

"Humble pie, I hope." Danielle smiled with exaggerated politeness.

On that bristly note they sat down to feast on Tida's superb meal, chicken curry with a side dish of yellow rice liberally flaked with bits of hot red pepper. They ate until tears streamed down their cheeks and they had consumed a half-gallon of water between them. Tida beamed approvingly as she cleared away the plates. She returned with dessert, mercifully nothing more elaborate than chunks of sweet fresh pineapple.

The standoff persisted through lunch. If anything, Ryan looked grimmer than before. Over coffee Danielle finally said, "I should probably leave Akan as soon as possible."

Silence.

"Ryan, you'll have to let me know your pilot's schedule so I can arrange—"

"Do you want to know what bugs the hell out of me the most about you, Danielle?" he began as if she'd never spoken.

She looked startled, then stubborn. "No, I do not want to know. I told you I'm leav—"

He overrode her again; the anger that had simmered all through lunch was boiling over. "I don't think you give a damn about Marie Sabatin's talent. She's just a symbol of what can be done—something you can brag about on the cocktail circuit back home. I get the feeling you care more about how your philanthropy's going to make you look to your superiors than the good you think you might do here. All your righteous talk about cultural integrity—sometimes I think it's just a lot of political rot."

The attack blistered her. Danielle felt wildly like crying, but she forbade herself that weakness. "The table's turned, hasn't it?" she said in a strained voice. "Before, I was the one who was so determined to see the worst in you. Now you're doing the same thing to me. My career's important to me, yes. I'll be the first to admit that. But I'm not an egomaniac about it."

"I didn't—"

"No, please, Ryan, let me finish." Her eyes were pleading with him despite herself. "Maybe you're right about one thing. Maybe I do regard Marie as a symbol. She's a symbol of what can be accomplished for the whole community."

"You seem to forget there are human beings behind the symbols. All these grand gestures mean damn all if you do. Danielle, all I'm asking is," he went on, fighting to hold back his impatience, overlaying it with gentleness, "when have you ever genuinely given something of yourself to just one person? When you get down to it, that's the only thing that counts in this life."

She shook her head. "My father taught me a lot of things. But somehow we...we never got around to any lessons like that." She struggled to keep her voice even. "Do you remember how we were joking the other night about quid pro quo—you give something only because you expect to get something in return? Well, that's how I've seen life. My parents' marriage was an alliance based on that philosophy." Danielle was saying things she'd never admitted aloud before. She knew she should stop, but something compelled her to go on. "My mother's family was newly rich with no connections, and my father had a terrific social background but no money. The match was a tremendous success—on the surface."

Ryan's eyes sought hers. "What about you and Hal?"

"As I said, I learned all the lessons my father had to teach. Compromise, maneuvering, getting not what you want but what would be best for everyone concerned—those are the terms of the game, Ryan.''

"And you accept them?"

"I never considered any other choice!" Her voice rose on a quavering note of passion. *Until now.* But she caught herself in time. Never could she allow herself to admit that, not when she knew how Ryan suspected everything she stood for.

"I don't trust that part of you your father has molded. All I see is a woman willing to do anything for the sake of a goal. And that scares me," he added in a low taut voice.

"Why should you worry so much about how you feel about me? I told you, I'm going back to Washington.''

He smiled grimly. "Maybe I don't believe I'll be getting off the hook that easily. Maybe I don't even trust you to mean it when you say you're leaving.''

Danielle scrambled up to a kneeling position on the pillows, leaning across the table. "You had your nerve calling me a Pollyanna last night, you—" she groped for the most rotten epithet she could think of "—you holier-than-thou bastard.''

"You're right. I apologize!" he shouted. "I shouldn't have called you that. Do you prefer Machiavelli, instead, or how about J.R.? You're just as—" He stopped in mid-tirade and clutched his chest. "Oh, damn, it hurts.''

Danielle leaped up and ran around the table to him, their differences forgotten. "Listen, Ryan, don't worry," she said breathlessly, squatting down beside him. "I took a CPR course last summer."

For all his pain and aggravation, amusement glimmered in his eyes. "What would I do without you?"

"Never mind. Just lie down," she ordered urgently, her hands going around his shoulders. "I know just what to do."

His mouth twitched. "You have a wicked tongue, Danielle. And I'll be delighted to take you up on that delicious proposition later. But not now." The grin fled, and he grimaced again. "Ask Tida...she'll know what I need."

She jumped up and ran to the kitchen. All it took was one word, "heart," and Tida reached for a bottle in the pantry. As the woman stirred up the concoction Danielle snuck a glance at the bottle. Her face went red. Antacid.

She carried it into the living room and found Ryan stretched out on the divan with one leg bent, one arm flung across his forehead. He took the glass and drank down the pink liquid.

"Revolting stuff."

"Heartburn," she said accusingly. "You had no business eating that hot curry."

"It wasn't the hot food—it was the hot-tempered company."

"Humph," she fumed, turning her back and going to stand at the window.

She was distracted by the activity down in the logging camp. The elephant was thrashing around in the undergrowth, his movements neat and economical for all his hulking size. Danielle saw with amazement that he was dragging out sawn-off limbs and stacking them in a pile as if they were twigs.

"Does that elephant have a name?" she asked over her shoulder.

"Mimi."

She turned to him in surprise. "The he's a she?"

"And quite feminine, too."

Danielle had to smile at that. "She does have a thing for women's handbags."

"You two have already met?"

When Danielle told him the story he laughed. The storm of their argument seemed to have blown over. Ryan got up off the divan.

"Don't you have to rest, or something?"

He grinned. "Ah, that's right. You did say you knew just the thing for me."

"Sorry, but my humanitarian instincts have just dried up."

"A little wine, some soft music and candlelight could remedy that."

The elephant brayed in the distance.

"Go on, Mimi's waiting for you. She needs you more than I do."

"Oh, you're very good." He laughed. "I knew you had to have a sense of humor lurking around in there somewhere."

With that he was off, whistling jauntily to himself, leaving Danielle to stare after him. She rattled around the house for a little while, until she got bored and finally followed Tida out to her vegetable patch.

The Iban woman looked up and smiled, still busily weeding. After a minute she patted the ground next to her and invited Danielle to help her if she wanted.

"Oh, what the heck. Why not?"

Danielle took the pointed steel tool Tida handed to her, and soon the two of them were working side by side in companionable silence. It was pleasurable to turn over the soil and have the rich loamy scent of it fill her nostrils. The sun got hot, and Danielle's back began to ache a little, but she kept at it, letting her thoughts wander idly here and there, until she felt completely relaxed.

It was late in the afternoon when Tida threw down her tools and with a gesture signified, "Enough!" Then she took a long look at Danielle and began to giggle.

Danielle glanced down at her clothing, understanding why. The once-immaculate silk shirt and shorts were thoroughly grubby, her knees were mud-caked and her chignon hung lopsidedly to the side of her head, all its pins worked loose. "I'm a mess," Danielle agreed with a rueful look. "I'll have to get my overnight bag from the boat."

Tida shook her head. She called to one of the boys at work down the hill.

Within minutes the boy came up with the bag. Danielle was dismayed, though, when she saw that it was soaking wet. Tida began to chew out the boy, but Danielle touched her arm, shaking her head. It was her own fault; she had left it in Mr. Sabatin's boat and forgotten all about it.

She opened the bag with a sinking heart. The clothes inside were a mess, too. Tida saw her distress and made it clear she wasn't to worry; Tida would take care of it. The efficient woman took her arm and showed her up the spiral staircase to Ryan's bedroom. Danielle went reluctantly, until Tida opened a door and showed her a rustic but functioning bathroom complete with a shower. She laughed her delight.

Pleased, Tida went to the spigots and turned them on.

"You mean it's hot, too? Good grief, I'm in heaven!"

Danielle reveled in the stream of hot water for a good fifteen minutes, refusing to worry if there would be enough for Ryan later. She found a bar of castile soap, along with a square of coconut husk he must use for a sponge, and she lathered up luxuriously, humming to herself. Afterward she wrapped herself in Ryan's oversized green bath towel and stepped into the bedroom, where Tida stood patiently like a lady-in-waiting. On the bed behind her lay a folded square of blue batik fabric. The dirty clothes were nowhere in sight.

With a little flourish Tida shook out the fabric, and Danielle realized she was about to get her first lesson in how to wear a sarong. Expertly Tida wrapped and tucked and turned, until Danielle felt like a fashion designer's mannequin. But when the woman at last finished her ministrations, Danielle found that her limbs felt amazingly light. She seemed to float within the confines of the graceful garment. Tida had cleverly draped it in keeping with the Westerner's curious custom of covering the breasts.

"It's wonderful. *Terimakasi!*" Danielle said over and over again, until both of them were laughing.

After Tida left, Danielle found her brush and comb and padded downstairs. A lantern had been left to burn in the window, spilling a narrow river of light onto the veranda. She went out and perched on the wooden rail, idly swinging one foot while she pulled the comb through her damp hair. A whispered breath of coolness fluttered up to her in the twilight. Night rapidly closed in on the jungle until no light remained but a salmon-colored rim of sky glowing through the trees on the far bank.

A few hundred yards down the hill, Ryan left the camp longhouse and started the climb home, his mind sorting through the various questions his foremen had raised at their weekly meeting. They were eager to know when the company would have the funds to buy its own helicopter. Natural businessmen, they had been quick to follow Ryan's discussion of capitalization expenses and the advantages of owning versus renting equipment.

Like Ryan, they had assumed the loan would be automatic.

Now, seven months later, Ryan had had to admit with some chagrin that the decision rested with the lady up on the hill. The men hadn't laughed as he had expected them to. In their society Iban women were pretty much equals in terms of decision making and property ownership. What perplexed his men was why he hadn't yet persuaded the lady of the sense of his plan.

As if Danielle were amenable to persuasion, friendly or otherwise! That grittiness of character was one of the things he liked in her, but enough was enough. He was getting tired of the way she divorced her personal feelings from every decision she made. He knew she had a gentler, giving side, but she fought it like a wildcat. Because she refused to believe that side of herself existed, she found his softer moods suspect, too. And the hell of it was, he wanted to give, to share something of himself with her.

Ryan remembered that last year on the ranch before gran had died. Exhausted and weak after battling illness and the inevitable onset of old age, the woman had grown more dependent on her grandson for everything. He had come to her weak and afraid as a boy, ten years earlier. He had become a man strong enough for her to lean on, and that had been a source of mortification for her, as well as pride. In the end he had outtoughed the gritty old lady, and she had died grudgingly, fighting him and fighting death all the way. Life with her had been a constant battle.

He had thought he never wanted to see another woman like that again. Now here was the lovely Danielle toughing *him* out, so that even their tender moments were battlegrounds. He shook his head. Maybe he needed that kind of tonic to shake him out of the rut he'd fallen into. Maybe Danielle was right about one thing—his guilt over the past was becoming a trap. He had to make some decisions—soon. Maybe he should let the Iban take over the logging operation, so he could move on to other things.

Maybe she was right about another thing, too. Why should he worry so much about what Danielle was, when she would be gone in less than twenty-four hours? Although he told himself he wanted her to stay, secretly he was relieved she had made the decision. There was no chance for them. Danielle was too distant, too full of herself.

What if they both succumbed? What then? Was she supposed to say thanks for the loving lesson as he put her on the plane?

Don't worry, mate. He laughed at himself. Not much chance of *her* succumbing. He climbed the last few yards up the cliff, and his ironic laughter stuck in his throat.

Slowly his eyes drank in the unexpected vision. She sat on the rail with her back half to him, face lifted to the evening sky. Spilled light from the bungalow outlined her faintly against the night, the long black hair falling free past bare white shoulders, the slender figure wrapped sensuously in soft fabric. He quickened his pace and vaulted up the veranda stairs.

Startled, Danielle turned. "I was just admiring the view," she said almost guiltily. "You have a knack for surrounding yourself with beauty. I almost feel I could sit here forever."

Ryan walked the length of the veranda toward her. "Beautiful things are my weakness," he replied softly, leaning against the post as his eyes leisurely took in the details of her. "I like your hair down like that, Danielle."

The moment was too intimate, too fraught with unanswered questions. "I was just going to put it back up." She reached for the pins in her lap.

As she lifted her hand to her hair, his hand closed around hers. "No. Don't."

He stood so close she could smell the fresh cleanness of sawdust where it clung to him, and beneath that the hint of other things—a scent of skin and sweat, faintly pungent, all male.

Disturbed by her reaction, she pulled her hand away and politely asked, "Are you hungry?"

"Mmm."

Little prickles of heat touched her all over. "I meant for dinner," she rushed on. "Tida left us cold boiled chicken and rice."

"Sounds appetizing."

"It was my suggestion. I can't understand why you like to flirt with trouble the way you do—eating all those spicy dishes when you know the effect they have."

He grinned as he helped her down from the railing. "I suppose a moment of pleasure outweighs the pain that follows." They went inside.

"You're a funny sort of man," Danielle said a little later as they faced each other across the low dining table.

"I don't see you laughing," he teased her, reaching for the small jug of wine to fill their cups.

She said seriously, "I propose a toast to Kilpatrick Forestry."

Ryan looked faintly disappointed. "Does this mean I've won?"

"Only round one. I won't be recommending that you be tarred and run out of town, at least," she teased him. "Now it's up to the bank."

"I'll drink to that." He lifted his glass and sipped the wine. It was strong and sweet, faintly milky with the undertaste of rice.

"What convinced you I'm not a big bad ogre?"

She was too tired for feinting, or perhaps the directness of these people was catching. For whatever reason, she replied, "You, I suppose."

Their eyes met over the flickering candlelight, the soft glow concealing as much as it revealed. Then she looked down, her fingers tracing the lip of the flower bowl. A brilliant flame-of-the-forest blossom seemed to mock the constraint between them.

"You trust me now?"

"The Iban seem to trust you," she parried, a glimmer of a smile touching her lips. "And they know you better than I do."

His crooked smile echoed her own. "Maybe it's time you got to know me better, too."

Letting the red blossom fall, she began to run her fingers lightly on the lace-covered table, subtly but surely edging away from the personal.

"Before I go, Ryan, I'll need a few things from you. Statistics on the number of trees you're cutting, the square mileage of your leasehold from the Ibans, proof of their involvement in the decision making, and so forth. Some of the men told me the fish have begun returning to the river, so I'd like a statement on that. It will help to show that even the damage Kwan did wasn't irreversible.''

"Are you going to mention my involvement with Kwan?''

Her eyes flicked up, and she was oddly relieved to see that he'd asked the question not out of concern, but curiosity. "I feel an obligation to, if just for comparison purposes, to outline the differences in your operating methods.''

"What about the anthropologist who filed the original complaint?''

"Dr. Strathmore? I think he's back home at the University of Chicago. I'll send him a copy of my report, along with my promise that I'll keep a close eye on possible infringement of the more primitive tribal groups inland. I'll remind him that the Ibans have had modern ties for a couple of generations.'' She paused and allowed herself a brief smile. "Even Tida was in Kuching forty or fifty years ago. And I'll remind him that the history of these peoples has been a record of adaptation to change and outside pressure. They've survived on Borneo for five hundred years. I doubt if your operation is going to seriously jeopardize them.''

Ryan looked up from the coffee he'd been twirling around and around in his cup. "There's nothing you haven't thought of, is there, Danielle?''

"That's my style, Ryan.'' She ignored the faint

sarcasm in his voice. "I like to make a clean break. There are no loose ends dangling when I wrap up an assignment."

His look was sharp. "You sound like the lady executive behind her desk again. The image doesn't fit here." He reached across to touch her hair where it fell softly forward. The light contact became a caress when his fingers lingered on her naked shoulders, gleaming like alabaster in the candlelight.

"I'm not real tonight, Ryan. I'm a chimera. This will all be gone come morning."

"But we still have tonight."

Danielle's heart ached. She had been doing so well rebuilding the wall. Dear God, why did he have to try to tear it down.... There was no purpose in it.

"What good is tonight! Ryan, don't you see? Whatever that magic is between us, it's...it's reserved for those moments when time is suspended, when there is no past or future. It's one of those dreams you hate to wake up from. But we wake up all the same." Her eyes flitted to the shadowy corners of the room, as if she were a captive bird seeking a way out.

"We make our own reality."

"No. You and I belong in a fantasy world." She tried to laugh. "What we have has nothing to do with cozy evenings around a fireplace or walking a dog together. For other people love is a comfortable part of their daily routine, something they take for granted. For us it's nothing more than a snatched moment of joy. We go our separate ways in relief."

"Then let's have that last moment, Danielle," he said, and she felt the hunger washing through his quiet voice. "Come upstairs with me. If I have to be content with memories, let's have this one last taste of a dream."

How tempting it sounded, to just let go and give of herself wholly, this once.

"And if I do, then what?"

She hadn't realized she'd said the words aloud until he replied, the low grating of his voice like a caress from his callused palms. "You ask too many questions, Danielle. Can't you trust your instincts for a change? They don't lie to you."

Ryan unfolded his long legs from beneath the table and got up, holding his hand out to her. With a sigh Danielle bent her head to blow out the sputtering flame. She took his hand, and together they went over to the lantern burning in the window and extinguished it, too.

Upstairs the bedroom was dark, but a faint silvery light pooled on the floor where the door to the balcony stood ajar.

"Let's go outside, Danielle. The night's beautiful."

Although the bed beckoned to them, she went willingly. She smiled to herself when she saw the white rope hammock slung from the wall to the railing, creaking gently in the wind. With Ryan it was always the unexpected.

He stood behind her at the rail, slipping his arms around her waist to hold her tight against him. His masculinity—his scent and the warm hard length of him against her own softer curves—enveloped her.

Leaning her head back against his chest, she stared up into the sky, brilliant with stars, the constellations unfamiliar to her. Nothing was quite the same here, not the water rushing below, not the black tangle of virgin jungle that spread like a dense tapestry on the opposite riverbank. The setting was wild and untamed, as free as she and Ryan were. Nothing could bind or leave its imprint for long, or so she thought.

He turned her around to face him, his hands mapping the curve of her hips. "You're beautiful, Danielle. I want you as I've wanted no other woman."

And hearing that low fluid baritone, she could believe no man had ever spoken to her before, that none had ever touched or held her, so deep and complete was his effect on her. There were only the two of them now, and the long lonely hours of the night.

His hands were freeing the end of the sarong, and with a low impatient exclamation he began to unravel the strip of fabric until it lay in tangles at their feet. She dropped into the hammock. Close beside her he undressed, and she followed every movement with her eyes, eager to feel that hard naked body next to hers. Reaching up, she pulled him down to her.

They lay side by side, eyes searching and faintly feverish, half pleading for release even as Danielle and Ryan knew they had come too far to turn back. The swaying bed was a delicate prison of their own creation. There were no bars or guards; there was only the sweet complicity of their senses holding them captive.

Ryan slid one hand behind her back, while the other cupped her face and pulled it close to his. He kissed her with surprising gentleness, tasting and savoring as if he meant this moment to last forever. His lips brushed her cheek in a slow back-and-forth motion, teasing and playful, yet charged with feeling. "Don't you understand how I need this?" he asked huskily between the nips he bestowed on her chin. "How I need this more than anything else right now?" He pressed his mouth to her throat.

His confession fed her desire like fallen wood in a forest feeds a raging fire. Hot licking flames consumed her, sweeping her along on a burning river that was as wild as the rushing waters below.

"Ryan, don't say any more. Please, just kiss me."

His mouth closed on hers, a soft slow invasion escalating to mutual ravishment. Hungry to feel his body more intimately against hers, Danielle shifted until she lay straddled half on top of him, her head on his chest. He stroked her hair, then slipped his hand beneath the silken fall to cup her nape and caress the smooth long column of her throat with his thumb.

A lazy sensual awareness breathed through his fingertips, communicating the pleasure he found in her womanliness, transmitting his need to give her something of himself. Every inch of her body became an instrument to be played and stroked, kissed and nuzzled until they both resonated with the sheer animal joy of it. He rubbed the backs of her legs with callused palms, the enticing curve of her calves and the sensitive hollows behind her knees, making her laugh in breathless, impatient delight.

In a playful mood now, she arched and caught his ankle with her own. But this game, too, became an achingly delightful reminder of the chemistry that could ignite them with one glance, with one toying touch. The fine brown hair on his legs chafed the silken smoothness of her calf. And the network of hard muscle beneath his skin was a potent reminder of his strength, now tempered in his slow, gentle arousal of her.

Still, she rebelled against the swaying of the hammock and the indolent drift of his fingers over the curves and hidden hollows of her body. She wanted more, wanted it now. Arching her back even more, she flung her head toward the stars, her palms flat against his chest. Beneath her was a living, breathing man, and she reveled in him, sharing his hunger and feeling herself burn from the heat in his loins, pressed to her own. She felt the burgeoning power of him, like a dormant bulb breaking through the earth after a harrowing winter of cold and emptiness, and it excited her to the marrow.

The physical bond was stronger than them both, a heady force exploding their senses, uniting them and mocking their pleas for separateness.

"Ah, Danielle, Danielle," he whispered her name over and over again. "You excite me, you move me like no woman's ever done before."

Slowly she dropped her gaze from the icy beauty of the stars. His eyes gleamed up out of the darkness, reminding her of how she had felt when she'd dug deep into the rich loamy earth and discovered something primitive and joyous.

Her lips parted expectantly; he lifted his hand to feel the sweet expelling of breath against his fingertips, then to trace the outline of her mouth, her full lower lip like a furled bud on the brink of blossoming. In that same wondering, savoring way he ran his finger down her nose and up again over the fragile skin, faintly shadowed, beneath her eyes.

She smiled down at him, willing his expressive hands to touch her in just that way all over, his discoveries a shared joy. And he did, letting his middle finger feather her jaw, her throat, her pale shoulders, and finally her breasts, pendant and full.

He pulled her to him, his mouth a tantalizing instrument of arousal as he pressed it to the ivory swell of flesh. He circled his tongue delicately around the crescent shadowed underside. He found each soft rosy nipple in turn and coaxed them with teasing darts and nips, until they were full and erect. The soft brush of his mustache against her skin was like an animal's pelt, hinting at wildness lurking beneath the surface.

Languidly she raised herself to sit bestride him, her black hair a disheveled gypsy's mane. With each breath she felt logic and reason slip away, her senses in mad interplay. Acutely she felt a breath of wind across her breast, felt its coolness against the hot moist brand of Ryan's kisses. And she felt his thighs beneath her, the smooth ridge of muscles a foil for her pliant buttocks. She was aware of the rivulet of desire deep inside her, the slide of his hands over her warm bare skin. Each part of her was a potent reminder of being female to his male, both as fiercely beautiful and elemental as the world around them.

And she laughed in sheer unabated delight. He responded to the silvery sound by tightening his hands around her waist and gently pushing her back until she lay deep in the hammock.

He rose above her. Her eyes caressed the hollows in his shoulders as he leaned forward, and they caressed his tapering waist, the dark line of hair arrowing downward provocatively.

She yearned to feel the weight of him on her, but Ryan wasn't done with his love play. Catching her bare foot in one hand, he bent low to kiss it, pressing his mouth to the cool pad of the ball and tracing the high beautiful arch with his tongue, making her laugh. And now she knew the sound pleased him. She laughed again; in reward his lips brushed the top of her foot; his teeth nipped a toe or two.

Not done with her yet, Ryan's mouth moved upward more slowly along her leg and over the smooth knob of her knee, then down the valley of her inner thigh. His lips brushed her intimately, and she exhaled, a long muted sigh of surrender.

"No more teasing, Ryan, please," she begged softly. "I want to feel you inside me."

The words poured over him like honey, and in a

haze of desire Ryan felt her fingertips digging into his haunches as she pulled him to her. His heart pounded; his loins ached for release. Still he held himself back, caring more for her pleasure than his own.

He entered her slowly, and her hips arched instinctively for her to receive him. She opened like a flower in the rain, the inner reaches of her femininity enfolding him in sweet darkness.

Danielle moaned against his throat, her pulse leaping in tandem with his. Languorously she rotated her hips, drawing him deeper and still deeper. The undulant rhythm of their joined bodies grew swifter and more urgent, spurring her to ecstasy. Nothing existed but Ryan inside her.

She tangled her fingers in his hair and cried out softly as the gathering tension propelled them toward fulfillment. She rose on a ravishing wave that swept her free of the bounds of ordinary life, then crested it in a shimmering flash.

Still reveling in her pleasure, Ryan took his own gradually. And Danielle was free to simply delight in this union of their flesh, in the powerful urge that bound them.

Afterward he lay spent against her, and she stroked his damp hair. She rubbed her knuckles gently down his cheek, enjoying the faint rasp of his unshaven skin. He caught her fingers and pressed his lips to her palm, savoring the vestige of musk and roses, the scent of her that he would always remember.

"We've come full circle, haven't we, Ryan?" she whispered, the soft creak of the hammock not quite masking the catch in her voice. "We've ended where we started, in each other's arms."

"I can't convince you to stay a few days longer at least?" he answered lazily. "From Kuala Lumpur we could drive down the coast to Malaka."

She shook her head, brushing her cheek against his thick hair. "It would only be postponing the inevitable. This night's been beautiful, but I don't think anything's changed between us."

Even as she said the words she hoped he would deny them. But he didn't even try to murmur a sweet lie. For all the pain it cost her, she loved him more for that.

The lyrics of one of those sad corny songs out of the fifties drifted through her mind.

"*Que sera, sera*. What will be, will be."

They were adults; they both knew the reality of their lives.

Still, she wrapped her arms around him and clung, wanting to hold back the dawn.

CHAPTER ELEVEN

COMING BACK TO THE CITY was something of a shock after Borneo's rain forests. The bustle, noise and press of humanity at Kuala Lumpur airport put the three of them in a subdued mood.

Harry Diamond was waiting with his Peugeot, dusty and disreputable-looking as ever. Danielle and Racha were settled in the back seat, Ryan in front beside his general manager. Even in the presence of his boss Harry stuck to his ritual. Verdi's passionate operatic score swirled around their heads, making conversation impossible.

Danielle was grateful for that. She wanted to hold on to her memories of the past two days a little longer. She refused to think about the future yet. Too many things had been left unspoken between her and Ryan. Both of them had withdrawn a little on the trip back from Borneo. Perhaps they realized the things their eyes had to say were too private to risk interception by onlookers.

So Danielle contented herself with staring out the window, her thoughts far away as she pictured the mountainous jungle where she and Ryan had walked on their last morning at camp. Little by little he'd

begun to open up to her, confiding the excitement he
felt each time he came back to Borneo; how the rain
forests were his last frontier, a challenge between him
and the elements that he had to meet, not for the
money, but out of personal pride.

"Do you understand what I'm trying to say, Danielle?"

She had reached out to gently brush the groove below his lips with her finger. "I think so."

"It's not just the culture that has to be protected.
The essence of the land itself has to be preserved. If
we're going to log here it has to be a systematic thing,
so we can let whole areas grow two or three hundred
years before they're touched again. I'd like to take up
my idea with the government sometime." He paused
and grinned, putting his arms around her. "Think
your connections would come in handy?"

She smiled up at him, feeling elated, curiously
buoyant. "I never thought I'd hear you asking for
my help, Ryan Kilpatrick."

"There are a lot of things I never thought I'd hear
myself saying or doing before you barged into my
life." Though he was laughing, his eyes communicated a more serious message.

"A little shaking up is good for you."

"You've done that all right, luv," and he had
lifted her chin to bring her parted lips closer to his.
As they'd kissed, their arms tightening around each
other, none of their differences or their fears had
seemed to matter.

The battered Peugeot bounced along the crowded

highway, and Danielle longed to keep that memory, that soaring feeling when for a little while she had felt a part of Ryan's cherished dreams and hopes, a part of him.

Once the car had stopped in front of the house, Danielle observed the tender, solicitous way he helped Racha from the car. The two women hadn't discussed their private feelings about Ryan. Yet Danielle sensed the subtle tension between them whenever he was around, as if the girl were afraid Danielle was going to steal away one of the props of her life. Danielle shook her head as she walked alone to the bungalow. *You had no right to intrude here,* she berated herself.

Exhausted from the trip, Racha hadn't appeared at lunch. So after the meal Danielle sought her out in her room, knocking softly on the door in case she was asleep. But Racha called out at once for her to come in.

The room was curiously devoid of mementos, as though the ailing woman had deliberately decided to leave no personal stamp. What warmth the space possessed came from Racha herself. She sat on the edge of the bed, a light shawl around her shoulders despite the moist tropical air drifting in through the window.

Danielle tried to smile. "We haven't had much chance to talk these past few days. I've. . . I've missed that."

"Often the things two peoples have to say to one another are not expressed in words," Racha an-

swered softly, her great dark eyes fixed on Danielle.
"You are in love with Ryan."

"I'm going to leave Malaysia, Racha. I . . . just
wanted you to know that."

Racha gestured for Danielle to sit down beside her.
"But you will return."

"No. I can't really. My life isn't here."

"But you will return," Racha persisted in her quiet
way, "because he is here."

Danielle sighed, no longer trying to deny anything.
"It's difficult. Racha, I know you love him, too."

"I loved him from the first moment I saw him,
when I was a girl of sixteen in Akan. He was with Mei
then, and oh, how I despised her." Racha uttered a
soft little laugh, as if looking back on herself from
a distance, as if that person she once was no longer
existed.

"Do you dislike me, too, Racha?"

"No." The gentle laughter had died away. "A woman cannot help the way she feels. A man cannot, either.
Ryan loves me as a man loves a child. But I have seen the
way he looks at you, Danielle. He loves you because
you are a woman. It hurts me." She paused before
going on. "But I cannot dislike you for that."

"I'm glad." Danielle reached out tentatively to
touch her friend's hand. "By the way, how are you
feeling?"

Again there was the surprise of Racha's whispery
laughter. "I think I have unburdened my problems
on you too much. You appear so worried. Still, I prefer this to how you were when you first arrived."

"I think you managed to get around my aloofness even then. I hope I've learned a few things from you. In some ways you're much wiser than I am, Racha."

"There is one good thing I can say about this heart of mine. It has forced me to slow down, to take the time to watch and observe. Danielle, I am happy you feel I have given you something."

"And all I've done is take things from you."

Racha shook her head. "Ryan is not mine."

"Isn't he?" Danielle stood up. "Well, I'd better be going. You have to rest, and I have some things to take care of." She was nearly to the door when Racha's voice halted her.

"Danielle, when do you leave Malaysia?"

"I haven't decided yet."

Racha looked as though she wanted to say something more, then changed her mind. She merely nodded.

Relieved, Danielle opened the door and went out into the corridor toward Ryan's private study. The door stood ajar, so she took the liberty of glancing inside. The room was empty. Just as well. She would take care of business first and discuss it with Ryan afterward.

She sat down before the highly polished teak desk, pulled the telephone toward her and dialed. "Operator? I'd like to place a collect call to the United States."

While she waited for the call to go through, she reviewed the harsh things Ryan had said about her. He'd been right on some counts. Considering what she was about to do, Danielle wondered uneasily if she was being driven by guilt, or if she was making this call because she genuinely cared about Racha's future.

A familiar voice came on the line. "Dad? Hello, it's me.... No, I'm not home. I'm still in Kuala Lumpur.... What? No, everything's gone fine. Listen, I have a big favor to ask you...."

Twenty minutes and two phone calls later, Ryan came into the office just as she was hanging up. She came around the desk toward him. "I hope you don't mind. I had to call the States."

He nodded. "No problem. My home is your home."

The remark was lightly made; still, there was something in his eyes that made her look down. "Listen, Ryan," she began nervously, "do you have a minute? There's something I want to discuss with you."

"Sure. Go ahead."

She reached behind him to push the door shut. "I prefer this to be private for now."

He whistled softly. "Serious business, I take it?"

She nodded and went to sit in the upright visitor's chair, while he perched on the desk edge.

"Okay, now shoot." He was watching her intently.

"Ryan, I want to take Racha Sabatin home with me to Washington." She saw him stiffen with surprise and hurried on. "That was what I was on the phone about just now. I've made arrangements for her to be admitted to George Washington University

Medical Center if she...and you are willing. Jay Amstel's head of the cardiac-surgery program there, and from what I understand he's one of the best in the country. He can tell Racha once and for all if surgery could benefit her. And if it can, well, then, Dr. Amstel's the man to do it.''

She stopped when she caught the look of suspicion in his eyes. ''Listen, Ryan, I know what you're thinking, but you're wrong. The only reason I'm doing this—the only reason—is because I've come to care about Racha very much. Ryan, how can I explain it to you?'' She swallowed hard. ''Racha trusted me. She confided her deepest concerns. I feel an obligation to live up to her opinion of me. And the only way I can think of doing this is by getting her together with the best surgeon I can find.''

''I've seen her condition deteriorating, but she'd never wanted to talk to me about it.'' He sighed in frustration. ''I'm glad she opened up to you at least.''

''She opened up to me because she considers me a stranger, Ryan. Because she knew I'd be going away and I wouldn't have to think about her after I was gone.''

''Danielle—''

Afraid of what he might say, she hurried on. ''You'll have to arrange for her to be examined by a doctor here in Kuala Lumpur, to certify her okay for travel...arrange for extra oxygen on the flight, just in case.'' She went on, one by one checking off all the foreseeable problems.

Aware that her crisp, businesslike monologue was a cover for her feelings, Ryan circumvented her defense by coming to perch on the arm of her chair.

"Why are you going to all this trouble?" he quietly asked.

She felt his eyes on her, but she refused to look up. "For her...for you, Ryan. I know how important she is to you."

"I appreciate your concern," he said huskily.

She stood up. "I'd better go. I have some repacking to do."

"Danielle, please, will you reconsider what I suggested the other night? I want to take you over to Malaka. We could take long walks on the beach, have breakfast in bed, do all the things ordinary lovers do. Our time together's been too short."

She closed her eyes to his persuasion, not wanting to meet that tawny gaze, to let her eyes rest on those hard, sunburnt features that had become so beloved. And in closing them she found another memory....

They were facing each other in sweet abashed intimacy after their night together at camp, sitting over breakfast without talking, content just to be with each other. She had stared down at her hand, the perfectly manicured, dusty-pink nails resting against the homespun lace. Across the table Ryan's tanned fingers, tense and strong, gripped his coffee cup. Her eyes took in the brush of fair hairs below his knuckles, the faint bruise on his left thumbnail from an old work injury. She knew even then that she was saving up the reality of this moment against a future when they would no longer be together. . . .

Danielle opened her eyes again. "Ryan, please," she pleaded, using the same words, the same husky tone she once had to beg far different things of him. "I don't want any more stolen moments. My life's been too full of them since I've come here. Don't you see? I have to get on with my life."

Misunderstanding her, he took the words as a denial of anything real between them. "So you're leaving, just like that?"

Her eyes flashed. "Didn't you do exactly the same to me once? I'm afraid that's how we're destined to connect, Ryan. We meet in stolen hours—they don't belong to us. You said it yourself at one point. We don't even belong together."

"Maybe we just haven't given it enough of a chance."

How she wanted to believe that! She was on the verge of saying so when Racha came into the study, her eyes moving with candid curiosity between them.

It was Ryan who broke the silence. "How would you like to go to America with Danielle, Racha?"

"You are not joking me?"

"I'm dead serious."

Danielle added, "My father has recommended an excellent heart surgeon, and our university hospital in Washington is one of the best. I've told Dr. Amstel about your condition. He would like to meet you. He feels there's a good chance he can help you." She smiled. "What do you say?"

Racha's eyes lit up. "I must sit and think. It is too much too fast."

"Talk it over with Ryan, then. You know he always has your best interests at heart."

He walked over to Danielle. "I'll see you out."

"No, don't bother."

"I want to." Outside in the hall he took her arm. "I just wanted to say thanks again. She looked like a kid on Christmas morning when you told her."

"I want her to be happy."

His eyes teased her a little. "What about me? Don't you care about my happiness, too?"

"Ryan. . ." she began warningly.

"No, just listen to me. Danielle, we need a few more days together at least. We have a lot to talk about."

"I don't want to talk. I just need to be alone. . .to think. I've decided to go up to Pinang and just relax for a while, try to get my priorities straight."

"'Priorities'!" he repeated in frustration. "You're talking to me, Danielle, not to some committee. I'm getting tired of your obsession with having everything neat, pat and well arranged in advance. You have to play by the rule book every time. But I have just one question for you. Don't you ever feel it's one hell of a lonely life? That's the kind of life your old man's lived, isn't it? And what does he have to show for it now—except a cold lifeless museum of a house and a daughter he's not even close to. The ex-diplomat ends up still playing the power game because it's easier than admitting he's lonely and afraid he might need someone, after all.'' Ryan's eyes bored into her. ''Danielle, aren't you afraid you're going to wind up the same way?''

''What's the alternative?'' she replied, her voice a taut whisper. ''To give up everything I've known for thirty years?''

''I'm not telling you to give up everything. I just—''

She shushed him with a finger to his lips. ''Ryan, please don't say anything more. I'm going. I'll be back in a few days to pick up Racha. That's as far ahead as I want to think for now.'' She turned and hurried down the corridor, not looking back.

Ryan slammed his fist against the wall, wondering what in hell she wanted from him. She had more or less accused him once of using his guilt over the past to postpone the future. Now, because of her, here he was at thirty-five, facing a thorny emotional cross-road. And she refused to face it with him.

Risky as it was, he was ready to tell Danielle he loved her, though God only knew why he did. She was a feisty, opinionated little snob, he thought in aggravation, and she was wild beneath that calm surface of hers. She gave him heartburn and pushed his limited patience to the brink. He owed her nothing. And yet she excited him to the marrow; in her eyes he found a whole world of feeling that he'd convinced himself couldn't exist.

But, no. The risk was not in loving Danielle; it lay in losing her to that other life a continent away. He would have no qualms about competing with another man, but these other things... her controlled world, the ruthless manner she hid behind, had been ingrained in her since childhood. He didn't know if what he had to offer could counter them.

The study door opened, and Racha poked her head out inquiringly. "Ryan?"

Relieved, he let himself be drawn back into his own familiar world.

Racha looked a little worried. "Mei Kwan phoned. She is coming here again. Will you see her?"

"Great. Just what I need."

"I can tell her you are away, that you are never coming back."

Racha's uncharacteristically hard tone amused him. "No, I'd better get it over with. Avoiding her wouldn't do any good. You know how slippery she is."

Racha nodded philosophically. "Then I will send her in when she arrives."

A half-hour later the door to his study opened, and Mei stood there, a ghost from the past in her mandarin-collared silk dress. Even her hair was the same, that thick fringe of bangs framing a face that had once seduced him with its fragile innocence.

"You pick strange bodyguards, Ryan-san, an old alcoholic and a naive girl." She smiled sweetly. "But, then, you always did have a soft heart."

He pushed the papers on his desk aside and laid his palms flat on the table. "What do you want, Mei?"

Her eyes dropped demurely. "You are the only friend I have, Ryan."

"Get to the point."

"You are the only one who can help me."

"Why in hell should I help you?"

She glided toward him. "Because you loved me once."

Her insinuating voice grated on him. "You've lost your touch, Mei. You used to be subtler and more clever than that. You worked on your father's weakness. Then you worked on mine. He paid for his greed, and I paid for my misguided love." His eyes were cold. "When are you going to start paying for your sins?"

Her bud-shaped lips hardened. "My type never pays, Ryan. Can I help it if you chose to be so blind? You could have told the court I was the one who was the driving force behind my father—that I had Kwan in my pocket."

"I didn't know until it was too late," he shot back in disgust. "Your innocent act was so perfect that up until the day you walked out, I believed you were just another victim of the whole sordid scheme."

She laughed, a musical sound that contradicted the ruthless selfishness underlying it. "Dreams die hard, Ryan-san. Still, you must care for me a little."

"You should have saved yourself the trip."

"For old time's sake, for the sake of the love we had," she simpered, "you must help me."

He stood up and came around the desk. "Now you're the one who's a fool. Don't you understand, Mei? I don't feel anything for you...except pity and contempt."

Her face contorting with anger, she reached up, slapped him hard.

He didn't flinch. "Get out."

She crumpled into the chair and began to cry, heartrending sobs that should have melted stone.

He was unmoved, and when she saw her sobbing had no effect, she stood up slowly, the crocodile tears drying on her cheeks. "I did not come here to beg, Ryan, but I will." Her black eyes flickered over his face. "Please, loan me five hundred. I need the money to get to Luzon. My uncle has a nightclub there, and he has promised me a job singing."

"Why don't you sell your Mercedes?"

"It is not mine. It is a...a friend's."

"Then why doesn't he pay your way?"

She licked her lips. "He does not know I am leaving."

Ryan stared down at her for a long time, then with a sigh finally said, "You really want to go to Luzon?"

She nodded, watching out of narrowed eyes as he went over to the intercom and pressed the buzzer. "Racha, get me Jim Black." He turned to Mei. "I'll get you to Luzon, but I'll be damned if I'll give you a penny."

She turned her back stiffly, listening to him on the phone. "Black, Kilpatrick here. I have a one-way cargo shipment out. High priority."

If it bothered her to hear herself described in those terms, she didn't show it. Turning back to him with a wheedling smile, she said, "Then just a hundred, please, Ryan. If I'm going to audition I have to have something to wear."

He suspected she was lying through her teeth, as usual, but he had no interest in confronting her. Reaching for his checkbook, he wrote out the amount and handed it over.

Without a word she took it and turned on her heel. As she opened the door into the hall, Harry Diamond nearly fell into the room. Mei smiled contemptuously at him and marched out without a backward glance.

Recovering his dignity, Harry hurried over to his boss. "You didn't give her anything, did you, old boy?"

"I gave her what she wanted—a one-way ticket out."

"Bravo. That's two in one day you've gotten rid of. Good show, good show."

Ryan smiled wryly. "Not quite, Harry. Danielle will be back in a week. She only went up to Pinang."

"Damn all! Won't you ever learn?"

"This isn't the same thing at all, Harry. But I wouldn't expect you to understand that."

DANIELLE MOVED ALONG the deserted beach at the very tip of Pinang Island, the fine sand gilded bronze by the setting sun. Dead north lay Thailand and the rest of Southeast Asia.

As she walked, she thought about Bangkok, where she had attended first and second grades at the American school. And years later, after her mother had died, she had accompanied her father on his tour of duty to what was then Cambodia, a key assignment for Davis because the Vietnam War had just been heating up.

Between tours they had always returned to Foxhall, the serene home port she had thought would always be there, comforting in its spacious, solid sameness. Now even that would be gone before too long. John Davis saw no point in maintaining the lovely old white elephant when he and his daughter spent so little time there.

Danielle wondered what she would be going home to emotionally. She was glad Racha was coming along. The Iban woman was her link to Ryan's world; she was Danielle's reminder of what friendship and caring could mean. In a way, Racha would be the proof that Ryan had been wrong about Danielle. She was learning what it meant to be a woman, to be a decent human being. She was happy and confident, at least, about the decision to bring Racha to the States. After the surgery Racha would be a new woman, too—every bit as sturdy as old Tida up at camp.

Suddenly Danielle smiled, thinking about the odd friendship that had sprung up between her and Tida; the two had absolutely nothing in common. Danielle made a mental note to send her something once she got back to the States, maybe a sophisticated Cardin scarf. She could almost hear Tida's mischievous, delighted laugh when she opened the package. Again Danielle marveled at how Racha and Tida had insinuated themselves into her guarded heart.

Inevitably her thoughts turned back to Ryan; he was never far from them. He was the catalyst, the spur for her to confront her feelings and free them. The problem was, she had no idea what good feeling would do to her.

As twilight deepened around her and the first stars began to emerge out of the indigo sky, Danielle turned and walked back along the shore. Her hotel was a luxurious little hideaway tucked into a private cove, the manicured grounds shaded by great casuarina trees. A perfect lovers' retreat, she thought ironically.

In the end she stayed a week, seven solitary days of lazing in the sun and trying not to think about the future.

One morning she borrowed snorkel, mask and fins and swam out through the low breakers drifting with the warm current. Twenty feet below her stretched a contained world of lacy coral growing in fantastic shapes. Danielle lost herself in that stony underwater garden. Taking deep breaths, she would dive down and run her fingers over the sharp coral, marveling at the exotically colored fish that swam fearlessly up to her mask. Resurfacing, she cleared the water from her snorkel, gasping in the fresh, salt-tanged air.

Jen should see me now, she speculated lazily, remembering how her secretary used to insist that Danielle take time off for at least a short vacation, and of course she never listened. Thinking of Jen also brought her father to mind. The two of them no more belonged together than she and Ryan did . . . but maybe they would be luckier.

Another day Danielle went into town and wandered down streets with names such as Jalan Gladstone. The jumble of Eastern and Western cultures colored the city's personality. In an hour's time she passed an Anglican cathedral, a Chinese snake temple, several Islamic mosques and one high-walled Hindu sanctuary. The strange fusion of cultures made it possible for Danielle to escape her own identity for a little while.

In the evening she rode the funicular twenty-five hundred feet up to the top of Pinang Hill. She took tea on a café terrace and drank in the panorama of jungled hills tumbling down toward the busy harbor, where steamers plied the two-mile journey to the mainland and Chinese junks drifted along the shore like exotic beetles with wings spread.

Another day she shopped leisurely, buying little gifts at the Tong Aik Emporium and the Barakbah Street Market. Each morning she woke up with the promise to do just as she pleased, to get in closer touch with herself.

Danielle had gotten the address of Racha's brother before she left Kuala Lumpur, and on her last evening in Pinang she went to visit Sing. Like Racha, he seemed caught between two worlds. His small apartment opened directly onto a busy market street, where trishaws and bicycles rushed past endlessly. Inside, the room was as sparsely furnished as a longhouse dwelling, with mats and rolled-up hammocks. In his wheelchair Sing maneuvered easily around the open space. That evening his nimble fingers were occupied with an electronic-components board he'd brought home from the factory to finish.

His cheerful smile and dark serious eyes were a reminder of Racha, except whereas she was fragile and almost painfully thin, Sing was powerfully muscled across the shoulders, in compensation for his legs. He, too, spoke English with a quiet singsong accent.

When he learned she had visited Akan and met his family, Sing warmed to Danielle very quickly. They spoke of many things, and the young Iban confided he was saving his money because he hoped to marry a girl who worked with him in the factory.

"Racha mentioned that Ryan helped you find this job," Danielle said at one point.

"He is a good guy. Once I felt bitter toward him," Sing admitted candidly, looking down at his legs. "Not now. I think Kwan used him as he used the Iban. But when it was over he did not run in shame. He stayed with my village to build something good. Ryan is like an Iban man, loyal and generous."

"Your whole family seems fond of him."

"I had hoped he would marry one of my sisters. But Marie is too silly, and Racha is too weak. A strong man needs a strong woman."

Danielle didn't answer that directly. "Sing, I am taking Racha back to the United States with me."

"Yes?"

"There is a surgeon who may be able to help her."

He looked skeptical. "And do you believe that afterward she will be strong?"

"Very strong."

Sing wheeled away suddenly to a corner of the room, to a narrow shelf decorated with a beautifully worked rattan basket. He withdrew something and wheeled back over to where Danielle sat cross-legged on a mat.

"Will you give this to my sister for me, please?" He handed her a small star-sapphire ring.

"Oh, it's stunning!"

Sing nodded. "The Nepali traders out in the market street sell these to the tourists. This one is genuine."

"Do you want me to tell Racha anything?"

"Will you ask her if she remembers when we were little and we would sit at the top of the kampong ladder? The sky before dark was like this sapphire. Sometimes we made wishes."

"What would you wish for?"

"More than anything, we wanted to know the outside world before we died."

"Your wishes came true."

"Racha wished, too, for a new heart. She wanted to bury the old one in a box under the longhouse. She said she would be a new girl then."

"I'll remind her of that," Danielle said softly, and slipped the ring over her little finger.

The next morning she caught a Malaysian Air Charter flight back to Kuala Lumpur, her restful idyll over.

RACHA AND HARRY DIAMOND were together in the office when Danielle walked in, her suitcase in one hand and an elegant paper shopping bag in the other.

"You should have rung us up," Harry reproached her. "Ryan would have wanted me to collect you from the airport."

"I wasn't sure I could stand *La Traviata* one more time, so I took a taxi," Danielle teased the prickly Englishman. "I don't know if this will turn your whole routine upside down, but I've brought you a little present." She rummaged in the bag and pulled out a small rectangular package.

Harry opened it suspiciously while Racha and Danielle exchanged amused glances. "Gershwin!" he exclaimed, examining the cassette tape as if it contained a bomb.

"A little opera, American style," Danielle replied, unfazed. "*Porgy and Bess* is my favorite."

His big nose wrinkled up thoughtfully above his waxed mustache. "It might have possibilities," he mused. "Perhaps on the drive over to Malaka...." Forgetting to thank her, Harry wandered out of the office.

"I brought you something, too," Danielle told Racha, still laughing.

The Iban woman tore off the wrappings eagerly and exclaimed in delight, "A little clock!"

"It's a travel alarm. I thought you'd need it for the trip." Danielle sought her friend's eyes. "You *are* coming to Washington, aren't you?"

Racha nodded. "It is my wish, more than anything."

Then, remembering Sing's token, Danielle handed it to Racha. "Sing told me how you and he would sit in the evening, making wishes on the evening star."

"He told you of them?" Racha smiled pensively, slipping the sapphire onto her ring finger. "I hope my second wish comes true, too."

"Of course it will," Danielle reassured her, so confident of it herself. "Did you get our flight reservations made?"

"Ten o'clock tomorrow morning. Harry will drive us to the airport—that is, if you can tolerate Wagner for an hour."

"I'll manage. Well...." She glanced around the office.

In response to Danielle's unasked question, Racha said, "Our Ryan is not home yet. But his pilot friends are already out by the pool, waiting. It is their poker day."

"Aren't you going to join them?" Danielle teased her.

"I have much to do," Racha replied seriously, "but you are welcome to, if you wish."

"If they're anything like American men, I don't think they'd appreciate a woman crashing the party. I'll just go on over to the guest house and rest awhile."

"Talib is still cleaning it, I am afraid. But there is fresh tea in the kitchen, and you can relax in the living room, if you like."

"Thanks. Would you like to join me?"

Racha smiled. "I hope we will have much time to talk once we are on the airplane tomorrow. For now I really must work."

In the living room Danielle kicked off her shoes and laid her head back against the sofa. The men were at the far side of the terrace, gathered around the patio table. From the sound of things their poker session was in full swing.

"I'll see you, mate, and raise you four." Swanson's deadpan drawl was unmistakable.

"Risky move, Swanson," Jim Black warned him.

"A bit of risk is what it's all about, isn't it? That's my philosophy, all right. Used to drive old Madge up the wall."

"Ever hear from your ex?"

"'Ell no. She's found 'erself a new man who'll sit with 'er in front of the telly every night and let 'er tuck 'im into bed by nine." The sneer in Swanson's voice didn't quite mask his anger and jealousy.

"A lot of rot," Black agreed. "That's why I never got married in the first place. What woman could take this kind of life?"

Harry must have joined the other two, because his impeccable, slightly aggrieved accents wafted in through the open sliding-glass door. "The last thing a man needs is a woman around to muck up his life. Ryan had to learn that the hard way. If he lets it happen again he's a ruddy fool. To top it off, that little cow Mei Kwan was sniffing around again. You would think it was enough that she let her father and Ryan take the punishment for her greed. But, no, she has the god-awful cheek to play on his sympathy again!"

"Too right you are, blokes. Except who could resist the lookers he attracts?" Swanson's chuckle was downright lascivious. "That cool-as-a-cucumber American number he's got here now...."

Danielle stood up, deciding she was getting just what she deserved for eavesdropping. She went outside, taking a wide detour around the pool area, and walked across the lawn to her tree house.

The warm fragrant air off the river blew away the traces of pine oil from the room. Talib, thorough and efficient as always, had done his afternoon's work and disappeared. Telling herself she would just nap a few minutes, Danielle lay down across the bed, not caring whether she wrinkled the emerald batik sundress she had bought that morning before leaving Pinang.

Hazily she dreamed, off and on, snatches of the men's conversation running through her mind. Men whose lives involved adventure and risk couldn't afford the luxury of wives. She dreamed of Swanson's wife, Madge, saw her being worn down emotionally while she waited for him to come down from the mountains—homesick in an unfamiliar culture and frightened. And then the wives got tired of waiting, went home to Australia or England or America. Over and over she heard Harry's voice: "Ryan had to learn that the hard way. If he lets it happen again he's a ruddy fool."

Danielle opened her eyes with a start. The room was bathed in shadow. Then she realized it must have been Ryan's soft knock that awakened her, and she wondered how long he'd been standing there staring down at her.

"You didn't come to dinner. I was concerned."

She sat up in the middle of the bed, running her fingers through her softly mussed hair, aware of the still intimacy of the moment. Their eyes met, and a thousand questions flashed between them.

All Ryan said was, "You look beautiful in that dress. I've never seen it before."

"I suppose I'm like any woman on holiday, dressing frivolously and doing all the things I wouldn't ordinarily do."

His smile eased his strained expression a little. "I'm all for it, so long as she has no regrets afterward."

She shrugged and stood up.

"Danielle, welcome back."

The caressive sound of his voice, no longer teasing, washed over her, but she wouldn't go to him. She was determined to hold him at arm's length.

"I brought you a present, too, Ryan," she said with feigned briskness, reaching into the bag beside the bed to pull out a small package.

Instead of handing it to him, she opened it herself with nervous fingers. A half-dozen paper-thin brass elephants, suspended by nylon threads, nestled in the tissue. She went over to the screened window and, after gently disentangling the threads, hung the wind chime from a hook. As the breeze touched it, the brass figures began to tremble against each other, filling the night air with a high, sweet music.

She turned back to Ryan. "I bought one for me, too," she admitted softly. "When I'm home again I'll hang the chimes near my bedroom window. The hot summer wind will touch the brass, and every time I hear that tinkle I'll remember the river rushing below your cottage...I'll remember the sound of the wind through the trees and the hammock's creak."

The intimate sensuality of her words sent desire

snaking through his belly and made his own voice husky. "I've done nothing but think about you all week, Danielle. I would dream of holding you in my arms, and I'd wake up feeling cold when you weren't there."

Why are we torturing each other like this? she thought in agony.

"Racha and I are flying out in the morning." She willed her expression to be distant.

"I know that. And I want you to call me the minute you know if the surgery's feasible. I'll fly out."

Danielle nodded stiffly. "She'll need you."

"What about you, Danielle? Can't you admit you might need me, too? I want to give this thing between us a chance."

Her pulse pounded against her temples. "You ask too much," she whispered. "It's impossible."

"Only if you want it to be."

She shook her head uncertainly.

"Dammit, Danielle. I'm in love with you. I'm tired of living alone."

"You're not alone. Your whole life is here. You have Racha and Harry, your friends—"

He raked his fingers through his hair. "That's a lot of rubbish, and you know it! Do you love me or don't you?"

What her heart had been saying all along, her lips couldn't speak aloud. With a long shuddering breath she turned away from him. Outside, the tropic night hummed with the sound of emerald cicadas and lizards stalking along the thatched walls.

"When I got back today, Ryan, your pilot friends were out by the pool, and I happened to overhear them talking. They're all either divorced or bachelors like you. You've created a male domain here where a woman has no place, except on your terms." She gave him a quick glance over her shoulder. "This is a different world, Ryan, and I don't think I fit in."

"You've lived in Southeast Asia."

"That was years ago. Before I'd built my own life elsewhere."

Something wistful in her voice touched him, and he came to stand behind her. They were so close now he could no more keep his hands from caressing her than he could have stilled his own heartbeat. His fingers closed gently around her tanned shoulders; he marveled at their round, silken softness. He lowered his head and let his lips and mustache graze the fragrant skin, savoring the beauty of this woman he had come to love.

Warmed by the magic of his touch, Danielle turned and clung to him, her cheek to his chest. "I can't believe my own naiveté," she whispered. "Somehow I always thought that once I fell in love my whole life would fall into place and I'd be certain of everything—you, me, our lives. But it isn't that way at all. It's only made me more confused."

Ryan tilted his head to look down at her. "You've never been in love before?"

"Only once." Her eyes were both troubled and amused. "I seem to keep making the same mistake.

This is twice now I've fallen in love with the same man.''

"I won't be fool enough to let you go this time," he murmured huskily, bending down to catch her mouth and kiss her deeply.

Her lips opened to him like violets after a storm, moist and soft and beckoning to be plundered. But when he went to lift her onto the bed she resisted.

"Danielle, I want to feel close to you again. I want to hold you in my arms. I want to make love to you one last time.''

The urgency in his voice reminded her of her own aching need, of how their bodies had moved in slow exquisite rhythm. Her breasts and thighs cried out for the pressure of his body, and she wanted nothing more than to feel the driving completion of his maleness.

But if she couldn't give herself wholly she would give nothing at all. She feared such a commitment would be too final and ultimate a surrender.

Did she love him—*did she*? With Hal it had never really been a question of love. He had simply always been there for her and always would be. She had felt safe and secure with him, knowing what he expected. She wasn't at all certain about Ryan. Hal had satisfied her partially because of her own power over him. With Ryan, could the power of love be enough? She believed he wanted her, without needing her.

Attuned to every nuance of her body, Ryan sensed her withdrawal, and he released her. "You've made a decision, haven't you?" he said quietly.

"Before I came here, Ryan, my father told me I would make the right decision. Maybe he knows me better than I know myself. He said I know where I belong," she told him in anguish. "Ryan, I'm leaving."

He gripped her arms—she shook him off. "Please, don't make this harder for me than it is!"

"Have it your own way, then." Hurt, he turned on his heel and left her alone.

After he'd gone Danielle stood at the window; her gaze followed him until he disappeared into the darkness. She felt as if a light had been extinguished, as if a part of her had gone with him.

CHAPTER TWELVE

AT SIX FORTY-FIVE Monday morning Danielle let herself into the dark office. Setting a small wrapped package on Jen's desk, she picked up the neatly bound stacks of mail and carried them into her office.

She read swiftly, tossing the junk, making notes and consulting her calendar. An hour later she was interrupted by her secretary's characteristic brisk knock.

Without waiting, Jen popped her head around the door. "Welcome home, Danni." She surveyed her boss's littered desktop. "And by the look of things you couldn't wait to get here."

"I was wide-awake at five, so I decided to come in," Danielle replied, her words punctuated by the ripping of another envelope. She looked up briefly to meet Jen's eyes. "You've handled all the routine stuff beautifully. Thanks."

"I need to talk to you, Danni."

"Can it wait fifteen minutes? I want to finish going through this last stack."

"You're still the boss."

Fifteen minutes later on the dot, Jen buzzed. "Do

I have the all clear to come in now? I'll bring you a cup of coffee, too, since I'm getting one, anyway.''

"Yes, thanks, Jen."

Danielle was circling dates on her engagement calendar when Jen came in, carrying two cups of coffee. Danielle tried not to look too inquisitive as Jen sat down opposite her.

"What's up, Jen?"

"Well, first I want to thank you for the necklace you brought me. I never saw coral carved into such delicate flower designs before. It's lovely.'' Jen paused, her lips quirking teasingly. "I always knew there was a good reason for my begging you to take a vacation.''

"You've done a terrific job for these past few years. I suppose it was time to let you know how much I appreciated it."

Jen gave her a strange look. "Danni, have you been talking to your father?"

"Not since I called him from Kuala Lumpur over the weekend. Why?"

"Did he mention his...or rather, I suppose I should say our plans?"

Danielle carefully set down her coffee cup. "What plans, Jen?"

The woman took a deep breath. "I'll be leaving here in a few weeks.''

"You're leaving Washington?"

"No, I meant I'll be leaving my job here with you," she corrected gently. "Your father's asked me to marry him.''

"I see." Danielle hoped she didn't look as stunned as she felt. "Isn't this a little sudden?"

"Danni, we're two grown people. I've known for years what I've wanted in a man. At last I've found it. John's everything I could have hoped for. Danni, you know how bored I was getting with these forty-year-olds who are still 'searching for themselves.' Besides," Jen added, her eyes crinkling impishly, "he always laughs at my jokes."

The playful words were met with silence, and Jen shifted uncomfortably. "Danni, for heaven's sake, say something. Say you're happy for us. Say you hate me!"

"I don't hate you."

Jen looked at her askance. "Don't tell me you're going to play snob again and tell me I'm not suitable material for a diplomat's wife."

"What good would that do? You'd only deny it," Danielle teased her back, aware that neither of them was wholly teasing. "There is one thing I'm curious about, Jen. Have you taken him to dance class with all your kids?"

"Yes, I have, as a matter of fact. He was more of a stuffed shirt about it than you were. But he's coming around."

The laughter in Jen's eyes animated her whole expression. She was radiant, down-to-earth, positively jolly. For all her experience with men and the world, she had an innocence about her that made it impossible to stay estranged from her for long.

Danielle tried to put herself in her father's shoes,

to imagine him watching Jen move across the old gymnasium floor, her every motion graceful and full of passion. She was his draw to life, just as John must be her steadying point, her connection to something solid.

Danielle picked up her coffee cup, met her friend's eyes over the rim. "Well, I suppose congratulations are in order."

"Congratulations for what—for my taking the starch out of his stuffed shirt, or for our engagement?"

Danielle smiled. "Both. Anyway, I suppose I owe you an apology."

"Forget it."

"No, I can't. I was pretty high-handed and rude to you before I left, and I'm sorry about it."

"Apology accepted."

They sipped their coffee in silence for a while.

"You know, Jen, he's changed in the short while you two have been together. I even sensed it in his voice on the phone the other night." She sighed. "I suppose I was so jealous of you because he's given you something he's always withheld from me and from my mother, too, I guess. Dad's given you a free, unconditional part of himself, when all along he's taught me to see life, even love, as a duty instead of pleasure."

"Danni, is that how you feel about Hal?" Jen's sympathetic eyes were troubled.

"I loved the potential of what we could be together someday, but I'm not sure if I ever loved him."

"Maybe it can still happen."

"It might have worked if...if I hadn't gotten a glimpse of what love and passion can be."

"You mean Kilpatrick, don't you?"

"I suppose dad's been talking to you about this."

"It wasn't so much that, Danni. I saw you and that Australian together. There was something so strong between you two that you could almost touch it. I figured there was a chance this would happen. So," she concluded practically, "what are you going to do?"

"Try to forget him."

"Aren't you kidding yourself, Danni?"

"No! Ryan and I went around and around on this. Our lives are just too different."

Jen bit her lip, sensing her friend's desolation. "I hate to see you this way. You've got to pick up the pieces. Maybe it's not too late with Hal." She hesitated. "To tell you the truth, John's been more or less badgering him."

"What! This is none of his damn business."

"Your father seems to think Hal must be at least partly to blame for the breakup. He's been giving him advice, and believe it or not John even managed to talk him into getting up on White Lightning again." Jen's chuckle was nearly irresistible, but Danielle didn't feel much like laughing.

"Dad's nothing if not determined."

"Come on, Danni. You have to give Hal a little credit, too. He wants you back in the worst way." She stood up. "Well, enough of that. I understand you brought a young Iban woman back with you?"

Danielle told her briefly about Racha, and when she was done Jen asked jokingly, "Any chance she'd like to come to work for you after her surgery? It would save us placing an ad in the *Post*."

"I don't think so. Besides, how could you wish me on anyone?"

"You do have a reputation as a real slave driver," Jen was nearly to the door when she turned around again and said solemnly, "I hope you'll call your father, Danni. He's anxious to hear about your trip."

"I'd rather see him over the weekend in person. Foxhall's sort of neutral ground. We can talk better there."

Jen nodded. "He'd like that."

"Oh, by the way, Jen, do you know if he's still planning to turn Foxhall over to the National Trust, now that you two are going to be married?"

"Yes, he is, Danni. We discussed it quite a bit, and we're planning to build something smaller. He thinks if you do marry Hal, your life-style will keep you in the city or overseas, anyway."

"When's the big day?"

"Three weeks from Saturday. We've decided to be married in the garden at Foxhall. A private ceremony—just my parents and you." Jen smiled almost shyly. "Would you like to be my maid of honor?"

"Thanks, but I have a feeling I'll be giving the groom away."

Jen chortled with delight. "He'll be honored."

DANIELLE WORKED through the rest of the day without a break. After reviewing her trip diary and research notes and thinking long and hard about Ryan's logging operation, she wrote up a tersely worded recommendation that he be granted the loan. She had come to believe in Ryan deeply, but the realization only made their separation all the more difficult to take.

Uncharacteristically, Danielle left the office early. She was anxious to get home to see how Racha was getting on. Letting herself into the town house, she found her guest bundled up in Danielle's fluffy white bathrobe. The heat in the apartment was turned up to at least eighty.

"Are you sure you feel like going out to dinner?" Danielle asked.

"Of course. We must celebrate my first night in Washington, do you not think so?"

"Yes, I think so. And I've got something very special in mind."

Racha marveled at the orderly, sane flow of traffic as they sped along the parkway down into Alexandria's Olde Town on the western shore of the Potomac. It was a blustery night, and Danielle had insisted on loaning the girl her hip-length sable jacket. Racha was still shivering a little, though.

Danielle's surprise was a dinner cruise up the Potomac, during which they dined on shrimp pilaf, while the city's most beautiful monuments loomed before them. Racha exclaimed over the pristine, needlelike profile of the Washington Monument, saying it reminded her of the minarets in Kuala Lumpur, and she nodded with pleasure at the pure classical dome of the Jefferson Memorial.

"It is good to know that other countries can create such harmony in their works," she observed with quiet satisfaction. "Before I thought it existed only in the mountains and rivers of Sarawak."

The two women sat up late that evening, talking. First thing Tuesday morning Danielle drove Racha over to the university medical center.

Dr. Amstel was a pleasant if intense-looking man of about John Davis's age. After the women sat down he launched into a clear and unemotional discussion of the various possible diagnoses for Racha's condition, and of the risks involved in surgery.

"Of course, I'm only speaking in generalities right now. We'll be able to discuss the specifics once Miss Sabatin's had a detailed physical examination and our usual battery of diagnostic tests. Do either of you have any questions at this point?"

"Yes, we do, Dr. Amstel," Danielle replied, looking to Racha for corroboration. "Will you want to admit her today? And if so, how long will the exam and all those tests you mentioned take?"

"A couple of days." He looked at Racha then. "If everything goes according to schedule, Miss Sabatin, and we find you a suitable candidate for surgery, you can be operated on by the first of the week."

Racha nodded, and Danielle suggested briskly, "Fine, then, I'd like to bring her home those free days in between. There's a lot we want to see and do."

"I wouldn't recommend it, Danielle. I'd prefer keeping an eye on the patient."

Encouraged by the reassuring squeeze Danielle

gave her hand, Racha spoke up. "I have survived twenty years, doctor. Do you think another three days will matter so much?"

"Besides," Danielle put in with a faint twinkle, "doesn't the patient's frame of mind count for something? Knowing Racha, she'd get bored and restless in a hospital room with all of Washington out there waiting to be explored."

"I see you have your father's persuasive knack," the surgeon conceded, his professional manner thawing a little. "All right, then, I'll agree to that if you promise to readmit her first thing Sunday morning."

"It's a deal, Dr. Amstel," Danielle said, standing up to shake his hand. "And I have to tell you again how deeply we appreciate what you're doing."

The man actually smiled. "It's nice to be able to do something for international goodwill. Miss Sabatin's a spunky young woman."

DANIELLE SPENT the rest of the morning at the office, though she found it hard to concentrate on work. She kept seeing Racha in the stark hospital bed, looking as small and lost as a child, her few personal possessions—a delicate gold watch and the sapphire ring from her brother on the bedside table—also looking a little lost and forlorn. Racha had tried to put on a brave, smiling face as Danielle left her. Yet Danielle sensed how frightened she was.

At ten-thirty Clay Perrin called Danielle into his office. Her boss was delighted with the precise, reasoned report she had submitted on the Kilpatrick

Forestry case; she was obviously her old self again.
Danielle wasn't so sure of that.

At noon she left the office, and after purchasing a
huge basket of anthurium and orchid blossoms at the
city's best florist's she hurried over to the hospital.
Racha's bed was empty. Somehow that empty bed,
with the slight indentation on the pillow, affected her
more deeply than leaving Racha alone that morning
had.

Danielle waited restlessly, going down to the gift
shop to buy a couple of glossy fashion magazines, a
selection of paperbacks, a teddy bear with an irresistible little face and anything else she could think of
that might appeal to Racha. When she returned upstairs the head nurse met her and explained that
Racha wouldn't be free for another two hours.

Danielle went back to the office, spent an hour re-
searching files in preparation for the next case Clay
had given her, opened the afternoon mail. One was a
letter inviting her to participate in an international
seminar the coming autumn in Paris, and the second
requested her presence as guest speaker at an International Monetary Fund luncheon two months away, to
discuss her role in safeguarding cultural heritage.

Ordinarily she would have fired off acceptances to
both events. Now she set them aside, not wanting to
commit herself that far into the future. She felt as
though her life were curiously in abeyance. The only
cultural heritage she wanted to safeguard was
Racha's—her right to live.

That afternoon Danielle had better luck when she

returned to the hospital. Racha was back in her room, not in bed but sitting in a chair in front of the window. The wistful expression on her face turned to one of delight when she saw Danielle.

"How's it going, Racha?"

"The tests have been much work. So far they have made me walk on a sidewalk and ride a bicycle, neither going anywhere. And they have taken X rays of my heart. But everyone is very kind."

Danielle smiled. "You're looking a little bored now."

"Oh, no. . . ."

Ignoring her denial, Danielle went on again, and unashamedly using her connections, wangled permission for Racha and her to visit the pediatric wards and other usually off-limits areas. Delighted by the prospect, Racha insisted on bringing the stuffed teddy bear as a present for the children.

Afterward the women went up to the hospital staff's rooftop patio overlooking the city. Danielle pointed out landmark after landmark to the smiling Racha, promising that they would see as many of them as they could.

True to his word, Dr. Amstel signed the patient-release forms on Wednesday morning, and Racha was free until Sunday. The surgeon wasn't in. He had left a message that surgery looked feasible and he would discuss the situation in more detail with her later.

Leaving Jen in charge of the office, Danielle enthusiastically took on the role of tour guide. She planned a day-long excursion that kept Racha off her feet and indoors as much as possible. They toured the White House and attended a matinee at Ford's Theater. On the drive home Racha dozed off. Concerned, Danielle asked if she wanted to forgo the evening's entertainment.

"No! You have promised me American basketball, and I would be disappointed if I did not see it."

So, after dining at Trader Vic's, they drove over to the Washington Coliseum to watch a fast-moving virtuoso performance by the Harlem Globetrotters.

"What did you think?" Danielle asked later as they walked back to the car.

"That you Americans have boundless energy," Racha said enviously.

"The Globetrotters have boundless energy," Danielle corrected with a smile. "I got exhausted just watching them."

Racha nodded solemnly. "I am glad you admit that, because I felt the same."

SATURDAY MORNING the women were up bright and early, dressed in cords and sweaters for their country excursion.

On the drive to Foxhall Danielle told story after story about the happy times she'd had there—Easter-egg hunts on the lawn, summer picnics with the Larkin kids, one old-fashioned Christmas when her mother had had the gardener decorate the house as it had been done in Civil War days, with Mountain

Farm laurel, long crowfoot vines, branches of magnolia and bunches of spice-scented berries.

She didn't tell Racha those few happy times had been sparsely scattered over twelve years. She didn't confide, as she had to Ryan, the emptiness she had sensed in her parents' marriage, the way her father had made her into a junior image of himself. She wanted to buffer her guest from the harshness of reality. Then she realized the unfairness of her attitude, because Racha was a woman, her equal and, more so with every day, her very dear friend. Still, she kept up the inane sparkly chatter, because Racha seemed to be enjoying it and because she was still unaccustomed to sharing her feelings.

As they turned into the curving drive Racha exclaimed over the giant English oaks, the branches forming a green canopy overhead. Danielle drove straight toward the stableyard.

Sam Larkin was out in front of the barn when they drove up. He greeted Danielle with a big grin, proceeded to tease her about falling off Lizzie B as if she'd never gone and fell into conversation with Racha as if he'd known the young Iban woman his whole life.

"Say, would you like to come over to see my place?" he asked Racha. "It's not as fancy as the Foxhall spread. It's more a cozy down-home farm— we've even got a few pigs and chickens."

"Sam," Danielle broke in laughingly, "Racha is no stranger to pigs and chickens. I'm the one who could use a few lessons in animal husbandry."

"I reckon you could, Danni," Sam shot back. "Any girl who'd help at foaling while she was wearing fancy cashmere can't be too smart."

Danielle pretended to be affronted. "Speaking of my goddaughter, where is she?"

Sam led the way around to the big hilly paddock, which caught the sun most of the day. Little Foxfire, her coat gleaming like garnets, came rushing down through the thick grass, tail and mane flying. Sam gave a low whistle, and she galloped toward them, gangly legs nearly flying out from under her. With an impatient whicker she nudged each of their hands in turn. Finally Sam came up with a couple of sugar cubes from deep inside his large khaki pockets.

"Oh, God, she's beautiful, Sam!" Danielle exclaimed, leaning down to hug the animal. But Foxfire was too frisky and full of high spirits to stand for that. She took off again at a skittish canter that made them all laugh.

Danielle stared after her longingly, remembering with wonder that this sturdy filly had only been a frail little armful a few months ago. Never had she felt so attached to something in her life. Her emotional life was growing richer and more complex day by day, but allowing herself to feel frightened her, too, because the more she loved the more she risked losing.

Sam interrupted her train of thought. "You know, Danni, you should take over this place after your dad gives it up."

"Not me, Sam." She shook her head wistfully. "I'm a city girl, remember?"

"Well, it sure looks like the outdoors and Malaysia agreed with you. Don't let Cora see that tan of yours. She'll be jealous for sure."

A clatter of hooves on the gravel path caused them to turn just as John Davis rode into the yard on Palanquin, the sturdy gray Hanoverian he'd paid a small fortune for in Germany some years back. Danielle watched as he swung out of the saddle and began to walk the stallion to cool him down.

"Want me to do that for you, John?" Sam called over to him.

"No, thanks, Sam! I know Cora's waiting breakfast for you."

"Well, ladies, it's been real nice. I guess I'll see you later."

"Mr. Larkin," Racha spoke up suddenly. "If you were serious about my visiting your pigs and chickens, I would truly like to see them. I am a little homesick for my village, and perhaps...."

" 'Nough said, Racha."

"Sam," Danielle interposed, "you might want to take Racha up to your place in dad's pickup. He won't mind."

He took the hint immediately. In contrast to his own strength and vitality, the small Iban woman looked as wispy as thistledown. A quarter-mile hike uphill would be too much for her. "I'll do that, Danni. See you later."

She nodded, staring after them as Sam put a fatherly arm around Racha's shoulders and asked heartily, "You ever eaten flapjacks and syrup? No? Then you're in for a real treat."

After they left Danielle went to join her father. "Hello, dad."

"Welcome home, Danni."

"Thank you," she said a trifle formally, falling into step beside him as he and Palanquin made their circuit around the yard. "It's good to be back."

"I'm relieved to hear that."

The implication irritated her. She didn't say anything more.

Davis broke the silence. "Well, how did it go? Did you give our friend Kilpatrick what he wanted?"

She ignored the double-edged thrust of the question. "He runs a clean operation in Akan. He's sensitive to the people and to their territorial grounds. I've given his company the okay."

"Are you speaking as an ICCI department head, or as a woman?"

"Clay Perrin was satisfied with my report." She was bristling. "Old Danni's back on the job."

"I'm sorry, Danni. I suppose I have no right to cross-examine you. Come on and help me unsaddle this guy and get him brushed down. Then we can go up to the house and really talk."

Although Danielle nodded, she couldn't help wondering if it wasn't a little late in their relationship for them to "really talk." Or was he referring to another of their usual logic-and-strategy sessions, a discussion of how she could most efficiently pick up the pieces of a life he believed she'd been on the verge of throwing away?

Later they faced each other before the library fire, sipping the Irish coffee Davis prided himself on making so well. His air was once again formal when he announced that he and Jen planned to be married. "All I ask, Danni," he went on, "is that you accept Jennifer as a friend and as a member of this family. I know she'll bring some much-needed warmth into our lives."

Danielle took that as a slap in the face, as if she'd been the aloof one down through the years. She snapped back, "Yes, it's too bad you didn't meet her twenty years earlier."

John Davis flushed. "You've made your point, Danni," he said quietly. "If there's been any lack of closeness between us, it's been my fault. I haven't been a perfect father—I'll be the first to admit that. Maybe if I'd had a son I wouldn't have been so hard on you. Call that patriarchal, if you will, but more than anything I wanted you to share my principles and ideals, I wanted you to make your mark in the world." He wasn't looking at her as he said that. His eyes were fixed on the flickering fire in the grate. "I raised you to be independent and strong, Danni, and I thought you'd be grateful for that much."

"Oh, dad! I am grateful. You've given me lessons. You've given me ideals. I just wish...." Hesitantly she touched his arm. "I just wish you'd given me more of yourself."

He bowed his head. "We're too much alike, you and I. I never saw how you must have needed that."

Both of them looked into the bright cheerful flames. "Oh, how I used to envy my friends, with their fathers who'd bring them teddy bears on their birthdays and cuddle and read them fairy tales at night. I was damned if I was going to let anyone know that, though. My pride was just too strong."

"I suppose it's a little late to become more fatherly now?"

His ruefulness touched her. "Maybe not, dad. We can at least talk about it now. Besides, you and Jen will have children. She wants them, I think, and maybe you'll take time to do things differently."

"Danni, I can't tell you how she's transformed me, the joy I feel when we're together. Jennifer's made me feel young again."

"You're lucky, then, because at the moment I'm feeling the opposite—a little too sophisticated, a little too wise, a little too clever for my own good."

"Is that why you're so taken with that child Racha?" he asked, newly perceptive.

"Mmm, I suppose you're right. The past few days it's as though I've been seeing Washington with fresh eyes. I've enjoyed it as much as Racha has."

Father and daughter drifted into silence once more. Feeling a little awkward after their unusually revealing conversation, Danielle turned away. "Well, I really should be going—"

"Wait, Danni. There's one other thing I wanted to discuss with you."

She met his gaze levelly. "I think I know what it is, and I really don't want to talk about it."

"For heaven's sake, have you at least had the courtesy to phone Hal and let him know you're back?"

"No."

"What are you waiting for?"

"I have no idea what to say to him."

"I'm certain he'll be willing to forgive your little fling."

Danielle's lips tightened; she couldn't help wondering how much Jen had passed on of their conversation. "It was not a 'little fling,'" she answered proudly. "Ryan's asked me to go back with him to Malaysia."

"Nonsense! I didn't raise you just to see you throw your life and career down the drain."

"I'm in love with him."

The flat statement startled her as much as it did her father. Perhaps it was Davis's dispassionate appraisal of her that had sparked the admission.

Davis recovered first. "At this stage of your life you can't afford the luxury of falling in love." His blue eyes assessed her. "Tell me, Danni, have you once stopped to consider what this Kilpatrick has to offer compared to what Hal can give you?"

Danielle's answering smile was ironic. "What is it Hal has to offer me, dad? I'm curious."

"Don't patronize me, Danni. You know damned well what; we went through this discussion two years ago, before we decided you'd accept his proposal. The man's offering you a partnership in his future. You share the same friends. Together you'll build up a network of allies and connections. He's a good man."

Despite the warmth of the room Danielle shivered. "I know he is, dad. But sometimes I've tried to picture us twenty years from now, and I get scared. I see a narrow track running on a straight line into the future. There are no surprises, no highs or lows. There's no misery, but no ecstasy, either.''

"Your joys will come out of your devotion to your career, your husband, your children.''

"How can you stand there and say that, when a minute ago you were telling me what Jen's given you! You're being hypocritical.''

"That's not it at all, Danni. I'll tell you what I'm really afraid of. I think you're using Kilpatrick to punish me and Hal both. Kilpatrick's given you an emotional anchor to hang on to, but how deep do your feelings go?''

"I feel closer to Ryan than I've ever felt to anyone else.''

"Maybe that's because you're two of a kind. I've met him, don't forget, and I know a little of his background. He's tough-minded, a loner, secure in and of himself. If he asked you to stay, why aren't you there with him now instead of here?''

"I don't know!''

"I'll tell you why. Because you have to prove you're tougher than he is. Any sign of weakness in him, and you'll be gone. You're in love with what Kilpatrick stands for. He's something you can't ever really possess. Danni, you're the type who has to keep winning. You have to have control. If you lose that you'll lose everything. That's the kind of woman you are.''

His words chilled her. She shook her head, holding on tight to the memories of her and Ryan together.

But the cold logic of Davis's words threatened to overpower the truth of what she had become, with Ryan's help—an alive, warm, giving woman.

Abruptly she set her cup down. "Dad, I'm sorry, but I really have to go. Racha's waiting."

He nodded. "I'm sorry I got off on that tirade. Forgive me?"

"There's nothing to forgive. Maybe you do know me better than I know myself."

"For God's sake, Danni, more than anything I want to know you better. I still don't really understand why you're rejecting Hal."

"I don't love him. I never have."

He sighed. "Maybe you're right. Maybe I am a hypocrite, trying to tell you love isn't important, when my love for Jennifer has changed my life."

"You realize, dad, this whole argument is pointless. I'm going to end my involvement with Ryan."

"I won't believe that until I see you walking down the aisle with Hal."

"I've got to run, dad," she said, shaking her head ruefully. "Racha's waiting for me."

"Yes, I'd forgotten. What's the word from the surgeon?"

"I'm meeting Dr. Amstel tomorrow morning after Racha's been readmitted."

"Let me know what happens."

"You're really interested?"

"Danni, I may have difficulty showing it, but whatever is important to you is important to me, too. I. . .I care."

Realizing how hard it must have been for him to voice his feelings, on impulse Danielle reached up and kissed him. "Thanks, dad."

He returned her embrace rather awkwardly, and then she was gone.

CHAPTER THIRTEEN

DANIELLE KNEW she would always look back on that week with Racha as a warm, precious time. Danielle had found innocence, a sense of wonderment about a world she had taken for granted. She had found a sister as much as a friend, and in a way she had become a child again—giggling over late-evening cups of hot cocoa; sitting cross-legged together on the bed in their nightgowns, leafing through old photograph albums. Only the present and the past existed for them. By implicit agreement neither broached the subject of the future or what it might mean for them.

Sunday morning outside the hospital room, the two women hugged tightly, taking sustenance from each other. At the nurses' station Danielle turned and waved one more time, smiling at Racha in her stylish jeans and the borrowed fur jacket that lent a high-fashion elegance to her fragility. Then Danielle took the elevator to the surgeon's office. Her thin boot heels tapped out a lonely echo past the silent wards.

Dr. Amstel looked drawn and a little tired when he raised his eyes from the stack of X-ray film on his desk.

"Sit down please, Danielle. We've got a problem."

Her whole body went tense. "What is it?"

"I'm afraid we've seriously underestimated the problem. Here, let me show you." He switched on the light board behind his desk, put up one of the films and gestured for her to come join him. "The last diagnostic we did on Miss Sabatin was a cardiac angiogram. We put a catheter into one of the arteries and injected a liquid contrast. You can see it here." Using his pen as a pointer, he traced the pear-shaped outline of Racha's heart on the X-ray film. "With contrast, the blood appears as this white stream we can follow visually through the various heart chambers."

Danielle bent closer to examine the film. "I'm not certain what you're trying to show me."

"I'm saying that what's involved here is far more than just a faulty valve. The septum itself, the wall that divides the chambers of the heart, has complex defects in it. A normal valve allows the blood to flow in only one direction, but in this case the blood is washing back across. The valve doesn't shut as it should." Dr. Amstel swiveled, selecting another film from the stack on his desk. "Here you can see the blood flowing through the incomplete septum, as well. With the blood mixing in the chambers and washing back across the valve, the heart simply cannot act as an efficient pump."

"That...that hole in the heart wall is hard to repair?"

The surgeon let out his breath in a long frustrated sigh. "In a patient Miss Sabatin's age it's very risky. In this country we treat congenital defects like this when the patients are still infants."

Danielle went back around the desk and sat down, her mouth grimly set. "You mean there's a chance Racha could die on the operating table tomorrow?"

"I won't mince words, Danielle. The chances are two to one she *will* die."

"Dear God," she whispered. "What do we do next, Dr. Amstel? Do you recommend we cancel surgery?"

"That's not my decision. It's hers. You'll have to advise her."

"For pity's sake, you're the surgeon! Can't you give me some guidance?"

He shrugged. "What can I say, Danielle? It's a difficult decision. Miss Sabatin is weak. Without surgery her chances of living even another four or five years aren't good. She'll get weaker and eventually be confined to absolute bed rest. It's not a pretty future for such a young woman."

Danielle's lips were trembling, but she fought for control. "Dr. Amstel," she pressed, "if Racha were your daughter, what would you do?"

He set down the pen he'd been absentmindedly toying with and met her gaze directly. "I'm a surgeon, Danielle. I live by the knive. If she were my wife or daughter or sister, I'd want to feel I had taken every possible step—however tremendous the risk—

to give her her life back. And not an invalid's life, either.''

Danielle nodded. ''Thank you, doctor. I'm...I'm sorry I snapped at you before.''

''Never mind. It's good for us surgeons to be confronted every so often. Unfortunately, sometimes we forget we're dealing with a human life rather than an abstract medical question.'' When he looked up again, Danielle saw the compassion in his eyes. ''Discuss this with her, Danielle. Come back and let me know what she's decided. All right?''

She nodded.

Outside in the empty corridor, Danielle leaned against the wall for support. She pushed her hands deep into the pocket of her raincoat, and her fingers closed around the telegram she had received that morning from Ryan. The five simple words were a talisman she clung to: ''I'll be there Sunday night.''

''Hurry, Ryan, please. I need you.'' The whispered words were a prayer, helping to hold back the tears of fear and frustration. Slowly she went back downstairs to Racha.

Gray light streamed in through the window, washing out some of the cheeriness the yellow walls and bedspread gave to the luxurious private room. A television host was enthusiastically describing a trek through the Himalayas, but Racha wasn't watching him. Her eyes were fixed on her sapphire ring on the bedside table.

Danielle hated to see her this way. Gone were the stylish fashions that had made Racha seem a sophisticated woman of the world. In the plain white hospital gown that was a little too big for her, she looked lost and forlorn.

Danielle forced herself to smile as she sat down beside her. "Are you all settled in?" Gently she stroked Racha's arm, noticing the goose bumps. "Still cold?"

"Just a little." Racha searched her friend's eyes. "What did the doctor say?"

Danielle looked away. "He wants me to talk to you about the surgery."

"Do not shield me, please. Ryan may treat me like a child, but I cannot let you try to do the same," Racha chastised her softly. "I want to hear...how is it you say—I want to hear it straight."

Taking a deep breath, Danielle nodded. Painstakingly she explained the cardiac angiogram and what the procedure had revealed. She described how Racha's heart looked on the X-ray film and exactly what the defect in the heart wall meant. She told her friend how risky the surgery would now be and what the future would probably hold if she elected not to have it.

Racha took it all in with a grave expression, but when she spoke her soft voice was surprisingly firm and strong. "Thank you for telling me the truth."

"I'm afraid for you," Danielle confessed, anguished. "I feel responsible."

Racha stilled Danielle's trembling hand, covering it with her own. Their fingers entwined tightly. "The decision to come here was mine alone. I am willing to take this risk because I want a fuller life. Right now I feel I am a shadow. With the surgery maybe I will die. But maybe, too, I will be a whole woman. I will live all of today with that hope." She smiled into her friend's eyes. "You are the one person who gave me that hope. I·think you are the only one who truly understands how very much I want this chance."

"But the terrible risks. . . ."

"I am willing."

Danielle bent her head and brushed her forehead against their twined fingers, hoping to absorb a little of Racha's serene strength, though she knew it should have been the other way around. Perhaps with friends it didn't matter. Who gave and who took was irrelevant because the burden was equally shared. She lifted her head and smiled tremulously, her own burden somewhat eased. "If you are willing, Racha, that's all that matters. I'll give Dr. Amstel your decision."

Racha nodded. "And will you ask him if I, too, may look at the pictures of my heart?"

"Of course!" As she stood up Danielle berated herself for not having thought of that on her own. She remembered how avidly Racha had poured over that old *Science* article in the Akan longhouse. How long ago that seemed.

A young nurse came in. "I'm afraid you'll have to leave now."

"I was just on my way. Tell me, do you think we can have the heat turned up in this room?"

"It's centrally controlled."

"Then we'll have to have a portable heater brought in."

"I'm sorry, but hospital rules don't allow that. I'll have to ask Dr.—"

Danielle overrode her. "Never mind. I'll take care of these things myself."

She leaned down to brush her lips one last time against Racha's forehead, squeezed her hand encouragingly and went out with a brisk step, determined to get the heater and the X rays Racha wanted to see. Danielle was relieved to have something positive to accomplish. She badly needed that bit of control, however illusory it was, when everything else seemed to be slipping away from her.

THE REST OF THAT DAY she sat by the phone in her town house, waiting for Ryan's call from the airport. It never came.

Danielle forced herself to eat a cup of canned soup and a few crackers at dinnertime, even though she wasn't in the least hungry. Then she drove through the rain to the hospital in time for evening visiting hours.

When Danielle came into the room, Racha looked expectantly past her shoulder. "Ryan?"

"He's been delayed, but he'll be here tomorrow morning before they take you into surgery. I promise," Danielle said calmly, hoping her own disappointment wasn't as pathetically obvious as Racha's was. "Well," she went on, stooping down to rub her hands in front of the efficient quartz heater radiating warmth throughout the room. "This is nice, isn't it? Are you warm enough now?"

"I am fine, Danielle," Racha answered gravely. "You may stop fussing like a mother hen."

Danielle bit her lip. "Was I?" She came to sit on the edge of the bed, and the two of them clasped hands. A gust of wind splattered rain against the window, breaking up the light from a neighboring building into a thousand prismlike droplets.

Danielle stared out into the night. "Did Ryan ever tell you the story of the time he was determined to save a stray lamb and got caught in a rainstorm? He's a very caring man."

Racha nodded and smiled. "But he was not always that way. Did he ever tell you about when he was a newcomer to his grandmother's farm and afraid of her, and he did not want to go out to take care of the animals? He would hide in the closet behind the clothes."

"You're kidding! Did he say whether his old granny took the strap to him when she found out?"

Racha laughed. "I do not know."

"Well, I know his gran pushed him the way my father pushed me, let me tell you." And with a smile Danielle launched into tales of her past, comparing them to the few stories Ryan had told her of his boyhood. Since he couldn't be there, she would take his place as best she could. Racha smiled and nodded at each story, invariably coming back with one of her own about Ryan. That evening he became another deep, shared bond between the two women, bringing them even closer.

Visiting hours were nearly over when Racha asked with sudden shyness, "Will you marry him, Danielle?"

"He hasn't asked me to."

"Ryan wants you with him there in Malaysia. Why wouldn't he want you to marry him?"

Danielle picked nervously at the bits of fluff on the gold blanket. "Perhaps he's wary," she replied, choosing each word with care. "Perhaps he wants to leave himself the option of a graceful exit if it looks like things aren't going to work out."

"I will have a talk with him, then," Racha said, her eyes bright, her expression adamant. "How can he expect things to work out if he will not offer himself fully? If he truly loves you, he would be foolish not to risk everything for that."

"It's not just him," Danielle confessed. "I'm not willing to take the risk, either."

"Then what is life for?"

Danielle had no answer to that, and they were both silent.

The same nurse who had asked Danielle to leave that morning now popped her head in and switched off the overhead light, leaving only the bedside lamp burning. "I'm sorry, but visiting hours are over."

Danielle turned back to smile at Racha. "Well, it looks like I'm getting kicked out again."

Racha sat up hurriedly to open the drawer by her bed. "I was going to wait to discuss this with Ryan. But since he is not here I will tell you." She lifted out the delicate gold watch. "If I die tomorrow—"

"Don't say that, Racha! Don't even think it."

"If I die tomorrow," the Iban woman went on with sweet stubbornness, "I want my sister, Marie, to be given this. She has been envious of my having it ever since Ryan gave it to me." One dimple flashed briefly, and then she grew serious again. "Second, Danielle, I wish for you to have the sapphire ring my brother gave me."

"I've got a better idea," Danielle replied softly. "You and I will make a wish on it together. Let's wish that we are friends until we are both old and gray. And when I'm eighty I'll come to visit you. We'll go up to Akan. We'll sit together at the top of the longhouse ladder. And when we look up at the evening star we'll wish that our grandchildren have as full and rich a life as ours have been."

For the first time tears sparkled in Racha's eyes. She could not speak. Reaching out, she clung fiercely to Danielle.

"Now sleep well, Racha," Danielle whispered with a catch in her throat. "You have to be rested for tomorrow. I'll bring Ryan. I promise."

Satisfied, Racha lay down, her eyes following Danielle out into the lighted corridor.

Quickly Danielle went into a telephone booth in the hospital reception area and gave the operator her credit-card number. "I'd like to place an overseas call to Malaysia...no, I don't mind. I'll wait."

As the minutes ticked away Danielle thought with growing misgiving of the brash promise she'd made to Racha. *Damn it, Ryan. Where are you!* Didn't he understand how much both women needed him now?

Her head snapped up when a brassy female voice crackled over the line. "Kilpatrick Forestry. State your business, please."

"Hello. I'd like to speak to Mr. Kilpatrick. This is Danielle Davis calling."

"You're too late, ducks. He's left town."

"Good. He's on his way to Washington, then?"

"Crikey! All he mentioned to me was something about an emergency up at camp."

"You're certain of that?"

"Miss, all I was hired to do was answer the telephone for a few weeks."

"May I speak to Harry Diamond, then?"

"He went with Kilpatrick."

"I see. Will you please tell Ryan I phoned?"

"Right-o, ducks."

The receiver crashed down summarily, and Danielle was left with a rather uncharitable image of a frowsy blonde making an absolute mess of things at the same front desk where Danielle had first met the gentle, efficient Racha.

Outside the hospital Danielle stood at the curb, buttoning her coat up around her throat. It had stopped raining. A few stars winked through the jagged frieze of storm clouds, pale against the city lights.

She looked up at the forboding sky, wondering where to go. After a week of laughter and shared confidences with Racha in her apartment, the place would be too unbearably lonely tonight. She knew she should go back to keep vigil by the phone, but the thought of waiting for it to ring held her back. Instead, she drove farther uptown to Hal's neighborhood.

For a long time she sat inside her parked car and stared up at the high-rise building where he lived, debating whether to go in. His lights were on. He was home. Danielle knew his weekly routine by heart, since it hadn't varied in the two and a half years since she'd known him. Sunday was Hal's day of rest. Her own life had been woven increasingly into that same unvarying pattern... until the unscheduled trip to Malaysia had changed everything.

But tonight, sitting alone in the dark inside the cold car, she remembered almost nostalgically the quiet backgammon sessions with him on Sunday evenings, the White Russian nightcaps they would sip companionably, before each went their separate ways the coming week. The placid relationship had suited Danielle just fine because she hadn't been asked to give too much. That life tempted her now, if for no other reason than because it could buffer her from all the upheavals she'd been prey to lately.

Hal opened the door in his bathrobe and slippers, a pipe between his teeth. He nearly dropped it when his mouth sagged in surprise. "Danni!"

"Hello, Hal. Aren't you going to invite me in?"

"Of course! Should I mix up a couple of our usual?" he asked, as if their weekly Sunday evening ritual had never been disturbed.

"Just black coffee, if you have it."

A few minutes later Hal brought a tray into the living room and sat down beside her on the sofa. "So," he began tentatively, "I take it you've finished with all that Malaysian business?"

The look Danielle gave him was full of irony. She had almost forgotten the allusions that passed for conversation between them. "Not quite, Hal. I've brought a young Iban woman back to Washington. She has a heart defect. A cardiac surgeon over at GWU is going to correct it."

"That was a nice gesture on your part," Hal said carefully.

"It's not a gesture, damn it! I really care about her."

Discomfitted by her emotional outburst, he took refuge in platitudes. "I'm sure everything will turn out for the best. It generally does."

Her eyes snapped at him impatiently, and out of the blue she asked, "Hal, were you ever sorry you were an only child?"

The question startled him. "Danni, what—"

"Were you?"

"No, why should I have been?" he answered with the air of someone humoring a crazy person. "They say an only child has a lot more advantages. Anyway, Danni, why are we talking about this? There are so many other important things we have to discuss."

She ignored that. "I never really missed having a brother or sister, either, until Racha showed me what it could have been like. We got so close this past week. I don't know how to describe it. She has such a poignant hunger for life.'' Danielle swirled the coffee in her cup, wishing she could talk about her own indefinable hungers.

But Hal, ever practical minded, shattered the mood. ''Your father thinks you're being a little foolish about this whole thing. Danni, you know if this girl dies your goodwill gesture is going to backfire in your face.''

'' 'Goodwill gesture'? Hal, aren't you listening to me! Racha's become a dear friend.''

''I'm sorry, Danni,'' he replied, not sounding overly apologetic, ''but you have to remember I haven't met her. You really can't expect me to understand.''

''No, I guess I can't.'' She stood up abruptly. ''I think I should be going, Hal. I have to be at the hospital early in the morning.''

''But we haven't even talked about anything yet.''

''Another time,'' she said wearily. ''I'm sure you've been managing your life fine without me the past few weeks.''

At the door Hal kissed her with his cool dry lips, a timid, questioning caress. ''No, I haven't. I've missed you. I'm glad you're home, Danni.''

''Are you?'' She smiled up at him ruefully. ''I was just thinking I don't know where home is anymore. Good night, Hal.''

She went out into the corridor, and he called after her, ''I'll phone you.''

She turned around. ''I'm not the same woman I was, Hal.''

"You'll be your old self again. John said so. Clay told you that, too, didn't he?"

"But you don't seem too sure, Hal."

"Danni...."

"Good night, Hal."

She got into the elevator, afraid to look back.

CHAPTER FOURTEEN

HER MUSCLES WERE stiff and cold after a night of sleeping curled up on the sofa, the telephone cradled beside her. Clear morning light poured through the uncurtained bay window. Danielle looked at her watch: only five-thirty, still two and a half hours until Racha would be wheeled into surgery. Shaking off her exhaustion, she went over to the window.

The cloudless sky cheered her; with the passing of the storm her optimism returned. She had brought Racha to one of the best physicians in the country, and Dr. Amstel's surgical ability would surmount the odds against her. Racha would survive because she had everything to live for, Danielle convinced herself. Ryan's absence still hurt, but she dismissed that, too. She would wing this crisis alone.

Danielle hurried upstairs to shower and change into fresh clothes. She almost put on a straight black skirt but decided it was too somber. Rummaging deep in the closet, she found a soft cherry wool sweater dress she'd never worn. An aunt had sent it to her a few Christmases before. It suited her mood that morning, and she was determined her confidence would spill over onto Racha.

At the hospital she met Dr. Amstel outside Racha's room. His unruffled, slightly detached manner bolstered Danielle considerably. Here was a kindred professional, able to put emotions aside and get down to the business at hand. That attitude was one she not only understood but lived by.

"How's she doing, doctor?"

"The nurses are prepping her now, and we've administered a mild sedative. But she's still alert. You'll be able to go in and see her soon."

"Thank you."

"Any last-minute questions?"

"I don't think so."

"Good. I'll go scrub, then."

He started to walk away, but she called after him. "Dr. Amstel...." He turned around. "Thanks again."

This time his serene smile didn't quite still the butterflies in her stomach. She went over to the recessed window, trying to calm herself by watching the city gear up for a new day.

A few minutes later the sound of rushing footsteps caught her attention. She turned anxiously, and there was Ryan. His hair was tousled and his suit rumpled after twenty hours in a plane, but he had brought in with him the scent of the outdoors, so that the hospital atmosphere no longer seemed quite so sterile. Danielle longed to throw herself into his arms and let his strength take over, but she fought the impulse.

"Thank God you finally got here," she said quietly. "Racha's been asking for you. What happened?"

"I missed the flight I was booked on." For all his anxiety, Ryan managed a fleeting crooked smile. "I insisted Harry drive me to the airport in my Land Rover instead of in his wreck and—I know he's never going to let me forget this—we had a flat. I caught the next plane out to San Francisco. Then we were delayed because of fog." He shook his head, his lips compressed. "It was a hellish trip. The whole time I was going mad thinking of the two of you here alone."

"Your receptionist told me you'd gone up to Akan on an emergency."

"She got that wrong, like everything else she's done this past week. Did you really believe I'd abandon you like that? Didn't you realize I'd be busting my tail to get here?" His eyes flickered toward the closed door of Racha's room. "Can I see her?"

An apology for her lack of faith seemed pointless, especially when they had far more urgent matters to discuss. "We'll be able to see her in a minute. But... first there's something I have to tell you." Swiftly Danielle explained what Dr. Amstel had said, watching Ryan's expression grow grimmer as the implications sank in.

He leaned one shoulder against the wall. "I had no idea it was so bad."

"Listen to me, Ryan. This surgeon's one of the best. I'm very confident."

He stared at her tiredly. Somehow he hadn't expected this briskness. All that had held him together on the long trip was the thought of taking Danielle in his arms and holding her. But he was afraid she didn't want that. He was afraid the city had taken hold again.

Then he noticed her upswept hair falling here and there in untidy tendrils. And, oddly, he took heart from that detail. Somehow it gave him reason to hope he hadn't lost her.

"Danielle, is everything all right?" He reached up to brush a wisp of hair behind her ear. She turned her head toward his hand, the move as instinctual as a flower turning toward the sun. For an instant they stood in deep, touching connection, her lips drinking in the rough warmth of him. "Ryan," she whispered. "I'm so glad you're here."

The door opened briskly, forcing them both to step back, and the tender moment was lost in other concerns. A middle-aged woman in a white uniform came out, her eyes behind metal-framed eyeglasses as calm and detached as Dr. Amstel's had been.

"You may go in to see the patient, but only for a few minutes," she admonished them as if they were children. "Doctor wants to get started at eight on the dot."

Danielle came into the room first, then stepped to one side to let Ryan go on alone. She watched him brush the back of his hand gently down the girl's cheek, and when Racha opened her eyes to find him there, her smile was radiant. They spoke in undertones. Ryan must have said something to amuse her, because Racha laughed softly.

Drawn by the two of them, Danielle moved toward

the bed. Racha looked up. The sedative was taking effect, making her groggy. "You kept your promise," she whispered. "He came. Danielle, thank you. I—"

"Shh," Danielle whispered, leaning down to kiss her cheek. "We can talk later. We'll be right here waiting for you, Racha."

The bossy nurse reappeared with two orderlies and a gurney. "You'll have to leave. We're going to transfer the patient now."

Outside, Danielle headed for the nurses' station and, after getting the information she wanted, came back to Ryan. "They say surgery will take several hours. Would you like to go down to the cafeteria to get some breakfast?"

He nodded. "It'll help pass the time away."

Downstairs they sat opposite each other at one of the long formica tables, two cups of black coffee in front of them. They were oblivious to the bustle of hospital personnel grabbing a quick bite before starting their shifts.

In the harsh fluorescent light Ryan's face seemed curiously defenseless and boyish, despite the deep lines of exhaustion etched around his eyes and mouth. She glanced at his hands, dark and supple against the white cup, and she remembered how they had sat this way together in happier times, when their newfound closeness had been a powerful bond. Lifting her cup, she sipped the strong bitter coffee, aware of his eyes on her.

"Danielle, you look tired."

"I was expecting your call all night."

"I'm sorry."

"It doesn't matter. The important thing is you got to see Racha."

"She's a tough little bird."

"Aren't we all?"

He let that one pass. "Did she get to see much of the city?"

"Yes. We had a wonderful time together."

"Are you glad to be back?"

Her brow furrowed slightly, and she refused to answer him directly. "There were a few little surprises in store for me. Do you remember my secretary, Jen Bondi? She and my father have been dating, and he's asked her to marry him."

"You're disappointed?"

"I'm more surprised than anything. Jen's not much older than I am."

"Did you and your father talk about us at all?"

Danielle bit her lip. "He's warned me not to throw my life away."

"You're going to listen to him?"

"I don't know, Ryan. I'm so confused. Sometimes I think the only thing that matters in the world is to be with you. But then I feel I'm needed here, that I have a real contribution to make." She sighed, frustrated. "The problem is I feel like an exile in both places, a ship without an anchor."

"Maybe I'm the one who needs an anchor, Danielle. I've been drifting too long."

His admission touched her. She had been so afraid

he didn't need her. How achingly sweet it was to find out she was wrong. They had so much to talk about. But not now. Not with Racha lying upstairs. Danielle looked at him and subtly shook her head. He seemed to understand, because he shifted the conversation to more neutral ground.

"You should have seen Racha at the basketball game, Ryan—she was on the edge of her seat the whole time. To her the players were 'black giants.' She made me laugh when she said that if they were in Sarawak they'd be trees instead of men, they were so tall."

Ryan smiled. "What else did you do?"

Danielle gave him a lively account of their week, glad to have something upbeat to talk about. "I had to be careful not to push her too much. She never wanted to stop. She soaks up new experiences like a sponge."

"How about the zoo? Did you take her there?"

"No. I was afraid it would make her homesick."

"Is that supposed to mean you think Harry and I are a couple of baboons?" he teased her.

"Not at all. Harry's more like a penguin, don't you think? Pretty comical beneath that stiff formality of his."

He smiled faintly at the apt comparison. "And what about me?"

"You, Ryan?" she mused. "You're just yourself."

"That doesn't disappoint you?"

" 'Disappoint' me?" She smiled into his eyes and

reached across the table to touch his hands, marveling at their strength and sensitivity. "Ryan, you're so full of surprises, I don't know what to expect next. I don't really know you."

"That's because you haven't given yourself a chance to."

Gently she withdrew. "We'd better get back upstairs, don't you think? They might be needing us."

It was a mistake to have hurried. Three hours passed and then four, until the small waiting area began to feel like a prison. They both started when the door of the operating theater swung open and a surgical resident in his green scrubs strode out.

"Is it over?" Ryan asked him in a taut voice.

"Not yet."

"How's it going?"

"You'd better talk to Dr. Amstel." With that he walked away, leaving them alone again.

Ryan began to pace like a caged tiger, while Danielle sat motionless on the green vinyl couch, her hands clasped in her lap. Never had she felt so helpless, so completely at the mercy of someone else's skills to make things right again.

If they had allowed her inside, she would have been there in an instant. Even that illusion of control and participation would have been better than this waiting without knowing. Her eyes were fixed on the swinging doors, willing them to open.

After an eternity Dr. Amstel came out, and Danielle hurried over to him. The surgeon's face was drawn. "We ran into more problems," he said tiredly. "The damage was even worse than the angiogram showed. We've got her sewn up and off the bypass pump. Her heart's beating on its own...barely."

Ryan seemed to tower over the slump-shouldered physician. "Will she make it, doctor?"

"I wish I could answer that," he replied quietly. "We're transferring her to postop intensive care."

"May we come up?" Danielle asked.

"You had better."

Hearing his worried tone, Danielle went cold all over, and she wanted to shake the man. What had happened to his calm, scientific detachment? How could he look so weary and defeated?

In a grim haze Danielle got into the elevator with Ryan, not even aware of his supporting hand beneath her elbow. She was too locked into her own frozen world of helplessness, inwardly raging at the surgeon and at fate.

The intensive-care unit was a windowless room dominated by ultrasophisticated monitoring equipment. A dozen beds ringed the nurses' control center, each one partitioned from the others by drawn curtains. Within those white pleated walls the patients waged their battles for survival in privacy.

Racha lay pale and motionless in one of the beds, her connection to the world a tenuous filament of wires, tubes and intravenous needles. Danielle and Ryan sat down on opposite sides of her bed.

Across the stark expanse of sheets he sat immobile, elbows on his knees, forehead pressed to his clasped hands. Danielle felt so distant from him; she didn't know if his head was bowed in prayer or despair. But she was focusing on the electronic monitor beside the bed. A series of red lines blipped feebly across the screen, marking Racha's faint heartbeat and pulse.

To Danielle it was as if her own lifeblood were draining away and she were powerless to stop it. Suddenly one of the lines began to jump across the screen in a jagged seesaw. It went dead.

At the control hub a warning buzzer sounded, and a tense voice cried, "Cardiac arrest! Bed six! Cardiac arrest!"

Seconds later Danielle and Ryan were shunted out of the way by the team responding to the urgent code. Numbly she watched from the far corner of the room, spectator to a nightmare—this couldn't be real.

A doctor rushed to the bedside and, leaning forward over Racha, jammed the base of his palm against Racha's chest, putting the full force of his weight behind each compression. Simultaneously a nurse bent over the bloodless lips and began to breathe her own precious oxygen into the woman's lungs, while a second nurse thrust a needle into Racha's arm.

"Give her 2.5ccs of adrenaline and an ampule of bicarb," a voice commanded sharply.

The tension mounted until Danielle felt as if she were being squeezed by powerful talons. The team worked feverishly. Ten minutes elapsed, and twenty, and the team's efforts became more desperate with each passing second. Danielle's eyes were transfixed on the cardiac monitor.

Summoned on his beeper, Dr. Amstel had come on a run to his patient's bedside. After a glance at the flat line on the screen, he went into whispered consultation with his colleague. Then Danielle saw the surgeon shake his head and put his hand on the younger man's shoulder.

She knew it was over. She had read it in the doctor's eyes before he came slowly over to where she and Ryan stood, helplessly looking on. "I'm sorry," he murmured, his face drawn. "We did the best we could."

Unable to accept that, Danielle went over to the bed and touched Racha's still-warm hand. She was too numb to feel anything but utter bewilderment. She wasn't aware of the cardiac team silently walking away, or of Ryan beside her. There was nothing but a great void inside.

As if from a distance she heard him say her name, and she looked up into his eyes. She saw his tears of anguish, the pain of loss etched in his features, but she couldn't help him. Her own expression was frozen, revealing nothing. Without answering him, she turned and walked stiffly away.

Out in the corridor a toddler sat crying on his mother's knee; over by the water fountain a couple of student nurses stood talking and giggling. Danielle was grateful for this flow of life around her, because for a moment she could pretend to forget the nightmare.

Again the window was her refuge. She stared down at the busy hospital entrance. A cabdriver honked in irritation at a florist's van that had cut him off, while a woman in a wheelchair with a newborn in her arms was being wheeled out to a waiting car by her solicitous husband.

Danielle started when she felt a hand on her arm. Ryan cleared his throat. "Let's get out of here," he said hoarsely, his eyes red rimmed from crying. "I despise hospitals."

She nodded.

WARM SPRING SUNSHINE bathed the wooden deck outside Danielle's kitchen. She had made a fresh pot of coffee and sliced a few apples to serve with the cheese she'd brought out. Neither of them touched the food.

Ryan stood at the edge of the deck with his back to her. His shirt was rolled up over his forearms, and he had thrust his hands deep into his trouser pockets. Squirrels scampered between the broad-leafed poplars out on the grounds, but he wasn't seeing them.

In his mind he saw Racha as a sixteen-year old, painfully shy, yet bright and full of promise; he saw her bent over a book in the dim kerosene light at her parents' house, oblivious to the noise and bustle around her. He heard her laughter when she struggled over unfamiliar syllables in English, and he remembered her quiet sobs when the little parrot she had trained to ride on her shoulder was killed by a ferret slinking around the kampong.

God, how it hurt to think of her gone, to never

again see the smile that lit up her eyes. He swallowed hard and turned to Danielle, wishing she would come to comfort him. He wanted to hold and be held, to have her caress away the tension gathering, ready to explode at his temples, to have them ease each other's pain.

But she sat curled up in the redwood lounge chair, dark head bent over a notebook in her lap. "What are you doing, Danielle?"

"Making notes."

"Don't you ever stop?"

Her head jerked up. "Ryan, you have to admit I was right about one thing."

"What are you talking about?"

She got up and perched on the deck rail next to him. "Akan needs a health clinic—I'm convinced of that more than ever. Do you realize if the village had had one twenty years ago Racha might be alive and healthy now?"

"But Akan didn't. And she *isn't* alive now," he replied stonily.

"I intend to change things, Ryan. I have the whole agenda jotted down. We'll call it the Racha Sabatin Memorial Clinic. I know I can get the financing for it. I have a friend in fund-raising who'd be willing to spearhead a drive. We could build it adjacent to the field you're using as a helipad. It would be per—"

"Will you shut up? Will you stop just one bloody minute and listen to yourself?"

Her eyes widened. "What's wrong?"

"Will you have the decency to let me grieve for someone I happened to love deeply? Or can't you understand that?''

She flinched as if he'd slapped her. "We all grieve in our own way, Ryan. I loved her, too.''

"I thought you did. I was beginning to believe that.''

"What good would it do to cry and tear my hair?'' she countered. "She's gone.''

"Is that all you have to say? You act like you're talking about a contract that's been completed, or some deal that's fallen through. You act like you don't care bloody hell who Racha was, about the hole she's left in our—in my life.'' His eyes raked her. "Are you made of stone? Don't you feel anything?''

Still clutching the notebook, Danielle got up and strode to the far end of the deck. Like an animal who had come too close to a fire and been burned, she was shying away from the source of her pain. She had let Ryan and Racha get close to her. Now the girl was dead. Was that what loving meant?

"You have your nerve lecturing me about feelings—'' she turned back to Ryan "—never in my life have I felt the pain I feel now. Before I met you I never could have cared for Racha the way I did. I wouldn't have bothered to reach out. I wouldn't have tried to help her, and she'd still be alive now. That's what my caring has done.''

Ryan came close. "You know you're not to blame for that. It was her decision. Racha wanted a chance at life. You gave her something no one but you even knew she wanted. And she loved you, Danielle. She was thrilled to think you had let down your guard enough to be her friend. If you retreat into yourself, you'll be betraying her.''

"I can't betray Racha. She's dead,'' Danielle said in a tight, controlled voice.

"But I'm alive. And you're betraying me. You're so busy trying to tough it out and do something to make up for your loss that you're denying your emotions altogether. For God's sake, Danielle, don't cheat us both. Let's help each other get through this agony.''

"No! This is my cross to bear. It has nothing to do with you.'' She turned away from him, covering her face with her hands. Yet she couldn't blot out the sound of his voice.

"Danielle, it has everything to do with me. Racha may be gone, but we're both still here. What about our love?'' His hands closed gently around her shoulders. As she felt his touch and heard his voice, she understood the intensity of her love for him. Rather than bringing her joy, the realization brought her only fear. She loved Ryan more deeply than she had ever loved a man; she and Racha had begun to love each other as only two women friends could. Danielle never wanted to be that vulnerable, that deeply hurt again.

"I don't want to care about you, Ryan,'' she said, her back stiff. "I don't want you to be a part of me.'' Hidden beneath her denial was her deepest fear. *Because if I lost you, I couldn't bear it.*

Already crushed by the loss of Racha, Ryan heard only, "I don't want you." When he urged her to face him, she shrugged him off. "Danielle, you've left me nothing to say. Should I go?"

Clinging blindly to her composure, she refused to reply. Ryan's hands dropped from her shoulders, yet still he stood there, waiting.

The seconds ticked away emptily.

"Goodbye, then, Danielle," he said at last. "There's nothing left here. I'm going home."

She heard him walk away, heard the front door slam behind him as he let himself out.

"Dear God, what have I done?" What had her damnable control given her but emptiness?

Slowly she turned back to the silent house, more lonely than she had ever been in her life. She began to cry, dry heaving sobs that left her deepest sorrows bottled up inside.

CHAPTER FIFTEEN

IN THE WEEKS after Ryan left, Danielle kept herself feverishly busy. She reviewed cases, initiated projects and sat in on several high-level staff meetings with the ICCI board. Her free time was spent lobbying for the health clinic she wanted to set up in Akan. Talking about the village helped keep it and Ryan alive in her mind and left her no time to grieve. No one looking at her would ever have suspected her businesslike front hid a heart in turmoil.

She never got home before nine. Dinner was a simple salad and canned soup. By ten she would stumble into bed, too exhausted even to watch the nightly news.

Meanwhile, her secretary took charge of screening and interviewing applicants for her own job. Jen did it with a good-humored efficiency that made Danielle realize how much she would miss her after she was gone. Finally the selection was narrowed down to three women, and Danielle met with each of them for an hour.

In the end Danielle hired Irene Morris, an attractive fifty-year-old widow determined to reenter the work force. Although the woman's secretarial skills were a little rusty, both Danielle and Jen were impressed by her levelheadedness and brisk sense of purpose.

"Gosh, I'm glad that's over with," Jen said to Danielle after Irene had left. "Believe me, I was starting to worry about who we'd find to take care of you."

"Yes, I noticed that with all three choices you went for a blend of motherliness and efficiency."

"Every woman exec needs that, especially one who insists on overworking herself," Jen said smartly, her gaze resting on the shadows beneath her boss's eyes.

"Never mind me. You've got enough things on your mind."

"Danni, why don't we take an hour off for lunch?"

"I owe you that much, at least," Danielle agreed, trying to smile. "We'll make it my treat."

"That's a deal, and I know just the place. There's a darling open-air café near Dupont Circle. I bet you haven't seen the sun in days."

So they lunched at the quaint little place Jen had chosen. Dappled sunshine filtered through the chestnut trees and warm May air fluttered the pink linen napkins on their table, but Danielle barely took notice of the lovely afternoon. She was remembering other afternoons she had spent with Racha, sightseeing and just talking together. All those simple joys had died with the girl.

Jen kept darting concerned looks across the table, and as soon as the waiter had brought their check she said, "I guess we'd better get back."

Danielle made an effort to shake off her gloomy mood. It wasn't fair to cloud Jen's happiness. "Not just yet. I'd like to buy you a trousseau present. There's a nice boutique around the corner."

"Oh, Danni, how thoughtful. You don't have to do this."

"I know. I want to."

After lunch they spent an hour browsing through the drifts of silk and lace in the luxurious little shop. Finally Jen chose a filmy, ice-blue teddy imported from France, edged with Valenciennes lace.

"I have the 'something borrowed' and 'something new,'" Jen said to Danielle with a twinkle as the saleswoman wrapped their purchase. "So this 'something blue' is just what I needed."

Impulsively she threw her arms around her boss's neck, hugging her. When Danielle didn't respond, the sparkle went out of Jen's eyes. "What is it, Danni?"

"I'm sorry. You just took me by surprise. I am happy for you, you know that."

"Then please don't drive me away."

Danielle nodded, blinking and staring at the ceiling, her throat beginning to burn with tears.

The saleswoman handed her the package, and she and Jen walked out. "Danni, we really should get back now," her friend said awkwardly. "I want to have the office all shipshape for your new secretary."

"No, take the rest of the afternoon off, Jen. I know you have a million things to do. I'll manage."

Jen brightened at once. "Thanks. Thanks again

for everything.... But Danni, are you sure you're okay?"

"Of course," Danielle replied briskly. "I just need to get back to work, is all." Jen nodded, waved and went on her way.

Back at the office, Danielle ran into Clay Perrin in the elevator. "Hi. Back from lunch?" he greeted her.

"Yes, I took Jen out. This is her last week, you know."

"I'd almost forgotten. When's the wedding?" he asked almost wistfully.

"Saturday."

"I think your father's one lucky man, Danni. I just wish I'd seen Jen first myself."

"Clay, Jen's been right under your nose for two years."

"Yes, well, I guess I never took the time to notice. Too busy."

The elevator stopped at Danielle's floor, and she got out. Before it closed again, she took in Clay's slightly rumpled air, the expanding waistline and receding hairline, the tired eyes that hinted at life passing him by. There had been a thread of loneliness running through his conversation. Once she used to think Clay and her father were two of a kind. Now she began to wonder uneasily if she hadn't been wrong; maybe it was she and Clay who were alike.

Walking to her office, Danielle had the sensation of looking at herself on a movie screen. Her emotional distance was precisely what had driven Ryan away. Never had she felt so cold and cut off from everything that mattered to her. But still she was unable to confront her feelings over Racha's death; they were frozen deep inside.

SATURDAY DAWNED warm and breezy at Foxhall, a sparkly morning full of the promise of summer. But the house itself had an autumnal air, as if the rooms knew they would soon be shuttered and lifeless.

Danielle sat up in the old Jenny Lind bed she had slept in as a child and looked around the room. Dust sheets had been spread over most of the furnishings. The night before, in the dark, she had tripped over a pile of boxes left beside the door.

The movers her father had hired started with the upper floors so that the rooms below would be left as is until after the wedding. Even so, Danielle had seen the sad transformation downstairs, too.

Late Friday evening she, her father and Jen had drunk a lighthearted toast in the library. Although a fire had crackled cheerily in the grate and the indented leather wing chair was as cozy as ever when Danielle curled up in it, the room wasn't the same. Some of the Davis Civil War memorabilia had been packed away, and there were lighter patches on the walls where her father's favorite photographs and antique English hunting prints had hung.

Danielle had felt as she had when Racha was dying: that she was losing a part of herself and was unable to stop it from happening.

Now with the morning sunlight pouring into her beloved old bedroom, she felt no differently. She was about to get up when she heard a faint knock at the door. Hurrying to open it, she found Jen smiling at her.

"Good morning, Danni," she whispered. "Do you think you could give me a hand? I'm so nervous I'm all thumbs, but I still have to put a few snaps in my going-away outfit."

"Of course, Jen. I'm not too great with needle and thread, but I'll try."

Like a child on Christmas morning, full of secrets and surprises, Jen led the way back to her room. The window had been thrown wide open to the day, and her crocheted wedding dress festooned the closet door like an ivory garland. The pale lacy teddy Danielle had bought her lay carelessly across a dresser top, while a brand-new suitcase sat open on the neatly made bed.

On the bedside table stood a crystal vase of long-stemmed roses, the delicate buds partly unfurled, a card beside them. As Jen chattered on happily, Danielle glanced down at the message. "To my darling Jennifer. May our love blossom forever. Your adoring John."

Danielle's eyes veered away from the private words, sweeping the room again—the whole atmosphere was joyous. If there had been dustcovers here, Jen must have folded them away. Danielle watched her pull out an emerald-green, surplice-bodiced dress from the closet and laughingly hold it up in front of her.

"What do you think, Danni? Will John like it? Green's his favorite color."

"Is it? I didn't know."

Jen must have sensed the other woman's pain, because she sat on the edge of the bed and gently pulled Danielle down beside her, her dark eyes questioning and full of concern. "What is it, Danni? Did I say something wrong?"

Danielle sighed. "Not really. I guess I'm just regretting the past a little bit. I couldn't help thinking about Racha, too. That week before she died, we spent it together this way—like a couple of sisters."

Jen's emotions were always close to the surface, and now tears welled up in her eyes. "Oh, Danni, I'm so sorry. I didn't realize you'd grown that close to her. I hope. . . I hope you and I can be that close."

Danielle nodded stiffly. Jen started to say something else, but Danielle didn't give her a chance. "I hope so, too, Jen. Now just get me that needle and thread, and I'll see what I can do with these snaps."

While Jen finished packing she cast occasional worried looks down at Danielle, whose head was bent in concentration over her sewing. "Danni," she asked finally. "You don't resent me, do you?"

Danielle's head came up. "Jen, no! Not anymore. I'm just envying you like crazy. Your happiness is making this whole house come alive. You're a very lucky woman."

Jen dropped the blouse she'd been folding and sat down beside her once more. "Danni, it's not just luck. I've told you this before. I knew what I wanted, and I went after it. I'd had a crush on John ever since he stopped by the office last winter, so when you invited me out to Foxhall, believe me, I jumped at the chance. As soon as I talked with him, I knew I could love him. There was no question in my mind. I wasn't interested in any flirting games or playing hard to get. I made it clear that when I was with him nothing else in the world mattered.''

"You make falling in love sound so simple. . .so inevitable.''

"Danni, I truly believe love comes along so rarely in a lifetime that you can't let it slip by. You can't let problems that circumstance throws in your way hold you back. If you really want something, for Pete's sake, it's worth going after. You have to be willing to fight for it, to give in a little if you have to.''

"The problem is, I don't know what I really want. As Racha would have said, my 'falldown' is that I want it all.'' Tears sparkled in her eyes as soon as she mentioned Racha's name, and Jen's arms went around her.

"Danni, I hate for John and me to leave you alone like this. Maybe we could postpone the honeymoon—''

"Jen Bondi, don't you even think it!'' Danielle stood up and laid the emerald dress in Jen's arms. "I'll be fine.''

Jen pursed her lips doubtfully, but she obviously knew better than to try to back her ex-boss into a corner. She nodded. "By the way, did John tell you he's invited Hal out for the wedding?''

"No, he didn't, but I should have guessed. Dad's invariably full of sly maneuvers.''

Jen rushed to her fiancé's defense. "John wants you to be happy, Danni. I know that's as important to him as anything else."

"Speaking of the groom," Danielle said wryly, "I think I'd better go and give him a few last words of advice."

That made Jen smile. "Go to him, Danni. He'll be thrilled. He does want to be closer to you."

After making a pot of coffee, Danielle visited her father in his room. He stood by the window in his navy velour bathrobe, his hands clasped behind his back.

"Good morning, dad. I made us some coffee."

"That was thoughtful of you, Danni."

She poured them each a cup and joined him by the window. Below, the formal gardens fell in neat terraces toward the pasture and woodlands beyond. Clipped box hedges formed a neat counterpoint to the riot of peonies, crocus, chrysanthemums and irises growing around the old pink Venetian wellhead. Beside it was a pergola entwined with climbing roses that would serve as the chapel. Danielle's gaze shifted to the upland pasture, where several of her father's horses stood in silhouette against the morning sky.

"Won't you miss all this, dad?"

"No, it's time for me to move on. I'm afraid of getting stagnant in my old age."

"I'm feeling just the opposite. I'd like to dig in right here and put down some roots."

Davis turned to look at his daughter. "I've invited

Hal Adams out today, Danni." She nodded, and he went on, "Hal's the one who could give you your sense of belonging."

She looked away, weary of the old argument. "I wish Foxhall could stay in the family, dad."

"It's the past."

"I know, but we've always traveled around so much. This is the only home I've really known. Even my town house isn't much more than a place to sleep at night. I've never invested very much of myself in it." As she talked her eyes roved the hilly pastures, on the lookout for Foxfire. "And what's strange," she added, "is that I never realized how strongly I felt that way until I met Ryan Kilpatrick."

Then Danielle was telling him about the old willow-patterned dishes that had belonged to Ryan's grandmother, about the lace tablecloth in his bungalow up at the logging camp. "I guess what he did was to bring part of his past with him to Malaysia; he gave himself a sense of continuity. I like that."

Davis pointedly ignored her references to the Australian. "You know, I don't have to sign the final papers, Danni. Foxhall is still in the family. It's yours if you want it." Then he couldn't resist adding, "You and Hal could be happy here...."

Her lips curved unwillingly. "I just might take you up on the offer—without Hal as a condition, I hope. You're still a wily negotiator, aren't you, dad?"

His smile was conspiratorial. "Oh, I don't know about that. I think Jennifer is having a mellowing effect on me."

"You're going to be happy with her, I know."

John Davis cleared his throat. "It means a lot to me to hear you say that, Danni."

"Well. . . I suppose I'd better get out of here and let you get ready."

She was nearly to the door when he spoke again. "Danni, there's just one more thing I need to say to you." She waited, curious. "I do love you."

The air between them was suddenly alive with long-suppressed emotion. "You've never said that to me before," she whispered at last.

"I never knew how."

She hurried across the room, and they hugged each other. "I love you, too. Good luck, dad, and I wish you all the happiness in the world."

"Danni, I want the same for you, you know."

She patted his lapels, trying her damndest not to cry.

BEES HUMMED in the warm, somnolent garden, while high in the green pasture horses whickered in contentment. The day was perfect for a garden wedding.

The minister, called out from his tiny Fairfax County church, read the marriage vows, his ruddy cheeks puffing out as he intoned the familiar words. Danielle saw the tears in Jennifer's mother's eyes. The woman was an older, slightly plump version of her daughter; she possessed the same warmth and good-natured gentleness, the same crinkling touch of humor around her dark expressive eyes. When Jen looked over at her mother, her own eyes began to shimmer with emotion.

The scene left a bittersweet ache in Danielle's heart, and she dropped her head for a moment. Hal stood stiffly by Danielle's side, his eyes fixed on John Davis as if the older man could somehow give him what he wanted.

The simple ceremony was over quickly, and the quiet afternoon was soon disrupted by happy tears and heartfelt wishes for the newlyweds' happiness. Before Danielle knew it, Jen and her father were off to the Bahamas, breaking with tradition slightly by sharing a car to the airport with the Bondis, who were en route home to New Jersey.

Danielle stood alone at the balcony rail long after the car had disappeared around the last bend in the long graveled driveway. At last she turned to face the empty house. She envisioned the Davises of generations past, when families were large and the gardens and terrace must have exploded with activity. She pictured the old-fashioned Christmases, the buggy rides and picnics and balls, and finally the tragedy of war. This house that had been so full of life would soon be lost to her. Even if her father relented and rescinded his gift to the National Trust, she knew she couldn't keep it up alone.

In a while she turned away and went down to the fenced pasturage. Imitating Sam Larkin's whistle, she called Foxfire down to her. The filly came running full tilt, abrim with energy, and impatiently nudged Danielle's hand. She gave the gangly little horse a sugar cube from her pocket, rubbed her wrinkled-up muzzle, then lightly slapped her burnished rump, sending her off to play again.

Danielle returned to the house with a heavy heart. In the foyer, the carefully arranged flowers on the antique dresser had already begun to wilt from the day's heat. She wandered into the living room, running her hands over familiar objects. The heavy chintz drapes had been taken down, so that for all the warmth of the late-spring day, the room seemed barren and cold.

Not wanting to stay and yet reluctant to leave, Danielle sought refuge in the cozy clutter of the library. She was startled to find Hal there, a drink in hand as he browsed among the shelves filled with her father's old law books. She had forgotten all about him.

He turned at the sound of her footsteps. "I'll bet John will be delighted to get out from under this albatross. Foxhall must have cost a fortune to keep up."

"He loved it here. So did I," she replied, each word reproaching him. "This place was one of the few things we allowed ourselves to be sentimental about without embarrassment."

Hal said nothing to that. Instead he reached into his pocket and pulled out a package. "By the way, I found this shoved way in the back of your mailbox when I stopped by your place this morning. I put the rest of the mail inside on the entry table, but I thought you'd want this. It looks like it must have been hand delivered."

Danielle's heart twisted when she saw her name spelled out in Racha's delicate, spidery script. Her fingers shaking, she opened the box and the folded note inside.

Dear Danielle, you will find this today when you arrive home from the hospital. I know you will be worried, but I implore you not to be. I will always be grateful that you have given me the gift of hope.

These are wind chimes. Our Ryan told me you like such things. Please put these in your kitchen window. When the wind touches them, I will be there with you.

Your Racha

Six porcelain hearts, white and fragile, tinkled against one another as she lifted them from the box. The sound was faintly sweet and sad. Examining the hearts more closely, she found one of them chipped.

Danielle closed her hands tightly around them. Without warning she felt the tears welling up from deep inside her, and they dropped down her cheeks. Her shoulders began to heave. She reached blindly for the leather footstool, lowering herself onto it. She cried as if her own heart would break.

Hal stared down at her bent head, thunderstruck. "Danni, what's wrong?" he demanded, touching her shoulder awkwardly.

She shook her head, unable to speak.

"Whatever it is, you'll get over it," he tried to console her, getting more nervous by the second.

She didn't hear him. "Hal, please, just put your arms around me. Hold me."

Stiffly he knelt down beside her, and she buried her face against his chest. But the more she clung to him, the more she longed for Ryan, longed for the healing grace of his arms enfolding her and his beloved lips kissing away her tears. Even through her anguish, Danielle had sensed Hal's embarrassed withdrawal, and she knew now how Ryan must have felt when she had done the same to him. She understood now how he had needed her then and how badly she needed him now.

She pulled away, reaching for a tissue. "Forgive me, Hal. I'm fine now."

"Danni...."

"No, really, I'm fine." She dabbed at the smear of mascara on his white shirt.

"I'll take you out to dinner," he said solicitously, now that the disturbing storm of emotion seemed to have passed.

"Thank you, but I want to be alone."

"I'm confused, Danni. You've never been this way before."

"Hal, I'm not the woman you thought you knew."

"I can't believe a person can change that much. I thought we were a team."

"Hal, you and I were business partners. If I let you think this is love, I'd be cheating you. You deserve someone who can give you more."

"It's really over, then?"

"It has to be. It's easier for me to say it now than to risk a lifetime of hurting you, of holding back."

His face went pale as he stood up, and she was afraid he would beg. But he had more dignity than that. Without another word, he turned and left.

After he'd gone Danielle wandered out to the garden to sit on the low brick wall. She stayed outside all afternoon, hoping to absorb some of the peace of her surroundings. A pair of brown thrushes called to each other across the hedge, while out in the woodlands a covey of bobwhite quail spread their wings and rose into the empty sky.

For the first time, Danielle was able to think about Racha without pain. If they had been sitting there together all afternoon, Racha would have found a hundred little things to exclaim over in delight. She had loved everything life had to offer, and in the brief time they had been together she had infected Danielle with her shy exuberance.

Knowing Racha had been a precious gift. And gradually she remembered what she had been thinking before Racha went into the hospital—that she wouldn't exchange the week they had spent together for anything. Racha was gone, but Danielle would feel the influence of her gentle, giving nature for the rest of her life.

Much later a cool wind sprang up, stirring the laurel leaves and carrying down with it the workmanlike hammering of a family of woodpeckers. Afternoon faded into twilight and a muted sunset. Feeling chilled, Danielle stood up, staring back at Foxhall. This might be home, she thought, but even home could be a lonely place.

Inevitably she thought of Ryan, as well, and how she had spurned the gift of his loving. If only there was some way she could make it up to him. Jen's words came back to her. "If you really want something, for Pete's sake, it's worth going after."

Inside the library again, Danielle built a small fire in the grate and lay down on the rug before it, staring into the flames. She knew what she had to do now. The simple, beautiful logic of the decision gave her heart wings.

CHAPTER SIXTEEN

THE TAXI DREW TO A HALT before the dark house, and Danielle paid the driver. Nervously she watched him speed away, following the cab's taillights until they disappeared through the trees.

The Malaysian night was alive with the sounds of myriad insects, at once familiar and strange, like the urgent beating of her own heart. She picked up her bag and walked around to the back of the main house. A sliver of moon illuminated the rock-bordered pool, to cast a silvered shadow across the grass.

She trailed the light down toward the river, excitement and fear feathering up her throat as soon as she saw the bungalow. Would he be there? Would he forgive her turning away from him?

She hurried now. The damp earth beneath her feet felt rich and full of promise, dormant ground ready to burst with life.

Without hesitation she ran up the ladder; the door yielded to her touch, and she slipped inside. For a long time she stood there, simply drinking in the sight of him.

Ryan lay sprawled on his stomach, the sheets

bunched around his waist. Moonlight slanted in through the bamboo screen, patterning his shoulders and back. A stray breeze wafted through, making the wind chimes laugh, a high, whispery sound.

"Danielle?" he murmured in his sleep.

Had he spoken her name, or had she just imagined it? Her heart pounding, she crossed the room and went to kneel beside the bed. She stroked his head with gentle fingers, contenting herself with the reality of him.

Slowly he opened his eyes and focused on her. "I thought I was dreaming," he said huskily. "Maybe I still am."

"No, Ryan. I'm here."

Sleepily he reached for her, pulling her into the warm circle of his arms. "God, how I've missed you, Danielle. These past weeks have been hell. I was so bloody scared I'd never see you again."

"It's been hellish for me, too, ever since you left," she told him softly. "I had to learn the hard way how much I need you."

Pulling himself up, he leaned on one elbow so he could drink in the vision of her beside him. Gently he took the pins from her hair and fanned it across the pillow. Her face was in shadow, but her eyes shone luminously. His fingers traced the beloved, familiar contours of eyes, nose and mouth as she spoke.

"I kept thinking about Racha, how much I loved her. When she died I was so angry at the world I didn't want to feel anything but bitterness—yet I denied the grief. That coldness was an ugly sickness inside me, and the worst part was that it spilled out onto everyone around me. I had to face the truth about myself—either I could go on as I was, withdrawn and miserable, or...."

"Or?"

She kissed his fingertips. "Or I could take my chances. I was so desperately afraid of losing you that I cut myself off from the joy of our love."

His hand lay still against her cheek. "That's why you drove me away?"

Her eyes clouded at the memory. "I loved you too much, Ryan. I just didn't have enough faith in myself or in life. Racha's dying made me feel I was falling into a dark valley. Now I know there will be other valleys. But as long as our love is strong, it can help pull me through."

She looked up at him, her eyes greedily absorbing him—the tanned skin taut over his cheekbones, the crooked smile half-hidden beneath his thick mustache, the faint wonder in his eyes as they met hers. And she smiled, too. "I realized that the joys of loving outweigh all the other agonies."

He bent to kiss the corner of her mouth and found it salty. "You've been crying." He brushed his thumbs down the imagined trail of her dried tears.

"I was so afraid you wouldn't be here. I was so afraid I'd be too late with my love."

He kissed the palms of her hands and slid his own hands beneath her blouse, his touch hard and warm against the small of her back. She clung to him, ready to give and to share, ready to open to him and hold nothing back.

Her passionate yearning excited him. "Danielle, you're beautiful. Have I ever told you how much I love to see your hair down? I've dreamed about this. I've been so hungry for you."

She caressed his face, tracing with one finger the sensuous droop of his lips. They parted, and he licked her fingers, letting his tongue circle and tease them. Their languorous love play aroused her, and she gave herself up to the pleasurable mounting tension, aware of his hands playing over her stomach, exploring the curving softness of her breasts.

Danielle slid her hands beneath his shirt now, eager to share in the bewitchery. She reveled in the familiar taste of him, burying her face in the fine down on his chest until it tickled her nose. And they both laughed.

Their laughter was at once a release and a deepening bond of intimacy that imbued the silent room, compelling their surroundings to bear witness and nurture their love.

Slowly they undressed each other in the shifting moonlight, making a game of planting kisses where the light patterned their bodies. His mouth drifted over her collarbone toward the shadowed undercurve of her breast, and she in turn followed somewhat breathlessly the pale light bisecting his torso. Her lips brushed the narrow downy line that glistened like a strand of silver down his belly. He smelled of spiced soap and of himself—a musky maleness that thrilled her. Her kisses were pinpoints of flame rushing them toward a burgeoning fire, causing him to groan in need. Her hair fell forward to curtain her face, so that the world glimmered darkly through a silken web twining them closer.

Rolling over onto his back, Ryan pulled her on top of him. With a startled intake of breath, she began to enjoy a whole new spectrum of sensations akin to a host of butterflies madly beating their wings across a hidden landscape. She moved her hips, imitating the butterflies' flight; Ryan reached up to grip her waist. He shuddered, and she stared down in wonder at his closed eyes, at the mouth that soundlessly formed her name and drew her into his private world of ecstasy.

She leaned forward, bracing her palms on his chest. Now she made the wings inside her take flight once more. She rose with them toward a night sky filled with shooting stars, willing Ryan to follow. And he did, his eyes devouring the fullness of her breasts and her hair strewn in wild abandon across her shoulders.

Exultant, Danielle felt her joy rising toward the vast dome of the imagined sky, for she knew that with him she had found a joy no one could take from her, ever.

With a sigh she sank down, spent, on his chest, content to listen to the slow, steady drumbeat of his heart.

"I love you, Ryan," she whispered finally. "Sometimes I feel as if I've known and loved you forever."

Gently Ryan stroked her hair until her eyelids fluttered down against his chest, and she slept.

SHE AWOKE to Ryan's cool lips against her temples, his fingers caressing her hair.

"Good morning, Sleeping Beauty. I don't think I'll ever get tired of watching you wake up."

Happiness flooded through her, and she reveled in the feel of his ticklish mustache when he pressed his mouth into the crook of her shoulder.

"How long can you stay, Danielle?"

"Forever, if you want me."

"You mean you've quit your job?"

"Ryan, you know me better than that!" Her eyes laughed up at him. "I've decided I can just as easily do my job here. Maybe not on quite such a scale, but enough to keep an active hand in. I think it's fair to warn you, though—you have to put up with my taking short trips back to Washington."

He grinned. "Once we're married, don't think I'm going to let you out of my sight that easily."

"That's reassuring, because there's one other thing."

"Ah, a catch. What is it?"

"Dad's given me Foxhall, and I'd like to spend a few months a year there."

Ryan lay back down, clasping his hands behind his head. "Will you fancy that? Me, a gentleman rancher. I never thought I'd see the day. At least I know from my last trip to Washington that my business can survive without me for a bit."

She stared at him in astonishment. "You're not teasing me? You'll come home with me, then."

"Danielle, my love, I'll move heaven and earth to be with you. Haven't you learned that yet?"

Wordlessly she leaned over to kiss him.

The delicious moment was interrupted by a shout from below.

"Is everything all right up there, old man?" Harry called. Ryan pulled on a pair of drawstring pants and went out onto the deck. "Talib was blathering something about a ghost lady in the night," the cantankerous Englishman went on.

Danielle heard Ryan's laughter, as well as his teasing retort. "Yes, everything's okay, Harry. I've just found myself a wife."

"Oh, fuss and bother. Women! Won't you ever learn?"

"You don't know what you're missing, Harry."

Danielle heard her lover's pleased laughter and smiled herself, absolutely content. Her eyes roamed lazily around the room. Sunlight poured in through the screened windows, touching her heap of clothes on the floor, the imprint of Ryan's body next to her in the bed.

The door opened again, and Ryan stood there, his long body silhouetted in the morning light. She saw his smile and the loving laughter in his eyes as he came toward her.

March's other absorbing
HARLEQUIN *SuperRomance* novel

A MOMENT OF MAGIC by Christina Crockett

For Susie Costain, designing Mardi Gras costumes set her free. To be creative was as necessary to her as the air she breathed.

Sy Avery understood Susie's dedication to her work. Being a gifted photographer, he, too, made certain sacrifices. But when the sacrifices included giving up precious time together—day and *night* —something had to be done.

Sy would never ask Susie to give up her work. He knew the price she had paid for her freedom—but neither knew it could cost her her life!

A contemporary love story for the woman of today

These two absorbing titles
will be published in April
by

HARLEQUIN
SuperRomance

A LASTING GIFT by Lynn Turner

Jennifer had been happy, married to Michael Page. He died after a tragic illness, and now all she wanted was to be left alone.

Then Nathan Page, Michael's younger brother, arrived, determined to take care of her. Tempers flared, but temper turned to tenderness when they admitted their mutual loss. Something special had begun. . . .

Nathan was first to realize he was in love—with his brother's widow. He knew he should leave. But Jennifer had already lost one love, and she could not let him go. . . .

RETURN OF THE DRIFTER by Melodie Adams

When Kathryn was seventeen, the fiery excitement of Judson Taylor's touch had seared itself into her imagination and flesh forever.

Seven years after she'd been devastated by his abandonment, she had risen from the ashes of her painful past. Kathryn finally had it all: her own boutique, an independent life-style and the love of a man touted to be Kansas's next governor.

And now Judd had returned, no longer the shiftless drifter she'd known, but the head of Monument Oil—a powerful man determined to set the record straight, no matter what it cost him . . . or her.

These books are
already available
from
HARLEQUIN
SuperRomance

SANDCASTLE DREAMS Robyn Anzelon
AFTER THE LIGHTNING Georgia Bockoven
WAKE THE MOON Shannon Clare
EDGE OF ILLUSION Casey Douglas
REACH THE SPLENDOUR Judith Duncan
SHADOWS IN THE SUN Jocelyn Haley
NOW, IN SEPTEMBER Meg Hudson
CRITIC'S CHOICE Catherine Kay
THE RIGHT WOMAN Jenny Loring
FORBIDDEN DESTINY Emily Mesta
TRUSTING Virginia Nielsen
AMETHYST FIRE Donna Saucier
A RED BIRD IN WINTER Lucy Snow
THE HELLION LaVyrle Spencer

If you experience any difficulty in obtaining any of
these titles, write to:

Harlequin SuperRomance, P.O. Box 236,
Croydon, Surrey CR9 3RU

HARLEQUIN *Love Affair*

Look out this month for

SECOND SIGHT   *Rebecca Flanders*

Normally, Jennifer Kiel was her town's head librarian, but on that bright autumn day Jennifer had donned cape and veil, transforming herself into Madame Voltaire, the fortune-teller of Southworth's annual fair. Somehow, Adam Wilson found his way to Madame Voltaire's tent—and two lives were changed forever.

For Jennifer, who suffered a "condition", who had led a quiet life, Adam was an unexpected gift. And for Adam, who had been running, trying to outdistance time, Jennifer was the miracle he had never thought he would find . . .

HIGH VALLEY OF THE SUN   *Laura Parris*

The advertising agency where Audrey Mathieson worked usually handled small accounts and had never worked for a client as prestigious as Harkness and Walker, architects of Nava del Sol. Why should Ken Walker use the company that employed her, Audrey wondered nervously.

For Ken had been Audrey's nemesis in high school, taunting her about her good grades and her infatuation with the class president, Alan Mathieson. Audrey could only assume that after all these years Ken had heard about her divorce and had now seized the opportunity to gloat . . .

STRANGE BEDFELLOWS   *Marie Ziobro*

The Missouri newspapers gave full coverage to the heroic rescue and to the mysterious woman who had snatched the small boy from the fire. Mary Fitzhugh, lying unconscious in a hospital bed, never saw the stories . . . but her husband did. And when Mary awoke, racked with pain, Jamie Fitzhugh was at her bedside.

After four years he had come after her. Not because he had finally chosen his wife over his mistress, but because he was running for Congress and Mary had suddenly become a political asset . . .